Blood of the Devil

BLOOD OF THE DEVIL

THE LIFE AND TIMES OF YELLOW BOY, MESCALERO APACHE, BOOK 2

W. MICHAEL FARMER

FIVE STAR

A part of Gale, a Cengage Company

Farmington Hills, Mich • San Francisco • New York • Waterville, Maine
Meriden, Conn • Mason, Ohio • Chicago

LIBRARY OF CONGRESS CATALOGING-IN-PUBLICATION DATA

Names: Farmer, W. Michael, 1944– author.
Title: Blood of the Devil / W. Michael Farmer.
Description: First edition. | Waterville, Maine : Five Star Publishing, a part of
    Cengage Learning, Inc., [2017] | Includes bibliographical references.
Identifiers: LCCN 2016058127 (print) | LCCN 2017004589 (ebook) | ISBN
    9781432834142 (hardcover) | ISBN 1432834142 (hardcover) | ISBN
    9781432834074 (ebook) | ISBN 143283407X (ebook) | ISBN 9781432836429
    (ebook) | ISBN 1432836420 (ebook)
Subjects: LCSH: Apache Indians History—History—19th century—Fiction. | Mescalero
    Indians—History—19th century—Fiction. | BISAC: FICTION / Historical. | FIC-
    TION / Action & Adventure. | GSAFD: Historical fiction.
Classification: LCC PS3606.A725 B58 2017 (print) | LCC PS3606.A725 (ebook) |
    DDC 813/.6—dc23
LC record available at https://lccn.loc.gov/2016058127

First Edition. First Printing: June 2017
Find us on Facebook– https://www.facebook.com/FiveStarCengage
Visit our website– http://www.gale.cengage.com/fivestar/
Contact Five Star™ Publishing at FiveStar@cengage.com

Printed in the United States of America
1 2 3 4 5 6 7 21 20 19 18 17

For Corky, my best friend and wife.

TABLE OF CONTENTS

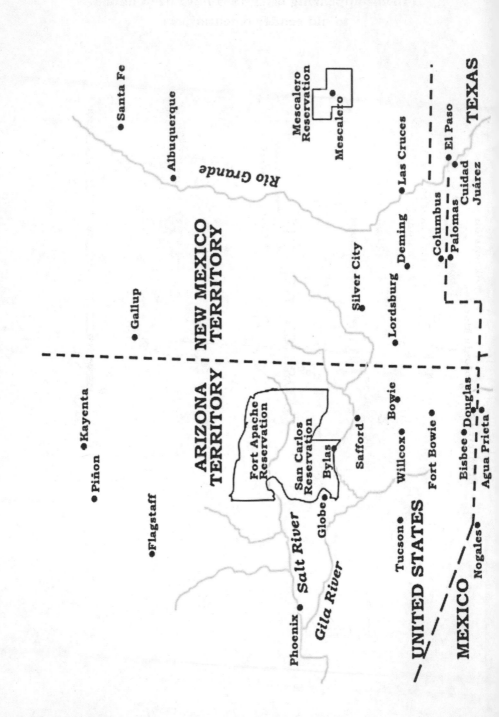

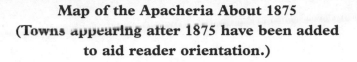

Map of the Apacheria About 1875
(Towns appearing after 1875 have been added to aid reader orientation.)

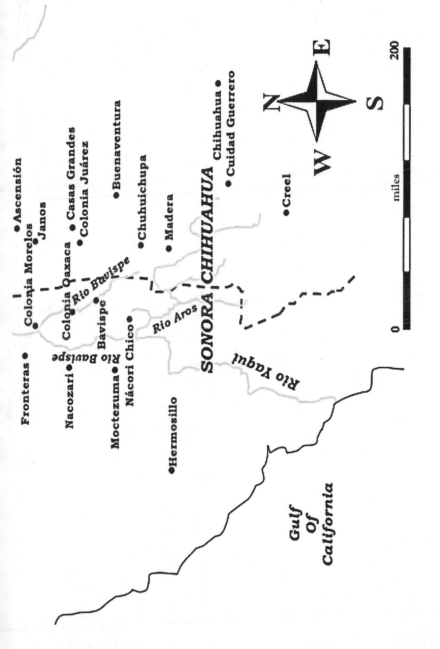

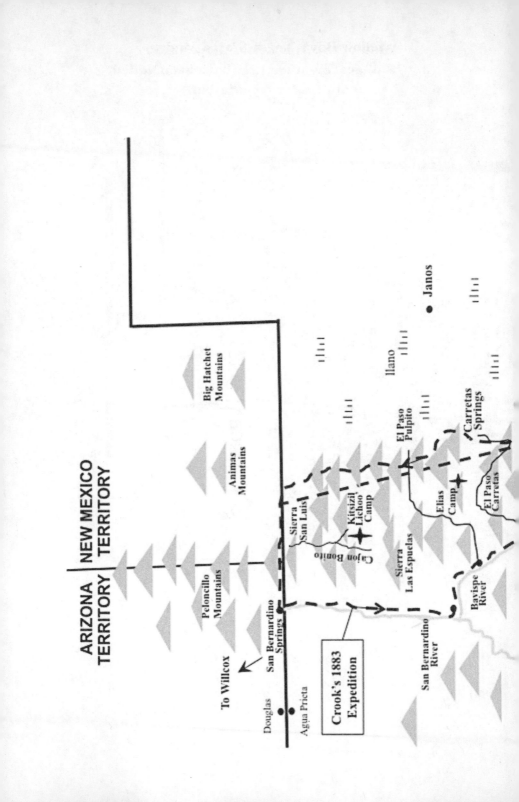

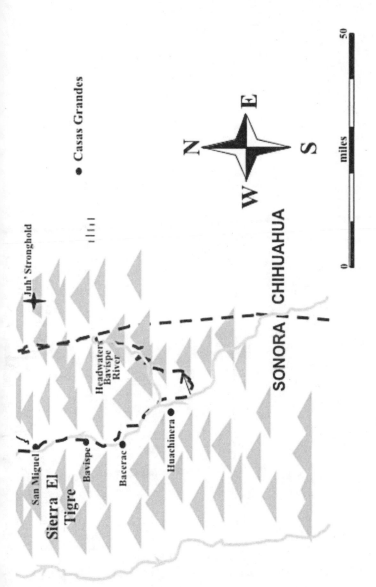

ACKNOWLEDGMENTS

A project of this magnitude is not done alone. I owe a debt of gratitude to many friends and associates who have supported and encouraged me in this work. There are several who deserve special mention.

Melissa Starr provided editorial reviews and many helpful questions, suggestions, and comments to enhance manuscript quality. Her work is much appreciated.

Bruce Kennedy's knowledge of the southwest and invaluable commentary made many helpful contributions to this story. I thank him for his support.

Lynda A. Sánchez's firsthand knowledge of Apache culture and history provided guiding light and clarity on many details. Her insights and comments on this story were invaluable. I owe her a debt of gratitude.

Pat and Mike Alexander have graciously opened their home to me during return visits to New Mexico for research and book tours, and they provided company on long roads across endless deserts and prairies and tall mountains. Friends such as these are rare and much appreciated.

Excellent descriptions of Apache culture, beliefs, and methods of raiding and war in the mid- to late-nineteenth century are provided by anthropologists, linguists, and historians. Some of the ones I found most helpful are provided in Additional Reading at the end of the story. The work by Eve Ball and her associates Lynda A. Sánchez and Nora Henn provided especially valuable insights into Apache life because they faithfully recorded the stories Eve's Apache friends remembered of the old days, and they remembered those days very well.

CHARACTERS

FICTIONAL CHARACTERS

Beela-chezzi (Crooked Fingers)—Friend of Yellow Boy

Calico Dove—Second wife of Kitsizil Lichoo'

Carmen Rosario—Mexican wife of Beela-chezzi

Chawn-clizzay (The Goat)—Sergeant in the Mescalero Tribal Police and friend of Yellow Boy

Deer Woman—Wife of Kah, former lover of Delgadito

Delgadito—Warrior who rode with Victorio and the first lover of Deer Woman

Falling Water—Daughter of Sleepy, a young widow

He Who Catches Horses—Mescalero Apache Monte gambler

Ish-kay-neh—Oldest boy in the camp of Yellow Boy, son of Sleepy

Juanita—Yellow Boy's first wife

Kah (Arrow)—Boyhood friend of Yellow Boy

Kitsizil Lichoo' (His Hair Red)—Adopted *Indah* son of Juh and friend of Yellow Boy

Klo-sen—Warrior who was killed by the witch, a friend of Yellow Boy

Little Rabbit—Yellow Boy's little brother

Lucky Star—Adopted Mexican child of Sons-ee-ah-ray, Yellow Boy's mother

Maria—Juanita's mother

Para-dee-ah-tran (The Contented)—First son of Kah and Deer Woman

15

Red Pony—Jicarilla warrior

Sangre del Diablo (Blood of the Devil)—Witch, scalp hunter, and leader of Comanches and *banditos*

Sergeant Sweeny Jones—US Cavalry officer, friend of Yellow Boy

Shiyé (My Son)—Little son of Carmen Rosario and adopted son of Beela-chezzi

Sleepy—Camp midwife, mother of Ish-kay-neh and Falling Water

Sons-ee-ah-ray (Morning Star)—Mother of Yellow Boy

Steps in Water—First wife of Kitsizil Lichoo'

Yibá (He Waits for Him)—Young Apache warrior, formerly named Ish-kay-neh

HISTORICAL CHARACTERS

Al Sieber—Chief of Scouts for General Crook

Captain Thomas Branigan—Chief of Mescalero Tribal Police for Major Llewellyn, who departed the reservation in November 1885

Cha—Leader of Mescalero Apaches in the Guadalupe Mountains

Chato—Chiricahua Apache chief

Chihuahua—Chiricahua Apache chief

General George A. Crook—Commander, US Army Department of Arizona, and known as *Nantan Lupan*, Chief Gray Wolf, by the Apaches

Dastine (Crouched and Ready)—Cibecue Apache scout

Elias (Jose Maria Elias also know as Nat-cul-bay-e)—Leader of a Sierra Madre Apache band

Fletcher J. Cowart—Agent at the Mescalero Reservation, who arrived in November 1885 and departed at the end of 1888

Haskehagola (Angry, He Starts Fights)—Apache scout

Jelikine (also known as Pine Pitch House)—Apache warrior, Geronimo's father-in-law

John Rope—Apache scout on General Crook's Sierra Madre Expedition in 1883

Joseph H. Blazer, Dr.—Owner and operator of Blazer's Mill and Store at the Mescalero Agency

Juh—Leader of *Nednhi* Apache band

Lieutenant Guilfoyle—Cavalry officer who chased Nana but never caught him

Major General George Crook—Commander of Sierra Madre Expedition in 1883

Major W. H. H. Llewellyn—Agent at the Mescalero Reservation, who arrived 16 June 1881 and departed end of 1884, also called "Tata Crooked Nose" by the Mescaleros

Mickey Free—Apache scout

"Miss Ida" Llewellyn—Wife of W.H. H. Llewellyn

Nah-da-ste—Geronimo's sister

Nana—Victorio's son-in-law and *Segundo* (second in command), an old and arthritic warrior

Nasta (He Knows A Lot)—Apache scout

Nautzile—Mescalero Apache chief

Nocadelklinny—Chiricahua Apache *di-yen* who brought the Ghost Dance to San Carlos

Tulan (Much Water)—Apache scout

Tzoe (also known as Peaches)—A White Mountain scout who led General Crook's expedition to Chiricahua camps in the Sierra Madre

Ussen—Creator God of the Apaches

Victorio—Mimbreño Apache chief

APACHE AND SPANISH WORDS AND PHRASES

Aashcho—friend
Ahéhye'e—thank you
Alcalde—mayor (Spanish)
Áshood—thank you
Baile—dance (Spanish)
Be'idest'íné—binoculars
Bronco—wild or untamed horse (Spanish)
Brujo—male witch (Spanish)
Búh—owl
Dahtiyé—humming bird
D'anté—greetings
Di-yen—medicine woman or man
Dos Cabezas—two heads (Spanish)
Enjuh—good
Googé—whip-poor-will
Hacendado—wealthy landowner (Spanish)
Haheh—puberty ceremony
Hondah—come in, you are welcome
Idiits'ag—I hear you
Indah—white men (literally "the living")
Indeh—the Apaches' name for themselves (literally "the dead")
Ish-tia-neh—woman
Jaadé—antelope
Ka-dish-day—goodbye
Kotulh—special tipi for the *Haheh* ceremony

Llano—dry prairie (Spanish)
Máquina—sawmill (literally "machine") (Spanish)
Nakai-yes—Mexicans
Nakai-yi—Mexican
Nantan Lupan—Chief Gray Wolf
Nednhi—southern band of Chiricahua Apaches
Nish'ii'—I see you
Pesh líí'beshkee'é—iron horseshoes
Pesh-klitso—gold (literally "yellow iron")
Pesh-lickoyee—nickel-plated or silver (literally "white iron")
Que paso?—What's happening? (Spanish)
Reata—rawhide rope (Spanish)
Río Grande—Great River (Spanish)
Shináá Cho—telescope (literally "big eye")
Shis-Indeh—the Apaches' name for their people (literally "People of the Woods")
Tejanos—Texans (Spanish)
Teniente—lieutenant
Tobaho—tobacco
Tsach—cradleboard
Tsélkani—mulberry wood
Tsii"edo'a'tl—Apache fiddle (literally "wood that sings")
Ugashé—go

APACHE RECKONING OF TIME & SEASONS

Harvest—used in the context of time, means a year
Handwidth (against the sky)—about an hour
Season of Little Eagles—early spring
Season of Many Leaves—late spring, early summer
Season of Large Leaves—midsummer
Season of Large Fruit—late summer, early fall
Season of Earth is Reddish Brown—late fall
Season of Ghost Face—lifeless winter

PREFACE

This novel continues an imagined autobiography of a Mescalero Apache warrior, Yellow Boy, who lived from about 1860 to 1951, a span of years that saw his people pushed to the brink of cultural extinction. They had to change or die as a people. The change demanded on the culture of the Mescaleros and other reservation Apaches over the period of the story in Book 2, 1880–1896, was great, but they evolved slowly. The Apache warrior, Yellow Boy, who tells his story about those years, was in his prime. He was a tribal policeman under Captain Thomas Branigan, a scout for General Crook, and a killer of the witch who had killed and scalped his people for money. These were the years that saw Victorio, the great warrior, surprised and wiped out by a Mexican army under General Joaquin Terrazas at Tres Castillos, and the breakout at San Carlos of the legendary Apache warriors Chihuahua, Loco, Chato, Pine Pitch House (also known as Jelikine), and Geronimo into the wilds of what Apaches called the Blue Mountains, the Sierra Madre, in Mexico.

General George Crook used a small army of Apache scouts who ran, rather than rode horses, over five hundred miles down valleys and across mountains in Sonora and Chihuahua for forty days to shepherd the runaways back to the reservations in a "good way." Three years later, Geronimo, out again with a quarter of the US Army chasing him and eighteen warriors across Mexico and the United States, finally surrendered. The entire band of Chiricahua Apaches, including the scouts who brought Geronimo in and those who never left the reservation, became prisoners of war for the next twenty-seven years in Florida, Alabama, and Oklahoma before most returned to New Mexico and the Mescalero Reservation. During these years, the blundering bureaucracy in Washington tried to force the Mescaleros and Jicarilla Apaches on to a common reservation, and failed; tried to crush the culture and spirit of the Mescaleros by forcing their children into American-European-style schools, and failed; and tried to steal their land, and failed. These were hard years with small victories that slowly led the Mescaleros to the other side of a wide river of change.

One certain victory for every Apache family was the birth of a strong, healthy child. Considered the best of times and filled with prayers like the one used in Chapter 13 and recorded by Grenville Goodwin in his *Social Organization of the Western Apache,* the child was introduced to its community with the Apache Cradleboard Ceremony.

The events in General Crook's Sierra Madre Expedition in 1883 as seen through the eyes of Yellow Boy, one of many scouts pursuing the Chiricahuas in Mexico, have their historical basis and timeline from stories told by scout John Rope to Grenville Goodwin in *Western Apache Raiding and Warfare* and from *An Apache Campaign in the Sierra Madre* by John G. Bourke. When John Rope's story differed from John Bourke's, I followed John Rope. A list of historical and fictional characters has been provided for the reader interested in learning more about those who played in one of the most daring and challenging military campaigns ever conducted by the US Army.

These stories are told through the eyes of Yellow Boy, who understood the changes that had to be made, learned from the whites, and grew in understanding and spirit in both cultures.

W. Michael Farmer
Smithfield, Virginia
May 2015

PROLOGUE

Yellow Boy, my Apache mentor and close friend for over fifty-five years, saved me from certain death in the winter desert when I was eight years old after I witnessed the murder of my father, Albert Fountain, in 1896. Yellow Boy helped Rufus Pike raise me, and they both helped me avenge my father and taught me to survive in the hard country of the southwest. In 1950, I persuaded Yellow Boy to tell me his life story.

Over the course of many afternoons and pots of coffee at his house in a canyon on the reservation, I wrote his story down as he told it in a mixture of Mescalero Apache, Spanish, and English in the whispery rasping voice of a vigorous old man. At the beginning of each session, I read back to him what I had written from the previous session, and after I explained the meaning of some of my fancy words, he usually agreed I had captured the essence of what he had said. When I missed what he meant, I rewrote it until he said it correctly told what happened.

This is his story as he told it and meant it to be heard. The story has been written in three books. Book 1, *Killer of Witch*es, covers the years 1865 to 1880. This Book, Book 2, covers the years 1881 to 1896, years when Yellow Boy, in his prime, had some of his greatest victories and hardest defeats.

—Dr. Henry Grace, 1953

CHAPTER 1
THE SEARCH BEGINS

The Stronghold of Juh, Great *Nednhi* Chiricahua Apache Leader, in the Sierra Madre of Northern Mexico, Early Summer, 1880

I am Yellow Boy, Killer of Witches, a Mescalero Apache grown to manhood in the Guadalupe Mountains in the land of the *Tejano*s. Once my People called me *Nah-kah-yen* (Keen-Sighted), but *Ussen,* the great Creator God of the Apaches, renamed me in a vision and gave me Power to use my Yellow Boy rifle. My rifle and I are one. What I can see, I never miss. I was given the Power to kill witches. This I reaffirmed to myself after singing my morning prayer to *Ussen* the day after I learned that the witch, Sangre del Diablo (Blood of the Devil), had killed his slaves, all women and children, after my warrior brother, Beela-chezzi, and I had freed them. This witch had killed, mutilated, and scalped many of our People, including my own father, for Nakai-yi (Mexican) gold. I had sworn vengeance against him, sworn to shoot out his eyes so he'd wander forever blind in the Happy Land.

We had wiped out most of his Comanche and *pistolero* followers and then plundered his stronghold after he and two Comanches barely escaped us. The warrior who brought us news of his killing the freed slaves also told us how to find Sangre del Diablo. His Comanches had gone to the camp of Elias three suns' ride in the Blue Mountains to the north. Juh promised to send one of his warriors with us to show us the way.

At Juh's insistence, Beela-chezzi and I waited four days before leaving after we swore to find and finish Sangre del Diablo and his Comanches. We waited in order to be wise, to see things as they truly were, and because, as Juh had said, we needed to make our minds smooth again before we took up the warpath.

In the time of waiting, I visited my mother, Sons-ee-ah-ray. She had adopted and named Lucky Star, a *Nakai-yi* (Mexican) slave child that Juh had given to me. As Sons-ee-ah-ray and I sat by her fire drinking piñon nut coffee she said, "I'm an old woman and have seen much since before the days you remember of Carlton's Bosque Redondo camp of suffering. Your attack on Sangre del Diablo and his band of Comanches and *Nakai-yi pistoleros* would make your father very proud. I know also your grandfather, though he died by the hand of the witch when you attacked him, was very proud to claim you as his grandson. The camp women have prayed many times for your safe return to Juanita, who at last carries your child in her belly. Truly you are a favored warrior."

"I won't rest until this witch walks blind in the Happy Land and is no more in the land of the living. Beela-chezzi and I are lucky to be alive. Sangre del Diablo is very powerful. Even Juh is afraid to attack him, afraid if he tries and fails, the witch will call the evil spirits on his whole band. Pray every day for *Ussen* to help us. Beela-chezzi and I must kill and blind this witch or we may all die."

Even in the weak light of her tipi, I saw the same fire in Sons-ee-ah-ray's eyes I remembered from my childhood. She nodded and said, "Don't worry, my son. *Ussen* will give you strength and make your Power even stronger when you need it. Come back to us when your vengeance is complete. While you hunt the witch, the women will protect the child who grows in the belly of your wife. We're all anxious for it to come. You'll return long before it's born."

"Hmmph. I believe my mother speaks true."

"Now go to your woman, comfort her mind with your strength and vision that your child might be born strong and ready, and smooth your mind to think clearly as you hunt the witch."

"My mother is a wise woman."

Juanita and I lay under the blankets and spoke long into the night about the child coming to us, a child we had awaited for over two harvests.

"Husband, be strong. Do nothing foolish to cause me to be left a widow as you look for your vengeance."

I smiled as she lay in the crook of my arm, and I stared at the milk river of stars I watched through the poles of the tipi top. "I've already seen how the witch dies in a dream. *Ussen*'s Power will protect me. Don't worry."

Juanita's warm body gave mine comfort just by its nearness, and I thought of the child she carried. I stroked the bare curve of her back and said, "Is it too early to consider who we will ask to do the baby's *tsach* (cradleboard)? It's the most important thing we'll do for our child after it's born."

I heard only the rhythm of her breathing for a while before she said, "No, it's not too early. I think a woman with wise hands and a good heart should make it. I think we should ask Sons-ee-ah-ray. Do you think she would make the *tsach*?"

I smiled again, "Woman, you see into my mind. She'd be proud to make it. Let's ask her when I return."

I drew Juanita closer to me and she said with a laughing

31

voice, "*Enjuh* (good). Now hold me close to you as we sleep. I think your trip will be long before you return to us."

I cleaned and oiled my rifle, tested its sights, counted my bullets, cleaned and straightened my arrows and fletched again those with feathers grown rough from use and blood, and sharpened my knife to slash fast and deep. Beela-chezzi and I spoke together a long time about how to best catch and kill Sangre del Diablo and his Comanches.

Pounding dried meat, nuts, and fruits together, Juanita made food I could eat on the trail without using a cooking fire, and she taught Beela-chezzi's new wife, Carmen Rosario, how to do this for her man.

Our ponies rested and ate their fill of good grass in the high meadows of Juh's stronghold.

With the help of Juh's *di-yen* (medicine man) we used a sweat lodge and let poisons leave our bodies and minds as we asked help from the mountain spirits and for *Ussen* to guide us. At last, with clear minds and renewed weapons, Beela-chezzi and I were ready to hunt and kill the witch.

On the fourth day, I stood on top of the stronghold cliffs and watched the edge of the sky turn blood red as the bright fire *Ussen* brings burning in the sun lifted out of darkness to once more bring us light and warmth. I lifted my hands and sang my morning prayer to *Ussen*. I sang it as Sons-ee-ah-ray had taught me when I was a small boy in General Carlton's prisoner of war camp at Bosque Redondo fifteen years earlier. Not far away on the same cliffs facing east, I could see the dim outline of Beela-chezzi, hands raised, giving voice to his own prayer to *Ussen*.

Soon, I joined him, and we saddled our ponies, hobbled them so they could continue to graze, and went to our separate lodges to have a morning meal, to speak with our women, and to await the warrior Juh promised for guiding us to the camp of the Apache warrior the *Nakai-yes* called Elias.

Juanita handed me a slice of beef and a gourd filled with wild potatoes flavored with wild onion and sage. "My man is ready to leave the stronghold? Your weapons, blanket, and trail food are ready? Is there anything else you need?"

I shook my head. "Beela-chezzi and I are ready."

Soon a dark outline appeared and waited outside our door. Juanita called, "You are welcome in our lodge."

I saw her eyes narrow and her hand cover her mouth as the warrior pulled back the door cover and stepped in to join us. I'm sure I must have looked as surprised as Juanita. This warrior was a little older than me, but his hair was long and red, and his skin was much lighter than ours. He smiled and nodded at us and said, "I'm called *Kitsizil Lichoo'* (His Hair Red) by my people and Pelo Rojo (Red Hair) by the *Nakai-yes.* Juh has asked I guide you to the camp of Elias."

Juanita recovered from her surprise and stood, motioning him to sit to my left. She said, "I'll tell Beela-chezzi you wait for him. Will you eat with us?"

Kitsizil Lichoo' said, "Yes, I'll eat. You're generous to strangers." Juanita handed him a gourd filled with meat and potatoes before she went to bring Beela-chezzi.

I said, "My people and I have taken sanctuary with Juh for over two moons now. How is it this is the first time we've seen Juh's son, Kitsizil Lichoo', an Apache not easy to miss?"

He laughed. "You haven't seen me because for three moons I've been in Sonora scouting the *Nakai-yi* mining camps in the Sierra El Tigre and just returned two nights ago to tell Juh what I've learned. He watches the *Nakai-yes* closely after they stole our women and children. With the help of Geronimo and others, we took them back. Each *Nakai-yi* village in the Sierra El Tigre will one day be a target of a Juh raid. He hates the *Nakai-*

yes and the *Indah* (white men)."

I nodded and said, "Why did Juh send you to guide us so soon after you returned to the stronghold?"

"He trusts me to get you there quickly. He says you hunt the witch, Sangre del Diablo, and have much power. If you come to his camp quickly, Elias will not have decided what to do with the witch, and you'll have a better chance of killing him."

"Hmmph. Then I'm glad you'll guide us. We have much to learn of the Blue Mountains."

We then ate quickly, speaking little, eager to be on our way. We were ready to ride when Beela-chezzi came.

CHAPTER 2
KITSIZIL LICHOO'

Standing near the edges of high places never made me want for courage. From the time I was a little one, I always liked to stand on high cliffs. In the high places, I can see far, and in the faraway places, I see my spirit. Riding the trails on the edges of high Blue Mountain cliffs, I first saw a spirit of gut-churning fear.

Following a trail along high canyon cliffs, giving views to the far horizon and straight down into deep dark canyons, the warrior Kitsizil Lichoo' led Beela-chezzi and me to the camp of Nat-cul-bay-e, known also to the *Nakai-yes* as Jose Maria Elias, in the Blue Mountains. My pony's hooves often landed only a hand span away from the edge of forever. One little slip, one foot in the wrong place, one unexpected jerk by me or the pony at the wrong place or time, and we would stumble into black, shadow-filled air or roll down steep mountainsides to be mangled beyond recognition.

Not losing courage and trusting my pony was a hard lesson to learn. It required the constant focus of my attention in much the same way as when I shot a rifle to hit a fast-moving target. Keeping an unchanging focus every moment meant keeping my mind and body in a good place, relaxed, yet ready to act faster than a striking snake.

It took two long days and a night of rest to reach the camp of Elias. The mountain ranges the *Indah* know in the north have their peaks running north and south with wide valleys in between. The Blue Mountains have high, blade-sharp ridges that run side-by-side north and south. Many angry, jagged boulders cover their sides, and the deep canyons between the ridges often have running streams or deep tanks of water at their bottoms. Blue oaks cover the ridge sides close to the canyon bottoms, but the ridge tops, like islands in the sky, have easy-to-find grass and tall pines. Many trails cross these ridges, but I think Kitsizil Lichoo' chose the highest, hardest ones to make us stronger.

At the end of the first day, we camped in tall pines on a high ridge but made no fire. Enemies on tops of other ridges can see light from even a small fire hidden by rocks. We believed we were better cold and living than warm and dead. Our hobbled horses grazed in tall grass at the edge of the trees. As golden light at the end of the day faded, we pulled together piles of pine straw to keep us warm while we slept. In the high darkness, sitting close together for warmth, we ate the trail food Carmen Rosario and Juanita made for us, listened to the night sounds of birds, wolves, coyotes, and singing insects, and spoke of our lives, as new friends will.

Kitsizil Lichoo', perhaps no more than three harvests older than me, moved and spoke like a chief who had Power. I liked him and wanted to know more about him.

"Kitsizil Lichoo', I would ask you about your life. Will you answer?"

I saw Kitsizil Lichoo' make a one-sided smile. "Speak. I will answer."

A *googé* (whip-poor-will) called from the top of the ridge, and far down the canyon, we heard Cougar scream like an *Indah* woman taken against her will.

"How old were you when you came to be Juh's son?"

"Juh took me from a stagecoach he ambushed between the

villages of Mesilla and Tucson." I frowned, and Kitsizil Lichoo' quickly added, "A stagecoach is what the *Indah* call a wagon for carrying them on long rides. I was with my mother that day and had lived through four harvests. I remember a gray beard who smelled of old sweat and whiskey riding with us on the wagon. When he laughed he showed ugly black teeth and sweat ran down the sides of his face into patchy black and gray whiskers, and a big, ugly growth of gray hair was under his nose. He told us many stories of what Apaches did to little boys and how they tortured captive women. Those stories made my mother make faces of fear and squeeze my hand tighter than normal.

"He died gagging and spitting blood early in the attack when an arrow flew through the window and stabbed deep into his throat. When the stage stopped in the middle of the *llano* (dry prairie) road, the driver and guard had been hit with many arrows and were slumped on the driver's seat. My mother, moaning and sobbing, looked through the stagecoach window and saw the Apaches coming. She feared them more than dying and pointed a pistol to kill me, but then she shot herself in an eye instead."

He paused for a moment and cupped his hand to his ear. We did the same. Far down in the canyon we could hear wolves snarling and growling, water splashing, and the faint bleat of a deer coming to its end.

Kitsizil Lichoo' continued his story. "Juh already had three wives, one not yet with a child, and he gave me to her. It was two harvests before I made words or noise after my mother died, but I listened and watched, and I spoke as a true *Nednhi* when my tongue worked again. I learned to live like an Apache. I played war and raiding games with the other children, learned the bow, knife, spear, and sling. I trained as they did, running long and hard every day, and I learned the ways of the People and *Ussen.*

"The *Nednhi* women thought my hair was pretty and that it brought them luck when they stroked it. They taught me to pray to *Ussen* every morning, made sure I had plenty to eat, and took good care of me. In time, I understood the *Nednhi* were my people, not the *Indah*. I had to work hard for the *Nednhi* women until Juh began to train me. It's been five harvests since I went on my first novice raid. Now, I wear a warrior's scars."

He turned to me and said, "I would ask to know more about your experience with this witch you seek in the camp of Elias. Will you answer?"

Even in the starlight shadows under the tall pine trees, I saw Beela-chezzi squint a warning that meant, *Answer carefully. We don't know this Apache with red hair.*

"I will answer." Beela-chezzi looked up to the stars in apparent disgust. But, to me, Kitsizil Lichoo' was a friend we must trust, not a stranger.

"You've likely heard how I showed Juh my Power by shooting the gourd off the top of the head of a running *Nakai-yi* slave child, the one my mother now calls Lucky Star." He nodded, and I continued, "That shot convinced Juh my Power was from *Ussen,* and he told me of the witch, Sangre del Diablo, the one who led the Comanches and *Nakai-yi pistoleros* when they wiped out and scalped most of Cha's Mescaleros in the Guadalupe Mountains, including my father. All three Mescalero warriors in our camp at Juh's stronghold rode with me to kill that witch. Only Beela-chezzi and I returned. Sangre del Diablo and two of his band escaped, still, we killed many of his warriors and *banditos.*"

I stopped for a moment as the memory of Beela-chezzi and me burying my grandfather and our friend, who were killed by Sangre del Diablo, blew to life the hot coals of fury still hot in my guts.

"A warrior, riding to Juh with word from Victorio, rested his pony in the Río Casas Grandes bosque and saw Sangre del Diablo and his two Comanches destroy three wagons filled with women and children and then burn their bodies. Those women and children were slaves Beela-chezzi and I had freed when we took the witch's *hacienda*. Before torching the bodies, the warrior heard Sangre del Diablo send the Comanches to the camp of Elias where he said he would go in three moons after he left a baby, who lived through the wagon massacre, with a woman in Casas Grandes and called more warriors to leave the Comanche reservation far out on the *llano* to come and join him." I knew Kitsizil Lichoo' heard the rage in my voice. I couldn't hide it. I spoke through clenched teeth.

Beela-chezzi sighed. "Victorio, the great chief who stayed at Mescalero for a while, is on a rampage trying to kill every *Nakai-yi* in Chihuahua and every *Indah* north of the border. Why would Sangre del Diablo save the life of a slave baby? Do you think he will use it to get back his *di-yen* power in a witch's feast of blood? Perhaps he will rape or mutilate it in front of his men. He's the worst of evil."

Kitsizil Lichoo' shrugged his shoulders and shook his head, but his face showed he hated the thought of what might happen to the child.

I said, "If the Comanches are in the camp of Elias, we'll find a way to kill them and not betray Elias's welcome. We'll wait for Sangre del Diablo to appear and then kill him. *Ussen* gave me Power to kill witches. My Power gives me the accuracy to shoot them in the eyes and send them forever blind to the Happy Land. This witch must die for all the evil he has done to my People and others. He'll die by my hand. I'll send him blind to the Happy Land of the grandfathers."

Wind shook the tops of the pines on our ridge, and I could feel the eyes of Kitsizil Lichoo' on me, but he said nothing for a long time, and I thought he had heard all he wanted and had nothing more to say. But then, he said, "Elias will give the Comanches and their witch wickiups and help them when they ask. I don't trust Elias. He's a fool who makes badly planned raids where warriors always die. Juh stays away from him. Perhaps the witch will turn on my People as he did on yours. I'll help you kill him and his Comanches before they can attack us."

"*Enjuh*. Kitsizil Lichoo' is a good friend. Beela-chezzi and I welcome you to our hunt for the witch."

CHAPTER 3
THE CAMP OF ELIAS

We kept our ponies back in the trees and studied the camp of Elias from behind boulders on top of a ridge. I counted over thirty wickiups scattered among the cottonwoods, willows, and scrub oak growing next to rushing water in a deep canyon. Although the sun was only halfway to the western mountains from the time of short shadows, the canyon floor was dark from its high wall shadows and made the camp hard to see. If Beela-chezzi and I had come alone, we might never have found it. Like other Apache camps, no noise gave it away. No horses snorting or neighing, no cattle bawling, no children playing, even the women chopping wood were hard to hear over the rush of the water. Kitsizil Lichoo' pointed with his nose to a man making a long saber-tipped lance next to the biggest wickiup in the rancheria. He had long hair, reaching to his waist and held out of his face with a blue bandanna. His muscular arms and big chest projected an image of strength and vigor. This was Elias.

Three women worked around his wickiup, and he occasionally spoke or motioned to one or the other to bring him something from the wickiup or to do some chore. A few warriors worked on their weapons or lounged in the camp, but we saw no Comanches among them.

We watched the camp until the sky began to catch the orange and pink colors of sunset, and then rode down the twisting trail off the ridge toward the camp. Playing children saw us coming and ran. As we passed the outer edge of the camp, warriors began appearing with bows, spears, and rifles in their hands, saying nothing, their obsidian-black eyes following our every move as we confidently rode to the place where Elias was finishing his lance. The men of the ranchería closed behind us, silent, waiting for a sign from Elias, who sat by the orange and yellow flames of a fire one of the women had lighted.

Kitsizil Lichoo', rifle in the crook of his arm, stopped his pony and said, "*D'anté*, Elias. Kitsizil Lichoo', son of Juh, brings Mescalero friends to speak with you. Will you share your fire with us?"

Elias set aside the nearly finished lance tipped with a long curving blade from a *Nakai-yi* sword and ran his eyes over Beela-chezzi and me a few moments before motioning us down from our ponies. Boys ran up to take our reins and lead them away.

Elias nodded toward us. "I know the son of Juh, Kitsizil Lichoo'. If you come from Juh, you have ridden far. How are the Mescaleros called?"

Beela-chezzi, being my senior, said, "I am Beela-chezzi of the Mescaleros." He turned toward me and said, "My brother is called Yellow Boy. He's a Killer of Witches. He'll speak for us."

Elias, his face a mask of indifference, motioned us to sit. At this sign of hospitality, the warriors who had followed us to his fire disappeared into the growing darkness.

"You have hunger from your long ride. Eat first, and then we will talk."

A woman appeared out of the wickiup with a haunch of roast venison, slices of mescal, a pot of mixed greens, potatoes, and chiles, and a basket of acorn bread. A young boy, maybe two harvests, held on to her skirt with one hand while he followed her and studied us with bright, unblinking eyes.

We had eaten only dry trail food after we left Juh's stronghold, and the smell of the cooking sent arrows of hunger deep in our bellies. The fiery pot filled with chiles, boiled yucca leaves mixed with algerita berries, potatoes, and onions added good flavor to the meat we sliced off the haunch with our knives and to the crunchy acorn bread we held in our fingers. We filled our bellies until we could eat no more. We put our gourds aside, cleaned our knives, rubbed the grease from our mouths and hands on our legs, and rested back against our elbows while Elias took his time to finish eating and studied Beela-chezzi and me as he asked Kitsizil Lichoo' about any news of Victorio and his raids against the *Indah* and the *Nakai-yes*.

Elias finally put his gourd to his lips, tipped it up, slurped the last of its juice, and then wiped the grease from his mouth to rub it on his legs. Another woman came and took the rest of the meal inside to the waiting women and children before she came back to clean up around the fire.

Elias pulled a small sack of tobacco from a parfleche near his tools and, dropping a few pinches of chopped tobacco into an oak leaf, rolled a cigarette. Lighting it, using a twig from his fire, he smoked to the four directions and passed it to us.

The cigarette finished, he said, "My Mescalero brothers have come far. What do they seek from Elias?"

Beela-chezzi nodded toward me to begin.

"Two harvests ago, my brother here and I lived in the camp of Cha across the great river in the mountains the *Nakai-yes* and *Tejano*s call Guadalupe. During the Season of Large Fruit, Cha went on a raid far to the south and west of the great river with most of our warriors. I was in the mountains to the west and north where *Ussen* gave me a vision and Power to use my rifle to send witches blind to the land of the grandfathers.

"A few days after my vision, I had a dream about a witch attacking my father's camp. I left the mountains and rode hard to warn them and to kill it, but I was too late. The day before, a

Comanche-*Nakai-yi* witch leading Comanches and *banditos* wiped out all in Cha's camp, taking their scalps to sell to the *Nakai-yes*. A few women and children escaped because they were away collecting nuts and juniper berries to save for the Ghost Face Season. My grandfather, who had a stiff, crooked knee, was able to escape by hiding in the brush. No other warrior in the camp survived the attack."

I heard Beela-chezzi sigh. I knew he still blamed himself for not being there to defend his wife and sons when the attack came. I noticed that Kitsizil Lichoo's eyes narrowed as he followed every blink and twitch of Elias's face. I struggled to keep the rage out of my voice, but I knew Elias heard it.

"I found those who survived and took them to the Mescalero Reservation where they would have food for the Ghost Face Season and be protected from the witch and *Indah*. Only Beela-chezzi and three other warriors returned to their families from Cha's raid across the great river. All they found were the ashes of their camp and signs of the bodies I buried in the cliff talus next to the camp. *Tejano* Rangers killed Cha and most of the other warriors. Beela-chezzi and the others returning saw our trail toward the reservation and went there the next year after snow cleared the passes in the Season of Little Eagles.

"That year, in the Season of Many Leaves, the Blue Coats came to the reservation to take our rifles and horses. They believed the Mescaleros helped provide Victorio with warriors, supplies, and ammunition. Maybe a few did, but most stayed away from Victorio. Our little band from Cha's camp escaped the soldiers on the reservation and crossed the great river to find the stronghold of Juh, where he told us of a witch living a long day's ride from the stronghold. The way Juh described him, the witch looked like the one my grandfather described, a painted giant with no hair, burning, killing, and scalping.

"My warrior brother here, Beela-chezzi, another warrior, my

grandfather, and I killed most of the witch's band, but he and two Comanches got away after sending a warrior and my grandfather to the Happy Land. Three days after we returned to Juh's stronghold, a warrior carrying a message from Victorio told Juh that, while he rested his pony in the bosque on the Río Casas Grandes, he saw a giant with no hair and two Comanches destroy three wagons filled with women and children on the trail to Casas Grandes."

Elias's eyes narrowed and he shook his head. "These are foolish men to throw away valuable captives like that. Why would the witch do that? Who knows if a witch can ever be trusted to do anything that makes sense?"

I saw Beela-chezzi's hands resting on the top of his knees curl into angry fists, but he said nothing as I continued.

"Those wagons carried the slaves we had freed after we attacked the witch and drove him off. The warrior told Juh he heard the giant tell the Comanches to go to camp of Elias in the Blue Mountains where he would join them in three moons. We're looking for those Comanches, and we ask if they've come here. That's all I have to say."

While I spoke, the eyes of Elias never left my face, and I looked straight into his. The frogs in the water and peepers on the trees and the night crickets began their songs and sang above the rush of rolling water. Kitsizil Lichoo' and Beela-chezzi sat in the shadows cast by the wavering flames and studied us both. I heard a child laugh, and I wondered if maybe Elias also laughed at us in secret. A voice spoke in my mind and told me not to trust him.

Elias stared into the fire a few moments and slowly shook his head. He turned to us, his arms crossed, his eyes looking away from mine to stare at the stars above the black ridgeline behind me.

"No Comanches came to my camp. If they had, I would tell

you. You have the right to face them warrior-to-warrior and take your revenge. I've heard of Sangre del Diablo, a very powerful warrior and witch. Juh fears him, and so do I. You did well against him, even if you didn't kill him and lost two of your brothers. Stay and wait for his Comanches. You're welcome here. Perhaps you can teach us all to shoot better."

Beela-chezzi said, "Elias is generous with his offer. We have women and children in the camp of Juh and must speak together to decide if we can wait. Tonight we'll rest in your camp. With the sunrise, we'll speak with you about what we'll do."

Elias nodded. "Beela-chezzi is wise. The first wickiup by the trail coming in is empty. Spread your blankets there. I'll send women with wood for your fire. Come for a meal at my fire when the sun rises. We'll speak then about what you have decided."

"Elias is a great chief and generous to guests in his rancheria. We'll come again when there is new light for the day."

We left Elias's fire and walked back down the trail to the wickiup he offered us. As soon as we were out of his hearing, Beela-chezzi said under his breath, "Elias fears the witch. He lies."

Two women, saying nothing, came, started a fire, and left us enough wood to keep it burning through the night. We spread our blankets, sat down, and enjoyed the bright, yellow heat in the cold, black air. I lighted a *cigarro,* and after we smoked, I said, "Why do you think Elias lies?"

Beela-chezzi said, "He watched you the way a rattlesnake watches a rabbit. He lies, but I don't know why. I know he fears the witch. Maybe he thinks if he provides him cover from us, the witch won't scalp him or witch his people."

I nodded. "I think you speak true. Somehow, we must learn his true mind."

Kitsizil Lichoo' smiled and said, "Wait until the fire burns down. I'll go bush crawling to a widow I know and consider for a wife. I'll learn what happens in this camp when I lie on her blanket."

The ashes in our fire were cold and the stars had turned around the North Star past the middle of the night. We heard the grass and twigs under Kitsizil Lichoo's blanket crackle before he slid its wool over his body and wrapped it close around his shoulders and neck. Beela-chezzi spoke into the cold blackness, "The widow speaks more than sighs at your coming?"

"She sighed plenty at my coming. After we took our pleasures, she whispered her secrets to me."

My mind awoke from its daze at the edge of sleep, stirred by the bait of his words. "Tell us!"

He leaned in close to us and spoke softly. "She says the Comanches left yesterday at the time of shortest shadows. The only trail they know to the camp comes in from the north and is the one they follow back to Casas Grandes. That is why we did not see them on the trail here from the south. They told Elias they would return with Sangre del Diablo and more warriors in three moons and how to find them in Casas Grandes if there was news for them. Elias thinks the witch will attack and try to wipe out his camp for scalps to sell for *Nakai-yi pesh-klitso* (gold), and the easiest way to stop an attack is to tell the witch where we are. Elias sends a rider to Casas Grandes tomorrow."

Beela-chezzi grunted, "Hmmph. How does she know all this? How does she know that he sends a rider to Casas Grandes and that he truly fears the witch?"

I heard Kitsizil Lichoo' snort and give a low-throated laugh. "Hah! Her mother is second wife to Elias, and her wickiup is next to the one where Elias sleeps. Tonight all his wives sat in the big wickiup listening to Elias in council. Children were playing their war games around the wickiups, whooping and laughing. My woman and I had only to be quiet while we enjoyed each other. I, too, heard most of the council when I lay with her."

I laughed with Beela-chezzi, and Kitsizil Lichoo' and said, "Apache women do like warriors with red hair. *Enjuh.* Tomorrow, let's tell Elias we need to return to the stronghold but will return in two moons to wait for Sangre del Diablo; he's already said we're welcome to wait.

"We'll leave after we speak to Elias and wait up the trail to see the rider before taking a short trail across the Blue Mountains. If we ride hard, we can get in front of him and wait for him near Casas Grandes. That way we can follow him to the house of the witch's woman."

They grunted, agreeing with me, and Beela-chezzi said, "It's a good plan."

CHAPTER 4
SANGRE DEL DIABLO

After we left his camp, Elias had a warrior follow us. When the shadows were shortest, the warrior disappeared. I took the *Shináá Cho* (literally, Big Eye—a telescope) and ran back down the trail to watch Elias's camp while Beela-chezzi and Kitsizil Lichoo' waited with the ponies in the trees on top of a high ridge. I ran the trail faster on foot than the warrior who had trailed us on a horse and nearly beat him back to the camp of Elias.

From the trees on the ridge above the camp, I watched the warrior speak with Elias. When he finished, Elias called to another warrior, who carried a single-shot rifle with a long barrel like those the Blue Coats used. He wore a holstered revolver backwards the way I'd seen *Indah* wear them at trading posts. He had an ammunition belt across his chest and shoulder, and wore his hair in one long braid that reached to his waist.

Elias spoke with him awhile and then listened with crossed arms as the warrior seemed to repeat what he heard Elias say. I saw Elias nod and then motion the warrior toward a trail along the canyon wall to the northeast, the same trail the Comanches had followed. The warrior's pony, big and red with a white blaze on its nose and a white right foot, made it easy to know the rider and the pony. I ran back up the trail to my friends before he rode the opposite trail out of the canyon.

★ ★ ★ ★ ★

We waited behind rocks on a ridge above Río Casas Grandes, taking turns using the *Shináá Cho* to study riders on the trail by the bosque. Directly below us, next to the trail, lay the burned remains of the wagons that had carried the women and children we had freed from the witch. The unburned pieces of the wagon frames looked like big black bones sticking up from a grave, and mingled with them were the real burned bones of those women and children. I stared at the black place for a long time, wondering if the bones would ever have their revenge, their justice. I hoped that *Ussen* would guide my bullets so Sangre del Diablo paid the full price for the evil he had done and that soon his bones too would burn.

A day and a night passed before we saw Elias's rider in late morning light, staying off the trail but still following the river toward Casas Grandes. We waited and then followed him, keeping the river bosque between him and us. He rode past Casas Grandes but soon stopped at the gate of a small *hacienda* east of the village. Two Comanches came through the gate, rifles cocked, motioning him to dismount. He put his hands where they could see them, swung a leg over his saddle horn, and slid off his pony. The rider and Comanches talked awhile, and then one of the Comanches went inside and returned with a scowling Sangre del Diablo. He stood with crossed arms listening to the rider from Elias, the red thunder in his face growing as he heard the message. With the *Shináá Cho*, I could see past the gate and into the front of the *hacienda* compound where a young Indian-Mexican woman, tall and built well for having children, paced in the wall shadows with a baby in her arms.

All three of our enemies and Elias's rider stood together in front of me. I wanted to shoot, but the rider from Elias kept moving around and getting in the way, and I did not want to risk killing him. We didn't need enemies in the camp of Elias, and the range was too far for a certain shot with the evening breeze off the hills swirling the weeds and grass. If I missed, I'd scatter Sangre del Diablo and his Comanches across the *llano* like quail seeing a coyote. I thought, *Patience. Patience. Ussen will give them to you.* Then Sangre del Diablo lowered his head, as though in thought, and walked back inside the *hacienda* compound. The Comanches led the Elias rider into the compound and closed the gate.

We waited. The sunset, a great blazing fire burning the sky black, left a long twilight trail, but the *hacienda* gate stayed closed. Toward the east a golden white glow was forming behind the mountains for a full moon rising.

Beela-chezzi said, "We need to be ready to ride. Comanches like to raid under big moons."

Kitsizil Lichoo' grimaced and scowled. He didn't like to ride at night. It was always dangerous to ride in the dark.

The moon big and glowing white floated above the distant mountains, bringing soft light and stark shadows. Slowly the *hacienda* gates swung open, and Elias's rider rode out toward the west and the Blue Mountains, but he used a different trail than that through the bosque along the river. The two Comanches rode north back up the Río Casas Grandes. Sangre del Diablo, on a big black stallion, rode with them until just past Casas Grandes before turning east toward the great river.

As we mounted, I said to Beela-chezzi, "*Ussen* gave me the Power to kill witches. The witch is mine. The Comanches are yours. I'll meet you at the stronghold after our work is finished."

Beela-chezzi nodded. "Take the witch, and satisfy us all with his blood."

He turned to Kitsizil Lichoo' and asked, "Will you help us, brother?"

Kitsizil Lichoo' nodded. "I'll help my brothers. These

51

Comanches one day will dare attack our people. They must die."

We rode up out of the bosque. On the moonlit *llano,* there was enough light to see dust streamers from the riders disappearing in the cold, black shadows in the distance, and we took up the chase. I knew that if Sangre del Diablo got across the great river too far in front of me, I could probably never catch him in the land of the *Tejanos.* It was unfamiliar land to me, and many more *Indah* rode the land than *Nakai-yes* in Chihuahua. I was much more likely to be seen or caught in the land of the *Indah.* I made it my goal to take him before he crossed the river. I had to take him before then. It was a matter of pride. I listened to my anger and not the head *Ussen* gave me, but I knew I had to be careful. If the witch saw me coming, he would wait in ambush and kill me.

CHAPTER 5
RACE TO THE GREAT RIVER

The land toward the great river east of Casas Grandes is hard, rocky, *llano* covered with cactus, creosote, and mesquite, great white sandy playas, and black mountains the old ones say were made in valleys of fire, leaving big rock cinders that cut you when you touch them unaware of their knife-sharp edges. The easiest, but longer, way to reach the great river from Casas Grandes is to ride north and then east and trail around the mountains and playas to the village on the great river, the one the *Nakai-yes* call El Paso del Norte, where the *Indah* live on the north side and the *Nakai-yes* on the south. Sangre del Diablo didn't take that trail. After a short ride north, he turned east to follow a dry, shallow arroyo toward a star-filled notch between two black bumps, mountains in the night. I hung far back as I trailed him. The bright moonlight let me see and follow the dust cloud kicked up by the big black in the cold, still air as he loped in long, easy strides that ate up the distance.

I thought of many things as I followed the witch. I wanted to use the Power the great Creator God, *Ussen,* had given me to help my People and be a Killer of Witches with my Yellow Boy Henry rifle, a rifle with *pesh-klitso* (yellow iron) around its trigger and loading lever. With my gift of Power, I could shoot out a witch's eyes with that rifle and send him blind to the land of the grandfathers. As I wound past mesquite, creosote, cactus, and ocotillo growing on the banks of the arroyo, images drifted through my mind of the night my father, Caballo Negro, gave me my first real bow and a buckskin quiver filled with arrows made by my grandfather, He Watches. That same night, He Watches also gave me the sharp knife I still carried. The next day, I began my warrior training. Caballo Negro had spoken to me about becoming a warrior. First, I had to learn to hunt. I had to discipline myself to wait a long time unmoving for a one-shot kill. I had to know the habits of the animals I hunted and have more patience and be more knowledgeable than an animal in its own territory. Now, I hunted the most dangerous animal of all, the witch, Sangre del Diablo, who had already killed my father, over three harvests earlier, and then He Watches, my friend Klo-sen, and nearly me almost a moon ago.

I remembered burying my father's body after Sangre del Diablo killed and mutilated him. I remembered the witch tying me to a cross like those the brown robes keep around their meeting places and wear on little *pesh-lickoyee* (silver) chains around their necks. I remembered He Watches hanging on a cross opposite me while the witch's owl tore out his eyes and killed him. He Watches suffered without a sound. He never gave the witch any pleasure in his suffering. He was a man of great courage, and I was proud to be his grandson. I remembered hanging on a cross, being tied there with green, wet rawhide that grew tight as it dried, pulling at my joints from my wrists to my shoulders, and thinking that I didn't have the courage to die as bravely as He Watches. But Beela-chezzi and Klo-sen had freed me. *Ussen* meant for me to live, and he'd given me another chance to kill Sangre del Diablo.

The moon reached the top of its arc and began to fall toward the mountains to the south and west. The arroyo in which Sangre del Diablo rode split around a cluster of hills in the middle of the star-filled notch between the two mountains; one arroyo branch went northeast, the other, southeast. Sangre del Diablo rode up between the hills and disappeared on the other side, following a wide grassy climb up through a low pass.

A voice in my mind spoke straight and clear. It said beware of an ambush, but the burning rage growing in me from thinking of the deaths of Caballo Negro and He Watches and Klosen made me deaf to its warning. I waited as long as I dared to ride through the low pass and not lose the witch on the other side. I knew the danger in going over the pass in the moonlight. With the moon still up, I would be outlined on the horizon.

I stopped to think. *I won't have a long exposure crossing the pass. I can't waste time looking for the witch's trail if I lose sight of him. Besides, wandering into his rifle's sights out on the* llano *could kill me, too. I have to go now.*

I urged my pony forward and let him pick his way around the rocks scattered on the faint trail up through the dry, brown grama grass to the top. We topped the pass. I instantly knew I had made a mistake. We were in black outline against the face of setting moon. I heard a sound like a fist hitting a belly. My pony shuddered, neighed in surprise, and staggered to its knees. I leaped off his back as he fell and I heard the thunder from the big rifle bullet that killed him echoing off the canyon walls below. The air stirred my hair as a second bullet whistled past my ear, followed by a second echoing roll of thunder.

I managed to keep my rifle as I hit ground and rolled to one side. I crabbed over to my pony, dead before it hit the ground, sliding a little way down the trail from the top of the pass and stopping a few paces beyond me. Even though I hid in deep shadow and knew the witch couldn't see me, I stayed low to find protection behind my pony's back. I strained to see through the darkness, but the same blackness that had probably saved me, blocked me from seeing anything.

I heard a wolf's howl and then two more before a deep, roaring laugh echoed off the wide canyon walls below. A loud voice I knew well said, "Apache fool! You think I didn't see you following me? I have much to do and must ride now, but I'll come back for you. Then I'll fill your mouth with your privates and cut your throat while you choke on them. I'll take your hair just as I took your father's hair!" Then he made his wolf howls and they faded in the distance until I heard them no more.

I thought, *witch, I'll come now. Even if you don't wait for me, I'll find you.*

My canteen survived the fall of my pony. I still had water. I checked my rifle. It was not broken, not even scarred by my fall. I saw light in the eastern sky. The sun was coming. I gathered myself and ran, ducking from shadow to shadow down the pass to the canyon, found the witch's trail, and followed it.

I knew that with the rising sun's light spreading long shadows, the witch would be well out of the hills and would stop to rest near water, hiding his pony and finding a hiding place where he could sleep.

I saw the green brush around water in the distance and knew that must be the place where he would stop. From a nearby ridge, a little above the tank, I used the *Shináá Cho* to study the country looking for where his trail might wind toward the east before I decided what to do.

The *Shináá Cho* showed the *llano* very dry, the creosote bushes not much more than bare sticks poking out of the ground, and prickly pear pads, dry and shriveled, made me glad I carried water. Sangre del Diablo knew the hidden desert water tanks and springs. I didn't know the country, which meant I couldn't get ahead of him and wait to ambush him at the next water. I had to follow and wait for him to make a mistake. It would take three, maybe four, days of running to reach the great river. Somewhere along the way, I knew I would have a chance to take him. I just needed to make us even, maybe even give myself an advantage. On foot I could probably outlast his pony in a long-distance run, and I believed if we were both on foot, I could run faster and longer than the witch. I might have more of an advantage in a foot race with him than if we were both on ponies. I had to decide how to keep him moving and not rest. A tired, sleepy man always made mistakes.

I used the *Shináá Cho* to study every hiding place around the water tank but did not see Sangre del Diablo or the black stallion anywhere. I decided to go down the back of the ridge, and circle the water tank out of sight, until I found his hiding place.

Crawling and slithering across the *llano,* I moved in a great circle around the sparkling pool of dark water as I looked for Sangre del Diablo's resting place. Almost reaching the ridge east of the water, and past the time when shadows are shortest, I finally saw his big, black pony, hobbled and grazing in a low place screened by a thicket of mesquite. I didn't move. I knew if I made any sound, the witch would be quick to find me, and, shooting from cover, he wouldn't miss as he had in the dim moonlight. I would wait until the late afternoon shadows favored me or the witch made a mistake.

The sun was falling into darkness, and the shadows grew long. The stallion raised his head from the grass and stared toward the ridge, his ears up, listening. At last, the witch stirred. I thought, *Now witch, I'll take you.*

I twisted slightly to look toward the west to judge how long the light would last, and then looked back toward the stallion. It had disappeared. I remembered it hadn't had water all day. Raising my eyes just above the brush, I saw the glint of the tank water reflecting the last golden light from the sun and the dark outline of the witch leading the pony toward it. The witch stayed on the stallion's far side away from me, making it impossible for me to see him, much less take a shot. The one chance I had to take the witch was to kill the pony and hope for a shot when it fell.

In the dimming light, I pulled back the rifle hammer to full cock, and rising to one knee, sighted on the stallion's head. The Henry roared in fire and smoke, its crack of thunder rolling to the ridge behind the water tanks and coming back to me. The top of the stallion's head exploded, and the pony collapsed, its life gone in an instant. I levered another round and, with my eye fixed on the sights, swung my rifle back and forth looking for a shot.

Sangre del Diablo had disappeared. Even in the low light, I could tell he didn't lie behind the black pony for cover. He had to be somewhere in the mesquite waiting for me to show myself so he could take a shot. Neither of us moved as we waited for the cover of cold blackness before the moon lighted up the night. I crawled to the dead pony before moonrise, took water, and waited for the moon to find his trail. He wouldn't wait to ambush me here. Running ahead to another place of water where he might see me on his trail, rather than guessing how I might move to catch him, was to his advantage.

For three nights and days, I followed Sangre del Diablo, drawing closer to him, looking for my chance to take him, but he carefully avoided places where I could ambush him and kept to well-hidden places, impossible to reach without him seeing and killing me first. I had guessed right. I could outrun him, but I needed my speed to follow him on the long trails while he took the shorter ones. I waited for my chance. My grandfather, He Watches, had taught me patience long ago, which was sometimes the only way to fight against a strong enemy.

After trailing the witch throughout the fourth night, I caught whiffs of the moldy smell of mud and felt water in the air from the great river. I knew he might try to cross the river in the early light, which meant I had to risk running in the land of the *Tejanos* if 1 chose to follow him. With the *Shináá Cho* in the early gray light, I caught a glimpse of him crossing a stretch of white sand and disappearing behind a line of mesquites. I had to get closer and take him or follow him across the river.

CHAPTER 6
DUEL

I waited, scanning the mesquite where Sangre del Diablo disappeared. Nothing moved, not even leaves in the lightly stirring air. The dawn light was growing brighter. I ran for the mesquite, desperate to take him before he crossed the great river. A brilliant flash of orange and white light thundered from the dark mesquite and hammered me backwards into a shallow dip in the sand. He fired fast, emptying his rifle, his bullets raising little fountains of sand where they hit. I don't think he could see me. All his other shots were wide or sailed high over my head.

Lying in the hollow, I stared up at the soft light filling the sky and felt a fool. Ambushed twice in the clear. I had not made such a childish error since my friends and I tried to ambush each other when we learned to fight using slings and rocks. My wound felt far worse than the sting from a rock hit, more like a red-hot blade cutting into my left side just below my ribs. The firing stopped. I cocked my rifle and waited, listening for the sound of bullets being loaded and moccasins crunching across the sand coming me to finish me. None came.

Blood, warm, somehow comforting in the cold air, slowly leaked down my side and covered the sand. I felt it on my back, making the sand warm and smooth, and I wondered if the witch had killed me. I moved my hand covering the leaking wound in the front to feel if the bullet had come out my back. I felt the hole in my back. It was a little larger than the one in front. The bullet had passed through. I thanked the spirits protecting me. A voice roared in my head, *You won't die! Get up and catch him!*

I raised my head and saw nothing between the mesquite and me. *I might live and still kill the witch.* Only *Ussen* knew. I crawled to a clump of prickly pear a few yards away. I skinned a few of its pads, squeezed the juice from some on the bullet hole, made a bandage from my bandanna, and slid a couple under the bandage over each bullet hole. I rested awhile and didn't feel as weak as I had lying in the sand hollow. The bleeding stopped, and, using my rifle as a staff, I managed to stand. I wobbled toward the mesquite, my rifle ready, but certain Sangre del Diablo had already gone.

On the eastern side of the mesquite thicket, I found where he had sat waiting for me. Cartridges shining like *pesh-klitso* lay scattered and gleaming on the white sand. There was enough light to see the great river's dark, green bosque four, maybe five, long bowshots away, and to see the path he made toward it. I wobbled down the path after him as fast as I could but grew weaker with every step.

By the time I entered the bosque, I was bleeding again and staggering to stand as my strength drained away. Even though the sun was coming, the light seemed to dim. I came to the great river's bank sweating so hard that it ran off my forehead and into my eyes, nearly blinding me. Using my shirtsleeve, I wiped the sweat from my eyes and, looking through the cottonwood trees, saw Sangre del Diablo wading across the river. He was nearly to the far bank. I sank to my knees and rested my rifle on a driftwood log. Through the sweat filling my eyes and the strangely fading light, I tried to see enough of the Yellow Boy's sights to shoot. He looked back, saw me, and threw up his rifle. I didn't hesitate. The Henry boomed and a black dot suddenly appeared on his upper chest that streamed blood down his chest and belly as he staggered backwards. Time stood still as wide eyes and a dropped jaw of surprise filled his face. He fell with a big splash and slowly rolled over facedown in the brown water that turned the color of a blood-red cloudy sunset around him.

The light was almost gone. I began sinking into a powerful, black sleep, watching the current carry his body downstream. My eyes stayed open as I sagged back off my knees to sit down and watch the witch float away. I thought, *You won't be blind in the Happy Land, witch, but at least you aren't here in the land of the living.* I watched him drift facedown in the great river, its current carrying him toward the far bank, but in the space of a few long breaths, he suddenly stood, the water rolling off his body and making him glisten even in the low light. Still holding his rifle, looking like a boy's toy in his big hands, he staggered into the brush on the far side. Darkness filled my eyes, and I left the day with the bitter thought that I had not killed him after all. Maybe he had killed me.

I felt the fire's warmth before I opened my eyes to see its wavy orange and yellow light flickering against the darkness. I heard the burble of the river nearby and the frogs and insects making their songs, saw white, twinkling points of pure white light in the blackness covering the leaves above me, and felt my throat burning for water. I had not yet passed to the Happy Land of the grandfathers. I lowered my eyes and looked across the fire. Surprise and a glad heart filled me to see the face of Kah (Arrow), a friend from since before we went on our trials to earn invitations from the warriors to serve them as novices on their raids. Grown to a strong warrior, Kah had been on a raid in Chihuahua with Cha when the witch with his Comanches and *banditos* destroyed our camp. He found what was left of us on the reservation, but after a few moons rode away to make war against the *Indah* and *Nakai-yes* with Victorio before the

Blue Coats came to steal our rifles and horses. I had not seen him since he left us.

Kah saw that I had awakened and nodded. "So Yellow Boy lives. It will take more than a Blue Coat or Mexican bullet to kill you." He stood and brought a Blue Coat canteen to give me water. It was from the great river and should have tasted a little sour, but it was the sweetest water I had tasted in a long time. In long gulping swallows, I drank it dry, and nodding, handed it back to him as he squatted near me, watching every move I made.

I wanted to sit up and face him but was too weak and spoke to the stars. "Never was water better. Kah, you saved my life, but the hole in me is not from a Blue Coat or Mexican bullet. It is from Sangre del Diablo, the witch who killed and scalped our people."

Kah frowned and cocked his head to one side as if mystified. "How did you come to find the witch in this place, and how did you miss killing him? Your Power would shoot out his eyes and send him to the grandfathers. Is your Power gone? Where is the witch now? I will kill him."

I put my hand down where the bullet hit me and found a poultice covered it. "I will answer all you ask, but first tell me how you found me and what you've done to my wound."

Kah's face, hardened by months of raiding and killing *Indahs*, *Nakai-yes*, and Blue Coats, cracked with a smile, and his eyes shone as I remembered from the old days. "*Ussen* makes the great wheel of life turn. I was scouting this country for Victorio, so he'd know where the Mexicans and Blue Coats were and could attack them to his advantage. A Blue Coat fort, the *Indah* call it Quitman, is a little south, down the river from here, and I was riding in the bosque to find a place where I can watch it. Victorio says he'll come soon for a raid and plans to make raids in the land of the *Indah* and *Tejanos*. I heard guns. One rifle shot many times, and then it was quiet. I thought that maybe a Blue Coat patrol was wasting bullets. I decided to kill them and take their supplies. I came near here, and two more shots sounded very close together, but there were no Blue Coats.

"I found you soon after the shots. I thought that maybe you were dead. I saw no others. You had bled much. I had to stop bleeding quickly or you'd die, so I built a little fire and made the end of my knife blade red, very hot, and used it to stop the bleeding in front and back. Then I used the prickly pear to heal the burns around your wound. I worried that you'd come awake and try to kill me because I burnt you, but you didn't wake up. We're both lucky. If the bullet had stayed in you, the wound would turn green and stink, and you would have died. I've seen this many times riding with Victorio. Now, will you answer my questions?"

I nodded and felt the prickly pear pads over the bullet holes, and sliding my finger under them, felt the crusted skin, sore and tender, where Kah had burned me to stop the bleeding. Yes, I was very lucky.

I groaned. "I'll answer you. In the Season of Little Eagles, the Blue Coats came one day at the time of shortest shadows from many directions to the reservation. They took our guns and horses. They thought the Mescaleros had supplied Victorio with bullets and horses, even warriors."

Kah muttered, "The fools."

"Yes, they were fools. Our little camp slipped away across the great river and went to Juh's stronghold on the flat-top mountain. He let us stay and showed us the witch's *hacienda*. Beela-chezzi, two others, and I tried to kill him and his band of Comanches and Mexicans. He nearly killed me, and he and two Comanches got away, but we killed all the others. Two of our warriors went to the Happy Land."

Kah squinted at me in disbelief. "I've seen you shoot. Why

64

did you miss?"

"I can't hit what I can't see. Beela-chezzi and I went back to Juh's camp. Three days later, a warrior sent by Victorio to ask Juh for help with bullets and horses said he was resting his pony in the Río Casas Grandes bosque and saw the witch. He heard him tell the Comanches that he would meet them in Elias's camp in the Blue Mountains in three moons and to stay there until he came. Juh sent a warrior, Kitsizil Lichoo', his son with the red hair, to show Beela-chezzi and me the trail to the camp. Elias welcomed us but said no Comanches had yet come."

A smile of disgust formed on half of Kah's face. "Elias lied."

"Yes, we all thought so. We told Elias we would return in two moons to wait for the Comanches and the witch. We left for Juh's stronghold, but stopped and watched the camp, and after a while saw a rider take another trail east. We followed him and found the witch with the two Comanches at a *hacienda* a little east of Casas Grandes. That night the witch and Comanches left the *hacienda*. I followed the witch east, and Beela-chezzi and Kitsizil Lichoo' followed the Comanches north.

"Four days ago, the witch ambushed me and killed my pony, and the next day I killed his. I wanted to catch him before he crossed the great river and disappeared into the land of the *Indah*. I made a child's mistake hurrying to catch him. He ambushed me again from the mesquite thicket four bowshots west of the bosque. I had enough strength to stagger to the bosque and see him wading across. He was almost to the far side. I was bleeding and sweating, and the darkness had almost taken me when I tried to aim. The witch saw me and brought his rifle up. Even half-blind, I was quicker than he was and shot him high in the chest. He fell backwards and then rose to the surface facedown in the river and floating to the far side. I thought maybe he was dead, but soon he stood up and staggered out of the water and into the trees. Blackness overcame me, and I slept until you woke me up. The witch and I have wounded each other and lived to fight another day."

Kah sat shaking his head. "*Ussen* watches out for you, Yellow Boy. Sleep. I'll watch through the night in case the witch comes back. I'll track him and kill him myself when the sun comes."

CHAPTER 7
KAH RETURNS

Birds calling in the trees and squawking flocks on the water woke me. The sun, a metallic orange egg fast turning yellow, lay just above the horizon. Kah had built up the fire. Tilting up my head and looking around, I didn't see him anywhere. I felt better than the day before, but my wound throbbed with every breath, and I had a thirst as though I had run all day in the desert with only pebbles in my mouth. Kah had left the *Indah* canteen next to my blanket, and I worked the plug off and drank half of it before I rolled off the blanket to my knees and managed to stand without falling into a pit of darkness.

My side felt like Kah was still sticking his red knife in it. Little flashes of light drifted before my eyes until I steadied myself and staggered to the bushes to do my morning business. It took the last strand of my will to keep from falling when I returned to the blanket. I lay down with no strength left and hoped Kah would return soon.

The fire died down to a few coals in the cool, moist air of the dark, green bosque, and I drifted in and out of consciousness, floating along like driftwood bobbing on the surface of the river. The sun shot its arrows through the trees as it rode toward the top of the sky, their pools of light, shimmering and bright, drifting across my body. Then suddenly, as if stepping out of a dream's mists, Kah stood at my feet watching me, his arms crossed, concern filling his face.

"How do you feel, Aashcho (my friend)?"

I spoke as if in a dream, slow and thick-tongued. "My side thumps with every breath, but doesn't bleed. I'm weak and can barely stand to visit the bushes. Where did you go and what have you learned?"

Kah nodded, his eyes never leaving me, and said, "I looked for the witch. I found where he came out of the water. Truly, he's a giant. I have never seen such tracks. I think you shot him good. I found little splashes of blood on bush leaves, and his path was crooked as he staggered forward."

"He's a giant, bald and ugly. He's over a forearm taller than you are, and you're tall for an Apache, even taller than I am. Where'd he go? Is he dead?"

"Not far from the river are a few *Tejano vaqueros* with a cattle herd headed for Blue Coat places along the river, places the *Indah* call Camp Rice and Fort Quitman. Blue Coats with dark faces and short, curly hair camp with them. Victorio thinks these are good places to take a Blue Coat fort and then ride deep into the land of the *Tejanos*. The witch's tracks say he took a horse from the drovers' herd and rode hard north and east. He's gone, and I'll never catch him, but the drovers might. They left their cattle to chase him."

I nodded. "They won't catch him. He's too smart for them. Vengeance must wait until he returns."

"How do you know he'll return?"

"He told the Comanches who were with him he'd go to the Comanche reservation, find warriors, and come back to take Apache scalps for *Nakai-yi pesh-klitso* and to find me. Our business isn't finished."

Kah looked at his feet and shook his head. "No, it isn't finished . . . if you live. I must get you back to Juh's camp before the Happy Land calls you. Do you think you can stay on a pony?"

"Yes."

"Good. The cattle herders will lose another pony tonight. Rest while I fix something to eat."

Kah roasted a rabbit and found some wild onions and potatoes for us to eat. I slept as the sun fell in the west. I awoke stronger, but my side still felt on fire. Kah took a tan mustang from the cattle herders, and, by the time a fingernail moon rose above the *Tejano* mountains, he had me on the mustang ready to ride. Kah made a rope halter for my pony so he could lead him. All I had to do was hold on to the saddle horn and stay on the pony. My wound burned like fire in my side, but I am an Apache, taught to endure and overcome suffering. I managed to stay in the saddle all that night.

We stopped at a small water seep to rest and water the ponies. Kah gave me water from the canteen, but he took none, saying he didn't need it. I lay down in the grass by the seep and tried to rest, but the fire in my side kept me awake and conjured up images of the witch and what he did to He Watches. I thought of Juanita and remembered what the witch said he would do to her if he found us. The thought tore at my heart and gave me the strength I needed to return to her and our coming child.

Dawn, a dusty golden glow on our backs, came, and still we rode. Flashes of black, the opposite of lightning in a storm from the season of rain and wind, closed my mind for moments at a time, but I held on with all my strength and did not fall from the saddle.

In the middle of the time between dawn and the sun's short-est shadows, we came to a Mexican water tank where a creaking wheel on a tower pulled water from the ground. The cattle tracks around it showed that many watered there. We knew *vaqueros* must use the water, too, but decided our need to rest the ponies greater than our fear of discovery. Kah watered the horses while I fell into deep sleep in the shade of thick creosotes growing tall and green from the water spilled from the tank.

We stayed by the water tank the rest of the day, Kah watchful and napping; me, weaker than when we left the river, locked in a deep, dreamless sleep. I finally opened my eyes to see the blood reds, purples, and oranges covering the sky as Kah shook me awake and gave me water. We ate all that was left of the food cache Juanita made for me when Kitsizil Lichoo', Beela-chezzi, and I left for the camp of Elias. I was weaker than the night before, and my side continued to burn and throb. Kah changed my poultice and said I was not bleeding, but that the place around the wound looked red and felt warm, which was not a good sign. He helped me mount, and we rode on through the night.

As the night sky began disappearing with the coming sun, we rode in the Río Casas Grandes bosque and, staying in the trees, rode around Casas Grandes village past the little *hacienda* where the witch had brought the baby. My strength nearly gone, I held on to the saddle horn as if it were my last link to life when Kah helped me down and hid me in the willows by the river.

He decided we were far enough from Casas Grandes that it was safe to build a small fire and make stew with the rest of the jerked beef he carried and plants growing near the river. We ate it as the sun began to fall toward the Blue Mountains, and I felt strength begin to return to my body. Still, Kah had to help me mount when we rode away from the river, its night sounds from frogs and insects filling the air.

I showed Kah the way to the witch's *hacienda* and told him that, while Beela-chezzi and I had taken much from the place, it still ought to hold much of use. He said, "Good. I'll tell Victorio and lead him here."

The night passed. The trail clear and easy, we traveled far and found the arroyo approaching the trail up to Juh's stronghold as the sun spread light on the *llano*. My side had grown numb. I felt nothing, but the black flashes to my mind came more frequently until one came and stayed. I slumped off my pony and fell in the sand in the arroyo. I was lucky and didn't hit a rock, break a bone, or crack my head.

Kah came back for me and drove the darkness from my mind. He helped me stand and mount his pony. He mounted behind me and put his left arm under my shoulders and around my chest, and we rode up the steep trail to Juh's stronghold that way. Juh's camp wickiups had no one living in them, but Kah saw plumes of smoke from the Mescalero tipis at the edge of the trees by the little stream and rode toward them. It had been the hardest ride of my life, and I could not have made it without the help of my friend.

CHAPTER 8
BEELA-CHEZZI'S STORY

The darkness left my head like black thunderclouds slowly parting for the sun. I opened my eyes and saw a rough, brown starburst of lodge poles surrounded by white and pointing toward a sky blotched with branches from pine trees. Although thirst filled my throat, my mouth watered at the smells of a meat stew and mesquite bean bread. I lowered my eyes and saw the concern and strength in the face of my woman. Juanita sat next to my blanket studying my face, her legs folded under her, her belly starting to swell with the child we had wanted for a long time.

"Yellow Boy, my man, is in our lodge. My heart has wings. His wound will heal, and his strength will return."

"My woman brings my heart the goodness of life. Is there water?"

She nodded and smiled, and holding my head up brought a water gourd to my lips. I drank it dry and nodded enough when she raised her brows to ask.

"I smell your stew pot and mesquite bread. I have great hunger. Is it ready?"

Her eyes sparkled with delight. "I'll bring it to you."

She helped me sit up and then lean back against a woven willow backrest she pulled in place before getting the stew and bread. I felt a fresh bandage over the bullet hole in my side and knew the smell of a poultice for which Kah could not find the herbs at the great river. She handed me a bowl of stew and the bread on a broad, green leaf. I ate as if I hadn't eaten in days, and I realized I hadn't had much to eat since I began the chase for the witch. Perhaps he wanted to kill his enemies through starvation.

I finished wiping the bowl clean with the last bite of bread, sighed, and said, "My woman makes the best of stews and bread. I thank her. How long have I slept?"

"Kah brought you to me three days ago. We feared you might not wake up. My stew pot says that is not so. My husband returns to the land of the living."

"The child in your belly, all is well?"

She smiled and nodded. "All is well. Your mother and Carmen Rosario tell me I can do no better. Now, tell me what happened with the witch."

I looked down and shook my head in disgust.

"We found his *hacienda* in Casas Grandes. Beela-chezzi and Kitsizil Lichoo' followed the Comanches that were with him north, and I followed the witch toward the great river, staying out of sight and looking for a place to ambush him. Somehow, he learned I was following him and ambushed me. He missed me but killed my pony. Later in the day, I managed to kill his pony, and then it was a foot race for the great river. I knew if he made it across the great river into the land of the *Tejanos,* I'd probably never catch him. There are too many *Indah* on the land, too many Blue Coats looking for us."

A breeze passed through the trees, and I heard the voice of my mother somewhere outside speaking to my little brother. I looked at my hands, sorry that I had to tell my wife what happened next.

"In the dawn light of the fourth day, I could see the great river's bosque and, in a hurry to stop him, I made another mistake and ran exposed across an open space. He was hiding in the mesquite thicket I ran for and shot me. The ground was sandy and I fell in a low place. His other bullets missed me. I waited, listening for him to come and finish me off. I was ready to kill him, but he ran for the river instead. When he didn't come, I crawled to my feet and got to the bosque in time to see him wading across the great river and nearly to the far side. My strength failing fast, I rested my rifle on a log, darkness filling my eyes. He turned to look over his shoulder and saw me. He threw up his rifle to shoot, but I was faster and shot him here in his upper chest. I thought I had killed him because he floated facedown in the river and drifted a little way, but soon he stood up and staggered up the bank on the far side. Then darkness filled my eyes until I woke by Kah's fire. He has told you the rest?"

She murmured, "Yes, Kah told me the rest. Will the witch come back?"

"He'll come back, and I'll shoot out his eyes."

She stroked my hand and curled her fingers around it. "I'm glad Yellow Boy lives to fight another day. The witch is powerful. It will take much strength to kill him. Now rest."

I nodded. "Before I do, tell me if Beela-chezzi and Kitsizil Lichoo' have returned."

"Yes. They came three days before you. Neither is hurt, and they say they've sent one of the two Comanches to the Happy Land, and they believe the other one is riding for the camp of Elias."

My eyelids, heavy with sleep, I said, "Hmmph. Good. I'll speak with them when I wake up."

Beela-chezzi, Kitsizil Lichoo', and I sat in my tipi and smoked one of my strong, black *cigarros*. After we blew smoke to the four directions, I said, "Tell me how you took the Comanche." Beela-chezzi looked at Kitsizil Lichoo', who dipped his head toward him, as if to say, *You tell it.*

Beela-chezzi gathered his thoughts and said, "The Comanches rode north along the Río Casas Grandes and then turned west as if they would ride back to the witch's *hacienda.* I told this to Kitsizil Lichoo', and we decided they planned to return and look for anything of worth left for the taking. We rode our ponies hard and fast to get ahead of them and stopped at the stone watchtower on the hill where we had watched the witch and his warriors before we attacked the *hacienda.*

"I studied the place using Blue Coat *be'idest'íné* (binoculars). The *hacienda,* burned black and crumbling, still had a few walls standing. White bones from those we killed lay scattered over the ground, picked clean by the big black birds and coyotes. We had left the stable standing after we loaded the slave women and children in wagons and sent them to Casas Grandes. When I'd searched the stable, looking for your Yellow Boy rifle on the night we freed you, I'd seen that the witch kept many good things there such as boxes of rifles, bullets, saddles, and even a big gun with many barrels riding on wheels. Because of this, I thought maybe the Comanches planned to guard the witch's treasure until he returned with more warriors. Looking back down the trail, I saw a small dust streamer on the wagon road to the *hacienda,* so we mounted and rode for the stable."

I smiled as I thought of what the Comanches must have thought when they opened the stable doors to stare down the rifle barrels held by Beela-chezzi and Kitsizil Lichoo'.

"Soon the Comanches came. We watched them through the cracks in the stable door. They watered their horses in the arroyo running in front of the *hacienda.* One of the Comanches walked over to the stable while the other began to unsaddle their ponies. The one at the stable door began to pull it open when the one unsaddling the ponies yelled, 'Careful! Fresh pony tracks!' We kicked the door open and killed that Comanche at the door before he could even raise his rifle. The other one ran and, hanging between their ponies, rode into the bosque lining the arroyo and up the other side. Like the wind, he rode out across the *llano* headed for the eastern hills. We ran for the arroyo. By the time we were through the brush on the other side, where we could get a shot, only streamers of dust in the distance showed him riding one horse and leading the other. Our ponies still hung their heads, worn out from getting to the *hacienda* first. We had no chance of catching him and didn't try. I think we'll see him again sometime and his luck will leave him. That's all I have to say."

"Juanita told me you think he's going to the camp of Elias. Why do you think this?"

"I watched his dust streamer awhile with the *be'idest'iné*, thinking he might come back to take us when we did not expect him. He made a long, swooping trail from the east back to the west and north toward the Blue Mountains. If I had wanted to go to Elias's camp, that's the direction I'd have taken. I think he'll try to hide there until the witch brings new warriors."

I looked at Kitsizil Lichoo'. He nodded.

I said, "Warrior with red hair, what do you think we should do?"

He didn't hesitate. "We must go to the camp of Elias and kill the Comanche before he fills the head of Elias with thoughts of coming after us, and I think we need to cache the supplies in the stable so Sangre del Diablo can't get them."

Beela-chezzi grinned. "In two days, I'll take pack ponies and helpers to get the witch's treasure. I know a big cave nearby where we can cache it."

I said, "Kitsizil Lichoo' and Beela-chezzi speak wise words. I also think we must do this. When I can ride, we'll go to the camp of Elias. Juanita tells me that after we left, Juh left the stronghold and followed Geronimo to sit with the Blue Coats in the dust at San Carlos. Will you follow your father there?"

Kitsizil Lichoo' made a face and shook his head. "If I go to San Carlos, the *Indah* will see my hair, know I have *Indah* blood, and insist that I leave the People. This I will not do. I'll start my own camp in the Blue Mountains north of the Elias camp. I know a good place, hard to find, well hidden. Some of Elias's warriors want to leave his camp, and others, even *Nakai-yes* and *Indahs*, seek the safety of a well-hidden camp. I'll have enough warriors to stay out of San Carlos, take cattle herds from the *hacendados* (wealthy land owners), and help Juh when he returns."

"You have a good plan. You think the *Indah* will let Juh leave San Carlos?"

"They won't let him, but Juh will return to his stronghold. He doesn't have much patience with *Indah* fools."

Beela-chezzi and I grinned, and as if with one voice, we said, "*Enjuh!*"

CHAPTER 9
KAH CHOOSES DEER WOMAN

The hole in my side healed, my strength slowly returning. I wanted to leave to return quickly to get the Comanches in Elias's camp, but Juanita and Kah said I was too weak for a long ride and might not make it. I looked at Juanita's swelling belly and decided to wait. Victorio's war against the *Indah* and *Nakai-yes* burned on both sides of the border, and he killed many. Our little camp, we the only ones left in Juh's stronghold, happy to see Kah, wanted him to stay. He had told us he could not linger and needed to return soon to the great river where Victorio planned to cross and raid into the land of the *Tejanos*. But for Kah, "soon" became ten days and then a moon.

He came one day to sit with me by the fire in front of Juanita's tipi and said nothing as he rolled tobacco in an oak leaf. After we smoked to the four directions, his solemn face told me he came to speak of important things. He said, "Juanita's belly fills with your child. She is well?"

"She feels good. Maria, her mother, thinks she will have an easy time and shows signs of making a strong baby."

"*Enjuh*. Have you decided when you'll return to the reservation?"

"She'll have the baby here. Victorio stirs the Blue Coats and Mexicans like an arrow in a nest of hornets. The Blue Coats will stay on the reservation until Victorio makes war no more. The *llano* in Chihuahua now is no place for a woman filled with a baby. We'll wait in the stronghold through the Ghost Face

78

Season until the Season of Many Leaves. Maybe then, I can go to the reservation and talk with my friend Blazer. He knows *Indah* hearts and can tell me when it will be safe to come back. When will you return to Victorio?"

Kah crossed his arms and slowly shook his head. "I want to stay with the People. They need me more than Victorio does. The Blue Coats come like floods in *arroyos* and sweep us away. We kill ten; a hundred, a thousand, more appear. The Mescaleros who left the reservation with Victorio, me among them, soon learned this. Some told Victorio they planned to leave and return to the reservation, that nothing could be done against so many, except shed the blood of a few *Indah,* and, for that, too many Mescaleros would die. Victorio killed them and asked the rest of us if we wanted to leave, too. We said no, but we lied. Will the people here take me back?"

I had to smile. "They're glad you came back. Stay. Help us hunt through the Ghost Face Season. Maybe we can go back to the reservation in the Season of Many Leaves."

Kah made a smile on one side of his face. "I'll stay. Deer Woman? You think she'll wait for Delgadito? He won't leave Victorio. He may not come back."

I thought a long time before I answered. I decided Kah deserved the truth and my honest opinion. "You know what she did with Delgadito. Whenever he bush crawled, she was there. She even tried to lay with me, and I refused her. I wanted Juanita, and she knew it. Still, she offered to lay with me. Now she has no man and her mother is poor. She is like a widow with little or nothing. Perhaps, if he returns, Delgadito will want her, but only as a second wife, not a first one. She knows this and is like an angry dog because of it. She'll take your offer. Be generous, and perhaps she'll stay loyal to you if Delgadito returns. She's a risk. You decide if you want to take it. If she's a good wife, you'll have gained much and have saved her from a long, hard life. She's a strong woman and can give you comfort and children. If she plays you the fool, cut off the end of her nose and be done with her."

Kah listened with a bowed head and nodded when I finished. "Will you represent me? Are four ponies enough?"

When I told Juanita of my talk with Kah and asked if Deer Woman would accept his proposal, she raised a brow and looked away. She turned back smiling and said, "Kah is a lucky man. Deer Woman will make a good wife for him."

Since Delgadito had ridden off with Victorio and his warriors, Deer Woman was dour and withdrawn, rarely saying much to anyone. I was sitting by my tipi as the sun fell into the far Blue Mountains. I saw the boy, Ish-kay-neh, lead Kah's pony, all washed and combed, to the front of the tipi of Deer Woman's mother, tie it there, and slip away. It was nearly dark when the tipi's door flap opened and Deer Woman stepped out with her water bucket. When she saw the pony, her free hand covered her mouth in surprise. She stood staring at it a little while before she recognized it, and then looked around to see if anyone was watching. Of course, we all were, but she saw no one, and taking her bucket, wandered off down the path to the little stream.

Kah's pony stood tied in front of the tipi of Deer Woman's mother all the next day. Sometimes in the sun, sometimes in the shade, swishing its tail against infuriating flies, it looked at each passerby, expecting to be watered, but no one gave it water. Sunset came and still the pony stood, its head hanging down in thirst and hunger.

I watched from my place in the moon's shadows, listening to the insects and tree peepers as the moon rode across the sky to the top of its arc and began to fall. The blanket covering the door to the tipi of Deer Woman's mother seemed to float up into the cool, night air, and from under it appeared Deer Woman. She walked to the pony. It lifted its head and ears expectantly as she approached, breathed her breath into its nostrils, scratched behind its ears, and taking the reins led it down the path to the creek.

When Deer Woman and the pony returned, she had a tied bundle of grama grass under her arm. She led the pony to the wickiup the women had made for Kah and, making no sound, spread the grass on the ground in front of it. It snorted with pleasure and began to eat while she rubbed it down with a few handfuls of grass before disappearing back to her mother's tipi.

Wearing the same shirt and vest in which I married, I went to negotiate the bride price with Deer Woman's mother. At the death of Sons-nah, her husband, during the witch's raid, Deer Woman's mother had seen any fortune she might have expected from the bride price of one of her daughters disappear. The esteem of Deer Woman by members of our band was low. It was known that she liked to lay with men, and Delgadito in particular. Her mother had learned this through overheard whispers and stories her "friends" told her. She knew the best Deer Woman could probably do now was to be chosen as second wife for Delgadito, which might be worth a few blankets, or at best a pony.

When I told her Kah asked for her daughter, she laughed when she realized that Delgadito was not asking for a second wife. I suppose she thought she might even double her best bride price for a young fool wanting a used woman. She said, "Deer Woman is worth two ponies. I won't take less."

I remembered He Watches telling me how happy it made Maria when he offered her five ponies for Juanita. She would have settled for three. I smiled and said, "Kah won't offer two ponies." Her face fell, and her sparkling eyes dimmed, and she said, "All right. One then."

But I shook my head, and she appeared on the edge of despair, ready to hear my counter offer or acceptance. I said, "Kah offers four ponies for Deer Woman. If they are accepted, he'll also provide cloth for a new tipi. What's your answer, Mother of Deer Woman?"

Tears flowed and her hands flew to her cheeks. She had to swallow several times before she could speak. "Kah has ransomed Deer Woman from disgrace and me from poverty and starvation. Yes, I'll accept his offer. They can marry in four suns after the women prepare a wedding feast and instruct my daughter in how best to care for her man."

So Kah took a wife. He told me he'd wanted her for a long time but never had the courage to ask for her. He didn't know how Delgadito would accept the marriage, and he didn't care. If Delgadito didn't like the union, then he and Kah could settle it with knives, and Kah was very fast, very good with a knife. The once-dour Deer Woman filled with life and gained a happy face almost overnight, and the couple seemed to leave their tipi in the early morning hours with glad hearts.

CHAPTER 10
PLANS

A moon had passed since Kah had taken Deer Woman as his wife. The Season of Large Fruit (late summer, early fall) had come, and the women and the few children among us were out before the sun and working into the firelit darkness, saving all the nuts, berries, fruits, roots, and wild potatoes they could harvest. The men hunted often for the women to save enough meat for us to live through the Ghost Face Season.

My bullet wound had healed but my side was still sore. Juanita rubbed it every night with a salve she made from willow bark, yucca, and other plants. I remember how good it felt to feel her hands on my belly and to see the smile on her face. I was fast getting my strength back, and I went hunting and target practicing every day to keep my shooting eye clear and my rifle steady.

Juanita's belly grew larger. Maria, her mother, told her it would probably be three more moons before our child came. My mother, Sons-ee-ah-ray, came with her adopted girl child, Lucky Star, the one I had won from Juh and given as a slave to Juanita, every day to help Juanita and ask how my wound healed. My mother had helped my father, Caballo Negro, many times with wounds he suffered as a natural part of being a warrior. She offered good advice about bad and good healing signs, and we were grateful.

Since Kitsizil Lichoo's people had left, and he had no woman, he hunted with us and ate with me at Juanita's fire.

Often at sundown, we sat and smoked and talked about places of wisdom and other tribes and strongholds in the Blue Mountains. One evening as we smoked and watched the sun turn the horizon clouds into brilliant orange and purple fire, I glanced at Juanita and saw her straighten up and brace her back with her hand. She was getting so big her back ached from her loaded front. I suddenly realized the shorter her time grew, the closer I needed to stay. We ought to find the Comanche who managed to escape Kitsizil Lichoo' and Beela-chezzi and lay plans for attacking the witch when he returned.

I asked Lucky Star, who was with Sons-ee-ah-ray helping Juanita sort and prepare the day's gathering of acorns and mesquite pods and piñon nuts, to run to the tipis of Kah and Beela-chezzi and ask them to join us. They soon came and, after we smoked to the four directions, sat cross-legged, waiting for me to speak.

I said, "Tonight I see my woman big with our first child, and I understand things we must do soon."

Beela-chezzi said, "What things are these, Yellow Boy? I also have worries."

"Take the last Comanche waiting for Sangre del Diablo and prepare for the witch coming with new warriors before snow fills the mountain passes. He might try to attack us now in the Season of Large Fruit, but I think he won't this season. He also heals from a wound, one that I gave him. This witch and his Comanches and *Nakai-yes* must be sent to the land of the grandfathers before he does to us what he did to our fathers. We must be on watch."

Heads nodded in agreement, faces hard and attentive. We all shivered in the cold breeze that swept up from the valley far below us, anticipating the excitement of facing the witch.

"I'll leave for the camp of Elias when the next sun comes. From Kitsizil Lichoo', I know the trail to his camp. None of you needs to come with me, but I'd be glad for your company and weapons skill against our enemies. The witch may have already come, or Elias might not be happy to see us and try to drive us away. It's a dangerous thing to do. I ask you, will you come on this raid?"

I looked around the fire at the eyes glittering in the firelight, and every head nodded yes.

"It's as I thought. I'm proud to call you my brothers. I have a special request for Kah."

He raised his brows and said, "Speak. I will listen."

"The witch knows the place of this stronghold, and I worry that he and his Comanches will come while we're not here to protect the camp. I ask that you stay to protect the women and little ones. I'll ask the boy, Ish-kay-neh, who'll soon be old enough to raid as a novice, to scout and help you. Will you do this, *Aashcho*?"

Kah squinted at me across the fire, made a smile on one side of his face, and slowly nodded.

"I know Yellow Boy thinks of me and Deer Woman, only married a moon and trying to make a child. I want to ride with my brothers, but what you say is true. We must be careful. Sangre del Diablo and all his Comanches must die, but we must not lose our families while we fight and kill him. Don't worry about the women and children. I'll guard them all as my own. Go, and I will stay."

Beela-chezzi, Kitsizil Lichoo', and I shook our right fists and said, *"Enjuh."*

Riding the high, rough trail to the camp of Elias from Juh's stronghold a second time left us at the end of the first day resting in the same tree cover on the same ridge as where we'd rested when we first rode to the camp of Elias. The night air was colder, and we heard more wolves as we sat back to back and ate our trail food before pulling pine straw over us for warmth in sleeping.

Juanita had asked me many questions about Kitsizil Lichoo' and his status with women I could not answer. Now they drifted through my mind and stirred my curiosity. I said, "Kitsizil Lichoo', here under the same trees where you told Beela-chezzi and me how an Apache with red hair came to be, I would ask another question, not my place to ask, but I ask it as a friend."

"Hmmph, Yellow Boy has the curiosity of Badger. Speak, and I'll answer."

"You have a woman, but she left with Juh before you returned?"

"Yes, I have a woman. She left with her family to follow Juh to San Carlos. She knows I wait here for her, and she will come when Juh leaves that shameful place."

"The woman in the camp of Elias, the widow you visited, you still plan to make her your second wife?"

"Hmmph. I have thought much on this. She is a good woman, works hard, smells good, and knows how to please a man under the blankets. But she has no child. I don't know if she can make one. She's a risk. My first wife says she doesn't care if I take her, but I haven't made up my mind. I'll know before we leave the camp of Elias. I think now maybe I'll take her and start my own camp north of Elias."

Beela-chezzi and I both turned to stare at him in the dim moonlight falling through the tall pine branches. A wolf howled nearby, and we felt for the triggers of our rifles.

Beela-chezzi said, "How will you do that? Your wife will want to stay with her mother. Why start your own camp?"

"My mother-in-law can come if she wants. My wife can leave me if she wants. I tell you, Geronimo won't stay at San Carlos. Juh won't stay at San Carlos. They'll leave. The Blue Coats will chase them as they run from the land of the *Indah* to the land of the *Nakai-yes*. I won't attack my mother's people or risk the Blue Coats capturing and taking me away from the People. I'll make my own camp in the Blue Mountains. My first wife doesn't want to come?" He shrugged his shoulders and said, "She can leave me and stay with her mother. I'll find another woman . . . or two."

We laughed, and I asked, "Where will you make your camp?"

"There's a place I've found less than a day's ride across the Blue Mountains to the *Indah* border. There are warriors in the camp of Elias who would leave if there were a better place to go because Elias does not plan his raids well and warriors die. If they don't want to raid with Elias, they can come with me."

"When will you do this?"

"When the snows leave the passes in the next Season of Many Leaves. There's no need for you to return to the reservation. Come, stay in my camp."

I nodded and said, "This we will think on. I'll do what my People want."

Kitsizil Lichoo' smiled. *"Enjuh."*

CHAPTER 11
BEELA-CHEZZI'S DUEL

Hiding in the trees on the trail high above the camp of Elias, I used the *Shináá Cho* to study people in the camp. Many more warriors were there than during our first visit. The women and children and a few old men were busy storing nuts, drying fruits and roots, and jerking meat to prepare for the Ghost Face Season. After several looks across the rancheria wickiups, I finally found Elias and several of the old men and warriors smoking and lounging in the shade by the stream at the camp edge. The stream's flow had slowed much. We couldn't hear it as we had on the first visit. I studied each of the old ones and warriors and remembered them from our first visit.

As I watched, a figure with long braids, holding a big bore Winchester in the crook of his arm, his waist wrapped in a fancy trade blanket, entered the up-close, circle view of the *Shináá Cho* and sat down by Elias. I had seen him before at the *hacienda* of Sangre del Diablo. Instinctively, I sensed the wind and estimated the range, but he was a target too far and a guest in the camp. Even if I could have shot him from where we sat, I wouldn't have done it. He was a guest in the camp and under the protection of Elias. To kill him like that would make sour feelings against us and make us targets of revenge attacks by Elias for many moons.

I handed the *Shináá Cho* to Beela-chezzi and Kitsizil Lichoo' and pointed where to look. They both grinned. Beela-chezzi said, "So we find you again, Comanche. Soon you die."

I pulled a grass stem to chew and, rocking back on my heels where I squatted, said, "How should we take him? He's a guest of Elias. Elias fears the witch and will not give up the Comanche unless we make him."

Kitsizil Lichoo', still staring through the *Shináá Cho,* nodded and said, "What you say is true. Elias would kill us before he let us kill the Comanche, regardless of our claims against him. The Comanche will hunt to help them and pay his keep until the witch comes. Let us wait until he leaves to hunt and then take him. In Elias's eyes, he just disappeared, and he can tell that with a clear eye to the witch."

Beela-chezzi nodded. "Hmmph. My brother speaks wise words. Let us watch the camp for a while and follow when the Comanche leaves. When he is alone, I'll kill him with my knife."

I nodded. Beela-chezzi was the best I had ever watched in a fight with knives. He could have killed many of the men in Cha's camp but always let his opponent live. "My brothers speak well. Let us watch and wait."

For three nights, patient hunters waiting for an animal to move, we slept in the pine straw, ate trail food, and quietly watched the camp with the *Shináá Cho.* Early on the morning of the fourth day, when the birds began to whistle in the gloom of the canyon, the Comanche left the rancheria, walked down to the brush fence corral, saddled a brown and white pinto, and rode off downstream. We followed, staying in the cover of the tall trees on the high ridges above him.

Three ridges downstream, he rode up toward the ridgeline on the opposite side. Near that ridgeline's top, we saw a place nearly bare of tall trees covered in grass growing tall and golden. With the *Shináá Cho,* I saw signs of deer, patches of grass cropped close, and bent grass mashed into resting places scattered across the meadow. Beela-chezzi and Kitsizil Lichoo' looked over the spot. Without saying anything, they handed me their reins and, taking their rifles, disappeared into the brush down the ridge toward the bottom of the canyon. This Comanche would not escape us again. I waited.

On top of the ridge across the stream, the Comanche rode to the southern end of the meadow, dismounted, and hobbled his pony in the thin grass growing in the shadows of the tall trees. He moved up the ridge a short distance and sat down on a large, flat rock to wait, his legs crossed and rifle lying across his knees. From where he sat, he had a clear view of the meadow grass and the deer trails leading into it.

I carefully kept glints off the *Shináá Cho* while I followed the progress of Beela-chezzi and Kitsizil Lichoo' up the ridge to close on the Comanche who sat peacefully with his face tilted toward the bright, late morning sun.

I watched and waited. The Comanche suddenly looked from the sky to Kitsizil Lichoo' who, as if by magic, suddenly stood not twenty paces in front of him, his rifle cocked and pointed at the Comanche's middle. They spoke, but were too far away for me to hear their voices, much less understand them. The Comanche took the rifle off his knees, laid it on the ground beside him, and slowly stood, his hands open and in front of his belly where Kitsizil Lichoo' could easily see them. They waited, staring at each other, not moving, two statues in the wilderness.

Beela-chezzi came down from the top of the ridge and entered the *Shináá Cho* circle of seeing. He spoke to the Comanche, who nodded, and laughing, pulled off his deerskin shirt and drew a big, long, knife from a sheath behind his back. Beela-chezzi drawing his knife, its blade shorter than the Comanche's but reflecting the sunlight like a mirror, spoke to Kitsizil Lichoo', stood his rifle against a nearby boulder, and advanced to face the Comanche standing on the big flat rock.

They circled, each carefully watching the other. I knew that one little mistake and he who made it was dead. Their fighting styles could not have been more different. The Comanche, his teeth clenched in an ugly grin, circled in a high crouch. His knife flipping easily between his left and right hands, weaving first one way and then another, slowly moving back and forth like a snake trying to hypnotize a bird. Beela-chezzi stood straight and relaxed, leaning slightly forward on the balls of his feet, arms dangling at his sides, his knife held lightly in the fingers of his left hand, his eyes locked on the Comanche's eyes.

The Comanche circled twice and another half turn before making a flashing thrust for Beela-chezzi's belly, but Beela-chezzi was already moving back left and to the side of the thrust as it flew by. His knife was faster than my eye could follow. A cut appeared on the Comanche that began at his belly and left a fine bead of blood up to his collarbone. The Comanche stepped back and continued to circle. He made a couple of thrusting feints that Beela-chezzi easily dodged. The bright red line from his belly to the Comanche's collarbone grew from a scratch's trickle to the flow of a deep cut across gut and muscle. I knew it had to weaken him. Even from where I sat, I could see the Comanche was in trouble. He feinted left and then swung his blade right in a slashing loop that just missed Beela-chezzi's throat. Again, the response from Beela-chezzi was blindingly fast. He cut the Comanche again, this time horizontally across the top of his belly. There was blood on Beela-chezzi, but I couldn't tell if it was his or the Comanche's.

They closed, each grabbing the other's knife wrist with his free hand and staggered back and forth trying to gain an advantage to drive their blade into their opponent. The Comanche threw a leg behind Beela-chezzi and, tripping him backwards, fell on top of him. The Comanche's blood-covered wrist slid out of Beela-chezzi's grasp, and his long blade slashed forward to stab into the stone where Beela-chezzi's head had lain only a moment before. At the same time, Beela-chezzi freed his knife wrist from the Comanche's weakening grip. I saw it flash in the sun before it stabbed deep into the Comanche's side, just below his ribs, and jerked up to release a shower of pulsing blood. The Comanche arched his back, grimaced with clenched teeth, and collapsed on Beela-chezzi. Neither warrior moved for a few moments that seemed longer than many seasons, and then Beela-chezzi rolled him off and staggered to stand, smeared and dripping from his face to his legs with dark red blood. He raised his hands still holding his knife and turned toward the sun singing a song of praise to *Ussen* for a great victory.

They left the Comanche as he fell, took his rifle, bullets, and pony, and began making their way down through the brush and oaks to the stream in the bottom of the canyon. Two great black birds already circled high overhead, and before my brothers joined me, many more filled the sky. Beela-chezzi stopped at the stream and washed the Comanche's blood from his body before jumping from one big boulder to the next in the fast flow to get to the other side. I studied him with the *Shináá Cho,* but I saw no wounds. I never knew another warrior, fighting with a knife, who had killed his opponents or made them surrender and yet never got cut himself.

Ever careful, in case someone from Elias's camp had wandered on to the ridge, Kitsizil Lichoo' covered Beela-chezzi with his rifle and waited until Beela-chezzi got to the other side to cover him when he crossed.

When Beela-chezzi and Kitsizil Lichoo' climbed the ridge back to me, I said, "Ho! The great warriors return. Only the witch remains for our vengeance. You've done well. Are you cut anywhere?"

Beela-chezzi shook his head. "The Comanche knew how to take scalps, but not how to fight with his knife." He looked up and saw the steadily darkening cloud of buzzards. "Let's return to our wives and children while the black birds feed on the bones of the evil one I have sent to the land of the grandfathers."

CHAPTER 12
DELGADITO RETURNS

Season of Earth is Reddish Brown brought cold nights and cool bright days. Juanita, swollen to bursting with our first child, moved slowly, but never complained as the women finished their final stores for the Ghost Face Season. She even spent time teaching my mother's adopted child, Lucky Star, how to be accurate with a sling and to shoot the little bow with reed arrows I made for her. My mother made a wise choice adopting Lucky Star, for the little girl worked hard to help her, learned the language of the People, and stayed quiet. After her puberty ceremony, she ought to bring a good bride price and be a dutiful daughter with a husband who could support them. Most of the time now, Sons-ee-ah-ray used her to keep an eye on my three-year-old brother, called Little Rabbit by my father.

One day I sat on a blanket in the season's brilliant light repairing arrows and making new ones. The oldest boy in camp, Ish-kay-neh, ran up the path toward me from the stronghold cliffs facing the rising sun. Lucky Star, who was at least six summers younger than he, was right on his heels. Ish-kay-neh called, "Killer of Witches! A rider comes on the trail toward the stronghold. I believe he rides like a Mescalero, but it's too far to tell."

Lucky Star joined him and said, "He rides a paint pony."

I thought, *a Mescalero? Who can this be?*

I pointed her to my tipi. "Go. Ask Juanita for my *Shináá Cho*, and bring it to me."

I said to Ish-kay-neh, "Show me this Mescalero you see riding for the stronghold."

I let Lucky Star carry the *Shináá Cho* as we trotted down the trail to the cliffs. When we reached the cliff lookout, she handed it to me, and she and Ish-kay-neh pointed toward a small dust streamer with a large black dot in front of it approaching the switchback trail up the side of the mountain. I studied the rider and decided he was Apache, and the way he sat his saddle said maybe he was Mescalero. I was amazed that the children next to me could discern the rider was Mescalero without the power of the *Shináá Cho* before their eyes. I watched as he approached, and I believed I knew who it was.

"Ish-kay-neh, run back to the camp and find Kah. I think I saw him working on a saddle near his tipi. Say that I ask he come see this rider."

The boy was off up the trail before the last words were out of my mouth. While we waited, I showed Lucky Star the great power of the *Shináá Cho.* She was so impressed, she spent the rest of the day looking through her curled fingers trying to make things look larger. I decided to find her a little *Shináá Cho* when we left the stronghold.

Using the *Shináá Cho,* Kah stared at the growing dot. I could tell from his clenched teeth that he thought the rider was the same warrior I had guessed. Delgadito, the warrior Deer Woman had expected to take her as first wife.

Kah said, "I knew this day must come. I just hoped we would have a child before he came back. Do you think Deer Woman still wants him?"

I shook my head. "Deer Woman isn't a crazy girl anymore. She's a grown woman who should have been married years ago. She has you now and knows she and her mother have done much better with you than with Delgadito."

"Then why do you think he left Victorio? He was a good killer on those raids. Now he comes here thinking he will let Deer Woman give him some comfort and leave again?" Kah's jaw muscles rippled in fury. "If he goes near her or says anything bad about her, I'll kill him in front of everyone like Beela-chezzi killed the Comanche."

"Hmmph. Give her a chance to prove herself to you. I think she wants to do that. If she turns to her old ways, then kill Delgadito, cut off her nose, and kick her out."

"*Aashcho* speaks wise words. I'll let Deer Woman prove herself."

Ish-kay-neh and Lucky Star sat nearby and kept their silence, but I could tell from the solemn look on the boy's face he had heard every word.

It was close to the time of shortest shadows when the struggling paint pony cleared the trail to the top of the stronghold, and a weary, bedraggled Delgadito slid from his back. Kah and I were there to meet him and to tell him Kah's news before we went to the camp.

He held up his hand in greeting. "*D'anté,* brothers! I have traveled far and bring news."

I frowned and said, "*D'anté,* brother. We can see you've ridden far and know you have been gone many moons. What have you come to tell us?"

Delgadito looked at the ground and shook his head. "*Nakai-yi* soldiers have wiped out Victorio and most of his fighting men at the place of little mountains the *Nakai-yes* call Tres Castillos. Only a few warriors scouting away from the camp and Nana, who searched for ammunition, escaped. I returned in time to see the black birds and coyotes feasting on many warriors gone to the Happy Land of the grandfathers. I came here to tell Juh and to ride with him in vengeance against the Mexicans."

Kah, his face grim, slowly shook his head. "Juh isn't here. He's joined Geronimo at San Carlos. We're here waiting until the Blue Coats leave the Mescalero reservation. We're ready for the Ghost Face Season. Stay with us. There's a tipi for you, and food enough if you hunt."

Delgadito puffed his cheeks and blew as if it were his last breath. He thought for a while and then said, "I never thought Juh or Geronimo would go back to San Carlos. I'll stay with you through the winter and maybe go back to the reservation." He grinned. "Where's Deer Woman? She'll keep me warm in the Ghost Face Season."

Kah kept his face a mask without a hint of what I knew he was feeling. "Deer Woman is in our tipi. She's my wife. If you stay here, respect that. If you don't, I'll kill you."

Delgadito grinned and sneered, "You'll kill no one . . ." He saw my hand close around the lever ring on my rifle. "There'll be no need. Only . . . how could you give a bride price for her when there are no half ponies?"

I saw Kah's hand curl around his knife handle. "Her bride price was four ponies. She was worth every one. I would have given more if I'd had them."

Delgadito snickered and said, curling his lower lip, "Yes, she's good . . . I enjoyed her very much."

I knew what Delgadito was trying to do, and I saw the color rising in Kah's neck and face and his hand tighten on his knife handle. Delgadito had his hand behind his back, and I was certain it held a weapon of some kind, maybe a pistol, since he had just come from raiding with Victorio. I cocked my rifle and poked it against Delgadito's chest. His eyes instantly swung from Kah's to mine, and he knew I meant business. His hands flew up in surrender. I said, "Deer Woman belongs to Kah now. You'll stay away from her and speak of her with respect. If you don't, you'll wander in the Happy Land without eyes. That's all

I have to say. It's all you need to know to be welcome here."

Delgadito's face turned the color of cold, gray ashes. He looked from me to Kah and said with palms out, "I'll speak no more evil of your wife."

Kah nodded and let his hand slide off the sheath of his knife.

The boy Ish-kay-neh had long since alerted the rest of the band that the warrior Delgadito was returning. The women continued to work, and the children played and helped them. All the while, they kept an eye on the path, waiting to greet the warrior who had ridden off to attack the *Indah* and *Nakai-yes* with Victorio. When we appeared, coming down the path, the women made a thin line on both sides and Beela-chezzi, now the elder in our band, waited at the end of the path.

They sang, "Our warrior comes. Our great warrior returns from war. Our great warrior comes down the path to us."

We stopped in front of Beela-chezzi, who said, "Our warrior returns from war. We welcome him. What is the news of Victorio's war?"

Delgadito slowly turned and looked at every face, his face sad and defeated.

"The war is no more. The *Nakai-yes* have wiped out our great chief at the place they call Tres Castillos. Only a few escaped. I was out scouting the country, looking for Blue Coats, and Nana was away looking for ammunition when it happened. Only a few others survived. I ask to stay through the Ghost Face Season with you. I'll hunt and bring in fresh meat while we wait for the Season of Many Leaves."

The younger children said nothing, but Ish-kay-neh and Moon on the Water, Juanita's little sister who was ten harvests, understood what Delgadito was telling us and looked at the ground to hide their sadness. The grown women covered their mouths as though their spirits might fly away

Beela-chezzi slowly shook his head and then said, "We're your People. You're welcome here. Stay with us as long as you need. The women are nearly finished storing supplies for the Ghost Face Season. They'll help you with a tipi when they finish. We're glad you weren't sent to the Happy Land with the great chief, Victorio. Eat at my fire tonight. I would hear more of what happened to him."

Delgadito said, "I thank the People for their care."

Deer Woman stood just behind the left shoulder of Kah, her face solemn, jaw slightly tilted up with pride, and her arms crossed. She didn't look away when Delgadito looked at her, but there were no hidden messages in her eyes. Delgadito's gaze did not linger at her and passed on to another.

CHAPTER 13
KICKING WREN COMES

Smoke from the orange coals in our tipi's fire pit drifted up and out into the black night filled with stars beyond counting. Juanita and I lay together under blankets sharing warmth between our bodies and our unborn child. We were content. The whole camp had feasted the return of Delgadito. It was a good thing to have another warrior in camp, especially during the Ghost Face Season, who could hunt and help provide fresh meat and protection against enemies who might come upon us. It was a good feast. At the feast, there had been no stolen glances, nothing to suggest the old days, between Deer Woman and Delgadito.

Juanita squeezed my arm as the baby moved. "Ummph. I think your son comes soon."

"Are you sure it's a boy? A daughter will also make me glad. You'll have help from a daughter when you're an old woman, and I'll have grandsons nearby. A son rides to his wife's lodge, sometimes far away."

"It's a boy who jumps inside me on my bladder. Our mothers say no girl kicks this much. Ummph!"

She turned, trying to find a better position in which to rest her belly and quiet the kicking child.

"What do you think of Delgadito's return? Do you think Deer Woman still wants him? Will he break his word to Kah and me so that we have to kill him and Kah will have to cut off the end of her nose?"

She was quiet so long I thought she had gone to the world of dreams, but then she said, "Delgadito's return is a good thing. He's a hardened warrior and can help protect the camp and train its boys. Deer Woman sees Delgadito with different eyes now and knows Kah is the better man for her, knows Delgadito would only betray her, knows *Ussen* has given her another chance. She won't betray Kah." She shifted again and settled with her head resting on my shoulder. I felt myself drifting toward sleep when she murmured, "I saw a large bird take wing this morning when I was bathing, and thought for a moment it was a great owl, but that's impossible, isn't it? That type of owl wouldn't show itself by day."

"No, it wouldn't," I said gently, and I said nothing more, but her words troubled me. I wondered if the witch could see us or work some evil on us through the eyes of the owl I had freed at his *hacienda*. Soon I heard her steady, deep breathing. My heart was glad *Ussen* had granted me Power to kill witches and given me a woman that filled my life with many good things.

I felt Juanita get up in the cold air to find the bushes. Far down the cliffs, I heard coyotes yip. It had become such a common thing for her to do in the past moon that I didn't even open my eyes when I felt her move. I waited to feel her chilled body return next to mine, but she didn't come.

I sat up. When my palm pushed against her side of the blankets, it landed on a soaked wet place. From the tipi entrance, I saw a fire growing in the pit outside the cloth-covered wickiup the women had made Juanita to birth our son, and there was a low glow through the canvas from a smaller fire pit inside. I saw shadows move inside the wickiup and heard a song from a birthing ceremony. Old Sleepy, mother of the widow Falling Water, was singing. She had been the midwife for the delivery of all but the adopted children in the camp. I knew all the women in the camp were there to help Juanita in her hard, happy time. It was my place to wait.

I looked at the stars and their turning around the one always pointing north. It was not long past the night's middle. I made a fire and propped the blanket up against the heat so the wet spot would dry faster. I used a twig from the fire to light my *cigarro,* blew smoke to the four directions, and asked *Ussen* to give Juanita a safe passage to our new life-way.

Memories came to me of my witch dream at Rufus Pike's rancho and the long, hard ride I made back to the Guadalupes only to find most of my People killed and scalped. I thought of Juanita and her sling and how she had helped me take horses from a *vaquero* camp for those who had escaped in that raid and how angry she was, thinking I had lain with Deer Woman, when the truth was I had not done such a thing. That memory made me smile. I thought of our first night together and how much pleasure she brought me in the blankets and in keeping our tipi strong and solid. I thought of all the things she did, all the things a woman of our People had to do to live, and thanked *Ussen* for the gift of a good woman.

The evil face of Sangre del Diablo floated before my eyes. I thought of his power and how he had almost killed me. I felt stirrings of fear as I thought how he might attack us from far away through the birth of our child. *Had Juanita really seen an owl?* Owls tell my People death soon comes. I wondered if the witch could somehow make our child die in the struggle to be born, or take Juanita by making her lose too much blood. Or if he might send a sickness and make the child sick so that it would die a few days after it was born. I knew of women who had died giving birth in Cha's camp and at Mescalero and of healthy children who had died early. I didn't have the power to fight a witch from far away. I could only pray that *Ussen* might give Juanita and the child Power to fight off any attack.

I shook my head to make Sangre del Diablo's face leave my mind. How could he know where I was or that Juanita was my wife? I thought, *Maybe I'm just making things up to worry about.* Then hurrying feet passed, and I looked out my tipi to see Sleepy's daughter, Falling Water, running to her mother's tipi. Soon she returned running with a basket filled with moss like women use at their moon time and a few bundles of dried herbs on top.

My mother, Sons-ee-ah-ray, came out of the birthing wickiup, kneeled to face the east, and raised her arms to sing a prayer.

"Come, child of Yellow Boy.

"Come, child of Juanita

"*Ussen,* give us this child.

"Give us the life of this mother.

"Give us this good woman and her child."

Sons-ee-ah-ray sang this prayer to the four directions, put wood on the outside fire, and went back in the wickiup. I wanted to run there and learn what was happening, but for our People, it was not a place for a man. I knew I must wait and be patient, but I wished many times that I had killed the witch. From the Happy Land, he could not possibly attack my wife and child. At some point, I drifted into an unquiet dream in which women were wailing and Sangre del Diablo laughed and howled like a wolf before roaring out a promise that he would take my wife and child. I jerked in my sleep, reached for my rifle, and Moon on the Water gasped. She had just entered our tipi, as if suddenly appearing out of the cold air, and stood before me.

I snapped awake from that evil vision in a cold sweat, looked through the tipi door, and saw liquid gold poured from a big round pot out on the far horizon.

Moon smiled with glittering eyes. "Sleepy says come. Your child awaits its father."

I wiped my eyes and felt my heart beat even faster. "Juanita?"

"She bled much, but she's strong. Your mother prayed. Sleepy used her medicine, and Juanita is still with us. She rests for a while. She has no pain. Your child is a fighter. It fought hard to leave its mother, but all is well. Come."

So witch, I thought, *your power is weak against my woman. She's a strong fighter.*

At the birthing wickiup, Maria, Sons-ee-ah-ray, and the other women, all except Sleepy, had already left to give us some privacy. Sleepy held our beautiful, dark-eyed child, its hair already thick and black, in a soft blanket. She had rubbed a thin layer of grease colored with red ocher on it to protect its skin. The baby didn't cry in the cold air but relaxed, waved its arms, and enjoyed kicking with the freedom of new life.

I dropped to my knees and looked into my wife's eyes. Juanita's face sagged with weariness, but her eyes sparkled, and she smiled when she said, "I lied to you, husband. Your first child is a daughter."

I laughed aloud. "*Enjuh!* Sons will come soon enough. You have no worries from the birth of our child?"

"I have none. The first sound our baby made was like that of a wren chirping in the trees. As much as it kicked to get out of me, Sleepy says we should call her Kicking Wren."

We both laughed. "It is a good name, a fitting one until we give her another." I nodded toward Sleepy. "We thank you, Grandmother, for all you have given us this night."

Sleepy, rhythmically rocking Kicking Wren in her arms, smiled and said, "This child is strong in her body and she has willpower. Raise her well, my son."

Juanita said, "I'll come back to our tipi before the sun hides again. Deer Woman says you're welcome at her fire for your meals. Go now. Kicking Wren is ready for her first meal."

With a nod to the two women and my first child, I left the

wickiup to offer my morning prayer to *Ussen* and to thank him for the safe passage of Kicking Wren to her new life. In the morning light, my dreams of Sangre del Diablo seemed distant, unimportant.

Juanita had asked Sons-ee-ah-ray to be the *di-yen* (medicine woman) who made the baby's *tsach* (cradleboard). Sons-ee-ah-ray gladly accepted the honor. She started work completing the *tsach* the morning Kicking Wren was born and worked steadily for the next two days to complete it, singing many prayers and performing ceremonies for each part as it was finished. She had many of its pieces ready before Kicking Wren was born and spent moons finding just the right materials. She sent me down to an arroyo near the stronghold entrance to collect black locust for the frame. She knew exactly how long the pieces needed to be by measuring the length from Juanita's elbow to her fist for the middle width and using ancient rules only women knew for the frame length based on how fast babies grew before they were set free from the *tsach*. She also had me find a piece of red cedar up on the mountain and split it into pieces for her to form the footboard, which she shaped with her knife, smoothed with sharp, black flint, and glued together to be laced into the slats.

I also had to provide her with a deerskin, and she worked for many days to make it softer than *Indah* cloth. Not knowing if Kicking Wren were a girl or boy she had collected both the narrow leaf yucca for a girl and sotol for a boy for the back slats and, with a piece of the soft buckskin, covered them with wild rice grass and mustard padding. On top of the buckskin, she laced fox fur to keep Kicking Wren warm in the Ghost Face Season. She cut the buckskin's outer wrap to hold the baby in place so that it laced from the right side, which was the custom if the *tsach* was for a girl.

The rainbow, the curved protective frame over the top of the child's head, she made by steaming arrow wood into semicircles and layering each as a rib on top of the other to the width of a hand so together they looked like a piece taken from a rough basket.

Before she finished the rainbow, she called me to her tipi and showed me four pieces of arrow wood she had planned to use that had unusual cracks in the grain. While she could probably still steam them into shape for the rainbow, they would have been weak and endangered Kicking Wren if the rainbow ever took a blow. Sons-ee-ah-ray asked that I find her more arrow wood without cracks so she could make the best and strongest of rainbows. I quickly found what she needed in my supply. But as Sons-ee-ah-ray put the cradleboard together and Juanita and I enjoyed our baby, deep in my mind, I worried that the cracked arrow wood showed that the witch, defeated now, was still working to take my child and curse my little family and me.

With the new arrow wood replacing that which was cracked, Sons-ee-ah-ray covered the rainbow with perfectly tanned buckskin and stitched it in place with deer sinew for additional strength and to hold feathers, strings of beads, and little colored stones and carved animals to bring Kicking Wren luck and to keep her entertained while Juanita did her chores. The rainbow protected Kicking Wren's head should the *tsach* fall. I have heard of this happening even when the *tsach* fell from a galloping pony. The frame reinforced with leather lacings, sturdy slats, footboard, and the well-made padding was strong enough to hang from a saddle when we traveled for fast escapes or to hang on a tree where Juanita could keep an eye on it while she worked.

Sons-ee-ah-ray had the *tsach* nearly completed by the end of the second day and was painting a half-moon and other symbolic decorations on the rainbow as she chanted and sang her songs for a long and productive life for her granddaughter.

Juanita had given Sons-ee-ah-ray two of her finest baskets for the *tsach*, and I, a fine new knife in a decorated sheath. Mother would have made the *tsach* for nothing, but custom said the *tsach* maker must not go unrewarded. We saw the beauty and strength of our baby's *tsach* and knew that Sons-ee-ah-ray had given us much in return.

On the fourth day after Kicking Wren was born, the whole camp gathered in the early morning light for Sons-ee-ah-ray's ceremony to bless and put Kicking Wren on her new *tsach*. As the sun floated above the far mountains, Sons-ee-ah-ray held the *tsach* toward the light and then, slowly turning south, pausing, then west, pausing, then north, pausing, finally to return to the sun. All the while, she sang a *tsach* ceremony song sung by my People for generations:

"Good like long life it moves back and forth.
"By means of White Water in a circle underneath,
   it is made.
"By means of White Water spread on it, it is
   made.
"By means of White Shell curved over it, it is
   made.
"Lightning dances alongside it, they say.
"By means of Lightning, it is fastened across.
"Its strings are made of rainbows, they say.
"Black Water Blanket is underneath to rest on:
"White Water Blanket is underneath to rest on.
"God, like long life the cradle is made.
"Sun, his chief rumbles inside they say . . ."

Sons-ee-ah-ray gently took Kicking Wren, sleeping in Juanita's arms, lifted her to face the sun, and sang to her softly as she again turned to the south and lifted her, turned to the west and lifted her, turned to the north and lifted her, and finally came back to the sun. Singing prayers to *Ussen* that sounded like those she had taught me when I was barely off a *tsach*, she unwrapped Kicking Wren from her blanket. The sudden exposure to the cold air made her tense, cringe, and wave her arms, but she made no sound. Sons-ee-ah-ray rubbed her with warm water and three times gently lifted her toward the *tsach*. The fourth time, she laid Kicking Wren within the *tsach*, covered her with her blanket on the warm fox fur, and laced her in, safe and sound.

Sons-ee-ah-ray motioned Juanita to her and, praying again to *Ussen* for a long life and safety for Juanita and Kicking Wren, touched them with the sacred yellow pollen on their foreheads and lips. She sang another prayer and then handed Kicking Wren in her *tsach* to her mother as they turned once more around the great circle.

When Sons-ee-ah-ray finished her ceremony, we had a great feast and ate good things, roasted mescal, bread from acorns and mesquite beans, honey, dried fruits, and roasted haunches of deer. It was a good day to be alive, but the threat of the witch stood like a shadow in my mind. I knew I had to find and send him to the Happy Land before he brought evil to us all, especially my family.

CHAPTER 14
BLAZER'S ADVICE

A hard Ghost Face Season filled with good times and bad dreams came after the birth of Kicking Wren. We didn't move down from the stronghold mountaintop to the *llano* where the cold, snow, and wind were much less furious. We stayed on top of the flat mountain in Juh's stronghold because none of us had any idea when the witch might come back. If we went down on the *llano* and camped near water, and he found us, we would be only five warriors defending fifteen women and children against two or three times our number. He would have a good chance of killing us all and taking our scalps. It was better to be a little cold than dead. Even if he returned with a hundred Comanches, he couldn't take us in Juh's stronghold. Still, I dreamed often he had somehow found us and moved among us unseen, bringing sickness and evil. I was in the sweat lodge often trying to learn what he might be doing or planning, but no visions came.

Our camp, deep in tall pine trees, had some shelter from the wind and snow, but high up on the flat mountain it was colder than our camp in Mescalero. To keep warm, we had to wrap in good, heavy *Nakai-yi* blankets and sit close to small, hot fires sifting down to red, glowing coals. The good times came watching Juanita nurse and care for Kicking Wren, sleeping close to them under the blankets, and knowing the satisfaction of successful hunts to keep bellies full in the camp. The younger children, tromping down packed snow paths from their lodges, came often to see and play with Kicking Wren, and they laughed with delight when she made faces back at theirs, laughed with them, or squirmed and chirped to be free of her *tsach*.

Beela-chezzi asked me to help teach and train his little adopted son, Shiyé (My Son), who did not yet have an adult name. The witch had been ready to sell Carmen Rosario, a *Nakai-yi* woman, Beela-chezzi's new wife and Shiyé's mother, to a place of whores in the City of Mules (Chihuahua City) before we burned his *hacienda* and set the slaves free. The child had the light of understanding behind his eyes and soon spoke our words better than Carmen Rosario, who was slow with her tongue, but quick with her hands. She'd learned to make baskets from Juanita. I made Shiyé a child's bow from *tsélkani* (mulberry) wood and blunt arrows from cane stems that grew along the water running through the camp.

On clear days when the wind wasn't bad, Shiyé and the other children developed quickness and accuracy in the snow playing the shooting games all Apache children have played since the time of the grandfathers. Many arrows were lost, but a child who learns to track the path of an arrow in the snow will soon learn to follow the tracks of animals and men on hard ground in the Season of Large Leaves (midsummer). The Season of Little Eagles, when the snow began melting, gave them another chance to find arrows escaping them in the snow and to fix ruined feathers so the shafts flew straight.

As the Ghost Face Season slipped away, I decided that with Victorio wiped out, the Blue Coats might leave the reservation. I spoke of this with Juanita one night by the fire as she nursed Kicking Wren and I cleaned the Henry rifle as Rufus Pike had taught me.

"Maybe Blue Coats on the reservation land have gone and taken the weak agent, Russell, with them. If we stay here, Kicking Wren will not know the mountains of her People, and the

Nakai-yes might come to kill us as they did Victorio. I believe the witch knows we're here, and he might come with his Comanches and *Nakai-yes* before I can find and kill him."

Juanita held her hand up for me to pause. Kicking Wren, full of milk, had stopped nursing and slept. Even with a hot fire, the night air in the tipi was cold. Juanita laid Kicking Wren close by the warm, slow-burning, orange and blue flames still coming from the fire pit coals. She covered the cradleboard with a blanket and then pulled a blanket over her shoulders and sat down next to me.

"Speak, husband. I think I already know the path of your words."

"Maybe the Season of Little Eagles will be a good time to return to the reservation. I would speak with Blazer to learn what the Blue Coats and Russell do. You're wise. What do you think we ought to do?"

She wrapped her arms around her knees and stared at the flames doing their slow dance in the fire pit. I finished cleaning the Henry, put it back in its scabbard, and put away the things I used in a parfleche she had made for them.

She looked at me from the corners of her eyes and slowly nodded. "I think of these things also. The reservation isn't the best of places, but it's much safer than this camp. Moon on the Water is afraid to return to the reservation because of what the Blue Coats did to us before you took us away. But she'll be strong, and Maria, our mother, will make her come with us. If the *Nednhis* decide to leave San Carlos and return here, the Blue Coats and *Nakai-yes* are sure to follow. Bullets will fly. Blood will flow. I think you should see Blazer when the warm winds come. If Blazer says it's good to return, then I say we ought to go back."

"Hmmph. My woman speaks my heart. I'll go when the warm winds come."

Blazer sat on his front porch enjoying the falling light and a pipe. The frogs and peepers were just beginning to tune up for their nightly chorus, and smells of steak and chiles, fried potatoes and onions, and hot apple pie still floated out open windows that were filled with the glow of soft, yellow light from lamps in the front of the house. The coming night was warmer than normal for the Season of Little Eagles.

I wanted to speak with Blazer in his barn so nobody saw or heard us. I rose up quietly out of the low light and murmured, "*D'anté*, Blazer. We go to barn and speak alone?"

He laughed through the brush pile of gray hair on his face. "Well, I'll be jennied. My old bones are glad to see you again, Yellow Boy. There's no need to go to the barn. Not many folks are around right now, and the new agent's not due for a moon or two. Sit down there on the steps. Can I get you anything? I think my woman still has a pot of coffee on the stove."

"Hmmph. Coffee, good."

He left his chair, went inside, and came back with a cup of coffee in each hand, gave one to me, and then sat down beside me. We talked a long time about many things. He said we were wise to slip away when the Blue Coats came. Most of the Blue Coats had gone away after the *Nakai-yes* wiped out Victorio. Some stayed at Fort Stanton but would come quickly if the agent called for them. The Mescaleros had had a hard winter. Some became sick, and some died, as there was not much food from Agent Russell and no guns to use in hunting. He looked off into the night and shook his head. "Why, I had to give 'em cattle to slaughter and corn for tortillas, and I sent my best shots out for game when the snow flew to help keep 'em fed."

As I listened, I knew Blazer was right. I was glad we had

gone to the land of the *Nakai-yes* far from the Blue Coats. Blazer blew the smoke from his pipe in a long, white stream against a black sky filled with more lights than I could ever count.

"I hear tell that the new agent comin' is called Llewellyn. They say he's from Nebraska out to the east on the plains, that he's a man of his word who uses common sense in dealin' with folks. If that's true, it'll be a good thing for everybody. Your People thinkin' about comin' back?"

"Hmmph. Baby on cradleboard better here than Juh stronghold. More safe."

"Baby? Did I hear you say baby?"

I smiled. I hadn't tried to speak much English in a long time, but suddenly, I was full of words. "Juanita gives us girl child. She kicks so much we think boy comes. First cry sounds like Wren in tree. Call her Kicking Wren. Women and children need safe place away from witch until I kill him, but no want to live by Blue Coat law."

Blazer nodded. "I don't blame 'em one bit. I'd be mighty glad to see you folks come back. You can even take your old camping spot you had before you left, and I'll help you get acquainted with the new agent."

"Blazer good friend to me and my People. Maybe we come back. Find work. Make money, buy Juanita and Kicking Wren warm blankets, and listen to *máquina* (sawmill) make flat wood for *Indah* house. No give up rifle."

Blazer nodded, "No give up rifle." He drank the rest of his coffee and listened to the peepers and insects. He knocked the ashes out of his pipe, and we smoked to the four directions using one of my *cigarros*. When the *cigarro* was gone, Blazer said, "So you didn't find the witch you wanted to send to the Happy Land of the grandfathers?"

"I find him."

It was hard for me to speak. I felt bitter water come up from my belly and go back down again. I said, "Juh showed Beela-chezzi, my grandfather, Klo-sen, and me, where to find witch's *hacienda*. Witch is giant, no hair on head, uses women shamefully. Witch surrounded by Comanche brothers and *Nakai-yi pistoleros*. Name Sangre del Diablo. He nearly killed all of us. Beela-chezzi and me, we survive. The witch and two Comanches escape, we kill all rest.

"One moon later, I track him from Casas Grandes. He rides to bring more Comanches from reservation in land of *Tejanos*. I am fool and run into his ambush. He wounds me. Still, I catch him crossing the great river. Shoot him in chest, but no kill. Not strong enough to follow him. No send him to Happy Land blind. I sleep in darkness until Kah finds me and fixes wound. He helps me back to Juh stronghold where Juanita makes me strong again.

"Kah no return to Victorio. Takes Deer Woman for wife. We know witch comes back. He tells his two Comanches he comes in three moons to Elias camp in Blue Mountains. We find both these Comanches and kill 'em. No find witch yet. Now want Juanita and Kicking Wren and others here safe before I try to kill witch again. That is all I have to say."

In the weak light from windows, I saw Blazer staring at me and slowly shaking his head. We listened to night sounds for a long time while he smoked before he said, "Go on. Bring your People back to the reservation. They'll be better off here."

CHAPTER 15
NANA

We returned to the reservation riding in white moonlight, ghosts unseen, passing *Nakai-yes* and *Indah* who hid behind their walls in the night and still thought maybe Victorio waited for them. We rested for two days by the water at the rancho of Rufus Pike, but we did not see him. He hadn't been there when I rode to see Blazer and returned to the stronghold, either. We found his mule tracks scattered along the trail like he was riding toward Mescalero.

From Rufus's rancho, we rode over the pass the *Indah* call Baylor, and across the *llano* of tall grass toward the mountains where the reservation lay. We rested in the little brown and orange mountains called Jarilla in front of the Sacramentos for a day before we rode again in the night for our canyon hidden on the reservation.

Returning to our canyon felt good, like seeing an old friend after being gone on a long raid. Juanita and the other women found a cache of food and supplies they had hidden in a cave during the Season of Earth is Reddish Brown before the Blue Coats came to the reservation. They made little fires that burned hot with no smoke, and we ate well and filled our bellies. We cut lodge poles up on the ridge above us, but we were careful to hide the places where we took them and did not cut too many in one place to tell knowing eyes we were there. The women hid our tipis in tall trees, and we made a corral for our ponies from brush so the fence and the ponies were hard to see, and hunters used their bows so the boom of a rifle didn't attract attention from passersby.

Ten suns after we returned, I rode the ridge trails to visit Blazer and learn more about the new agent. I left my pony in the trees above the place where the *máquina* sawed wood for the *Indah*. Once more, it was early in the night when I found Blazer. Many frogs and insects sang on the little river running past the *máquina* and through the agency grounds, but not much water ran there. Blazer sat in his rocking chair on the wooden floor in front of his house while he smoked and watched the night.

When I appeared, I said, "Blazer, we come back, stay in same canyon we stay before."

He laughed. "Well, Yellow Boy, you're like magic. One minute, there's nothing, and then you appear like the wind made you. My heart is glad your people have returned. Let's have a smoke and talk. Come sit with me."

I sat with him and lighted one of my *cigarros*.

Blazer said, "I'm looking after things until the new agent shows up in maybe three or four suns. Bring your people in, and I'll enroll 'em and give you some supplies. When the agent comes, I'll let you know to come in, and you can see him and decide for yourself if you like him. Just be sure your warriors know to keep their rifles out of sight. There're still a few Blue Coats here to keep an eye on things, and they get nervous when they see an Apache with a rifle he's not supposed to have."

"Hmmph. This I will do. We come tomorrow for supplies."

Blazer and the clerk at his store smiled when they saw us, and the *Indah* women who were buying supplies there laughed much and made noises and faces to make Kicking Wren laugh. The clerk gave money for two of Juanita baskets, and as Shiyé's uncle and teacher, I used some of it to buy Beela-chezzi's son a knife to go with the bow and arrows I had made for him in

Juh's stronghold. I thought of He Watches and how proud I had been when he gave me my first knife. I was seven harvests, and that was one or two more than Shiyé had, but he had a grown-up spirit that made him ready to learn the use of a long knife. His mother, Carmen Rosario, once a slave to Sangre del Diablo, was happy with her choice of Beela-chezzi as her man and father to her son. She kept her head covered and face nearly hidden so the *Indah* in the store wouldn't think she was a *Nakai-yi* captive and tell the Blue Coats to take her back.

Delgadito kept his word with Kah and stayed away from Deer Woman all during the Ghost Face Season and through the Season of Many Leaves when we came back to the reservation. He hunted often and kept the tipis of women who had no warrior without hunger. Sleepy and Falling Water often invited him to eat with them at their tipi. Juanita told me that Falling Water thought Delgadito might want her for his wife and that she would accept him, but he had not made any move to give her mother a bride present when we settled in our canyon on the reservation.

Two suns after we returned from our visit with Blazer, Delgadito came to sit with me while I sat in the shade of a tall pine showing Shiyé how to make his own arrows and handle his big new knife. I told the boy to run and play with Lucky Star but to put away the big knife first.

From his vest pocket, Delgadito pulled a new bag of tobacco he had bought at Blazer's store and an oak leaf to roll a cigarette. He smoked to the four directions and passed it to me. I smoked to the four directions, and we passed it back and forth until it was gone, after which he didn't waste sunlight with unimportant words.

"Yesterday, I hunted in the Rinconada. I found Nana's camp there."

"Nana's in the Rinconada again? That's where he camped when he stayed the winter before Victorio came. Does he plan to stay on the reservation? How many warriors does he have?"

"He won't stay. He doesn't trust the Blue Coats or the agent. He has fifteen warriors with him, and they're all Warm Springs Apaches, not like Victorio's mix of Apaches, Navajos, and Comanches." He paused for a moment and stared up the ridge. "While I was there, a handful of Mescalero warriors slipped over the ridge to come and talk with him. When they left, they were excited and laughing. You know what that means."

I nodded. "How many Mescalero warriors do you think might go out with him?"

Delgadito shrugged.

"Ten, twenty, who can tell? Nana speaks well of you. He says for you to come for a visit."

"Will you go out with him?"

Delgadito's eyes narrowed, and he spoke through clenched teeth.

"The *Indah* and Blue Coats don't treat us fairly. They took Mescalero rifles and ponies without cause. We still have many scores to settle and blood to spill. I'll go."

"You'll be making a mistake. Falling Water waits for your bride price offer. She's a good woman. She works hard, makes good baskets, makes White Eye money for her family. You'd have a good life with her, and the People need you here, not being shot at or killed by Blue Coats or *Indah*."

He looked up on the ridge, studying the trees, then nodded. "I know Yellow Boy speaks wise words, and I'll think on them. Will you visit Nana?"

"I'll go to Nana."

I followed the same trail through the tall, whispering pines that Juanita and I had followed in the Ghost Face Season when we visited Nana and his people hidden in their wickiups in a small canyon adjoining the Rinconada. When I found their canyon, I had to look hard to see their wickiups and, had I not known they were there, I would have missed them. Three warriors coming from deep in the canyon saw me and stopped. One disappeared toward a large wickiup set back in the tall pines. The others stood calmly, their rifles in the crooks of their arms.

One said, "Ho, Brother. You come to our camp. What do you want?"

"I'm Yellow Boy of the Mescalero. Nana asks that I come to speak with him. I'm here but I don't see Nana."

The warrior who had gone to the large wickiup reappeared behind an arthritic old man whose hip joints made him slow and tottering. Nana squinted toward me and smiled.

He called in a loud voice, "Ho, Yellow Boy! *Nish'ii'* (I see you), my son. Come to my wickiup, and we'll smoke."

I grinned as I slid from my pony, and the three warriors disappeared. His greeting was the same one he had used to surprise me when he crept up close to my lodge early one morning nearly two harvests earlier. I liked visiting Nana. He was old in his body but timeless in his skill, and, from what Delgadito told me, he could still sit a horse and ride hard all day as well as any warrior in his prime.

We sat in front of his wickiup in cool shade. He made an oak leaf cigarette, and we smoked to the four directions. He asked after Juanita and said Delgadito had told him we had a girl child. We laughed over the memory of when he'd camped here before and his warriors had taken back supplies the agent Godfroy had stolen. They'd given some back to my People, and some, they kept cached. I asked him how he had been lucky enough to miss the massacre of Victorio in the land of the *Nakai-yes*.

He looked at me, and then stared down the canyon and said,

"My Power saved me. My gift of Power has always been to find ammunition when the people need it. I don't think Victorio and his warriors had more than thirty bullets between them. We were desperate to find many bullets quick as we rode, riding north from the Río Conchos and east of the City of Mules out on the *llano*. We had made many raids, killed many *Indah* and *Nakai-yes*, and the Blue Coats and *Nakai-yes* chased us hard. We all needed rest and food before we could cross the *llano* to the Blue Mountains and hide from those who chased us. Three warriors brought us a herd of about thirty cattle. If we could hide in peace for three or four days we could slaughter the cattle and cut the meat in thin slices so it dried quickly in the hot sun, and we could pack it to live on until we were safe in the Blue Mountains. Victorio decided to drive the cattle to a small lake and grass for our ponies at a place he knew called Tres Castillos. He sent me and Blanco off to find bullets and to bring them where he camped at Tres Castillos."

Breeze blowing through the tall pines near Nana's wickiup sounded like a sigh for a story I knew did not end well.

Nana said, "The *Nakai-yes* under Terrazas had nearly a thousand men, and the Blue Coats with their dark-skin soldiers and Apache scouts were nearby. With so many men, Terrazas was not afraid of the Apaches and sent the Blue Coats back across the border.

"Somehow Terrazas figured out where Victorio was headed and laid an ambush for us near the lake. The *Nakai-yes* started firing on Victorio and our band as the long shadows came, and kept it up for a long time after the Apache stopped shooting back. I know this because an old grandmother here with us was there. She played dead by smearing the blood of her dead grandson on her face and neck to convince the *Nakai-yi* soldiers she was near the Happy Land. She was lucky they didn't throw her in the fire with the other bodies. The 'brave' *Nakai-yes* shot many women and children when the warriors couldn't fight back. Most of the women and children who lived were taken to the City of Mules and sold into slavery; many, sent to labor and die in the mines, some, to the *haciendas,* some to farms far south.

"Blanco, a few others who had been out hunting, and I were the only men who survived, and several of the women and children managed to escape, too. They looked to me to be their leader. I had returned with many bullets. I still have most of them, as the light was coming at the end of that night. But I was too late.

"No shots sounded in the early morning stillness. Blanco and I saw a big fire from a long way off. When we crept in close enough we saw *Nakai-yes* burning bodies of women and children that were killed. But they left many warrior bodies for the coyotes, wolves, and buzzards."

I thought of the bones I had seen of the slaves the witch had killed and burned near Casas Grandes and knew what I might see if I went to Tres Castillos.

"What did you do, Grandfather?"

Nana said, "We waited three days before I sent warriors to bury those who had been left for the coyotes and wolves. We had to be careful. The *Nakai-yes* knew our burial customs and might be waiting in ambush, but they were gone. The warriors found Victorio and several others lying by boulders. They had been wounded many times. Some, the *Nakai-yes* had killed with their long knives. Others killed themselves with their knives rather than become slaves or be thrown in the *Nakai-yi* fire. Victorio, his pistol, rifle, and bullet belt, all empty, had his knife in his heart. There were many warriors who died by their knives after their bullets were gone. We had nothing we could dig with and covered them with stones and big flat rocks. Victorio died as warrior, died as Mangas and Cochise had wanted to die years before, but *Ussen* had not given them that gift. Victorio died a good death, a warrior's death, fighting until he entered the Happy Land. I've grieved for my father-in-law all through the Ghost Face Season, but I know he watches and waits for me to join him when my time comes."

He stopped and looked off down the canyon, apparently reliving the experience. After a few moments, he began to speak again, slowly at first, as if coming out of a dream. He said, "Now I'll do my own raid. Maybe I'll die in it. We'll see, but I want only the best warriors to go out with me. I ask you to help me kill the *Indah*, kill the Blue Coats, kill the *Nakai-yes*, kill anyone who gets in our way, and we will take anything that makes us strong and rich to the land of the Blue Mountains. Come with me, Yellow Boy."

I shook my head and didn't hesitate to answer.

"I won't do this."

He frowned and said, "Why not?"

"I have an enemy who nearly killed me. *Ussen* says I must send him blind to the Happy Land. I have a girl child still on the cradleboard and more children to make with her mother. Our little band still lives; it needs all its warriors. You already take one from us. You take Delgadito. You take other Mescaleros from the reservation. Maybe you'll bring soldiers back like they came before and make everyone on the reservation suffer. No, I won't go. Nana is a great warrior. I think he'll raid over many long trails, take much, and kill many. But many warriors will die or suffer from bullet wounds or long knife cuts before Nana slips into the Blue Mountains. I won't chance that and leave my woman with no man to care for her. That is all I have to say."

Nana picked up a twig and poked at the fire a little while, and then stared up the ridge from where I'd come. He said, "Every man must do what his medicine says is best for him. Delgadito has no woman and comes to get good things for his future bride. You already have an enemy to kill and a woman and child to care for. I have a band of warriors who want to take what they can from the *Indah* and wipe out many. This we'll do in a moon or two after we've rested. I ask my friend Yellow Boy to let us stay here as long as we need and leave without a fight."

I stared at him a moment, and then said, "Leave no trail from the reservation. Let the Mescaleros live in peace. Do nothing to bring the Blue Coats back. I won't stop you or tell others of your presence here. May the great Power of *Ussen* be with you."

Nana shook his fist and said, "*Ussen* will give us Power to kill our enemies."

CHAPTER 16
TATA CROOKED NOSE

Nana and his warriors kept their peace while they hid in the Rinconada. If other Mescaleros knew he hid there, they said nothing, and I saw him no more after we smoked. A moon passed, and then one cold morning as dawn faded into bright light, I saw Delgadito ride over the ridge toward the Rinconada where I had counted twenty-five Mescalero warriors ride in twos and threes during the past five days. I knew many of them would never return. I had smoked with Delgadito several times, discussing whether he should stay or leave, and he often turned his eyes to the tipi of Sleepy and Falling Water as he considered my words. But the anger in his blood against the *Nakai-yes* and *Indah* led him to follow Nana and give up a good woman.

The day Delgadito left, word came from Blazer that it was a good time to see the new agent, Llewellyn. The Mescaleros in the other camps had begun to call him "Tata Crooked Nose" because he had a big crooked nose and, standing, towered above them. But he showed us he was a wise man, hard, just, and fair, a man we could trust to keep his word.

I found Juanita under the pines bathing Kicking Wren in the little burbling water that ran by our campsite.

"*Ish-tia-neh* (Woman), I go to the agency to meet the new agent, the one the other Mescaleros call Tata Crooked Nose. Do you want to ride with me?"

She looked at Kicking Wren happily splashing the water with her feet, then lifted her brows toward me and smiled.

124

"Our supplies are good. I saw Tata Crooked Nose on my last trip with the women for supplies. It's a good name. He has a quiet spirit. I think you'll like him. Your evening meal will be ready when you return. Kicking Wren and her mother will wait for you."

"Hmmph. *Enjuh.*"

I left my rifle and pistol in the tipi before riding over the ridges to Blazer's house. After Blazer and I had a little talk about what he thought of Tata Crooked Nose, we walked to the agency building to meet him.

The agency house had a place inside with tables and chairs where a woman sold hot food to *Indah* travelers. Tata Crooked Nose and a shorter, darker man, a little older than he, with a big bush of hair under his nose and eyes that stared through you, ate there when the sun was at the time of shortest shadows. Blazer and I walked up to their table, and they both stood, smiling and looking over every detail about me as they stuck out their hands for a shake. Tata Crooked Nose's height reminded me of Sangre del Diablo, both very tall, but unlike bald Sangre del Diablo, he had a big, ugly hair bush growing under his hooked nose, which hung off his face like a bird's beak. The words and the sound of his voice were respectful.

The custom in those days was to address the agents as "Major," as if they were army chiefs, and to address the chiefs of their police staff as "Captain." Blazer said, "Major Llewellyn, Captain Branigan, this is my friend Yellow Boy, the marksman I mentioned to you who so impressed Al Sieber with his shooting and good sense."

I took their offered hands and gave each one two solid pumps of their arms as Rufus Pike had taught me to do when shaking hands with an *Indah*. He told me this was an old *Indah* custom from the days when they carried long knives and offered their hands for peace instead of their knives for a fight. I said, "I am called Yellow Boy. Our band's tipis stand beyond the ridges west of this place."

Llewellyn nodded and said, "Please, Yellow Boy, you and Dr. Blazer sit down. Speak with us while we eat. Will you have something to eat with us?"

Blazer nodded, and I said, "I always eat when food given."

Tata Crooked Nose waved at the serving woman in the kitchen to bring two more plates and then began his meal again. While we ate, he asked me many questions, and I saw Branigan frown at some of my answers, especially about how Rufus Pike had taught me to shoot. I heard him say under his breath, "Traitor."

After we finished eating and drank an extra cup of coffee, Tata Crooked Nose said, "Captain Branigan is in charge of the tribal police. Since you decided you want to stay here rather than follow Al Sieber to the reservations over in Arizona, he wants to speak with you about being a tribal policeman. Are you interested?"

I looked at Branigan and said, "A tribal policeman must cut his hair?"

He smiled and shook his head. "No, my men don't have to cut their hair."

"Hmmph. I keep my rifle and carry it where I go?"

He nodded. "You keep your rifle and carry it, if you like. I'll give you a bandolier of ammunition for it and a pistol, horse, saddle, and bridle, and you'll make the same money as the troopers at Fort Stanton. You must wear at least the vest from the policeman clothes I give you so the other Mescaleros know that you stand for me and do what I ask to keep the peace on the reservation."

"This I can do."

"But, you cannot be a policeman to *Indah* who come on the

reservation unless I tell you directly to do that. If an *Indah* makes trouble, you find me. I'll handle it. Do you understand this?"

"Hmmph. I understand. When am I policeman?"

"You give your word you'll do what I say as long as you're a policeman?"

"It is so. This I will do as long as I am policeman."

"Good. Come to this building at sunrise tomorrow. I'll give you your equipment, let you pick out a horse, and tell you what to do for your first policeman work."

We talked some about problems on the reservation, mainly theft of our horses in Nogal Canyon and men who made whiskey and sold it to the Mescaleros.

After we finished eating, Tata Crooked Nose and Branigan stood and held out their hands to leave us and go back to their places in the agency building. I nodded that I understood and again pumped hands with Branigan and Tata Crooked Nose as a sign that I would keep my word.

After they were gone, Blazer stood taking this all in with a big smile. "Those are good men. I think you'll like being a policeman for Captain Branigan, and you can keep your rifle without worrying the army might try to take it from you."

"This we will learn, Blazer. Now I go back to Juanita's tipi and eat what she makes for me."

"Good. I'll speak with you tomorrow."

The shadows through the pines from the sun falling behind the western ridges painted the sky soft purple with orange and red patches and streaks across distant clouds, making the bright, yellow, tipi cooking fires easy to see up the canyon. As Juanita promised, my evening meal of mescal, venison, acorn bread, and juniper berries was ready.

We watched Kicking Wren play with the beaded strings on

her cradleboard while we ate, saying little. At last, Juanita asked, "Did you speak with Tata Crooked Nose?"

"Hmmph."

"Is he a good agent?"

I shrugged. "We have to wait and see. Perhaps he won't steal our supplies like the other agents or give us over to the cavalry as Russell did. Blazer thinks he'll do good."

She was quiet for a while as the darkness grew deeper under the trees and the night crickets and frogs by the stream grew louder. Kicking Wren yawned and began to chew on her fist. A cool breeze rolled off the ridges, and in her nearby tipi, I heard Sons-ee-ah-ray give an old woman's cackle at something Lucky Star said.

Juanita's eyes followed my face as she said, "When will you start work for Captain Branigan and become a tribal policeman? You liked him I know."

My lower jaw dropped. How did she know these things?

"Are you a *di-yen,* seeing what happens far away?"

She giggled and said, "I'm no *di-yen.* I listen and watch. Branigan and Tata Crooked Nose speak straight. I heard them say they need policemen, and I heard Blazer tell them how you impressed Al Sieber that day you shot for him and how you have light behind your eyes. I know this is *Indah* work you want to do. When will you begin?"

I stared in the fire for a moment and said, "Tomorrow at sunrise."

"*Enjuh.* I will be out of the blankets early to give you something to eat from my fire. See Kicking Wren sleeps and the night is full of good sounds. Husband, come to my blankets. Kicking Wren will soon need a baby brother."

I thought, *I should get a policeman's job more often.*

CHAPTER 17
TRIBAL POLICEMAN

Captain Branigan was a good police chief. For the first ten suns I was a policeman, he had me ride with an old warrior, Chawnclizzay (the Goat), who had worked with Agent Russell, and was now Branigan's sergeant, to keep order before the soldiers came to disarm and unhorse the Mescaleros. He asked Chawnclizzay to teach me the best ways to handle tribal disturbances that ranged from disputes over women to arguments over card games to controlling and preventing *tiswin* or *Indah* whiskey drunks. I learned much from the old man and knew I had much more to learn when Branigan sent word for me to come speak to him.

I came to Branigan's door just as the sun poured golden light through his back window, and the night water that collected on the glass rolled down in tiny rivers to form little puddles on the sill. He was already working. He saw me standing at the door, nodded, got his old floppy trooper's hat, and led me out on the porch. Blazer's sawmill was just beginning to cut planks off logs, and the air was cool and comfortable, a fine bright morning from *Ussen*.

Branigan nodded toward the western ridges. "You live over beyond that ridgeline, don't you?"

"Hmmph. Just before the Rinconada, there I live with our little band."

"Soldiers tell me they see young warriors disappearing over the western mountains and not coming back. Some soldiers believe they are leaving to join Nana. Peso and Choneska, maybe you know them, two of Chief Nautzile's best warriors, have been leading soldiers looking for Nana's camp, but they haven't found it."

"Peso and Choneska I know. Strong warriors."

He paused to pack his pipe and light it with a yellow flame from a big sulfur match while he studied me with a squint from under his big, dark, bushy brows. A good, orange-glowing coal started in his pipe's bowl. After taking a few good puffs and deliberately tamping the ashes with the butt end of his knife, he said, "You live on the side of the reservation where Nana's said to be hiding, and those young bucks disappear. You got any idea where he hides? That old man must be past seventy. I heard he limps badly when he walks. His warrior days must be long gone. I'm thinkin' the young men go see him for advice and then take off for fun and blood. If you can find him, we might be able to keep more young men from running off and getting themselves killed. You want to move around on the western range for a while and see what you can find?"

"I will look for Nana."

"Good. If you see his camp, come back and tell me." He took a long draw from his pipe and grinned. "The soldiers will convince him to stay and advise the young men not to go out."

The tone of Branigan's voice told me he was Coyote, the trickster, waiting, but I knew how to play Coyote's game, too.

"I will look for Nana and tell you when I find him."

Branigan nodded. "Good. Show you're a better tracker than Peso or Choneska. You might save the lives of some young men who ride over that last ridge into the Rinconada. Go now."

"Hmmph. I go." I thought, *What you really mean, Indah chief, is I save Indah lives if I find Nana.*

For three suns I rode over the western range of the reservation and out into the Rinconada. I looked in all the right places where the Blue Coats thought he might hide, and I left a good trail in case Branigan sent someone to follow me, but I never went to Nana's camp. I rode by the canyon where his wickiups stood looking like part of the natural brush, and I even saw two of his warriors look out from behind piñons to watch me. On the morning of the seventh sun, I saw his wickiups empty, and he and his band gone. I rode through the camp, counted wickiups, and looked in the horse corral to learn how well they rode and judged by their tracks and the dryness of the horse apples that they had left early the night before. It was time to tell Branigan I had found Nana's camp.

I rode hard over the ridges back to the agency, letting brush rub my clothes and pony, making us both look like we rode in a hurry. I tied my lathered pony to the hitching post in front of the big building and ran inside to stop before the open door of Branigan's place. He spoke to Peso and Choneska and waved for me to come in when he saw how hard I had been riding. He raised his big, bushy eyebrows in question.

I said, "Nana's camp on edge of Rinconada. All gone. Leave last sundown. Women and children go, too. Maybe twenty-five Mescaleros with Nana's fifteen warriors."

Branigan clenched his teeth and slammed his fist against his table. His anger made Peso and Choneska jump and look at me with wide eyes. He said, "Damn! I hate to hear that. Blood's gonna flow until we can bridle that old man. I've got to send a telegram to Fort Stanton. They'll want to be after him as fast as they can." He wrote out a note with big flourishing letters and then said, as he ran out the door in long, swinging strides, "Back in a minute, boys. Got to get this on the wire."

Peso looked at me and said, "You found Nana's camp back in that little canyon on the Rinconada?"

I looked him in the eye and said, "I did, and he was there twenty suns ago."

Peso and Choneska looked at each other and laughed. Peso said, "For a young man, you're a pretty good scout. Come see me sometime, and we'll talk over a smoke."

I nodded just as Branigan returned to sit in his chair and begin filling his pipe.

In seven suns, stories filled the reservation about the power of Nana's raid and how a soldier chief named *Teniente* (Lieutenant) Guilfoyle chased him hard, but never caught him in the wide trail of death and destruction he and his warriors left. Even Tata Crooked Nose's woman, called by our People "Miss Ida," who came to the agency house nearly a moon after him, passed a *Nakai-yi* covered wagon that was stopped close to the White Sands, horses gone, and the hand of a dead man hanging out from under the cover. When her driver stopped to check, he found another *Nakai-yi* and a woman piled up dead inside. Miss Ida, she's one lucky woman. If she had come earlier, she would have been in that wagon, too.

Nana's raid lasted about a moon. The story we heard about the last fight in his raid came from a trooper at Fort Stanton who told it to Branigan. He said *Teniente* Smith and some Blue Coat buffalo soldiers had the last fight with Nana close to the land of the *Nakai-yes* and that Smith and half his troopers went to the Happy Land.

All during Nana's long raid, I kept a tally of what Nana and his warriors did, and it made every warrior on the reservation proud they were Apaches. Nana killed at least fifty *Indah*, some said three hundred, but I didn't believe it, and drove off nearly

two hundred horses and mules before he disappeared into the
land of the *Nakai-yes.*

Not long before the Season of Earth is Reddish Brown, Branigan sent for me again. I went to the agency the same day I
heard him call for me. On the agency porch, he waved for me to
sit on a bench next to him and said, "Yellow Boy, your brothers,
the other policemen, tell me you have eyes like Cougar and see
well in the night. Do they speak the truth?"

"Hmmph. My eyes good when night comes and a little
moonlight shows the way. Not so good when no moon."

"I've seen you shoot, and I know you can hit anything you
can see. If you can see at night and can shoot half as good as
you do durin' the day, then I have a special job for a man with
your talents. What say you?"

"You say go, I go. What you want?"

"Remember I said when you started work as a policeman
that you stay away from the *Indah* as a policeman unless I
specifically said so?"

"I know your words."

"Well, sir, I'm now specifically tellin' you I want an *Indah*
policeman and a tribal policeman in the same body for this
work."

"You say I can shoot *Indah,* if they not do as I say?"

"I say I want you to shoot whoever steals Mescalero horses. I
ain't supposed to let you boys shoot the White Eyes. But in this
case, I will. Some bad White Eye gangs over in Lincoln County
come here over the ridges, and maybe some Texas gangs out of
the White Sands around La Luz. Under a full moon, they steal
horses wherever they find 'em. Mostly they raid Nogal Canyon.
It's gonna stop. Major Llewellyn and me ain't gonna tolerate it.
If I use just one shooter, the sheriff won't believe the tribal
police shot them boys. If a few of them gang members gets their

tails shot off, they'll run to the sheriff and claim the Mescaleros shot 'em when they just rode through. Sheriff from Lincoln will come nose around and ask us a few questions, but Llewellyn and me will claim we know the location of all the tribal policemen and other warriors on them nights. The sheriff will go away, tell them boys there ain't nothin' happenin' on the reservation, and they're gonna think twice about stealin' your horses.

"You know that narrow spot up Nogal Canyon where the creek runs over on one side?"

"Hmmph. Know place."

Branigan grinned and nodded. "Good. We're gonna start keepin' the herd up the canyon above it. Anybody steals ponies outta Nogal, they're gonna have to drive 'em by that narrow spot to get off the reservation and down in the basin. I want you to find yourself a place to shoot from there at the narrows. When they come, and they're gonna come, I want you to pick off as many as you can except for one. Leave one alive to spread around what happened. You want the job?"

I didn't have to think much about it. Stopping *Indahs* from stealing Mescalero ponies was warrior's work. Breaking up *tiswin* drunks, not so much. "I take job. Shoot *Indah* who take ponies."

Branigan grinned and nodded. He pulled out his pipe and tobacco and said, "Good. Let's you and me smoke on it."

"*Enjuh*. We smoke. When you want me to guard Nogal Canyon?"

Branigan began filling his pipe. "I want you on watch when it gets dark."

I nodded and looked in his eyes. "I be ready."

134

CHAPTER 18
COYOTE WAITS

I followed the wagon road through the reservation down the valley toward Tularosa and took the trail south across Río Tularosa into Nogal Canyon. Entering the canyon, the trail ran along the hills on the east side, while the little stream running out of the canyon was on the west side. The place Branigan thought would be a good one for an ambush was on an east-side hill where the canyon narrowed until it was no more than two long bowshots (about two hundred yards) across, a distance easy to cover with my rifle. The place Branigan chose had junipers and pines growing across the canyon floor. I saw those might provide the raiders cover when bullets flew. I moved on up the canyon to the top of the next hill so I had a clear shot across the canyon between the trail on the east side and the little creek on the west. The distance east to west across the canyon floor didn't increase more than fifty or sixty yards, which meant the distance was a shot I'd rarely miss, even in the dark.

I tied my pony in some junipers on the backside of the hill out of sight from the trail, and then made a nest with juniper needles that would keep me warm as I waited. There was still a little light left when I finished my nest, so I used it to find and stack a few rocks into a low wall for me to lie behind for cover in case the raiders returned fire.

The canyon grew cool as the sun went down, and it was soon cold enough to see my breath. I wrapped my blanket around my shoulders and legs and sat in my nest with my back against a juniper tree and my rifle across my knees, staring down the trail and waiting for the moon to rise and the *Indahs* who would die for stealing our ponies. For some, my rifle would certainly make this their last raid. In darkness blacker than a witch's soul, I ate from the bag of venison jerky, nuts, and dried fruit Juanita had made for me, a bag that I always carried on my saddle for when I had to stay out longer than a day. I finished my meal, and checked the loads in my rifle and pistol.

Coyotes called from near the water on the west side of the canyon, and an occasional night bird screeched. Little animals scrambled, sniffing through the brush, making the dry grass snap and crack, but it was too cold for most frogs and insects to make much noise. I saw the faint glow of the moon behind the mountains and shivered in expectation and excitement that this night I might help end the *Indah* and *Nakai-yi* raids on our horses.

As the moon floated up over the eastern ridges, rising like a feather carried on an easy breeze, I thought of my life and how good the spirits were to us when Juanita and I might have been childless, or how my daughter might have been born without her father if Sangre del Diablo's shot had killed me at the great river. Without thinking, my hand brushed the fresh scar from the witch's bullet, which puckered and ached when the air was cold.

What if Kah had not come along and saved me from bleeding out? I owed Kah much and hoped *Ussen* gave him and Deer Woman a child soon. I wondered if Delgadito had lived through Nana's long raid or if wolves and coyotes in some high, lonely place chewed his bones. I believed that if he came back, he would take Falling Water as his wife and support her and her mother, Sleepy. Delgadito had a wild and free heart. It would be hard for a woman to change him if she dared try. I didn't know Falling Water well enough to guess if she had that kind of courage and wisdom, and as I thought about it, I didn't know if Delgadito had the courage and wisdom to let her make him a better man.

I heard horses whinny and a light rumble of galloping hooves up the trail behind the hill in front of me. I crawled to my rock fence, stretched out on my belly, and covered my back and head with my blanket, making me nearly impossible to see. I rested my rifle's barrel on a rock in the little wall I had made and checked again my sight pictures against brush and stones scattered in the canyon and on the trail around the hill in front of me in the dim light of the rising quarter moon. The shadows were confusing in some cases, and the light low, which made it harder, so it took longer for me to point on a target than I had thought when Branigan asked if I wanted to take this work.

I sighted my rifle on the place where the riders would come around the trail curve toward me and waited. The sound of running ponies grew louder, and then one, a brown and white pinto, mane and tail flying in the cold night air, looking like a living shadow, was around the curve and charging down the road below me. Another, a big black with a blaze face, raced past my sights, and then two big grays came running side-by-side. Behind them came a big red pony, its shiny coat like a mirror in the moonlight. Driving on came a dark figure on a black and white pinto swinging and snapping a length of *reata* (rawhide rope) and whistling loud like a *googé* (whip-poor-will).

I didn't hesitate. I sighted on the figure, closed my eyes for an instant, so I'd still be able to see in the night after its flash as I squeezed the trigger, and fired. The rifle's thunder filled the canyon and came echoing back. In the low, white light, I saw the pinto had no rider. I levered a new cartridge into the chamber and waited, but no more riders came. Taking my blanket and rifle, I walked to my pony, tightened the cinches, and swung into the saddle. I stayed in the juniper shadows as I rode down the hillside and up the trail to the curve. The pinto had stopped a couple of hundred yards down the trail from where I rode off the hill. It stood watching me, ears up, reins hanging down to the trail dust. I moved with care. His rider might yet try to kill me. Coyote, the trickster, always waits.

I waited in the deep shadows of a big cottonwood tree, studying the trail up the canyon trying to find the *Indah* I knew I had hit. Then, not fifty yards away, in little spots of moonlight, the shadow of a small juniper lying on the trail moved a little when there was no breeze.

I swung down from my pony, cocked the Henry rifle and put its stock butt to my shoulder, and, pointing the rifle across the back of my pony directly at the then-unmoving shadow, advanced up the trail, keeping the pony between me and the shadow. When I was fifteen yards away, I saw the rider's bare legs outlined in the trail dust and heard a gurgle each time he tried to breathe.

A wave of great sadness washed over me, and a bitter taste filled my mouth like that of the Río Pecos when I was no more than five harvests old at Bosque Redondo. I had shot and probably killed an *Indeh* brother stealing ponies. I hated to think that I had spilled *Indeh* blood for a few ponies. Good warriors shouldn't die like that. Even worse, it might be a boy trying to make himself a name at the wrong place and time.

Keeping my rifle ready, I advanced on the shadow in the dust and came to look down at the face of Delgadito. A dark, perfectly round hole was just below his right nipple, the blood leaking out of it filled with bubbles. I heard the rattling, wheezing sound of air coming out of the wound as he took slow gasps, waiting for the night to stay black forever.

I kneeled beside him. He managed to mumble as he looked in my face, "So, it is you Yellow Boy. I thought either the luckiest or the best marksman had killed me. I'm glad it was the best marksman. I thank *Ussen* for an *Indeh* friend to kill me and not some miserable *Indah* with a lucky shot." He took a wheezing breath and coughed a little, blood covering his lips, pain rippling across his face. "Don't look so grim, *Aashcho.* I draw near the Happy Land. It's a good night to die. Kill the witch, send him blind . . ."

His breath flew away in a long sigh and did not return.

I sat down in the cold and dust beside him and felt more alone than when I had found my father, Caballo Negro, scalped by Sangre del Diablo's band. Delgadito had a good death, I gave it to him, but I didn't want him to go. I picked up a handful of dust and let it fall through my fingers, wondering if this bit of earth was where we all ended up. I laid my rifle across my knees and found a *cigarro* in my policeman's vest. Cupping my hands close to my body to keep down the initial flash from the match, I struck it with my thumbnail as I had seen my father do many times when I was a boy. I lighted the *cigarro* and made smoke to the four directions, asking *Ussen* to make Delgadito's journey to the Happy Land of the grandfathers a good one.

I wrapped Delgadito in my blanket and tied his body across his pony. I led them up the trail into the high country and left him in a cliff wall shelf I covered with rocks to keep the animals from his bones, and sacrificed his pony beside it for him to ride in the Happy Land. I found sage and other herbs and made a fire to purify myself in its smoke. *Ussen* had told me in my vision that part of my Power made sure I would never have Ghost Sickness as a Killer of Witches. Still I felt the need to bathe in the purifying smoke. A man I knew and respected had died by my hand. Coyote waits.

CHAPTER 19
GOOD TIMES

I told Branigan what had happened with the ambush, except I didn't tell him the man I had killed was Delgadito or that I knew him. I went home to Juanita, heavy hearted. She watched me sit by the fire for ten suns, ignoring her and Kicking Wren, as I wrestled with what I had done.

One evening we were alone. Moon on the Water had taken Kicking Wren to visit and play with Maria and her. I sat gazing into the fire, unable to stop thinking about what it meant to have killed Delgadito. I had never thought about the men I had killed before, and it churned my guts to think about the man, not a friend or an enemy, I had wiped out for a few horses.

Juanita sat cross-legged across the fire from me and worked on a basket with black, diamond patterns beginning to form in the coils made from yucca fibers interwoven with sumac stems. The crackling fire's yellow light shone off her raven's wing hair. I saw her cast a curious glance toward me, pause, and then continue her work. She finished a round on the basket and puffed her cheeks. Laying the basket in her lap and crossing her arms, she said, "My man no longer laughs with pleasure to see the day come or enjoys his woman and child. He spends his hours staring at the fire. Why?"

I looked into her eyes a moment, nodded, and then lighted a *cigarro,* blew smoke to the four directions, and offered it to Juanita, who smoked to the four directions and then coughed a little before handing it back. She studied me and waited.

"I killed Delgadito."

Her fingers went to her mouth. "Why did you do this?"

I clenched my teeth to speak the truth and sighed. "I was waiting one night on a hill in Nogal Canyon to ambush *Indah* horse raiders less than a moon ago. Branigan told me I could shoot *Indah* if they stole our ponies. A figure came driving away Mescalero ponies, stealing them. I shot at him. I thought he rode like an *Indeh*, but I could not be sure. I couldn't clearly see him, but he was raiding our ponies. I shot. In the darkness, I did this, and I didn't miss.

"I found him in the dust on the trail out of Nogal." Pointing to the spot below my right nipple, I said, "My bullet hit him here. He lived long enough to tell me he was glad *Ussen* let a true warrior kill him rather than some sorry *Indah*. I didn't want to kill him, but I did what Branigan said, shoot the raider, even if it is an *Indah*. Now, I think, maybe from now on, I must only shoot for myself and not for the *Indah* tribal police chief. Maybe I must find other work. I don't want to be the cause of *Indeh* blood because an *Indah* says so."

She stared at me awhile, and then lowering her hand from in front of her mouth, wise Juanita said, "Husband, Delgadito left us because you said his hatred against the Blue Coats was more important to him than the family he might make with Falling Water. He raided and killed many *Indah* and *Nakai-yes* riding with Nana. You killed him trying to steal ponies from his own people. He had no loyalty to this band or to any other Mescaleros. I'm sorry he died, but he chose to leave and to steal our ponies. He chose the price paid for taking his own people's ponies."

I knew Juanita spoke the truth, and soon my time of staring at the fire finished. A man made a choice to live or die raiding. I had chosen a different path, made a different choice, and if those choices crossed, like trails in the wilderness, one likely disappeared.

Before the Season of Little Eagles, Juanita took Kicking Wren off her cradleboard and soon she was finding her way into everything in the tipi. Juanita's mother, Maria, who by custom I was never supposed to see, looked after the child while Juanita worked at her chores and spent many long hours making the beautiful, coiled baskets and trays she sold or traded at Blazer's store. Moon on the Water sat with her often and worked on her own baskets, learning how to make the design patterns and how to sew close weaves for making a beautiful basket that another woman, *Indah* or *Indeh,* might want enough to trade or pay *Indah* money for.

In the Season of Earth is Reddish Brown, Ish-kay-neh, who was soon to be a novice warrior, worked on a shallow cave hidden behind junipers in the cliffs near our tipis. It was big enough for everyone in the band to sit in and visit around a fire. He made a place for a fire back from the opening and well out of the wind and surrounded it by rocks to hold the ashes and coals in place. Then he made a latticework of poles with a little door across the front and covered the lattice with brush to help hold in the heat from the fire. As the Ghost Face Season days passed and the men and Ish-kay-neh hunted, we brought deer and elk hides that could wait for the women to tan and finish and tied them to the lattice, and that helped keep the place even warmer. Two or three times, we had a hard snow after a warm time and caught many deer snowed in under tall pine trees. We killed enough to get through the Ghost Face Season without using much in supplies from the agency, and we even had feasts in our cave meeting place after the women worked in it to stretch and finish the hides rather than let them freeze until the Season of Little Eagles when the warm winds came.

Ish-kay-neh worked every day during Earth is Reddish Brown cutting a big supply of firewood for the Ghost Face Season. Our band used the cave often, and all the work he did serving us drew him closer to being a grown man of great respect by our People.

In those times when we sat around the cave fire, the children begged Beela-chezzi to tell them stories of the old days, and he did. He was a very good storyteller, and he told them tales of raids Cha and his warriors made out of our camps in the Guadalupe Mountains on the *Indah* and *Nakai-yes*. He told them how he and I survived our attack on the witch, Sangre del Diablo. The wind moaned and snow flew outside, and their eyes grew wide, and their mouths dropped open as they listened to every word. We all listened. It wasn't just a tale for the children. Even I listened, and I was part of the story.

Kah knew all the Coyote stories, and the children's favorite was Coyote and Bear. The way Kah used to tell it, Bear was chief at a camp where nobody could keep the fat when they killed game. Bear Chief wanted it all. Every day, he sent his two Bear Boys out among the people of the camp, and they gave the boys all the fat.

One day Coyote visited Bear Chief's camp. He liked what he saw and decided to bring his own camp over. After they made their camp, one of Bear Chief's people came to the camp and asked him if he knew the rules of their camp. Coyote said no. "Well," the visitor said, "in this whole camp, no one is supposed to keep the fat of any kind. That is the way of our Bear Chief."

Old Coyote said, "I'm not going to give any fat to your chief if I kill the game."

The visitor said, "You'd better, or he'll come and punish you."

That made Coyote angry, and the visitor returned to his own camp.

Next day, Coyote went hunting. He took a nice, fat, young buck. Coyote brought the deer back quickly, and Bear Chief, seeing him, sent his two Bear Boys to get the fat.

When the boys came, Coyote stepped out of his tipi and asked them what they wanted.

The Bear Boys said, "We came after the fat. All of it from the deer you brought in."

"No!" said Coyote.

One of Bear Boys said, "Our papa is chief here. We won't go until you give us that fat!"

"I say no. You two boys go home."

But they wouldn't go and kept asking for the fat. Coyote got a stick and gave the Bear Boys a good whipping. They both started to cry and ran back to the camp of Bear Chief.

Old Coyote was pretty smart. He knew that Bear Chief would come for a visit soon, so he built a big fire and scattered some pieces of deerskin large enough to cover the palm of his hand around the fire, and he put some pebbles in the fire.

When the Bear Boys went home to their papa, he asked them why they came back without any fat and why they were crying.

They said, "That new camper down there is the cause of all this."

Bear Chief got real mad when he heard this, and he went down to Coyote's camp, where Coyote had this big fire going, and all the people went down to see what would happen.

Bear Chief came growling and saying he wanted the fat. Coyote said, "No, this fat belongs to me. I killed the deer and brought it in."

Bear Chief got very angry. He said, "You whipped my boys, too. So, first I'll finish with you, and then I'll take the fat!"

Old Coyote was brave. He stood his ground by the hot fire. The Bear Chief started around one way, but Coyote ran to the other side. As they circled the fire, Coyote said to Bear Chief,

"I'm not afraid of you, either. Open your mouth wider, it won't scare me!"

Coyote kept saying that while he circled the fire, and he picked up the hot pebbles with one of the pieces of deerskin he put near the fire. He threw the hot pebbles into Bear Chief's mouth while he snarled and growled. Bear Chief, very angry, didn't notice the hot pebbles thrown in his mouth. He kept up the chase, round and round the fire. Coyote kept throwing hot pebbles in his mouth until, soon, the hot pebbles began to work, and Bear Chief dropped dead.

Then Mother Bear came down to see for herself why Bear Chief did not come home. She saw Bear Chief lying dead and became very sad and angry. She went after Coyote, but Coyote circled around and did the same thing with Mother Bear. He raced around the fire, first one way and then another, making fun of old Mother Bear. He mocked her, and she chased him harder, roaring loud, and Coyote threw hot pebbles into her mouth like he had with Bear Chief. Soon old Mother Bear dropped dead, too.

Old Coyote was the hero then. He'd killed both bears. He'd won the fight and won back the fat for the whole camp. Everyone was happy, and they had a big feast because they could eat all the fat they wanted. No one ever again tried to take all the fat. And the two Bear Boys had to make their own living, hunting their own food.

Beela-chezzi worked with Ish-kay-neh, now fourteen harvests, training him to be a warrior and preparing his own son, Shiyé, and my little brother, Little Rabbit, to begin training. He made them run every day, even in the snow, and jump in the stream to bathe in the early morning, even if they had to jump through a little ice frozen on the top of the stream. As hard as his training was for the boys, neither Shiyé, Little Rabbit, nor Ish-kay-neh complained, and they worked hard at what Beela-chezzi told them to do. I helped with their training by showing them how to make arrows fletched and marked so anyone knew who they belonged to and how to tip them with blunt ends for bird hunting, or, for big game, sharp points filed from iron barrel hoops. I also showed them how to make bows from *tsélkani* strong enough to kill an elk or a man, and how to hunt and catch the little animals like rabbits that tasted good roasted over the fire or in a stew pot. I gave them the bows and arrows I made with them watching. Good students, they learned well how to make their own. I was glad to help these good boys, but my heart was sad. They would not know the pleasures of riding with the warriors on raids as novices, or as warriors. I wondered what tests would prove their manhood for the women and all the Mescaleros.

Juanita and I were under the blankets many times that Ghost Face Season, but no baby grew in her belly, and her face was marked with lines of sadness. I told her *Ussen* would choose the best time for a baby in her belly. She smiled and nodded she understood, but her eyes said something different.

Warm winds came, and the snow melted, filling the creeks to overflowing. The sky was brilliant blue again, not covered with clouds, and the grass down the canyon was a deep, dark green that matched the pines. The Season of Little Eagles passed into the Season of Many Leaves, and the streams once filled with melted snow grew small again and easy to cross. People all over the reservation came out of their camps and canyons ready to gamble, play, or fight, and Branigan's police, me included, were busy keeping order.

With the streams nearly back to normal, our little camp went to the agency to collect supplies, and those with *Indah* money or things to trade visited Blazer's store. Juanita had a nice collection of baskets she'd made for trade, and Blazer's clerk gave her a good price for them.

While she bargained inside, I sat and smoked on the store porch, feeling the warm light on my face, my eyes nearly closed in the pleasure of the day. Through the slits of my eyes, I saw Branigan come out of the agency building. He saw me and came walking in my direction. I stood to meet him. We spoke of the Ghost Face Season and the coming Season of Many Leaves and of wild Apaches and *Indah* raiders we would have to fight that year.

Another Ghost Face Season came, and Kicking Wren, a great pleasure for Juanita and me, and still less than three harvests old, did well playing with the other children much older than she. Ish-kay-neh ran long distances by himself, did well in arrow shooting, slinging rocks, and throwing rocks by hand with boys his age from other bands. His victories showed he had paid close attention to what we taught him of the old ways, customs, and stories about doing a thing right and well. In an earlier time, he would have been ready to go on raids as a novice, but now there were no more raids, at least none anyone would admit. Beela-chezzi, Kah, and I smoked often by the fire, sharing the ideas we had trying to decide how to test the maturity of the boys growing to manhood in our little band without the benefits of learning by helping warriors on raids.

Deer Woman had her first child, a son, in the Season of Large Leaves (midsummer). Kah strutted around our camp for a moon with his chest out and a smile that nearly touched his ears. Sleepy made the child a *tsach,* and after the ceremony, Kah named him Para-dee-ah-tran (The Contented) because he almost never cried or whimpered from the day of his birth. Deer Woman never had to hang his cradleboard in a tree to teach him the need for quiet. After Para-dee-ah-tran was born, Deer Woman was sweeter and more content than at any time I

147

had known her since her *Haheh* (puberty ceremony), and she and Juanita became close friends once more after more than four harvests of carefully avoiding each other.

Sitting by the fire while the wind moaned and the snow flew, I smoked a *cigarro* and watched my girl child play with a little doll I had carved for her, and Juanita taught Moon on the Water tricks for making the tight, beautiful baskets for which she, Juanita, was well known. I thought of the year past and felt content. We didn't have an easy life, but our little band had not gone hungry. I had been shot at but never hit, and there was no word from anywhere of the witch, Sangre del Diablo. I hoped, maybe, I had killed him after all. All the children were growing strong and healthy and learning the old ways, and the Blue Coats didn't bother the People as long as we did nothing that appeared threatening.

We had heard of the breakout at San Carlos by Juh and Geronimo, how they had escaped into the Blue Mountains in the last Ghost Face Season, only to return and stir up the People of Loco and Chihuahua at San Carlos and lead them in a breakout that left many *Indah* and *Nakai-yes* dead on both sides of the border. But the Mescaleros stayed peaceful and far away from the Chiricahuas, who left a path filled with blood, smoke, and destruction.

Sitting there by the fire, thinking of our good fortune, I forgot that Coyote watches. The trickster waits until you are sleeping in your thoughts and then plays a trick that you never dreamed would happen, especially after a year's good fortune.

CHAPTER 20
SERGEANT SWEENY JONES

In the time the *Indah* called 1883, we again rode our horses early in the Season of Little Eagles, and the whole camp went to Blazer's store, the women to get their supplies, the children to play games with children from other camps, our nearly grown boy to enter bow shooting, racing, and riding contests with others close to his age, and the men to smoke, gamble, watch the sawmill, and listen to the latest gossip about the agency. I waited on the store porch and smoked a *cigarro*, listening to the others, while Juanita and Moon on the Water bought supplies from my pay as a policeman and bargained for good prices on their baskets so they could buy the pretty things they wanted.

I saw Branigan come out of the agency building followed by a Blue Coat with three yellow stripes on his coat sleeves. The trooper cut his brown hair, bleached white by the sun, short, and he stood straight as a well-made arrow.

Branigan motioned me to come over to the agency steps. He held up his palm as I approached and said, "*D'anté*, Yellow Boy. The winter has been long. Your People are well?"

"*D'anté*, Branigan. My People are well. No come to agency when very cold and snow blows hard in the Ghost Face Season. Hard to get over the ridges in deep snow. I stay with them as you said. There was no trouble even with many games of Monte."

Branigan nodded and turned to the Blue Coat. "Sergeant Sweeny Jones, our friend is Yellow Boy, a Mescalero policeman, the man you asked to see."

Sweeny Jones nodded and stuck out his hand for a shake, and I gave it two solid pumps. He said, "*D'anté,* Yellow Boy. Mr. Al Sieber wanted me to stop here and talk to ya after I carried some dispatches from General Crook to the commander at Fort Stanton. I'm on the way back to meet up with Sieber and General Crook at Willcox over to Arizona Territory."

"Hmmph. Al Sieber and me have good talk after he see me shoot. Why Al Sieber say you talk to me? I know you?"

Sergeant Jones grinned.

"Naw, we ain't never met, but you shore impressed Mr. Al Sieber with your shootin' and good sense. You probably heard last year about the breakout at San Carlos by Chihuahua, Geronimo, Juh, and them other bloodthirsty banditos. They've been raidin' outta their camps in the Sierra Madre down to Mexico. Lieutenant Davis caught us a White Mountain Apache Chato had taken last year during the breakout. He wanted to stay, but his wives was Chiricahuas and wanted to leave with ol' Chato, who didn't give 'im much choice, if ya know what I mean. He calls hisself Tzoe, but he's got such purty, rosy cheeks and smooth skin us troopers jest call 'im 'Peaches.' "

Branigan motioned us over to sit on a bench, and Jones stopped talking long enough to cut a chew, pop it in his cheek, and get it softened up so he could spit and chew. The air was cold, but the sun was bright and warming. Horses stomped and nickered in the stone corral where the Blue Coats once held my People in horse apples a hand-length deep until they were nearly all sick. Whoops and yells drifted down the valley from men playing hoop-and-pole on a flat place up the wagon road from the agency. While Sweeny Jones got his tobacco going, I sat down, leaned my back against a porch post, and lighted another *cigarro.* Branigan sat in a rocking chair with his arms crossed, watching and waiting for Jones, who first spat a long stream of brown juice out on to the road and then continued.

"Ole Peaches says he knows where the Chiricahua camps are in the Sierra Madre and promised General Crook he'd lead us to 'em. General Crook, he spent most of the winter getting things worked out with the Mexicans so's we'n go down there without them givin' us any trouble. In about a month, he's gonna take a few troopers and a whole lot of scouts and either get them Apaches to come back to San Carlos or wipe 'em out. Mr. Al Sieber says the general is taking a big gamble, damned if he does, damned if he don't, but it's gotta be done, or folks on the border is gonna be bleeding for a long the time, and the US Cavalry is gonna look mighty foolish chasin' ghosts the rest of its days.

"Mr. Al Sieber asked me to stop by the reservation here and see if you and a few other Mescaleros want to join up for this here little ride General Crook is about to take with his Apache scouts. He told me he wants you to come. Says there's a special job he has in mind that you'd be perfect for with your shootin' skills and all. Army pays thirteen dollars a month, gives you a uniform just like I'm a wearing, two bandoliers of cartridges, a Springfield rollin' block carbine, a canteen, shirt, pants, and a few other gewgaws you'd probably find right handy. I already asked Mr. Branigan there if he'd give ya time off from the policeman job you're a workin', and he said he thought he could do without you for three to six months, but no more. You'd be back here well 'fore the snow flies, so that ain't a problem. How 'bout it? You gonna help us with them Chiricahuas down to Mexico?"

I sat there feeling the warmth of the sun, like the closeness of Juanita, and smoked and thought about going into Mexico to face the Chiricahua and their friends. Thinking about how the Chiricahua scouts had nearly killed us at Rufus Pike's rancho when we left the reservation to escape the Blue Coats made me feel this trip might be a chance for a little payback. Sweeny Jones had stirred my memory of wild and free times. My friends, Kah and Beela-chezzi, would keep meat on the rack for Juanita and the other women while I was gone. I wanted to go. I wanted to see Al Sieber again, meet General Crook, the man the Apaches had come to call Nantan Lupan (General Gray Wolf), and learn about this special job Al Sieber said he thought I was perfect for. Besides all this, if the witch had returned to Mexico with more Comanches, I might have a chance of finding him again and, if *Ussen* helped me, sending him to the land of the grandfathers blind.

I said to Sergeant Sweeny Jones, "I go. Talk to Al Sieber. Maybe I go to Mexico and scout Blue Mountains with Nantan Lupan. I take my wife back to our camp first. Now she in Blazer's store selling baskets. When we ride?"

Branigan's dark face got a little darker, and Sergeant Sweeny Jones grinned and nodded. Branigan said, "I was hopin' you'd stay, but maybe you can earn your keep in Mexico and help out the general. Just don't let the Chiricahuas put a bullet in you when you ain't lookin'."

The camp returned to its tipis the next day, and I had told Juanita what I planned to do. She wasn't happy about me being gone for a long time, but she told me to do what I thought best, and she put together a good bag of trail food for me. Kah and Beela-chezzi promised to keep her, Kicking Wren, and my other women well provisioned while I was gone.

Sweeny Jones tried for two days to recruit other Mescaleros for the expedition, but none wanted to become a scout and work for the Blue Coats against the Chiricahua. The third morning after I'd met Sweeny Jones, we met again in front of the agency and rode down the wagon trail toward Tularosa in the early morning light, the air still cold enough to see our breath.

We were halfway to Tularosa when the sun brought bright light letting us see the blaze of white sands, which looked like a great, white cloud against the foot of mountains the *Indah* and *Nakai-yes* called San Andres. A thin, green line of mesquite and creosote bushes showed where the white sand ended. On the long trail we rode in those days, I liked seeing that land the best.

Sweeny Jones was a good horseman. He knew how to ride far in a day and not kill his pony by using the walk, trot, gallop style the Apaches had used for years when not on raids. On raids, they rode until their ponies were ready to drop, then stole fresh ones. In two days riding southwest, we crossed the great river and rode out across the *llano* covered in grama grass, creosote bushes, and mesquite. Scattered among them, gourds were making new leaves on vines creeping in every direction away from long afternoon shadows, and the stalks on yuccas, filled with pods ready to flower, reached for the sky. I tried to remember where I saw the largest crowds of yuccas, so I might bring the women back for mescal when I returned.

We rode into the army camp at Willcox near the end of the fifth day on our ride out of Mescalero. There were Blue Coat tents, large and small, arranged in straight rows near the iron wagon tracks that ran in from the northeast, tents for packers scattered near corrals for more mules than I had seen anywhere, and off to one side, fires started by distinct groups of Apaches, a few wearing Blue Coats. I had seen Apaches in Blue Coats before, including some at Fort Stanton near the reservation, but the sight of them still left a bad taste in my mouth. In the center of the camp were mounds of supplies, harnesses for packs, canteens, blankets, and guarded by troopers, boxes of ammunition and rifles.

At the head of the Blue Coat tents stood a big tent with a fire and stools in front, a cooking fire with pots hung from a tripod, and a frame supporting a side of roasting beef. The sides of the tent were rolled up to let in any breeze, and I saw an old *Indah* with a long, gray beard sitting at a table and looking at a big, thin, white skin covered with long wiggling marks drawn on it. I soon learned the *Indah* called it a map. As we rode past, Sweeny Jones looked at me and grinned. "That there is the general's tent, and that's who you Apaches call Nantan Lupan, General Gray Wolf." I looked back at Nantan Lupan and wondered how such an old man could still be a big chief leading the Blue Coats against the Chiricahuas in Mexico.

As we rode though the camp, no one paid any attention to us. All walked quick on their own trails. We stopped by another big tent close by the fires of the Apaches who cooked their evening meal. Sweeny Jones swung down from his pony, motioned for me to dismount, and said, "Wait here." He went in the tent while I looked over the Apaches by their fires. Most of them, I could tell by the way they talked and dressed, were Chiricahuas, but a few others were mixed in who looked a little different, and when I heard their voices, they said their words in a different way from the Chiricahuas, which made them even harder to understand. These were, I later learned from talking with Al Sieber, White Mountain, Yuma, Mohave, and Tonto scouts. By the time we returned from the Blue Mountains, I knew them all very well.

As I studied the scouts and wondered why he had asked me to come, Sweeny Jones came out of the tent followed by Al Sieber who grinned at me through the brushy pile of hair under his nose. He said, "Yellow Boy. You did come. I hoped you would."

CHAPTER 21
TZOE AND THE SNAKE

Al Sieber and I sat by his fire and smoked while the sun, four
fingers (about an hour) above the horizon, warmed our backs
and made long shadows. He told me how Nantan Lupan
listened to the Apache chiefs after he returned from warring
with the plains tribes. The chiefs told him how the agents
cheated the People of their rations and how the People did
nothing at San Carlos except wait around for the next issue of
rations. The People needed action and were restless. If Chihuahua and the Warm Springs chiefs came for them, they would
probably go without resistance, many *Indah* and *Nakai-yes*
would die, and the border would burn and bleed for a long
time.

Sieber said that, after listening to the chiefs, General Crook
made things much better on the reservation, but knew if the
renegades stayed in the *Nakai-yi*'s Blue Mountains, there'd
always be trouble. He had to make them come back, by talk,
which he preferred, or by blood and steel, wiping out many. Too
many Blue Coats guarded the *Indah* on this land for the Apaches
to live free, even in the Blue Mountains.

Blue Coats alone couldn't find the Apaches, and scouts alone
wouldn't force them to come back. Nantan Lupan decided to
go after the Apaches in the Blue Mountains with many scouts
and a few Blue Coats. He spent moons talking with the *Nakai-
yes* in Chihuahua and Sonora until they finally agreed he could

155

cross the border to chase the Apaches hidden deep in the Blue Mountains.

Sieber poured us some coffee and sat back down, blowing over the top of his cup to cool it. He took a swallow and said, "The biggest problem Nantan Lupan faced after the Mexicans agreed to let him cross the border was finding the Chiricahua camps."

I nodded, tasted the bitter coffee, felt it hot and scalding the inside of my mouth, and said, "Nantan Lupan has light in his eyes, but he will never find Chiricahua in the Blue Mountains. Looking for Apache camps like trying to find snake in black cave. How will he do this?"

Sieber grinned. "Well, he got real lucky, luckier I'd say than a cowboy with less than a dollar in his pocket winding up with the queen bee in a whorehouse."

I didn't understand what Sieber meant and frowned. He just laughed and waved his hand like he'd said nothing.

"There's a White Mountain Apache warrior named Tzoe who married a couple of Chiricahua sisters in Chato's band. Last year when Chato left with the others, Tzoe didn't want to go, but his wives swore they weren't gonna be left behind, and Chato made him an offer he couldn't refuse." At this, he winked and grinned, for what I did not know, and continued, "So he left with the rest. Three moons ago Chato came north looking to steal ammunition and brought Tzoe with him. Tzoe's best friend, who rode with them, was killed during a raid on a charcoal camp, and it sent Tzoe to a dark place."

I nodded. I knew Tzoe's heart. I had mourned a long time after my close friend Klo-sen, and my grandfather, He Watches, who died fighting the witch, went to the grandfathers' Happy Land. I said, "Hard thing to lose good friend. Tzoe fights no more? Goes back to wives? Sits in wickiup with long face? What he do?"

Sieber pulled out his pipe, stuffed it with tobacco, and lit it with a match while he studied my face. "Tzoe had a long talk with Chato and said that his medicine had told him he ought to go back to San Carlos and look after the Warm Springs People. Chato let him go, and the others with them gave him enough food to get back to San Carlos."

The sky was blazing in a fiery sunset. Oranges, reds, and purples streamed against far clouds just above the horizon. Blue Coats and scouts were at their cooking fires. Somewhere a mule brayed and horses snorted and stamped in a nearby rope corral. Sieber lowered his pipe, took a big swallow of coffee, and continued.

"Tzoe was in an abandoned camp about twelve miles from San Carlos when Lieutenant Davis and his scouts caught him. He didn't put up a fight. One of my scouts told me Tzoe grinned when he saw Davis. The lieutenant put him in leg irons, took him back to the reservation, and questioned him about who he was and what the breakaway Apaches were doing. Tzoe answered every question and told Davis most of the Apaches wanted to come back but their leaders wouldn't let 'em."

I nodded and said, "Victorio killed Mescaleros riding with him who wanted to go back to reservation. Victorio made bad medicine. Maybe that medicine kills 'im. Every warrior ought to make his own choice."

Sieber blew a stream of blue pipe smoke toward the stars in the cool, falling, night air. "Lieutenant Davis believed Tzoe spoke the truth and asked if he would lead Nantan Lupan to the Chiricahua camps in the Blue Mountains. Davis told me Tzoe didn't think more'n a minute before he said he would. Davis telegraphed Nantan Lupan what he had learned. Nantan Lupan told the lieutenant to send Tzoe down here to Willcox where he could talk to him face-to-face and decide if he spoke the truth. Davis sent him, and Nantan Lupan believed him. He had the guide he needed to find the Chiricahua camps in the Blue Mountains. So you see all the rushin' around gettin' ready to go down into Mexico after the breakaways. Nantan Lupan is usin' nearly two hundred Apaches and about fifty troopers for this here little ride."

"Hmmph. Al Sieber, you have two hundred Apaches already. Why you want me?"

"Lieutenant Davis, who's been put in charge of the reservation while Captain Crawford rides the Blue Mountains with his scouts, has informers all over San Carlos to help him know what the People are sayin' or if they're plannin' trouble. What he's heard is that Crawford has at least two or three scouts that favor the breakaway chiefs and don't want to see 'em have to come back. They don't know Tzoe is guidin' us to the Chiricahua camps. If they find out, they might try to kill him. He's a warrior and can take care of himself. Problem is, he's our only reliable guide. There's two or three others who claim to know the way, but they ain't anxious to guide us, and I wouldn't trust 'em anyway. We could end up in the Pacific Ocean if they showed us the way. Tzoe? I trust him. He wants his wives back and wants the chasin' around to end.

"To be on the safe side, I think there needs to be somebody to watch his back so we don't lose him to some scout tryin' to protect a cousin or brother down there in the Blue Mountains. I think you're that somebody. I want you to join the scouts for this expedition. Your big work's gonna be protectin' Tzoe. Besides, we need the best scouts we can find, and I think you fit the bill. How about it, Yellow Boy?"

I stared at the fire, thinking. I wanted to go. I wanted to learn more about the Blue Mountains and where the Chiricahuas camped than I had learned on the trips to Elias's camp, trying to find the Comanches and witch. I might even get lucky and find the witch's camp if he'd come back with more Comanches and was hiding in the Blue Mountains. My spirit wanted to stay close to Juanita and Kicking Wren, but the Apache raids had to stop.

Stars were lighting on the eastern horizon, and far out on the *llano* two coyotes howled. *Yes,* I thought, *Coyote waits, just like he did for Delgadito.*

I looked in Sieber's eyes and nodded. "Hmmph. I go with Nantan Lupan to Blue Mountains. Protect Tzoe from attack. Bring back Chiricahua. When we go?"

Sieber grinned. "I'm mighty glad to hear that, Yellow Boy. We leave here in two days and go on down to San Bernardino Springs for a few days to shake out the real players for the campaign, and then we head down the San Bernardino Valley toward the Río Bavispe. We'll get you signed up and your equipment issued tomorrow. You'n make some extry moccasins and meet the rest of the scouts. How about some supper? I'm hungry."

"Supper good thing. Belly makes growling wolf noises."

The night before we left for San Bernardino Springs, the wind came up. By sunrise, it carried clouds of dust blowing over the big, nearby *playa,* stinging our skin like switches on our legs when we were small boys and the warriors chased us, making us run far and fast. All that dust and wind made it hard to see and hear the Blue Coat chief.

Teniente (Lieutenant) Gatewood, a Blue Coat officer, commanded all the scouts at Willcox. At the command of the scout leaders with three yellow stripes on their coats, we gathered in one place and waited, huddled over with our backs against the wind until the wagons were filled with ammunition, food supplies, and water, and the pack mules were harnessed and ready. The wagon freighters and mule packers, fast and efficient, soon pulled up to wait beside us.

159

Teniente Gatewood rode across the front of the scouts, and the sergeants yelled against the whistle of the wind for us to stand and get ready. He rode back and forth in front of us two times and looked over every scout before he stopped on the far side of us and raised his right arm. I saw the scouts tense, like just before a race. Gatewood threw his arm forward and yelled, "*Ugashé* (Go)!"

We scattered forward, quail running from a coyote, each of us finding our own path. I stayed close to Tzoe, but I didn't expect any trouble until we came near the Chiricahua camps far away in the Blue Mountains. We could keep our pace, which was slightly slower than a horse could trot, all day if needed. That night I heard Sieber tell the Blue Coat officer, Bourke, that we covered almost exactly four miles on the hour. Every day we ran fifteen or twenty miles and stopped to let the much slower freight wagons catch up with us. It took five days to reach San Bernardino Springs, but the scouts ran just a little more than half a day each day.

When we ran down the San Bernardino Valley in the land of the *Nakai-yes,* all the supplies were on mules, and even then, the trooper horses and mules worked hard to keep up with us. Sieber told Bourke he knew we could run forty miles or more a day, every day, if we had to.

We stopped to rest when the sun had raised halfway between first light and the time of shortest shadows. Mesquites made us shade on the edge of an arroyo, and we smoked and relaxed, lying on the sloping brown sand of the arroyo banks while we waited for the wagons hauling supplies, the pack train mules, and Blue Coats to catch up.

I studied all the scouts, especially Tzoe. He sat by himself, minding his business, his eyes sagging with sadness. He was near my age, a fine-featured, strong warrior. No unmarried woman would avoid him. None of the others scouts paid him any attention. Sieber had pointed him out to me the day after I arrived and said he had told no one else of our arrangement, including Tzoe. He wanted Tzoe to become my friend before he told him a stranger watched his back. Sieber feared that if it came out that Tzoe guided us, and that I kept a protective eye on him, plans might be hatched to kill both of us.

As I watched Tzoe, he stood and turned to climb the arroyo bank behind him for probably some alone time in bushes far from the rest of us. The arroyo banks were little more than head high, their sand, steep and soft, so he stretched his arm across the top of the bank and grabbed the trunk of a small mesquite to pull himself over the top.

A rattlesnake had already claimed the mesquite's shade. Seeing Tzoe's hand reach past it to the tree, it coiled and began its loud, unmistakable rattle as soon as Tzoe's head cleared the top of the bank. The snake's head, less than an arm's length from his face, even closer to the arm holding the mesquite, was in a perfect position to strike and kill him. Every scout in the arroyo froze to watch the action. We all knew if Tzoe didn't quickly get away from the snake, it would strike, but if he moved it would strike. Here in the wilderness without a strong medicine man to drive away the snake's demon spirit, Tzoe wouldn't last long. It would be the end of Nantan Lupan's best guide for rounding up the Chiricahuas in the *Nakai-yi* country.

From my seat on the opposite bank of the arroyo, I saw the rattlesnake's head, speckled by the sunlight filtering through the mesquite leaves, and heard the rattling stop and then start again, harder than before. I didn't have to think about shooting. In one motion, the butt of my rifle came to my shoulder. As the snake's head filled my sights, it disappeared in thunder and smoke. The bullet flew so close to the side of Tzoe's head, his hair twisted like a dust devil wind had passed by.

Silence hung in the hot, dry air like just before shooting

begins in an ambush, until someone said, "Tzoe has no need to go to the bushes now!" We all, including Tzoe, laughed. He pulled up farther on the bank top and, grabbing the bloody snake's body, threw it off into the brush, and then turned to ease back down the bank. The barrel of my rifle still had little wisps of smoke drifting out the end. He knew where the shot came from.

He walked over to where I sat and grinning, said, "*Ahéhye'e* (thank you). I'm Tzoe of the White Mountain band. Yesterday another scout told me your name is Yellow Boy. You must be the same one who, as I heard Juh tell the other chiefs, never missed and had the Power to go after the *Nakai-yi* Comanche witch Juh would not attack. You are the same warrior?"

"I'm the same warrior. I'm glad *Ussen* gave me the Power to kill the snake and you're not hurt. Do you want to smoke thanks to *Ussen* with me?"

He nodded. "Yes, I want to smoke to *Ussen* with you. I owe you my life for *Ussen*'s gift to you."

I pulled a *cigarro* from my shirt pocket and lighted it with a match I started with my thumbnail. Off to the east we heard faint yells of, "*Jaadé! Jaadé!*" (Antelope! Antelope!). Soon there was the distinct, distant thump, thump from the Springfield .45-70 carbines the scouts carried. We all grinned and nodded, happy to have antelope for our meal that night.

CHAPTER 22
INTO MEXICO

Tzoe convinced Nantan Lupan he had told the truth, and the Blue Coats made him a sergeant. Being sergeant made it look natural for him to lead us in the direction of the Chiricahua camps. After his meeting with the snake, he led his scouts on until we camped near *Dos Cabezas* (Two Heads) Mine. The land around the mine had water and good grazing for the horses and mules. We made our little individual campfires and, with clouds saying it might rain, set up wickiups over beds we made of pulled grass, and waited for the wagons, mule pack trains, and Blue Coats.

We saw the wagons coming from a long way off. They made a long, high, dust cloud like those I'd seen as a boy when I sat with my grandfather, He Watches, scanning the eastern road from the top of Guadalupe cliffs. I watched them come with the *Shináá Cho* and saw the dust covering the wagoners' faces and clothes with a fine powder, which made them look like mountain spirits at a dance and forced them to wear bandannas over their mouths and noses to breathe. Two columns of Blue Coats followed by pack mules led the wagons. Every foot, hoof, and wheel was adding to the dust and sand in the still, evening air, when the Blue Coats reached us.

We cooked some of the antelope heads, hearts, livers, and haunches, along with cottontail rabbits and quail our fast runners caught. When the Blue Coats, wagon freighters, and mule packers were ready to eat we gave them coffee, tortillas, and

163

meat we didn't use.

Sergeant Sweeny Jones, Al Sieber, and Mickey Free ate at our fire. Mickey Free, an *Indah-Nakai-yi* interpreter, had only one eye. He had been taken by Apaches at the age of twelve and later freed by Blue Coats. *Teniente* Bascom had started a war, spilling much *Indah* blood by accusing Cochise of taking Mickey Free, when he had not, and then hanging innocent warriors. I had made friends with his good friends, Tzoe and John Rope, a White Mountain scout. I liked Mickey Free, and soon we became friends as we joked around the fire. After supper, we sat, smoked, and talked while we enjoyed our full bellies.

Mickey Free, slurping his coffee, looked across the fire at Tzoe and grinned. He said, "Grandson (a term of affection between friends), what story do our brothers tell me about you going face-to-face with Rattlesnake at your first rest today?"

Tzoe's cheeks turned redder than normal. He grinned and nodded. Al Sieber frowned and stared hard at Mickey Free and then Tzoe. Sweeny Jones's eyes grew wide, and his jaw dropped. He leaned forward, one ear cocked toward Sergeant Tzoe.

Tzoe said, "Your brothers tell you true, Mickey Free. We stopped to rest in the shade of mesquites on the edge of an arroyo. I needed some alone time in the bushes and began to climb up the bank of the arroyo. When my head cleared the top of the bank, Rattlesnake lay coiled and waiting for me. He didn't like me bothering his nap, and he started to rattle, his head no more than an arm's length from my nose. One good strike and he would have killed me for certain. I knew, if I moved, he would strike and could not miss my face. His anger grew when I froze, staring at him, and wondering how long before I went to the Happy Land."

Sieber shook his head and asked, "What'd you do? If you ain't bit, you sure as the devil oughta been."

Tzoe smiled and nodded toward me. "No, Rattlesnake did

not strike. My friend Yellow Boy sat across from me on the far arroyo bank. In less time than it takes to draw a breath, he shot the head off Rattlesnake."

Sieber's frown went away. He grinned and cut his eyes to me and then to Tzoe. He laughed good and slapped his leg the way the *Indah* do when they feel good about a laugh. He said, "I knew that bringing a shooter like Yellow Boy along on this ride was a good idea. Bet you didn't need to go to the bushes after that."

We all laughed, but Tzoe just looked at the ground and shook his head.

From a few wickiups over sounded the melodic hum of music from a bow across the strings of a *tsii"edo'a'tl* (wood that sings), what the *Indah* called an Apache fiddle, played by a scout singing softly near his fire. Its strings were horsehairs, and its body made from the husk of a mescal plant. Its gentle rhythm filled the night as we listened and felt easy. Its song made me think of Juanita and the days I courted her. I wished her nearby. I hoped she and Kicking Wren stayed safe while I followed this trail.

We ran four more days and came to San Bernardino Springs on the border of the land of the *Nakai-yes*. Some Blue Coats had already come to guard extra supplies and send out patrols with scouts to stop the Chiricahuas, who tried to come north and raid *Indah* ranchos and mines or ambush Blue Coat patrols for bullets and ponies. A Blue Coat named Captain Crawford had also come with another hundred scouts.

I looked over the scouts riding with Captain Crawford, thinking I might see a friend or enemy. One stood a head taller than most of those around him, and I immediately recognized the scowling, pox-scarred face of Soldado Fiero, the sergeant who led the Chiricahua scouts to catch or destroy my little Mescalero band after we'd escaped the reservation when the Blue

Coats came to disarm and unhorse us. I was ready to kill him when Juanita knocked him senseless with a stone from her sling. The last time I saw him, he was still in the dream world where Juanita sent him, his men carrying him back to Mescalero. He still wore his blue coat as Captain Crawford looked over his scouts, but he no longer had three yellow stripes on his sleeves. I wondered if failure to catch us, and returning with a big knot on an aching head, led to his loss of those yellow stripes. I decided to avoid any trouble with him if I could. Thanks to Juanita's skill with a sling, I don't think he ever saw me at Rufus's ranch. Still, word of my skill with my rifle might give him some hint that I was the one responsible for sending him dreaming back to the Blue Coats and enough reason to come looking for me. It was his choice. I was ready, no matter what he chose.

Nantan Lupan worked the Blue Coats and scouts hard for the next three days, from dawn until moonrise, making sure only the fittest mules and horses and scouts crossed the border, and that the mules carried enough for every man, but no more. Every Blue Coat and scout carried forty bullets on a belt or bandolier, a blanket, and his weapons. The mules carried pots, hard bread, coffee, and bacon, which most scouts refused to eat, and an extra one hundred sixty bullets for each scout.

Five mule trains and their packers, fifty Blue Coats, and nearly two hundred scouts from the Chiricahua, White Mountain, Tonto, Mojave, and Yuma bands ran or rode into the land of the *Nakai-yes* at dawn on the fourth day. A young *di-yen* with us who had strong Power told us that we would have great success and our spirits wanted to play.

We followed the Río San Bernardino south, covering about the same distance each day we had on the runs from Willcox. Our camping place the first night lay where a small creek coming from the east ran into the San Bernardino. We hunted as we ran and came into camp with more than enough deer and turkey to feed us all.

The San Bernardino Valley was a patchwork of many colors. The trail followed the Río San Bernardino, which ran through mostly flat desert country where everything was bigger, sharper, and deadlier than in the deserts northeast across the border, until it emptied into the Río Bavispe. The creosote bushes were much bigger than those in the north, and their blooming made veils of little white flowers, good for the eyes and sweet to smell. Great patches of prickly pear cactus, ocotillo covered with red blossoms reaching for the sky, and mesquite with light green leaves standing out against those of the much darker, feathery creosotes filled the valley.

We followed the Río Bavispe flowing through deep twisting canyons. The land along the river was filled with arroyos and canyons, forming hard-to-climb, rocky ridges and arroyo bottoms filled with soft, easy-to-break caliche over deep sand. Even the strongest mules struggled on the trail up the Río Bavispe.

We passed many villages abandoned because of Apache raids. Dust-filled irrigation ditches crisscrossed fields where crops had once grown. The crops had gone to scattered seed competing with weeds. The villages where the *Nakai-yes* continued to live had dirty, black-eyed children wearing rags, and the livestock and dogs showed rib bones of hunger. The droopy, sad faces of the adults filled with fear when we ran past them.

After four suns of running from San Bernardino Springs, we made camp against the mountains east of Bavispe. The Río Bavispe was filled with cool pools, their surfaces like mirrors. We bathed and swam in the still, deep water. Losing the dirt we had gathered, washing our hair, and feeling clean again made a fine reward for a hard day's run. Al Sieber rode over to a cattle herd grazing near Bavispe. He drove back ten boney cows for us to butcher. The cattle didn't look so good, but the smell of their meat grilling over our fires made our stomachs howl. We ate like wolves, the juice from the meat running down our chins and forearms. We rubbed the grease from our fingers and forearms on our legs and moccasins to keep them supple for the hard running still to come, and grilled all the meat left from our meal to feed the Blue Coats and mule packers when they finally came in at dark.

The *alcalde* (mayor) of Bavispe rode a white pony over to our camp. He dismounted where Sieber talked to Mickey Free, stuck out his chin in defiance, and said in a trembling voice, "*Señor, por favor,* you owe my village for the cattle you took. We are poor and fight the Apaches a long time and have little. You don't pay? You steal food from our mouths."

He grinned and nodded when Al Sieber gave him enough pesos to pay for the boney cattle. The *alcalde,* his voice not trembling anymore, invited everyone, including the scouts, to a *baile* (dance) in the village that night. I stayed in camp, but several went. They included Sieber, a few *Indah* Blue Coats, and some scouts, who together consumed a couple of jugs of strong mescal. The mescal followed like a ghost haunting them and pounding their heads when we left Bavispe, still running south in the shallow darkness and early morning mists off the Río.

The village of Huachinera lay a day's run south toward the source of the Río Bavispe. We made camp that night just east of Huachinera in a canyon at the foot of a high mountain. The next morning, we began the hard run up the trail toward the top of the mountain. The trail followed a steep ridge to the top. I was used to following ridge trails when I went to the camp of Elias with Beela-chezzi and Kitsizil Lichoo'. But unlike the others, this trail seemed to have an overpowering presence hovering over it like ghosts somehow left by the Chiricahuas, of all people, who flinched at even the word *ghost*.

The trail climbed up into the morning light, following long straight stretches and then switchbacks. On the south side of the trail were drop-offs so high that big pine trees in the canyons looked like little black insects against the brown and red sand in the arroyos.

High up on the ridge, a mule made a bad step and, struggling and heehawing to stay on the trail, went off the edge, pack and all, leaving his packer shaking his head in disgust. Wailing in fear and desperation, it kicked and twisted against the wind on the way to the bottom until it smashed into the rocks below and was crushed under its pack, which somehow stayed lashed upright on its back. It was so far to the bottom of the canyon no one bothered to go after it, and we lost several more on the climb to the top.

After much hard running, we finally reached the top of the mountain. We rested there and could see far up the valley we had run the day before and trace the Río Bavispe almost all the way back to Bavispe. Three boney cows, their heads hanging down and barely moving, stood in the shade of the tall pines on top of the mountain. We guessed they had escaped from the herds taken from the *Nakai-yes* and driven by the Chiricahuas to their camps for slaughter, but they didn't escape our knives. The meat was tough and not much on the bones, but the hearts, livers, and heads made us a good meal when we camped that night.

Tzoe and a couple of others who had been with the Chiricahuas for a while knew the best places to camp. We went down from the mountaintop a short distance where a spring flowed back in the big pines. There we made our next camp.

This was Chiricahua country, so we had to be more careful than a man reaching for pups in a dark wolf's den. Oak made long lasting coals in fires built under the trees to disperse the smoke. By making the fires early and cooking for the night's meal, only coals survived to make light and give heat for sleeping after sunset. Light from a small open flame in the Blue Mountains shows from far away. Scouts kept a lookout in every direction for Chiricahuas.

Since leaving San Bernardino Springs, Sergeant Sweeny Jones came to our fire several times for an evening meal. We ate and told many stories of times fighting enemies. I came to know Sweeny Jones like I did Rufus Pike, and I liked them both. I counted Rufus, Sweeny Jones, and Dr. Blazer among my friends, even if they were *Indah*.

Sweeny Jones told me of the great respect he had for Nantan Lupan and his scouts. The scouts had fought in the Tonto Basin War ten years earlier. In those days, the scouts came from Apaches, Yavapais, Walapais, and even the Paiutes, who despised Apaches. He said Nantan Lupan soon learned that Apaches were by far the most reliable and courageous of all the tribes he used. He came to depend on Apaches more than the others.

That night as we sat under trees listening to the night birds, insects, tree peepers, and the occasional coyote bark, I asked Sweeny Jones if he knew Soldado Fiero. He nodded slowly, the shadows from the orange coals under a light layer of gray ash wandering across his lively face.

He said, "Yes, wished I didn't, but I do. Three years ago, when General Hatch tried to disarm and unhorse all the Mescaleros, a few of 'em sneaked off, and the general sent some Chiricahua scouts under Sergeant Soldado Fiero to bring 'em back. When them Chiricahuas came back, ol' Fiero's face was black and blue, and they didn't have no prisoners. He looked like somebody had cold-cocked him on the side of his head with a hammer. He claimed that his head was a-hurtin' bad and he needed some firewater to ease the pain, and the Mescaleros they's a chasin' got clean away. He claimed he knowed where they went, but he couldn't git permission to go after 'em again.

General Hatch took his stripes away after he showed up drunk at a drill, said he could earn 'em back by showin' his courage when they faced Victorio. He never got a chance to face Victorio. I 'spect he's mighty lucky in that regard, since the Mexicans got to Victorio first. Now, Soldado Fiero hankers to come along on this here expedition, so he'n show his bravery an' git his stripes back. Only thing, Chato is a cousin or half-brother to Soldado Fiero. I can't figure which. Word around the night fires says Soldado ain't above killin' Tzoe and claimin' the Chiricahuas did it, if it comes down to helpin' Chato escape. You better stay away from him. He ain't nothin' but trouble, and he has a big thirst for firewater."

"Hmmph. I hear you, Sweeny Jones. I watch Soldado Fiero good around Apache camps."

Chapter 23
Chihuahua's Camp

Al Sieber and the other scout leaders had a long powwow with Nantan Lupan. He agreed to change how we operated. We spent four days by the spring baking bread and making dried meat in the middle of the day so no one saw our fires. We also made up fruit and nut mixes, so we wouldn't have to cook when we stopped.

Fifty scouts went on ahead and looked for the Chiricahua camps while the rest followed with the pack mules. Tzoe, my new friends, John Rope and Tulan (Much Water), and Soldado Fiero and I were among the fifty chosen. If we found a camp, runners were to race back to tell the others to move up quick and help take the village. I stayed near the front of the line to watch Tzoe, who led us.

We left the camp single file: first, ten scouts and then a mule; next, ten scouts and then a mule. We repeated the same pattern until we were lined out down the trail and crossing a canyon toward a mountain to the southeast. We soon found old tracks and a horse left behind in very poor shape. We butchered him and were able to use some of the meat and liver. After that, we were nearly always in sight of some animal, dead or dying, that had fallen off the steep trail. Others wandered free, lost from the herds the Chiricahuas pushed across the mountains. The Chiricahuas didn't retrieve cloth streamers, hides, and many other things lost on the steep trails.

We followed the tracks for three days. Two pack mules carrying a lot of supplies caught up with us. We sent a message that the others needed to come where we had camped while we went on to an old Chiricahua camp Tzoe knew in a canyon near the headwaters of the Río Bavispe. There under many tall pines we found tracks from a big dance. Much Water, who was of the Warm Springs band, said the tracks looked like those made in a war dance. From the dance center, the tracks led off in many different directions. I knew this trick. As a child, I had escaped Bosque Redondo with my parents when bands of Apaches ran off in different directions so the Blue Coats wouldn't know who to follow or where the tracks might lead.

The next day we ran along the side of the mountain until the middle of the afternoon, when we stopped to eat and rest. I sat at a place where it was easy to see through the trees to the top of a mountain across the valley. I took out the *Shináá Cho* and studied the dark green treetops and a few bare spots on the mountain across the valley. Tzoe and Much Water also searched the far mountain with their Blue Coat *be'idest'iné*.

We saw the Chiricahua camp on top of a ridge across the valley at about the same time. There was a big, flat place near the camp where Chiricahua horses, lots of them, grazed. I scrambled back to tell the others, and they came to see for themselves. Looking at the camp with the *Shináá Cho,* I saw many Chiricahuas. I thought, *Now, we'll see if Soldado Fiero just makes a big wind about getting back his stripes or if he tries to kill Tzoe.*

Sieber studied the Chiricahuas before he called two of the strongest runners to find those far behind and tell them to hurry up, ride all night if need be, and come plenty quick. I was glad we had cooked up much bread and made trail food. We sat back in the darkness and cold air wrapped in our blankets and filled our bellies, watched the Chiricahua camp in the low glow from their fire coals, listened to the wolves and other night animals, and whispered to each other what we planned to do in the coming fight. Late in the night, we drifted off to sleep. The snorting of mules, the creak of harness and saddles, and the stomp of hooves woke me. Crawford and the rest had come. Gray light began to show on the far horizon. Crawford ordered the Blue Coats to tie their horses back down the trail out of sight of the Chiricahuas, and the scouts to eat and rest.

Light came, filling the mountainsides with shadows and yellow pools of light. Birds began to call. Morning water sparkled in spider webs across the bushes. We saw much smoke from cooking fires in the Chiricahua camp. Sieber divided us into three groups. First, one group went straight down the trail leading into the camp. The great warrior Alchesay, now a sergeant, led it. Second, a group ran down the north side valley in order to come up behind the horse herd. I ran with a third group down the valley and around a low ridge with the second group, but then we left them and ran up a shallow stream and then up the trail the Chiricahuas used for watering the horses.

Much Water, well in front of the rest of us, and true to his name, stopped at some bushes near the trail to make water. He saw two Chiricahuas riding down the trail and ran back to warn us. We disappeared into the brush along the side of the trail and waited to take them. Someone in the second group fired a shot. It echoed down the canyon, but the Chiricahuas riding toward us never seemed to hear it and kept coming.

Scouts started firing at the two Chiricahua riders. They jumped off their mules, scrambled into the brush on the far side, and disappeared. We ran on up the trail, but stopped to drink at the last place there was any water in the stream before running up to where the horse herd grazed. Some of the scouts complained their knees hurt. They said they had to run slow, behind everyone else going up the trail. Tzoe told me later that those scouts always did that. They were afraid. He said he ought to make them run in front, but we didn't have time to cure them of their fear. When we were far enough up the trail to see the place where the horses grazed, we saw three Chiricahuas herding some toward new grass, and behind them rode a boy and a girl each leading a horse.

Up the trail, Much Water and John Rope crawled to the edge of the brush. They stayed out of sight, waiting for the boy and girl to ride by. When the young ones rode even with them, Much Water, a Warm Springs Apache who talked like them, said, "Hold! Come over here."

The boy and girl stopped. They looked toward the brush from where the voice came, and squinting and moving their heads this way and that tried, but didn't see who called them. Much Water, command filling his voice, said, "Come here! Hurry up."

They dropped their lead ropes and rode over toward the voices in the brush. When they reached the edge of the brush, Much Water and John Rope charged out and snatched them off their ponies. Much Water took the boy, and John Rope took the girl. Much Water knew the girl's father and swapped the boy for her. In those days, children taken in wartime belonged to those who took them. Kept, traded, or sold, but we didn't consider them much in the way of loot.

After we took the boy and girl, we scouts ran out of the brush and yelled for the three Chiricahuas on ponies to stop, but they wheeled and raced off into the pine trees on the other side of the trail. Our shots made branches fly off around them like some giant spirit whacking the trees with an ax as it chased them. We shot only one rider. It was hard to hit anything, shooting through those trees at a moving target, but Rufus had taught me well. I didn't miss. The other two got away until John Rope saw the moccasins of one hiding under a bush and pulled him out. He was only a boy, and he wasn't hurt. Several of the scouts ran up to John and asked for him, but John said, "No, I found the boy. He stays with me."

We ran up the trail to the horse herd and then into the camp. Nearly all the Chiricahua we saw the day before had run off. They had been slaughtering cattle. Meat and hides were drying everywhere on bushes, and a large store of cut-up mescal was drying. That night Tzoe told me that the shot starting the attack was an accident. A sergeant, who had his rifle cocked and ready to fire, was climbing up a steep place, slipped, and pulled the trigger when he lunged forward to keep his balance. Tzoe said we had attacked the camp of the great chief, Chihuahua, and that the Chiricahuas had just come back with a big herd taken from a *Nakai-yi rancho* five days ride to the south. There was much booty in the camp. I found a couple of *pesh-lickoyee* (nickel-plated) Winchester rifles, several revolvers, and nearly a full case of ammunition. I kept it all, not sure how I'd get it back unless I could trade some of my booty with one of the mule packers and have him carry it back to San Bernardino. The nights had been very cold high in the mountains. I didn't think more than the time it took to blink before taking a couple of good, warm Mexican blankets, and I found a pocket watch, which I didn't know how to use, but also kept.

A young gray mule watched me through the bushes. I put my booty in a pile so the other scouts knew it was mine, and went for the mule. It tried to run when I approached him. He wore a fine silver-trimmed saddle and a practically new bridle. The bridle reins caught in the brush when he wheeled to run and held him tight for me. I liked him. He had good, strong confirmation, and he watched me unafraid. I spoke to him in a calm voice. I held his jaw, breathed in his breath, and let him take in mine. He relaxed and let me lead him to my loot and load him up. I tied him to a juniper tree on the edge of the camp and returned.

On the other side of the camp, three scouts from San Carlos

led by Soldado Fiero approached an old woman whose face had more wrinkles than the Blue Mountains have ridges. She was on her knees cutting up meat. When the scouts came up, she laid aside her knife and stood up with the bloody palms of her hands out and said, "You from San Carlos. I know you Soldado Fiero. I quit the Blue Mountains. Go back with you. Don't shoot me." Soldado Fiero angrily kicked her meat and knife off into the bushes, stared at her a moment, and said, "Time for the Happy Land old woman." He shot her in the chest, right in the heart. She fell backwards, dead before she hit the ground, a twisted smile of defiance on her face and her eyes still open, laughing at the stupid scout, even in death.

I clenched my teeth and sighted down the Henry ready to kill Soldado Fiero. There was no cause for that murder. Some White Mountain scouts ran up to him and asked, "Why did you kill that old woman? You shouldn't have done that." He stuck out his lower lip, shrugged his shoulders, and said, "I came after Chiricahuas, and I'm going to kill them. Get back my stripes."

One of the sergeants yelled for the San Carlos scouts to go surround the horse herd and drive them toward the camp. Two Chiricahua men up in some boulders above the herd took a couple of shots at the scouts, but did no harm. They yelled, "All right. You do us this way now. We'll do you the same way another time."

Tzoe led his scouts up the trail to take a mule corral, but we found no mules. John Rope found another child there, not long off the cradleboard, hiding behind a pine tree where her mother had left her. That made two children he had caught for the day. He gave her to a scout who laughed and gave her to Nasta (He Knows A Lot), who was riding a horse. He kept her in front of him and rode down the hill, singing the victory dance song from the old days, as though he had taken a big prize. All the other scouts laughed with him.

Nantan Lupan told us to destroy everything in the camp we didn't want. We took most of the meat and some of the mescal but destroyed many baskets full of big juniper berries the Chiricahua women had gathered for winter. After the fires began burning the food supplies, the smoke rising high for the escaped Chiricahuas to see, Nantan Lupan led us out of camp and up the trail some distance to a saddle between two mountains. The scouts, in a good mood, shot their rifles into the air to show it. We made camp on the far end of the saddle near a spring.

John Rope had saved some of the meat drying in the camp and had wrapped it in a hide with some grease. He called to Mickey Free, Tzoe, the two children he had caught, and me to come eat some of the meat he was cooking.

A scout had tried to buy the boy from John Rope because he thought the child belonged to the sister of his friend Naiche, youngest son of Cochise. John Rope had said no to him earlier in the day, but after we ate, the scout came to our fire and said, "My cousin, give me that boy like I asked. I want him. I'll pay you good for him. Eighty dollars and a silver saddle, I'll give you for him."

John Rope shook his head. "No, I won't sell him. I won't do the boy that way."

The scout made another offer, and then another. Still, John Rope said no. Then Mickey Free said, "Don't ask for the boy like that. We are on the warpath now. We don't know if the boy belongs to the daughter of your friend or not. Go away and leave John Rope alone."

The scout scowled, nodded, and went back to his fire.

The boy, listening to all this, seemed to relax a little and said to John Rope, "What kind of people are you? Why do you all wear those red headbands?"

John raised his chin a little and looked the boy in the eye. "Blue Coat scouts, we wear the red headbands so we don't shoot those on our side. We come hard after your people."

The boy started to cry, but the girl just sat there quietly listening. I thought, *She could be Kicking Wren in a few years,* and I felt bad for the Chiricahuas.

John Rope said, "If you try to run away, I'm going to shoot you, so you'd better stay with me." I'm sure he was joking, but the children didn't think so.

I hid my grin behind my hand. He wore two bandoliers holding fifty cartridges each and had used only six all day, and he'd shot three of those cartridges celebrating after we took the camp.

The girl's eyes grew wide. "My friend, don't shoot him."

John nodded. "I won't as long as he does what I say. He might even live to return to San Carlos."

Later that evening, Nantan Lupan sent word to the fires we made that he wanted all the Chiricahuas to lie down together and sleep in the same place. I gave the girl and boy two of the blankets I kept so they would sleep warm. Scouts guarded them so they couldn't slip away. A bright moon filled the night, and fifteen other scouts guarded positions around the camp to protect from any Chiricahua raids.

The next morning, Nantan Lupan had the prisoners brought to his tent. He asked the oldest girl which horse we had taken was the best. She pointed out a big gray one. A scout had taken it. Nantan Lupan sent for the horse, but the scout wouldn't give it up. Nantan Lupan growled to the scout chief to bring the horse right then. He brought it quickly, and the scout who had taken it stood near to watch what would happen next. Another scout saddled the horse for the two oldest girls. Nantan Lupan gave them food and *tobaho* for Chihuahua. He said, "Go. Find Chihuahua. Tell him we only come to take his people back to San Carlos, not to make war on them. The raid on his camp yesterday was an accident. It did not mean war. Tell him where this camp is and that I want the Chiricahuas to come in for a talk."

As the girls mounted, Much Water, holding the horse, said to the oldest girl, "Tell my brother and sister that I say to them, come to the camp quick. Don't wait around and make us come after you. It will be bad for you if we do." Then he and twelve scouts led them back to their camp and let them leave to follow the Chiricahua tracks and find Chihuahua. Much Water and the scouts came back and said they saw signs some Chiricahuas had looked for things in the camp, but had gone back toward the top of the mountain across the southern side valley.

CHAPTER 24
WE BE FRIENDS

It was quiet the night after the two girls left to find Chihuahua. None of the Chiricahuas we caught in their camp tried to escape, and none came to free those we held. Mists gathered in the canyons and rose above the saddle where we camped, blocking out the stars and screening the mountainsides from us in the early morning light, as the camp began stirring. The rising sun drove away the mists and bathed us in its gold light. We cooked more of the meat we took the day before and warmed pieces of mescal to feed our growling bellies.

New guards watched the Chiricahuas, and while scouts, Chiricahuas, and Blue Coats ate, packers, who were up earlier than the rest, fed the stock. It was a peaceful camp, a calm before the storm we all expected. The girls who left to find Chihuahua had told Much Water that many of the camp's warriors and their chiefs were off raiding the *Nakai-yes*. The oldest girl said they were due back in three or four days. She said she didn't know what the warriors might do, but that she and the others were disheartened that the Blue Coats, led by her own people, came for them in their safe places in the Blue Mountains. She knew now that they were not safe anywhere.

When Much Water told us this at John Rope's fire, I remembered how I felt after my parents and I escaped Bosque Redondo. We went to live in Cha's camp in the Guadalupe Mountains, a place the Blue Coats never found. It was a safe place for a long time, and then the witch came and wiped them out. The land there didn't make me feel good anymore. I knew how the Chiricahuas must feel.

Halfway to the time of shortest shadows, the camp suddenly grew quiet. Two women were coming to us through the trees down the mountainside next to our camp. The younger was dressed in her finest leather skirt and top with long fringe and many beads. She waved a white piece of cloth and covered her head. The guards let them come. Much Water recognized his sisters. He went to them and led them to our fire, but said nothing. A few scouts gathered around our fire and studied them awhile before going about their business. Much Water gave them slices of meat we had been roasting and some mescal he had saved. They were hungry and ate it fast, their black eyes flitting around our camp, taking in every detail. Al Sieber came and spoke off to the side with Much Water. Sieber motioned first to the women and then to the mountainside before he went to the tent where Nantan Lupan sat smoking his pipe and watching us.

Their hunger gone, the women waved away offers of more meat and mescal. Much Water, his voice betraying no anger, said to his oldest sister, "We've been all over these mountains looking for you people, not to kill you, but to take you back to San Carlos to be friends. Tell this to Chihuahua."

She studied Much Water's face, looked around the camp once more, and nodded, saying something I didn't hear, and then she left and disappeared into the trees up the mountainside. The time of shortest shadows passed, and another woman walked down a trail from the top of the mountains. John Rope and Tzoe studied her through their Blue Coat *Shináá Cho*. Tzoe immediately recognized her as Geronimo's sister, Nah-da-ste.

She looked neither left nor right, walking past the guards and up to Nantan Lupan's tent. I was among the scouts who gathered around it. Mickey Free spoke to her, and then went into the tent to come back out quick with Nantan Lupan, who nodded to her and said, "You're welcome in our camp. We come as friends to take you and your people back to San Carlos."

She said, "You took white horse with *Nakai-yi* saddle with black saddlebags and silver bit and bridle. If you want Chihuahua for friend, give back to me."

Nantan Lupan looked at Al Sieber, who jerked his head toward a couple of scouts to follow him to the horses and mules grazing on the eastern slope of the saddle. Nantan Lupan said, "If we have this animal and the things it carried, we'll give them all to you to return. Will your people return with us, or will they fight?"

She looked at the ground and shook her head. "Not know. Scouts come, make us sick in hearts. Tzoe, once with us, now shows you our paths across the Blue Mountains. His wives wail.

"Many warriors raid *Nakai-yes* now. Return in four, maybe five, days. Warriors' anger make them want to fight, but you have great advantage. You hold their food for Ghost Face. You hold their wives and children and old ones.

"If *Indah* on reservation treat Chihuahua and Loco right, they go back to San Carlos. They not want to leave anyway. Lying *Indah* stealing from us make them do it. I not know what Geronimo and Chato do. They stay angry at *Nakai-yes* and *Indah*. Juh join them, but most his warriors already gone to Happy Land."

Nantan Lupan's eyes never left her. He stroked the fur growing on his face. It spread out on his chest like a big bush. He thought for a time and then nodded. "I believe you. We also look for a captive. A raid near the village of Lordsburg a few moons ago took a young *Indah* boy. He has maybe six harvests. Have you seen such a child?"

Now her eyes never left Nantan Lupan's. "Yes, I know child. Chato and Bonito take him in raid. Call him Charlie. He run away with old women who raise him for Chato when scouts first attack us. Charlie comes when old women return."

Al Sieber returned leading the white horse with Spanish saddle, black saddlebags, and silver bit she described. He gave her the reins and nodded toward Nantan Lupan who said, "Here's the pony and other things Chihuahua said we must give you to be friends. Dried meat and hard bread lie in the saddlebags. Take it and go. Tell Chihuahua that Nantan Lupan waits here for him to come visit me as a friend."

She swung up on the saddle and, before disappearing on the trail back up the mountain, said, "I give Chihuahua the words you speak."

When the shadows grew long and the sun was not far from the western mountaintops, we first heard and then saw six women coming down the mountainside waving white flags and yelling, "No shoot! No Shoot!" They stopped and hid in the brush still calling for us not to shoot. Mickey Free stood near the guards and yelled, "Come! We be friends!"

First one, then another and another, came out of the brush, slowly and carefully, one step at a time, ready to run like deer sensing danger. The guards waved them on until all six were in camp and eating by a fire. Mickey Free spoke with them, but they had nothing new to add to what we already knew.

Another quiet night passed. We expected to fight the Chiricahua warriors returning from their raids and talked much around our fires about how they would attack and how we should wipe them out. Al Sieber sent scouts back along every trail Tzoe knew the Chiricahua might use returning to their camps. He hoped to find the warriors before they found us. I knew that after learning Tzoe had led us here, the Chiricahuas would want to come after him. The only questions were when and how they tried, and if my shooting skills were good enough to keep him alive.

When shadows were shortest, we saw the white horse we had sent with Nah-da-ste the day before galloping up the south canyon toward us. It disappeared into the trees up the mountain-side nearest the camp, but soon reappeared on the trail, running straight and hard for our camp. The *Shináá Cho* showed a warrior rode the horse. The horse had red cloth tied to its tail and bridle and the warrior had a red band around his head. Two pistols were stuck in his belt and a red streamer flew on a long spear he carried. He rode his pony right up to the fire of some scouts nearest the trail and skidded to stop. They hopped backwards like crows avoiding a rattlesnake, rifles ready, not knowing what to expect. Tzoe, who followed the rider all the way into camp with his Blue Coat *be'idest'iné*, said, "Chihuahua."

Chihuahua said in a loud voice, "Show me your chief!" A scout pointed toward Nantan Lupan's tent with scouts around it, and the warrior charged through them. They had to jump like the others to get out of the way. Chihuahua rode the white horse hard right up to the tent. Mickey Free ran to the tent and was standing there when Nantan Lupan came out scowling, his shirt off and suspenders hanging off the top of his pants.

Chihuahua stabbed his spear into the ground beside his pony, dismounted, and walked over to Nantan Lupan. They looked each other over and then shook hands. It was hard to hear what they said. I moved a little closer and made out most of it.

I heard Chihuahua say, "If you want me for a friend, why did you kill that old woman, my aunt? If I tried to make friends with someone, I wouldn't raid their camp and shoot their relatives. It sounds to me like you're lying when you speak about being friends."

Nantan Lupan shook his head. "The attack was a mistake." I

thought, *Nantan Lupan bends the truth like a bow. He wants the Chiricahuas to understand what's coming if they don't return to San Carlos.* I heard Nantan Lupan say, "I want no war. Take this sack of food and this tobacco with you. Go. Bring in your people. We'll protect them and bring you safely back to San Carlos where you'll be safe. I speak true."

Chihuahua, saying nothing, stared at Nantan Lupan. Al Sieber, who knew Chihuahua, handed him a sack of food and gave him some *cigarros*. He took the sack and *cigarros,* swung up on the white horse, and rode him fast and hard out of the camp.

When the sun was halfway from the shortest shadows to the western mountaintops, Much Water's sisters came back. The older one told us that Chihuahua had returned and said, "It's no good with all these scouts and Blue Coats here. We have to move far away and hide from them."

His women didn't want to go away. They hid all right, but from him. Chihuahua still moved the camp a little distance so it was harder to find. As the shadows grew long, Chiricahua women began coming into our camp, including the ones we sent out earlier to find Chihuahua.

As the night came, a young Chiricahua woman came in crying. She saw the little girl John Rope had taken at the empty mule corral sitting by our fire with us. She ran up and took the girl in her arms, hugging her and saying bad things about the White Mountain scouts who had attacked the camp.

Mickey Free stood up, crossed his arms, and glared at her with his good eye. He said through clenched teeth, "You're no good! You ran off and left your baby in this wild place to men attacking your camp. You deserve to have your guts eaten out by a coyote. This man takes good care of your baby, and you say bad things about him, about all of us. We ought to kick you out of here and keep that baby."

She buried her face in the child's hair and cried some more, saying, "No, no, I was a fool. Fear took hold of me then. My mind did not know what to do. Now, I no leave without her."

Mickey Free looked over at John Rope, who nodded and said, "Go on and take her. Go sit with the other Chiricahua women. They have good rations now. Leave us to eat in peace."

She took the child and went to the other women, but the next night, when John Rope started his fire to cook, the young woman sent the child back over to eat with us, saying, "Go. That man will feed you. He's your friend."

The next day Nantan Lupan moved our camp to a little open grassy place closer to the foot of the mountain from where we camped on the saddle. A good spring and enough room for the Chiricahuas coming in to make a shelter and have plenty of water made it an easier place to camp, but it was harder to defend because a steep ridge ran on the east side of the camp and made it easier for us to be attacked than in the saddle where we had just camped.

Chiricahua women continued to come down from the mountains and out of the brush during that day and the following one. Mickey Free said Chihuahua had told Nantan Lupan to give him a few days while he went out and rounded up his people and told them to come in and surrender. Chihuahua had not come back. We figured he had decided to wait and ride with the returning warriors when they attacked us, but it didn't matter. We were ready for them.

The day before the warriors returned, the Chiricahua women cut up flour sacks and hung long white streamers on poles around the camp. They said it showed the warriors we didn't want to fight. We made our own defenses better and more dependable than the white cloth. We made rock piles and stacked pine logs to get behind when the shooting started.

The night came, cold and clear. We cooked and ate our fill.

Who knew? Maybe we wouldn't eat again for a long time. We cleaned and loaded our rifles and pistols and put on both our cartridge belts before wrapping in our blankets to try sleeping.

The women told us not to get up until sunrise so the Chiricahua men could see us. The women spent the night calling up to warriors they believed were on the mountains. They told them why Nantan Lupan and his scouts were there and that they didn't want any fighting, but they wanted the Chiricahuas to be friends with them.

After a while the women grew quiet. Except for the orange coals turning to gray ash in the fire pits, there was no light except from myriad stars, and the moon took its time to rise above the mountains. A wolf howled and his cousin answered. The scouts near my fire didn't sleep, and I didn't either. We lay there and waited. When early daylight came, the women began calling to their men and chiefs, Ka-ya-ten-nae, Geronimo, Chato, and Bonito, telling them they wanted them to be friends with Nantan Lupan. When it was good light and easy to see, we started our fires, went about our business, ate, and waited.

CHAPTER 25
GERONIMO

They called to us from the top of the high ridge, their outlines dark, their voices rising in the sunlight. They reminded me of big buzzards in the top of trees waiting for a dying animal to move no more. We camped too far away to understand what they were saying, but most of the scouts, including me, thought they said bad things, and we said so.

Nah-da-ste, sister of Geronimo, listening to them, heard us talking. She said, "They call for scouts to come talk."

Much Water made a face, "What do they want to talk about?"

Nah-da-ste shook her head. "They not say. I find out."

She returned after the sun was halfway to shortest shadows. Her face made a frown, and, shaking her head, she said, "They say only they want scouts to come talk."

Many scouts saw her come back and didn't want to go. They thought the returning warriors waited in ambush and wanted blood revenge for our attack.

Tzoe said, "I believe they want to talk. They want a straight story from us about why we come here. I showed you the way. I won't hide now that we're here. What we do is right. I'll go."

In the deathly stillness, no one moved. I stepped forward with my Yellow Boy rifle cradled in the crook of my arm. "I go with Tzoe."

Two other scouts stepped forward: Dastine (Crouched and Ready), a Cibecue Apache who had family related to Jelikine, who was Geronimo's father-in-law; and Haskehagola (Angry,

He Starts Fights), also a Cibecue and brother-in-law to Chato.

Jelikine, a mighty warrior, stood no taller than an old-fashioned, single-shot rifle. When he spoke, the other Chiricahua chiefs listened to him. We learned after the warriors came in early that morning that he came down from the ridge and crawled in close to our camp. He knew from hearing the voices of the scouts and the way they said words which ones came from San Carlos or belonged to the Tontos or White Mountain Apaches.

We loaded our rifles, put our bandoliers over our shoulders, buckled on our pistols, stuck our knives behind our belts, and tied white streamers on the ends of our rifles to show we didn't want to fight. It was a steep climb, slipping and sliding, up the ridge through oaks and junipers and around a few shelves of boulders.

When Tzoe, who led us, neared the top of the ridge, chiefs backed up by more than thirty warriors appeared out of the trees and approached us. I knew none of them, chiefs or warriors, and they didn't know me. I studied their dark, angry faces and wondered why I had chosen to risk my life and the survival of my wife and child to return wild and free men to a place *Indah,* who never knew them or how they lived, said they must stay.

Chato, his eyes narrowed, came forward and motioned to Tzoe and Haskehagola, his brothers-in-law, to join him. "So, brothers," Chato said, "your medicine takes you away from us and back to San Carlos. Now it brings you back with Blue Coats to our strongholds in the land of *Nakai-yes.* Your wives wailed in grief when you did not return with me. Now they howl in rage that you come back. Your medicine betrays us. Why have you done this?"

Tzoe and Haskehagola didn't flinch at Chato's hard words. Tzoe said, "We come as friends and brothers, not to make war, but to bring you back to San Carlos. You gave your word to the *Indah* you would come and stay. Now you have run away because the agents cheat us of what the *Indah* promised. You raid *Nakai-yes* and *Indah* ranchos north of the border. Nantan Lupan returns and makes things right at the reservations. Better you return than see your lives and families destroyed. We come to help you. You're our brothers. Take us to your fire that we can sit, smoke, and speak straight as brothers."

Chato's eyes glittered like shiny, black flint. He studied their faces, and then the anger in his face turned to sadness. He nodded and led them to a little fire under tall pine trees near the middle of the ridge where they were alone. Jelikine motioned Dastine to his fire where they also spoke alone.

An older warrior, his mouth nothing more than a slash, narrowed eyes missing nothing, walked up to me. I thought he was likely a chief because the others stepped out of his way and he wore a war hat covered with turkey feathers surrounding two eagle feathers in the middle on top.

The warrior stared at me long enough that I considered him rude and wondered if he wanted to fight. He finally said, "I've never seen you. You're Mescalero. Why do you, whose people have no belly to fight the *Indah* and Blue Coats, come to our strongholds with these dogs and an old worn out rifle? Do you want an early start to the Happy Land?"

I returned his rude look, looking him straight in the eyes, and said, "I'm Yellow Boy. The Blue Coat chief of scouts asked me to come because I hit where I shoot."

A crooked smile filled his lips. "I hit where I shoot, too, Mescalero. Perhaps the Blue Coat chief of scouts will pay me to chase myself in the Blue Mountains." The warriors standing behind him grinned. "Come to my fire, and we'll talk. You came because we asked Nah-da-ste to send us scouts. We want to learn why you come to attack us when we've done nothing to you." He turned toward the fire. I didn't move.

"I'll come to your fire when I know who speaks and shows no respect to a stranger."

He stopped and looked over his shoulder at me. "The *Nakai-yes* call me Geronimo. I'm a *di-yen* of the *Bedonkohe Nednhi* Apaches."

Geronimo sat by his fire with me and rolled *tobaho* in an oak leaf. We smoked to the four directions and drank piñon nut coffee made for us by a woman from Chihuahua's camp the warriors had found hiding in the brush. Three *Nakai-yi* women and a baby huddled together on the back edge of the camp away from the warriors. They looked falling-down weary and dirty. Their clothes were nearly torn to pieces from running through brush for the past three days, and they didn't look like they had eaten much in that time.

Geronimo saw me looking at them and smiled. "You want those *Nakai-yi* women? We had planned to take and trade them in Janos for our women the *Nakai-yi* Garcia took from us at the Corralitos fight. Maybe we will yet trade them for something worthwhile. Wait and see." He paused and frowned. "Now tell me why you come here. What does Nantan Lupan want from the *Bedonkohe Nednhi*?"

"This is my first ride with Nantan Lupan and his scouts. I came because Al Sieber saw me shoot and said he wanted me for a scout. When Al Sieber began planning this trip, he sent for me and said they might need someone who can shoot to help bring the Chiricahuas back to the reservations. He knew Geronimo would not want to leave the Blue Mountains, but he knew you would do the right thing for the *Bedonkohe Nednhi*. Nantan Lupan told Chihuahua the Blue Coats come as friends to take you back. He doesn't want war. Come down to his camp and talk. Hear his words yourself."

He shook his head. "I left the warpath against the *Indah* because my warriors had grown weary. They did not want to fight anymore. I went to San Carlos and worked in the fields as I promised. The *Indah* agents had only to keep their word and give my women their promised rations. They did not. They didn't do as Nantan Lupan or Clum, the agent who took me in chains to San Carlos, said they would. Carr led his Blue Coats to Nocadelklinny's camp on Cibecue Creek and murdered him. Nocadelklinny did nothing to them. He just danced and prayed for dead chiefs and warriors to come back. Carr must have believed he had the power to bring them back. Maybe that's why he killed him. I knew it was time to leave the reservation, and we did. We had to take the warpath again."

Geronimo picked up a twig and drew symbols I didn't understand in dust by the fire.

"I grew good melons and made canals from the river at San Carlos to carry water to them and make them good. Now it is all gone because *Indah* lie. They don't keep their word. We left San Carlos to be free of bad agents and a bad place to live. What's wrong with freedom? Why do you chase us for the Blue Coats? Without you, they would never find us."

I had thought about this since Al Sieber saw me shoot and wanted me for the scouts. "I didn't take Al Sieber's offer for a long time. My little band went back to the reservation in the Season of Little Eagles after the *Nakai-yes* wiped out Victorio. A new agent, Tata Crooked Nose, had come. He treats us good. Branigan leads the tribal police to keep peace. He asked me to join them. I did this. I don't want Mescaleros killing each other or *Indah* killing them. One day a Blue Coat sergeant came and spoke to Branigan who let him speak with me. The Blue Coat said Al Sieber asked him to find me and that I go with him to the *Indah* village called Willcox to see Sieber.

"I had not seen that country in a long time. Much of that

road and Willcox I had never seen. I went to see Al Sieber. He asked me to go to the Blue Mountains with Nantan Lupan to find the Chiricahuas and bring them back to San Carlos. The Blue Coats and *Indah* are too many and too strong. We must learn to be friends with them, or the *Shis-Indeh* will disappear and be no more. It's a hard thing to do. I decided to help Al Sieber and learn what I could from the Blue Coats. As a scout, I can use the Power *Ussen* gave me to help the *Shis-Indeh* learn *Indah* ways and grow strong again. I won't let my family and my little band be wiped out by the Blue Coats or witches."

Geronimo stared at the fire a long time. At last he said, "The Chiricahua prosper here in the Blue Mountains where we thought the Blue Coats and their scouts can't come. Now you bring them here. My Power showed me this three days ago while we ate our evening meal. We had taken many horses and cattle. It felt like a rock had hit my head after my Power showed me Blue Coats had come and taken our camp. I told the warriors what I saw. I don't think they all believed me until we came back and found you here. But I knew I saw the truth. I've thought since that day about what we should do." He paused, stared at the fire, and scratched in the dust. High above, an eagle circled on the wind and called to us.

"You are called Yellow Boy? Juh told me of a Mescalero with a little band who had escaped the reservation and camped with him in his stronghold. This Mescalero had great Power from *Ussen* for using a rifle. Juh said he hunted a *Nakai-yi*–Comanche mongrel witch who had wiped out most of his father's band. You are this Yellow Boy?"

I nodded. "I came close to killing the witch. My brothers and I killed many of his Comanches and *Nakai-yi pistoleros,* and I wounded the witch, Sangre del Diablo, but he got away across the great river. Now, like Coyote, I watch and wait for him to return. My Power tells me he will come, and I will kill him.

Perhaps he lives even now in the Blue Mountains. One day I'll send him blind to the land of the grandfathers. Can your Power see him here in the Blue Mountains?"

He shook his head and said, "He hasn't attacked us. I don't see him in the Blue Mountains. My Power says soon he comes. Be ready. Now listen to me. You're young and strong. Make many children with your wives. Don't scout for Al Sieber against the *Shis-Indeh*. There are enough fools to do this already. Leave the Chiricahuas alone, and you'll live a long time. Use the Power *Ussen* gave you. A time comes you'll need it to help an *Indah* boy who will bring good medicine to help our people. That is all I have to say."

I didn't understand what he meant about an *Indah* boy who would help our people, but before I could ask him, he looked over my shoulder at the other fires behind us and said, "The other scouts leave. Go with them."

I turned to see Tzoe, Dastine, and Haskehagola leaving the fires of Chato and Jelikine. I nodded to Geronimo and followed them. We slid down the trail we had come up, saying nothing among ourselves of what had passed between the warriors and us on the ridge. It was a time for thinking and a time for praying to *Ussen*.

CHAPTER 26
THE WARNING

Tzoe, Dastine, Haskehagola, and I returned to our fires, but said little to answer the questioning stares from the other scouts. We were glad we didn't have to shoot our way out of the Chiricahua camp and had come back alive and unharmed.

We had just finished a cup of coffee when we heard a yell in the shadows of the tall pine trees where the path up the ridge began. A Chiricahua warrior ran toward us, brandishing his rifle, pumping it toward the sun, and giving a loud, lusty chant of salute. Every scout who saw him cocked his rifle, ready to shoot if he tried to shoot first. He ran straight for Much Water's fire. Much Water walked out to meet him, a frown of uncertainty painting his face. Nearing Much Water, the warrior laid down his rifle and unbuckled his bandolier of cartridges to toss them on the ground beside his rifle.

He ran up to Much Water and said, "My brother, you've been looking for me. Now I'm with you again as if I belong to you."

A happy grin painted Much Water's face, and they embraced. They walked back to Much Water's fire and, sitting down, made a cigarette, smoked to the four directions, and began to talk. It felt as if a blinding fog had lifted from the camp and the sun had sent columns of light streaming to us.

Soon Chiricahua warriors from the top of the ridge were drifting into camp and sitting down at the fires of their women and children. By half the sun's ride between the time of shortest shadows and dark, all the Chiricahua on the ridge, except the chiefs, had come in.

Nantan Lupan left our camp and went alone to hunt birds in tall grass on a slope nearby. When I said that Chiricahua who still hid might try to attack him, Sieber told us Nantan Lupan did this to show the Chiricahua he had no fear and that he was not getting ready to fight them. He had shot several birds when the chiefs rose up in the grass near him. One grabbed his shotgun, another, his sack of birds, and there he stood surrounded by the best fighting men the Apaches had.

Chato snarled, "You shoot toward us. You want war."

Nantan Lupan looked them in the eye and shook his head. "I hunt only birds for my supper." He smiled and said, "I couldn't be shooting at you. Who can see an Apache who hides?"

Mickey Free saw the chiefs surround Nantan Lupan and snatch away his gun and birds. He ran down the slope and through their circle to the side of Nantan Lupan calling, "No shoot! No shoot," waving his hands palms out to show he was also unarmed.

The chiefs relaxed a little, and Nantan Lupan said, "Mickey Free speaks true when he tells me your words and you mine. Let's go down to the shade by the running water and speak together as friends."

Chato looked at Geronimo, who gazed off down the valley and said nothing. He looked at the others, and they all gave little nods. Chato said to Mickey Free as he stared at Nantan Lupan and pointed to a tree line on a little stream burbling below them, "We talk. Shade good there."

They talked together until the shadows grew long, and then with Nantan Lupan, the chiefs came back to the camp and went to the fires of their People. The scouts and Chiricahuas mixed as friends, and there was peace in the camp.

As the darkness came, the sounds of the camp sounded different from Blue Coats, scouts, and packers on the march, ready for war. Now children laughed and played, babies cried, axes thumped against trees to make firewood, horses neighed and mules brayed, women chattered back and forth, cattle bellowed, and bells on pack mules rang as they were brought in for grooming after a day's grazing.

In the dim light of the long shadows, the three *Nakai-yi* women and nursing baby I saw on the ridge top came stumbling out of the tree line. Blue Coats and scouts ran to help and comfort them. One who spoke good *Nakai-yi* told them they were free and welcome in Nantan Lupan's camp and that they would be cared for and returned to their people. Their eyes grew wide and little streams of water flowed down their cheeks. They could not believe that they had been miraculously freed from a life as Apache slaves dragged from camp to camp until the *Nakai-yes* traded captive Apaches for them. They raised their arms and shouted thanks to the God hung on a cross of the brown robes.

A Blue Coat chief wrote down the names of the *Nakai-yi* women and baby in a book. He showed them a private place to wash and a fire they could share with food to eat. The Blue Coat chiefs gave them clothes and pairs of high-top boots to wear. They pulled off their sandals, which were torn to pieces after running for days in the mountains, threw them in the fire, and thanked again the God of the brown robes for being freed from the Chiricahua.

All the next day Chiricahuas came in, some from Chihuahua's camp, some from Loco's camp, and others from the camps of the chiefs who had spent the afternoon with Nantan Lupan. Al Sieber told the scouts and Chiricahua men that with all the Chiricahua in the camp, the supplies the pack trains had brought would run out before we returned to San Carlos. He said the Chiricahuas needed to round up and slaughter as many of their cattle as they could, dry and jerk the meat, and cook and save all the mescal and other supplies they could find for the return trip.

The next day, we moved the camp half a day across the mountains to the headwaters of the Río Bavispe. The water at the new camp was in a few deep pools, clear and cold, with a thin stream between them. The women washed the little children and babies near the camp. We all washed and swam, the women and girls in a private place downstream a little way; Blue Coats, scouts, and Chiricahua warriors farther upstream around a bend in the stream. It was good to feel the water take away dirt and sweat I had worn for a long time.

That night the scouts danced in many of the old social dances with the Chiricahua. We made drums from cook pots partly filled with water and covered with soaked pieces of cloth stretched tight and tied off with wct rawhide. Willow sticks with a loop tied on one end kept the beat on our make-do drumheads, making good sound for the dances. We danced nearly every night on the way back and had good times.

We stayed in this camp several days while the women made food ready for the return to San Carlos. The women jerked meat from slaughtered cattle and a few ponies and served the best inside parts to their families. Much mescal was roasted and packed for mules to carry.

The Chiricahua men thought of themselves as great card players, but the scouts were far better. The scouts took much *Indah* or *Nakai-yi* money in gold, silver, and paper from the Chiricahuas playing Monte, *cunquián, tzi-chis,* and *mushka* with cards they cut from thin, stiff horsehide, painted with the card pictures. I liked the cards and traded one of the pistols I found for a set, and I watched how the good players won most of the games to understand how to use them to take some of the *Indah* or *Nakai-yi* money from the Chiricahua who didn't yet understand its value.

Small groups of Chiricahua continued coming down the trails to the *río* where we camped. I looked up from watching a card game and saw an old chief, wearing an *Indah* scout hat, lead seventeen of his people down a ridge trail and into camp. I knew Nana the instant I saw him. On the trail, he sat his horse easily, but when he dismounted, his ancient legs, joints nearly frozen from age, made him slow and tottering.

A Blue Coat officer and several scouts went to meet him. I started to go greet him, but something whispered in my mind, *Wait,* and I did. The officer gave Nana's people a place for their fires, and the women and children went to work. Nana's face was a mask of indifference, but I saw that his eyes pulled in every detail about the camp. He smoked with the Blue Coat officers. After speaking with the Blue Coats, he sat with the other chiefs until the sun took the daylight over the far mountains.

That night, as the fires burned low and the social dancing finished, it was my turn to help keep watch on the camp. I climbed to a ledge that poked out of the trees and made a good place to sit partway up the ridge. I could see up and down the river, trails leading in from the east, and virtually all the fires in the camp. It was cold, but I kept warm by keeping a blanket over my shoulders and back and one wrapped around my waist.

Somewhere to the north, a wolf howled, and the ponies and mules seemed restless in the grass where they grazed. I kept a close eye on them, expecting they would hear trouble a long time before I did. The sky glowed with white light behind the eastern mountains as the moon readied to show its face.

A voice near my ear said, *"Nish'ii'* (I see you), Grandson." It took all my discipline not to jerk around in surprise, but I had to smile. Nana had again surprised me in the dark here in the Blue Mountains as he had when he first appeared at the reservation three years earlier.

"Idiits'ag (I hear you), Grandfather. My eyes filled with memories of Mescalero when I saw you ride in with your People. Come. Join me. Let's speak together while I watch the camp."

His blanket fell beside mine, and he groaned as his stiff joints lowered him to sit beside me. He pulled his blanket over his shoulders, stared out over the camp, and sighed.

"You wear the red headband of Sieber's scouts. I was surprised to see this when I rode in with my People today. How long have you fought against us? I know it is after the *Nakai-yes* wiped out Victorio. Juh told me of your battle with the witch, Sangre del Diablo. Tell me of your days."

I noticed something below was making the horses nervous as they pranced and snorted in their rope corral. My eyes strained to see, but all I saw were scouts approaching to calm them. I picked up a small stone and flipped it off the ledges into the trees below us and that made some night birds fly out squawking at being disturbed.

"I'm a scout only since the time Nantan Lupan begins looking for you in the Blue Mountains. When Nantan Lupan brings you back to San Carlos, I'll return to my Juanita and our baby girl child, Kicking Wren. I still chase the witch. We found him in Casas Grandes after my friends and I went looking for him in the camp of Elias in the Blue Mountains to the north. I chased him to the great river where he put a bullet in me, and I put one in him, but he crossed the great river and hid in the land of the *Indah*. I wait to send him blind to the Happy Land when he comes again.

"Juh left his camp and went to San Carlos, but we stayed through a Ghost Face Season there and then returned to Mescalero. A new agent had come, one the Mescaleros call 'Tata Crooked Nose.' He spoke true and made things right after the Blue Coats left. His chief of tribal police is Captain Branigan. He too speaks true. I became a tribal policeman."

The horses in the rope corral, approached by scouts, seemed to relax and returned to grazing.

"Sieber asked that I come with the scouts to the Blue Mountains to bring the Chiricahuas back to San Carlos. Before Nantan Lupan came, he spoke with the chiefs and sent the crooked agents away and found work for the People to do besides raiding. It's a good thing he does. You need to leave the Blue Mountains and see your people grow strong again at San Carlos. That is all I have to say."

Nana laughed deep from his belly, shaking his head. "Nantan Lupan's heart is in the right place, but the *Indah* are too greedy to keep even Nantan Lupan's word, and too many Apaches, like Geronimo, still seek revenge for peace to last. But for Nantan Lupan and his scouts, we'll return to San Carlos, live in the dirt, and beg for bread and blankets until we can stand it no more.

"Sieber has many scouts. They led Nantan Lupan straight to our camps. Why does Sieber ask you to come when he has many others?"

I saw his eyes even in the moonlight shadows, narrow and questioning, watching to see if I spoke true.

"I have given my word I will not say."

He nodded. "Grandson keeps his word. *Enjuh.* I know your Power with the rifle. Sieber knows your Power. I'm a chief because I know, if an arrow fits the bow, it will shoot true and straight a long way.

"Now, hear me. Beware of Soldado Fiero. He does not keep his word. Beware of Geronimo. He thinks the White Mountain scouts betrayed us, and he's willing to die to send them to the Happy Land. He sets a trap for tomorrow night at the dancing. Jelikine, his father-in-law, told him not to do what he plans. He will do it anyway. There will be blood. Watch your back. That is all I have to say."

I waved my palm horizontal to the ground in gratitude. "I owe you much, Grandfather. *Enjuh.*"

He grunted as he slid back on his blanket, put his hand on my shoulder, and pushed up to stand. I heard the leaves and twigs fall from his blanket as he shook it before throwing it over his shoulders, and then Nana vanished into the night, leaving me to think over his warnings.

When the moon began to fall in the west, Haskehagola took my place on the shelf. I made my way down to the camp in the cold night air and lay down wrapped in my blanket with my feet toward our fire pit to warm them by its coals.

Shadows pointing west were long, the sun sending spears of light to the dark places, and mists still floated on the cold air. The camp was beginning to stir when Sieber sent word for me to come to his fire. He poured me coffee in a metal Blue Coat cup, and we sat down on a log.

"In three days, we'll leave here to return to San Carlos. Nan-tan Lupan will return on the east side of the mountains rather than go the way we came. He doesn't want to risk the *Nakai-yes* attacking the Chiricahua and will use the mountains to hide them as long as he can. Tzoe says there are springs with enough water for one-day camps along the trails on the east side.

"I have reason not to trust Soldado Fiero. I want you to watch him close, especially around Tzoe. Do you understand the meaning of my words?"

I nodded. "I understand. Now hear me. I do not trust Geronimo. Don't let the White Mountains dance with the Chiricahuas tonight."

Sieber looked at me from under his brows, frowning, and then nodded. "A scout, *Ja'ndezi* (Long Ears), died this morning from a snake bite. There'll be no dancing tonight."

"*Enjuh.*"

Early the next day, Geronimo and the Chiricahua chiefs told Nantan Lupan their people wouldn't answer their signals to come in because they thought the scouts tried to fool them. They asked for permission to go and gather their people and for the young men to gather all the livestock they could find and bring it in from canyons where they had hidden it. Nantan Lupan let them go, but told them he marched for San Carlos in three days. Geronimo told him he would not leave the land of the *Nakai-yes* until he had all his people gathered together. Nantan Lupan said for them to meet him at the mouth of Guadalupe Canyon.

CHAPTER 27
SOLDADO FIERO

After Geronimo and the Chiricahua chiefs left the camp to look for their People, cattle, and horses, I sat with Tzoe, Dastine, and Much Water at John Rope's fire. Tzoe told us about the trail north along the east side of the Blue Mountains. He said it was long but not as steep as the one we used to come in from the south and west. I sat against a log as we smoked, talked, and listened, and I watched Soldado Fiero at a nearby fire with other scouts. I noticed he glanced at us often, while Tzoe drew in the dust to show us the way he remembered the trail across the mountains toward Carretas.

Tzoe said, "We sit in this canyon here near the beginnings of Río Bavispe. Up the ridge on the other side of the *río* here, there's a trail that runs north along the west side of the ridges through junipers and a few tall pines and then turns east through a high pass and back around to the east side of the ridges, which begin bending toward the east away from this *río*. The trail stays close to the ridge tops, crosses, winds around some deep canyons, and comes out on the eastern *llano* at springs near the village of Carretas. From there, we can follow the Río Janos around to the *Nakai-yi* border and then west into Guadalupe Canyon and come out at San Bernardino Springs.

"I think I remember how the trail goes, but I have not seen it for many seasons. Nantan Lupan told Geronimo and the chiefs he moves slowly with the People. There are many women and children. They'll need water for themselves and the ponies and mules. All the supplies they make now will not be enough because they are slow. We'll need to hunt every day and find water for the camps along the way. Al Sieber says he thinks there'll be nearly four hundred Apaches returning to San Carlos. They're our brothers. We must take good care of them."

Chiricahua women worked hard packing mescal, dried meat, dried berries, roots, potatoes, and fruit, and nuts. Warriors, who had not gone out with Geronimo and the chiefs, gathered scattered ponies, mules, and cattle nearby into manageable groups, determined which ones they thought could make the long walk across the rough country back to San Carlos, and slaughtered the rest. Blue Coats cleaned their weapons, studied maps, and worked with packers sorting out what to leave and what to take back. Scouts stayed by their fires and, in the shade, cleaned their guns, sharpened their knives, arranged with the mule packers to have the booty they had taken from the Chiricahua loaded on the mule pack trains, and helped the Chiricahuas when they asked. I saw Soldado Fiero, like Tzoe, had taken little from the Chiricahuas but was always close by when anyone needed help with heavy baskets and parfleches filled with food for the trail or family goods.

I watched and helped Tzoe for the next two days. He was everywhere, spending time with the Chiricahuas and doing his work as a scout sergeant. It seemed that where Tzoe was, there was Soldado Fiero, always within sight. Given what Nana and Sieber told me, like Coyote, I watched and waited.

On the third morning after the chiefs and many of their warriors left, the canyon camp lay covered with mists off the river. The coming sun was fast driving it away when I returned to the fire of John Rope from my morning bath and swim. Much Water and Dastine were taking their turn cooking for us. They had pieces of meat speared on the end of sticks stuck in the ground and tilted over the fire; the smell of the meat's grease dripping in the fire made my belly growl like Wolf, and soon we were cutting the meat off the sticks and feeling its good, savory juices run down our throats.

It was a good morning to be alive. I expected Tzoe to come to our fire and tell us what the Blue Coat officers wanted from us that day. I looked toward the place where the Blue Coat officers and scout sergeants usually met and saw one or two men lounging there, but not Tzoe.

I said, "Tzoe doesn't come to tell us what the Blue Coat chiefs want from us today?"

Much Water said, "Ummph. He comes a short time while you swim. Says be ready. Nantan Lupan may go today if enough Chiricahuas are ready. Tzoe says he goes to hunt. Maybe finds big black tail deer the Chiricahuas will eat, maybe makes wives happy again so he can sleep inside wickiup instead of by scout fires. Maybe Tzoe needs mo' betta wives than those two."

I glanced toward the fire where Soldado Fiero slept. His blanket lay rolled up, ready to go. His friends ate their morning meal, but Soldado Fiero wasn't there. The meat I had just eaten turned sour in my belly. I had to find Tzoe quick.

"Does Tzoe say where he hunts? I saw big deer back up the canyon at our last camp."

"Ummph. Tzoe follows the *rio* to high places. He says big deer go there."

"I want to see the *rio* in high places. I'll find him and help him with his meat."

"Ummph. Don't look like a deer. You might not come back."

I followed the river upstream. There was only a little water that flowed between deep pools, long stretches of sand, and places of rushing water where stones of all sizes had collected during big runoffs in the hard rains that came with the Season of Large

Leaves. A little upstream from the main camp where the women bathed, I found tracks winding round the pools and in the long reaches of sand along the edge. The distance between individual footprints said the track maker was casually walking, occasionally pausing to look back or to survey the canyon sides. The tracks didn't go far before the stream forked, one stream up into the high mountains to the northwest and the other to the southeast. The tracks turned toward the high mountains.

A second set of tracks came from the junipers, where the river split, and followed the ones I followed, stopping behind boulders when the first set stopped before continuing. The river wound through a canyon in dark, morning shadows being chased away by arrows of light shot from the rising sun. They struck rough, black canyon cliffs streaked in reds and grays, making splashes of gold on the canyon sides. It was cool and calm down by the burbling water, its big, still pool surfaces black, perfect mirrors as the light grew.

I walked in the shadows and listened for calls or flights from startled birds, but there were none. Looking upstream across a stretch of sand between two pools, I saw only one set of tracks. The second set of tracks stopped behind a tumbled pile of boulders and then disappeared. I studied the brush and exposed ground even with the boulders on both sides of the stream until I saw weeds on the west side of the stream, which had been pushed down earlier, slowly bending back straight.

Three or four hundred yards further upstream, the riverbed made two sharp left turns around a ridge before winding north again. Soldado Fiero must have run over the ridge to get in front of Tzoe where he could ambush him when Tzoe followed the river around the ridge. I could run forward and hope to catch Tzoe in time to warn him about Soldado Fiero's ambush, or I could run over the ridge, find Soldado Fiero, and stop his ambush. Time was against me. I had to take the fastest way to stop Tzoe's murder. I chose to find Soldado Fiero and began the hard run up the ridge.

Juniper sparsely covered the western side of the ridge, but high shelves of rock I had to run around made the climb to the ridge top slower than I had thought, and the high mountain air made it hard to breathe as I fought against weary weights settling in my bones and muscles. I made the top of the ridge and sank to one knee to let my wind come back. I looked around but saw no sign of any recent passersby. I tried to look down in the bend of the river between the two turns where I hoped Tzoe was, but the ridge end blocked my view of the streambed.

I stayed low and worked my way over the top of the ridge until I could see the river pools far below me. The river coming off the second left turn around the ridge ran straight until it made a right turn up into a high-walled canyon reaching for the top of the mountains. At the place where the river curved into a new canyon stood a thick stand of junipers. For someone looking downstream, it was a good place to hide, watch, and wait for an ambush victim. I didn't see any signs of Soldado Fiero, but I knew he must be there. I didn't see Tzoe coming up the river. My heart pounded from the hard climbing and knowing I had to move fast or Tzoe would die.

I crept along, just below the ridgeline, until I crossed the disturbed grass and earth Soldado Fiero had made going down to the juniper stand at the river's edge. Far downstream from the junipers, I saw the tiny figure of Tzoe. I guessed he would be over two hundred yards in range from Soldado Fiero's rifle when he came into view. Since Soldado Fiero planned an ambush, I knew he would wait until he had a shot he couldn't miss, a range less than a hundred, or maybe even fifty, yards.

I scrambled along the side of the ridge through the thick junipers as Tzoe leisurely walked up the river, stopping often to study the sandy banks for tracks or looking up the sides of the canyon. I crossed Soldado Fiero's trail and ran on from the ridge until I was almost directly above the stand of junipers where I guessed he waited. The junipers and other brush gave me good cover as I came down the ridge. Still, I worried that Tzoe might see me and give me away, ensuring we'd both be shot.

A hundred yards from Soldado Fiero's grove of junipers, I found a place that gave me a clear line of sight to them and some protection if bullets flew in my direction. Tzoe, in a very dangerous position, would come within a hundred yards of the grove. I jerked out the *Shináá Cho* and studied the dark shadows where I thought Soldado Fiero waited. He was not there. Desperate, I searched other places under the junipers, but he wasn't there, either.

My guts felt in free fall. He had to be close. I scanned the low cliffs on the east side of the river. Directly across the stream, I saw bushes bent down and rocks and dirt scrambled in places going up the cliffs. I scanned along the top of the rock bluffs, about the same height as me on the other side.

Soladado Fiero lay about two hundred yards away on the far side of some small boulders. I saw only the top of his head, the barrel and forestock of his rifle, and the fingers of his left hand wrapped around it. I guessed he had decided to crawl there in order to watch for Tzoe rounding the ridge end and maybe have a better position for a close, sure shot. Lucky for us, he waited. Lucky for us, I found him, and the range was only two hundred yards. Tzoe wandered ever closer to the place where I knew Soldado Fiero would shoot. I had to take a quick shot, or Tzoe would die.

I had made many long, hard shots before. I pulled back the hammer on the Henry and aimed for the top of Soldado's head. I remembered how Soldado Fiero had baited me with my wife and our band of Mescaleros after we escaped the reservation and how he had killed the old woman in the first camp we raided for Nantan Lupan. *Ussen* creates the same chances for all warriors. It is like the turning of the stars. A warrior waits for his chance to come and makes old wrongs right. The thought of making things even with Soldado Fiero gave me a great feeling of satisfaction.

The crack of doom thundered from the Henry and echoed down the canyon. The brilliant, golden light of the sun showed on a red mist where the top of Soldado Fiero's head had been. Tzoe dived behind a jumble of boulders near some large junipers on the edge of the river. Not sure from where the shot came, he crouched down quickly looking in every direction, uncertain which side of the boulders offered protection.

I called to him, "Ho! Tzoe! It is your brother, Yellow Boy. I've taken the life of one who waited to kill you. I'm on the west side of the river. Don't shoot. I'll come to you."

He crabbed around to the far side of the boulders from where my voice came and yelled, "Come!"

I told Tzoe Soldado Fiero had been ready to kill him when I shot. He nodded and said, "I thought the fool might try something like that. I'm a lucky man to have you for a friend. Come, I would be sure this enemy is dead."

We climbed up the west bank to Soldado Fiero's hiding place and found him facedown behind the boulder where he had hidden. The smells of death, loose bowels and the metallic smell of blood, were strong. The top of his head was gone. My .44-40 caliber bullet had done a crude scalping job and insects were already crawling for what was left of the crown of his head.

Tzoe stared at the body for a moment, shook his head, and said, "Soldado Fiero wasn't the coyote he thought he was thanks to you, *Aashcho*. I owe you much."

I said, "What you see is the Power of *Ussen* making debts long due, right."

CHAPTER 28
LONG MARCH OUT OF THE
BLUE MOUNTAINS

Tzoe and I spoke to Al Sieber when we returned to camp. He listened and nodded as I told him what had happened. When I finished, he sat and puffed his pipe for a time and then said, "Yellow Boy, you did a good thing. You saved the life of a good man and ended the life of one who was not true to his word. I've killed other scouts for less. Say no more about this, and none will look for revenge. I'll report Soldado Fiero as killed by unknown fighters, and that will be the end of that traitor." He waved his hand parallel to the ground. "Go in peace. There's a long, hard march before us. We start in the morning." He made a half smile and said, "Moses leads us out of the wilderness to the promised land."

Tzoe and I frowned. "Where is Nantan Lupan? Who is this General Moses? Where's this promised land?"

Sieber laughed a deep belly laugh. "I made a joke. It's a story the brown robes tell of a great chief, Moses, who, with *Ussen's* help, freed his tribe from slavery and, for forty years, led them through a wilderness to a better place. Nantan Lupan is like Moses for the Apaches at San Carlos."

Tzoe and I looked at each other. We didn't understand what Sieber meant, but we nodded and then walked back to John Rope's fire.

The next day, Nantan Lupan began leading the long walk back to San Carlos. The *Nakai-yi* women and baby, still weak, rode on mules, as did old Chiricahuas, weak women, and young children. We left at sunrise, crossing the river and following the trail up the ridge Tzoe had told us we would take. The first day, we did not travel far and stopped by the time of shortest shadows. We had gone no farther than a warrior might easily run in the sun traveling a hand's width against the horizon.

The trail was long and hard. Scouts hunted every day to add to the supplies that weren't nearly enough to carry us all the way back to San Bernardino. On parts of the trail, water was scarce, and scouts, Chiricahuas, and Blue Coats all went thirsty. We passed through a burned place in the trees that left us black and dirty, and we won a fight against a range fire on the eastern *llano* that nearly burnt us up. As we came down out of the mountains for the springs at Carretas, all the supplies had run out, but the scouts found enough game to keep us fed, for there was plenty of game in the mountains.

We camped one night near the springs at Carretas. Cooking fires from the scouts and Chiricahuas made a long string of yellow lights scattered far down the trail, their little columns of white smoke rising in the still, cold night air. At John Rope's fire, we finished a roasted haunch from a deer Dastine had taken. We spoke of many things we had seen along the trail.

Much Water said, "I saw something very strange today while I was hunting. There's a rancho in a canyon back up the trail. I didn't go near it because I didn't want to stir up the *Nakai-yes* who lived there, but I did watch it for a while with my *be'idest'iné*. There were posts stuck in the ground with crosspieces fixed to the top where big hunting birds, an eagle, a couple of hawks, and even a great owl roosted with their heads covered. The owl made me cringe just to look at it. Even stranger, there seemed to be Indians working there with *Nakai-yes*. It was a fine *hacienda*, and it had a big, new corral filled with fine ponies, and many cattle grazed along the stream running below it. I don't understand why the Chiricahuas had not already taken the stock. Maybe the Indians and *Nakai-yes* watch them carefully, but that never stopped Geronimo and the chiefs before. It's strange."

I said, "Much Water, what tribe of Indians were the ones you saw? Were they Tarahumaries?"

Much Water shook his head, "No, not Tarahumaries. When I first saw them, I thought they were Comanches. But that makes no sense. Comanches ride the *llano* to the east across the great river, and now they are on the reservation with Quanah Parker and not even raiding the *Nakai-yes*. They wouldn't be in the Blue Mountains. I think my eyes deceive me."

I could only think, *So, at last, I find you, witch!*

"Can you show me how to find this canyon where you saw them? I want to watch them for myself with my *Shináá Cho.*"

Much Water nodded and with his finger drew a trail in the dust and showed me the canyon where he had seen the *hacienda* with the Comanches. The others around the fire paid little attention to Much Water's story or map, but I memorized it.

The next morning, in the mists and gloom of the coming dawn, I rode back up the trail and found the canyon where Much Water said he saw the Comanches and big hunting birds. I also found the *hacienda* he had seen. Truly, the Indians were Comanches. I watched the *hacienda* until there was good light, but I saw no hunting birds, only the big posts with the crosspieces.

The gates to the *hacienda* compound swung open and, as if in a dream, Sangre del Diablo, bald, naked to the waist, tattoos twisting over his arms and torso, walked out carrying a hooded golden eagle on a leather covered forearm. I threw my rifle to my shoulder, cocked it, and was ready to shoot when I realized if the Comanches came after me, the Chiricahuas would scatter like quail before a coyote and the expedition to bring them back to San Carlos would be a failure. Slowly the rifle came down and I tasted bitter disappointment as I thought, *I have to wait a little while, witch, but I'll be back.*

I memorized the path back to the *hacienda* from the trail Nantan Lupan followed, and I thanked *Ussen* for showing me the witch and his new *hacienda*. From the lessons I had learned attacking him before, I would think carefully this time about how I would kill him.

In twelve suns, we returned to San Bernardino Springs. The Blue Coats and scouts waiting there saw us coming from a long way off and started cooking all kinds of food for us. After we took care of the animals, we all lined up, Blue Coats, Chiricahuas, and scouts alike. There were so many, we had to eat in shifts, and, even then, some didn't get any food. The next day, we moved to a place with big oaks and much shade, and everyone cooked, as they needed.

Two wagons, each pulled by four mules, came to the place of the oaks. Al Sieber said they came to take Nantan Lupan, some of the Blue Coat officers, and the *Nakai-yi* women and baby to Tucson. Before he left, he called all the scouts to the wagons before the sun was high, but the light was bright and the air, still and cool. Nantan Lupan stood in a wagon and talked to us. He said many *Indah* believed we would never return from the land of the *Nakai-yes* alive. He said many of us thought we would never catch the Chiricahuas, but we did, and we came back from the land of the *Nakai-yes* with most of the Chiricahuas. He told us to go on to San Carlos and keep watch over them. Then he sat down, and the wagons rolled off down the road in a little cloud of white dust.

Al Sieber asked me to his fire the night after Nantan Lupan left. We drank his good coffee and smoked to the four directions. He said, "You're a good man, Yellow Boy, the best shot, including me, I ever saw. You saved the life of Tzoe twice, exactly as I needed. I want you to stay with me in the scouts. Your friends and Sergeant Tzoe plan to stay for a while longer. They also want you to stay. But I know you have a good woman and baby waiting for you at Mescalero and that you'll leave the scouts as soon as you can. You left your pony at Willcox. Stay with us until you get your pony. I'll make tracks on a paper that say you completed your service, and I'll put it with the tracks on the papers the Blue Coats keep. I'll get and pay the Blue Coat money you have coming for your good work. That way nothing will hold you up when you're ready to leave. Yellow Boy wants this? You're always welcome in the scouts. We still have much left to do."

"Hmmph. Sieber speaks good words. I go to Willcox. Get my pony. I leave with what you give me. You need me no more. You have plenty scouts. The Chiricahuas no more make war and raid."

Sieber crossed his arms and nodded, staring at the low, flickering flames in his fire pit. "Yes, the Chiricahuas are quiet now, but only *Ussen*, the chiefs, and Geronimo know for how long."

We left the big oaks the next day with wagons carrying the children, old ones, and the Chiricahuas' goods, and made Willcox in the same time we had taken to go to San Bernardino Springs over forty-five suns earlier. The Blue Coat soldiers at Willcox had taken good care of my pony. He was sleek and fat and needed a long, hard run. I gave him his run the same evening we came in. After so many days of running, I felt like I was flying through the fast-cooling air as the sun fell behind the mountains, looking like a great, fuzzy golden ball in the far, gray haze.

Al Sieber made the tracks on paper that said I did what I promised the Blue Coats. He gave me the money Blue Coats paid a scout and a little more. He said I earned it, and he told me to keep my scout coat but to return the other things.

I claimed my guns, blankets, and mule from the packer who kept and led the mule I had taken from the Chiricahuas. He said that mule was smart and offered to buy it from me, but I needed it to carry my case of cartridges, new guns, saddle, and *Nakai-yi* blankets. I hadn't worn my scout jacket on most of the trip, and it had stayed clean and in good shape, but the rest of my clothes, like those of the other scouts, were in rags. A store-owner in Willcox drove a big wagonload of clothes and other supplies out to our camp, so the other scouts and I spent some of our money on new clothes. I bought a shirt, pants, vest, a bandanna, and saddlebags to hold part of my hoard of new ammunition. The rags I burned.

To be safe, I decided to travel at night. Before I left, my scout friends and I shared a meal. I admired and respected my new friends. They were men who kept their word and remembered their friends. I told them there was always a place at my fire for them.

As I cinched my saddle, ready to leave, Tzoe appeared out of the darkness.

"You saved my life twice this time out, Yellow Boy. I owe you much, and I'm in your debt. Call on me when I can help you."

I waved my hand parallel to the ground and said, "I'm glad *Ussen* gave me the Power to help you, Brother. I've learned much. Be careful around the Chiricahuas. I hear they shot Jelikine in the head because he wouldn't help them with the dance ambush they planned for us and told them it was bad medicine. I'll see you again when *Ussen* needs our Power."

Tzoe nodded and grasped my forearm and I his. He said, "When *Ussen* needs our Power."

★ ★ ★ ★ ★

The moon was full during my ride toward the great river. I rode hard in the night, anxious to return to Juanita and Kicking Wren. I rested near springs and tanks during the day, and all the time, I watched and listened for Blue Coats, *banditos,* and renegade Indians. But I saw no signs of anyone, except for an occasional *vaquero's* fire off in the distance.

As dawn brought light to the sky on the third day, I sat on my pony and waited for Rufus Pike to come walking fast to visit the little house with the door hanging open close to the corral. When I had stayed with him, learning how to shoot, he always went there before he did anything else.

It was cool and quiet, the high, thin clouds a color of light blue turquoise. Even the birds had not yet begun their songs. Back up the canyon, I heard a cow bawl, and before me, in black outline, stood the mountain where *Ussen* gave me my Power. Night water lay sparkling on spider webs woven on the creosote bush by his porch. This was a place of wisdom Rufus had made for me with his clear eyes and good stories of the old days.

Rufus came out his door yawning and pulling the straps that held up his pants over his shoulders. Surprised, he jumped back into the doorway when he saw me, and then a big smile filled his face.

"Well, I'll be danged," he said, laughing, "You disappear and then reappear faster'n any ghost I ever seen, Yellow Boy. How ya doin'? I'll be right back." He jumped off the porch and ran for the little house.

He wasn't gone long, but already the sun had begun filling the canyon with brilliant pools of light when he came out of the little house and followed the path back to his big house. He walked up and, taking hold of my pony's bridle, said, "It's mighty good to see ya, my old *amigo.* Come on in after you take

219

care of your pony. You both look like you been ridin' hard for a long time."

I nodded. "This I will do, Rufus Pike."

I put my pony and mule in the corral, rubbed them down with a few handfuls of grama grass, and found some oats in Rufus's lean-to for them. I didn't think Rufus would mind if I took a little feed, and he didn't. By the time I had taken care of my animals and bathed in the water tank, I smelled steak on the old, black iron stove in Rufus's house and went to join him. I was hungry.

We sat in the porch shade and ate steaks and beans from *pesh-lickoyee* (white iron) plates. I hadn't eaten this well since I'd left the reservation with Sweeny Jones. Rufus finished his morning meal before me, put down his plate, took a long slurp of his hot coffee, and said, "It's been a year or two since I seen you last. I saw some unshod pony tracks here around the cabin a time or two while I's gone to help a woman over to Lincoln. Figured it musta been you stoppin' by goin' somewheres. Are you and your People back to the reservation now that most of the Blue Coats is gone?"

I told Rufus of the fight with the witch, of the birth of Kicking Wren, of Tata Crooked Nose and Captain Branigan, that I was a tribal policeman, how I had killed Delgadito thinking he was an *Indah,* and about the run into Mexico with Crook's scouts to bring back the Chiricahuas. Rufus listened, drinking his coffee and slowly shaking his head as if it were hard to believe all the things I told him.

Rufus said, "Dang! Ain't no moss gonna grow on yore back."

I didn't understand what he meant and frowned, but he waved his hand that it meant nothing and said, "So it sounds like you know where the witch is a livin' that killed yore daddy. What you gonna do? I know you're goin' back to get him. I mean, when and what're you plannin' to do?"

I shook my head. "This I still think on. My brothers and me, we go maybe plenty quick when I get back to reservation. Captain Branigan lets us go, we go. He says we no go, then we wait until Season of Earth is Reddish Brown and then disappear for a while. This time, Sangre del Diablo no run away. I send him to the Happy Land blind. No more Sangre del Diablo in the land of the *Nakai-yes.*"

"Well, when you decide, I want to go with you. Maybe my ole buffalo boomer can reach out and get him for you, and it's one I owe him for yore daddy."

"Ummph. When I decide to go, I tell you, Rufus Pike. Maybe you go. Maybe you change mind. Go or stay, *Ussen* wants me to kill this witch. Now, I have question for you."

"Okay?"

"I smoked and had talk with Geronimo before he and chiefs talked to Nantan Lupan and decided to return to San Carlos . . ."

Rufus spat a long, brown stream of juice off the porch. "Geronimo? He's a no good, murderin' outlaw. Why he even murdered a *Nakai-yi* boy he raised as his own. Caught him an' his family out herdin' sheep alone. Asked him to take off the fine warm coat his wife made for him so it wouldn't get blood on it and kilt 'em ever'one. If'n I'd been in Mexico with you and seen him, by damn, he wouldn't a come back."

"Many *Indah,* even many *Indeh,* think as you do, Rufus. Geronimo is *di-yen.* His Power is to see what comes. He said I would have 'wives,' but I have only Juanita. No room in my life for another woman, even if Juanita agrees. He also said I would help an *Indah* boy who would help our people. I no understand his words. He speak in riddles, in visions I no see. His words also riddles to you?"

Rufus spat again and stared off into the gray-brown distance across the valley of the great river. He finally shook his head. "I understand nothing of what Geronimo told you. If his Power truly lets him foretell events, you'll know soon enough. Seems to me he's just runnin' his mouth."

Perhaps Rufus spoke true. I didn't know, and neither did he.

I rested a day with Rufus, and even shot some on his target range at the back of his canyon. My memories of what I learned there were very strong. Late in the afternoon of the second day, I saddled my pony and loaded my mule, told Rufus I would be back when I could, and rode off for the reservation and my wife and child.

CHAPTER 29
RETURN

I waited, sitting on my pony in the deep shadows of the trees in the early morning light. A little earlier, just before light appeared above the mountains, a thin curl of smoke twisted out of Juanita's tipi into the high pine branches above it. Now the sun threw long spears of bright, yellow light passing through the tall tree branches and caught in the mists settled in the bottom of the canyon.

The blanket covering the opening of the tipi pulled back and Juanita stepped out into the cool canyon air, pulling a light blanket over her shoulders, and disappeared down the path along the little stream running through our camp to the place where the women bathed. She usually went there first in the mornings before the others came, even though it was colder then than later in the day. Soon she was back, shivering under the thin blanket, her hair drying long and loose, and her face pink, almost red from the cold water. Birds were beginning to make their morning calls, and I could hear muffled voices in some of the tipis near me and horses snorting and beginning to mill about on the other side of the brush corral fence.

Juanita went to the woodpile near her tipi and pulled the ax out of the big log she used for a chopping block. Flipping the blanket off her shoulders, she pulled a piece of log off the small stack of wood nearby, laid it on the chopping block, and with a puffing grunt and hard swing with both hands, cleanly split it into two pieces. Her back to me, she readied one of the split pieces for splitting again. I rode out of the shadows.

"My woman uses an ax better than many men." She turned toward me, looking this way and that before seeing me at the edge of the shadows. The hand holding the ax dropped to her side, and the fingers of the other flew to her lips. I heard her whisper, "Yellow Boy!"

For the People, it is unseemly to show affection in front of others, but since few were stirring, she ran to me in the shadows and threw her strong arms around me. We hugged and kissed as men and their women long separated do in private. I wanted her then, and she wanted me, but we knew that must come later. Her ear lay against my chest, and her hair, still damp, felt cooler than the morning air.

"My husband has returned. I hear the beating of his heart and feel his strength and Power with my arms."

"I've returned to my woman and daughter. I never left them, for they stayed in my heart. Tell me all is good, and I'll be satisfied."

"All is good, husband. Your daughter is a strong walker and runner already. Come. See your daughter walk and run. Moon on the Water stays with me at night to help keep watch over our tipi and Kicking Wren. Moon grows old enough to have her *Haheh* ceremony anytime. Soon you may have a new brother-in-law to help you. I have mesquite bread baking and a piece of deer Kah brought us ready for the fire."

"Woman, I rode all night to eat the good things from your fire."

She laughed. "Your belly sounds like a hungry wolf. Take your pony to the corral. Soon we'll eat.

I had been gone with General Crook's scouts less than two moons, but Kicking Wren was shy when she saw me come through the door. Moon on the Water smiled, and handing her up to me said, *"D'anté,* Brother. Your family is happy for your return from the Blue Mountains. Kicking Wren wants her father."

Kicking Wren felt small and warm in my arms. I held her high and looked at her face, but at first, she wouldn't look at me. I rubbed her back, and she smiled as I sat down next to the fire, played with her hands, and nuzzled her behind her ears, making her giggle. Before Juanita had my morning meal ready, Kicking Wren and I were old friends as she chattered away, sitting between my crossed legs and making words only the women in our tipis understood.

Captain Branigan sat at the table where he made tracks on paper for the agency police. I stopped at the doorway and waited for him to see me. He looked up, smiled under the big bush of hair below his nose, and waved me inside his work and council room at the agency. He stuck out his hand, and we pumped arms twice.

"Yellow Boy, you return! Good! I read in the papers how General Crook and his scouts brought back the Chiricahuas with almost no bloodshed. For a while, we thought they had wiped you out. Sit down. Sit down and tell me about your adventures."

I sat in the chair in front of his table. He went to get coffee off the stove in the back and brought me back a cup before I began my story. I told him all of it, except for finding the witch outside of Carretas. He sat and smoked his pipe, nodding at the wise way General Crook handled Geronimo and the chiefs, and frowning at how hard the trails were in the Blue Mountains.

When I finished my story, Branigan said, "General Crook and his scouts, you among them, have done this country a great service. As a former army officer, I can see where the general took a big gamble, but it paid off in a big way. I'm glad you got back unharmed, and Agent Llewellyn will be glad to see you, too. Are you ready to go back to work as a policeman? I've got your badge right here in my desk drawer."

"Wait two moons. Work in the land of the *Nakai-yes*. Need three brothers in camp to go with me. Need paper with tracks says it good we leave reservation. Brothers and me make sure we no break *Indah* or *Nakai-yi* laws. You give paper with tracks?"

Branigan took a swallow of coffee and studied me while he thought on my request. "Two moons and three friends to go with you into Mexico after you were in on rounding up the Chiricahuas in the Sierra Madre, eh?" He raised his brows and grinned. "You must have found a pretty good stash of Chiricahua loot."

I said nothing. *Indah* did not believe in witches or the Powers *Ussen* gives.

"Things have been pretty quiet around here. If you want to wait a couple more months before you start work again, I don't see any problem with that. You risked your life going after the Chiricahuas. For all I know, they might still want to shoot you for comin' after 'em. Who are the three men you want to go with you?"

"Two warriors, Kah and Beela-chezzi, and a boy, Ish-kay-neh, ready to follow warriors."

"You ain't plannin' any raids down there in Mexico, are you?"

"No raids. Work to do in land of *Nakai-yes*."

Branigan must have understood I wouldn't tell him more. He pulled open his table drawer, took out a white sheet of paper, and began to make tracks the *Indah* and some *Nakai-yes* knew how to read. When he finished, he folded the paper twice and handed it to me. He said, "That paper says you are free to leave the reservation for two moons with the names of the warriors and boy I've listed. If any Blue Coat or *Indah* with a badge asks if you have permission to be off the reservation, show him that paper. If you're going to Mexico, don't get caught. They'll either kill you or make you a slave in the mines, and we'll never find you. Keep that paper safe. It's important. I expect to see you back here on the reservation within two moons. Go in peace." He stood and extended his hand. I've never understood why the *Indah* like to pump arms so much. I took his hand and gave it two pumps.

"We come back plenty quick. *Ka-dish-day* (Goodbye)."

The night warm and comforting, the stars like a river of milk, children played their night games around and in the stream. Kicking Wren played with them. Not many moons off the *tsach*, she walked and ran easily, Moon on the Water watching her while Juanita and the other women gossiped and worked on baskets. Beela-chezzi, Kah, and Ish-kay-neh sat with me in the flickering shadows made by my small council fire off in the trees away from the women and children. I lighted a *cigarro*, smoked to the four directions, and passed it around my circle of friends. When it came to Ish-kay-neh, he took it and looked in my direction for approval. I nodded. Even if he hadn't done a single apprentice raid, he'd earned our respect after the Blue Coats took over the reservation. He deserved a place in our little circle.

When we finished smoking, I said, "Brothers, thank you for all you've done while I scouted for General Crook. Most of the Chiricahuas are back on the reservations, and there will be a time of peace before they leave for the Blue Mountains again."

They all nodded and, as if with one voice, said, *"Enjuh."*

They waited for me to speak, the only sounds, children playing, frogs, and insects in the trees and brush, and the soft snap of the fire.

I took a deep breath, almost trembling with excitement, and

said, "On the long walk back, I found the witch's new *hacienda*."

Beela-chezzi's eyes became narrow slits and he asked, "Are you sure it's his *hacienda*? If it's his place, show us, and we'll help you kill him. We've all waited a long time for this."

"I'm certain it is Sangre del Diablo's *hacienda*. Listen, about eight fingers above the horizon run-time from the springs at Carretas up the canyon that splits off from Higueros Canyon where the Río Carretas runs, my friend Much Water told me he saw a strange *hacienda*, and he watched it for a time with his *be'idest'iné*. He saw Indians, Comanches, and *pistoleros* among them working around a corral. He saw big hunting birds, an eagle, hawks, and an owl, with covers on their heads, roosting on crosspieces across the tops of posts in the ground. He told me this when we camped at the springs at Carretas. Early the next morning, I rode the trail Much Water said he rode and watched the *hacienda* he described with the *Shináá Cho*. I saw the posts for the birds he described, but there were no birds. I saw Comanches around the place. I waited, and then I saw Sangre del Diablo with a golden eagle on his arm go to one of the posts. I almost shot him, but feared if I did the Comanches would come after me, attack the Chiricahuas, and scatter them. The expedition to bring them back would fail. I decided to wait. I tell you, this *hacienda* is where Sangre del Diablo has returned to the land of the *Nakai-yes*."

My brothers all leaned toward me, listening. Kah said, "You have a plan?"

I reached behind me and tossed an *Indah* flour sack in front of them. It landed with a little puff of dust and lay there lumpy and unmoving. They leaned back from it and frowned as though it might have snakes. I laughed and said, "Nothing is inside that will hurt you. Ish-kay-neh, show us what is inside."

The boy didn't want to touch it, but clenching his teeth, he crabbed over to it, pulled the drawstring, reached inside, and brought out a string of bright red chile peppers to hold up in the fire's yellow light. They all turned their heads to look at me as if they thought the Mountain Spirits had made me crazy.

Kah said, "These peppers are your plan? The light behind your eyes is no more. I knew something was wrong when you rode off for the scouts."

I said, "Listen to me first. If you still think I'm crazy, tie me up and take me to the agency. Kitsizil Lichoo' and I often sat together on cliff's edges at Juh's stronghold in the evenings, smoked to the four directions, and watched the light change over the mountains while I healed from the bullet wound Sangre del Diablo gave me. We told each other stories of our fathers and raids we made. He told me a story about how only a handful of harvests earlier, some of Juh's *Nednhi* women and children went collecting mescal and other foods down on the *llano*. They were attacked and taken captive. *Nakai-yes* sold them as slaves to work in mines to the south.

The *Nednhi* and *Bedonkohe*, led by Juh and Geronimo, searched and found them being worked to death at a *pesh-lickoyee* (silver) mine near a village. They looked in bad shape because they refused to eat. They wanted to die if they had to stay slaves. The *Nednhi* and *Bedonkohe* watched the village for a while and learned that, every seven days, the *Nakai-yes* all went in this special building together and watched a brown robe make a ceremony. While this went on, the *Nakai-yes* left only a guard or two at the place where the slaves were locked up every day after their work."

Beela-chezzi crossed his arms and smiled. "I remember this story, and now I understand what you intend to do. These other two have not heard it. Tell them what happened."

Up on the ridge, a coyote called his brothers, who answered him from another ridge. I thought, *Coyote waits, witch. Soon we come.*

229

"The *Nednhi* and *Bedonkohe* waited until a day came when the village gathered inside the place of the black robes. Then they quietly killed the guards next to the place of slaves and blocked the doors to the house of the brown robes. Geronimo's brother, Fun, climbed on the roof of the place the brown robes used to make ceremonies. He had cut a hole there the night before. He had a mixture of chopped up chiles, wood shavings, and *ocote* (pinesap) that he lighted and then dropped in the hole, which he covered with a blanket, to keep the smoke trapped inside. Smoke from burning chile will kill you if you breathe too much. The *Nednhi* and *Bedonkohe* covered up all the windows to the place. The *Nakai-yes* begged and screamed for the doors to open while they coughed and choked and gagged as the smoke grew thicker. After a while, the *Nednhi* and *Bedonkohe* heard the *Nakai-yes* no more. The *Nednhi* and *Bedonkohe* freed their women and children, and the warriors started landslides that rolled down the sides of the canyon burying the village. Kitsizil Lichoo' said they had a big celebration when they all came back. The *Nednhi* and *Bedonkohe* still tell this story around their fires.

"I think we use chiles to make smoke in the *hacienda* of Sangre del Diablo and his Comanches. If they have even a little in their face they will be blind and in a hurry to run from the smoke. We kill them, every one, when they come out. I have spoken to our friend, Rufus Pike, and he wants to come with us. He has a good eye for targets with his big thunder gun. He alone can kill many Comanches."

I opened the blanket beside me and gave the rifles I took as booty to Kah and Beela-chezzi and a revolver to Ish-kay-neh. They gripped and stared at them with boyish delight. Their weapons needed much work to shoot right, and no *Indah* would do that for an Apache. The revolver was Ish-kay-neh's first gun, and he held it like an egg.

"I have bullets for those weapons, and you, too, will kill many Comanches. I will blind and send Sangre del Diablo to the Happy Land as I have promised *Ussen*. What do you tell me? Will you help me end this witch who killed our fathers and mothers, brothers and sisters, and sold their hair?"

Their eyes glittered in the firelight as they all leaned in to listen to my words. The boy, Ish-kay-neh, was the most excited, and he practically shouted, "Yellow Boy, we'll help! The witch will go blind to the Happy Land, and his Comanches will be no more."

We shook our fists and yelled, *"Enjuh!"*

The women looked up from their baskets and smiled. The children stopped their play, listening for more, and when none came, began their games again.

Beela-chezzi, Kah, and I spoke together alone later that night. I said, "We need to give Ish-kay-neh a new name so he can be done with his childhood, and I want to count this trip as his fourth and last in apprenticeship raids with warriors. He did well and acted as a warrior when we took the women and little ones from the Blue Coats, when we outfoxed the Chiricahua wolves at the rancho of Rufus Pike, and when we returned to Mescalero. This raid we'll go on to kill the witch may be the last we can do now that we no longer fight the Blue Coats and *Indah*. I say, if he does well as an apprentice on this raid, he will have been on four raids and he should become a warrior and be treated like one of us."

Beela-chezzi stroked his chin with the thumb and forefinger of his right hand and stared into the fire. Kah crossed his arms and stared at the milky river of stars above us. Beela-chezzi looked at Kah and then me and nodded.

"Ummph. You speak true. I have trained Ish-kay-neh in warrior skills and watched him through the times of which you

231

speak. He has strength. He learns well and fast. I agree with you. Let this raid count as his fourth apprenticeship ride."

Beela-chezzi and I looked at Kah who smiled, shrugged his shoulders, and said, "I, too, think the boy is ready. What name shall we give him?"

I said, "I waited a long time for my name. Maybe the *Nakai-yes* will name him if he becomes a fierce warrior, but I think, Yibá (He Waits for Him) is a good name. It says he waited like a good hunter for his name to come."

Beela-chezzi and Kah nodded. Beela-chezzi said, "Yellow Boy makes a good name for Ish-kay-neh. Before we leave, let's hold a feast and give it to him for all to hear."

Kah nodded. "That will be a good time, a good thing. Ish-kay-neh will like his new name."

CHAPTER 30
THE TRAIL TO CARRETAS

We took a week to get ready for our attack against Sangre del Diablo. Yibá took delight in his new name and was humbled that we respected him enough to use this ride as his last apprentice raid. I used two boxes of cartridges teaching him how to load, aim, and shoot his new revolver. He needed many more days of practice, days we didn't have, to become accurate and deadly with it. I told him he could carry it, but to be sure and carry, like the rest of us, his bow. Up close, an expert, as we were, with a bow and arrow was as deadly as a man with a gun.

We spoke with our women and told them what we planned. They smiled and said this time they knew the witch would die. They began making sacks of trail food for us and practicing the traditions they followed when we were on the war trail, such as stacking their woodpiles in a certain way and praying twice a day.

I rode to the agency and found my policeman friend, Chawnclizzay, who had taught me much. I asked him to keep an eye on our women and children. He said I honored him by asking him to do this. I gave him one of my Chiricahua revolvers to show my gratitude for his help.

Our dances done and feasting complete, the moon barely a dim glow behind the mountains, we left our women and children and disappeared into the darkness. We traveled at night and took the shortest trails, determined to avoid *Indah* and Blue Coats. We crossed the reservation ridges to the Tularosa wagon road, and keeping a fast pace in the moonlight, ate up the distance. We pushed our ponies that first night, making the Jarilla Mountains before sunrise, and resting at the same little spring we'd used during the escape from Mescalero when the Blue Coats took over the reservation and sent their Chiricahua scouts after us. We kept watch across our back trail and the open range as the dawn drove away the night, while Yibá, as the warrior apprentice, took care of the horses and made a hot meal. Soon we would not be willing to risk a small fire.

It was the Season of Large Leaves and very hot in the basin during daytime. The only things showing green on the *llano* were the creosote bushes and mesquite, and these were beginning to wilt, lose leaves, or turn brown from lack of water.

Water in the desert tanks was low, and the springs were mere seeps, all waiting for the rains to come near the beginning of the Season of Large Fruit. Soon our women and children would cut mescal bulbs from under the yucca plants, and bake them in big, deep pits under a cover of leaves and dirt for three or four days. The heat for baking came from burning coals covered with rocks under leaves lining the pit bottoms. When done, the baked mescal tasted sweet and sticky like *Indah* molasses smoked by a fire, and we all ate too much. The women dried and cut the leftovers into slabs that supplied us enough food to last through the Ghost Face Season, even with game scarce. We watched for places where the mescal was plentiful so we could bring the women to it when we returned from our raid against the witch.

From the Jarillas we studied the *llano* as far as *Shináá Cho* let us see into the far, gray air, but we saw no sign of *Indah* or Blue Coats. Smoke did not even rise out ranch house chimneys close to the tall, rough, orange and brown mountains the *Indah* called Organ. The day looked peaceful, but we took no chances. We divided times to keep watch between us, and those not keeping watch slept in the shadows of cliff shelves near the spring where it was cool. As the ending day fell into the west, we all got up and readied our ponies to ride. Since Rufus Pike's rancho was only about half as far as what we had ridden the night before, it would be an easy trot for the ponies to make Rufus's rancho before he got up to run for the little house by the corral.

Out on the *llano*, the night was clear and cold, the moon bright, and the trail clear all the way to the springs where we had waited for the Chiricahua wolves chasing us after the Blue Coats took over the reservation. We rested the ponies there and then rode over the pass Rufus called Baylor and on down the wagon road running on the west side of the Organs to Rufus's rancho.

Our ponies walked into the bare place in front of Rufus's ranch house. The stars showed it would be awhile before Rufus opened his door to run for the little house. We rode on back to the pasture where the People had stayed near the big pool of water Rufus had made for his cattle by damming up a spring flowing into an arroyo. We unsaddled, rubbed down our ponies, and put hobbles on them so they wouldn't wander far. We bathed and then walked back to the ranch house to wait on Rufus. A light touch of gray and a few scattered pools of yellow light began to form in the valley.

The bed Rufus used creaked inside as he sat up and coughed. A match popped into flame, and an oil lantern filled the house with smoky, yellow light. Rufus pulled the latch on the door and pushed it, squeaking and complaining, open. He stuck his head out the doorway and grinned.

"Howdy, boys. Let me take my mornin' walk, and I'll whomp us up somethin' to eat soon as I git back." He came out the door in the long red pants he called long johns, and he wore his old campaign hat and mule-ear boots. He had that smell of horse and sweat the *Indah* have when they don't wash for a long time. I was glad I was upwind of him.

We grinned, watching him trot off. I called after him, "Rufus, we surprise you many times with early visits. Why you no surprised now?"

"I's awake, listenin', when you boys rode out to the pasture. A big cat's been after my calves. Figured it must be you or yore People, and you'd scare off the cat and let me git a little snooze 'fore I had to git up."

He reached the little house, stepped in, and pulled the door closed. We waited.

While we ate, I told Rufus what we planned, and, his eyes glittering, he said, "Well, I'm a comin', too. I reckon you'n use my ol' thunder boomer to chop down a few Comanches, can't ya?"

"Maybe you come with us?"

"Couldn't be kept away. When ya leavin'?"

"Tonight we go. Branigan give paper to leave reservation for two moons. Nine suns gone already while we make ready and ride here."

Rufus scraped the last spoonful of beans from his pie pan plate, filled his face, chewed like a happy cow with calf, then winked and said, "Get some rest, boys. Me an' my ol' gray mule'll be ready."

We rode away from Rufus's ranch house when the sun was low in the west, filling the sky with brilliant reds fading to oranges and purples. We crossed the Río Grande at a cattle crossing south of Mesilla village and followed the great river south, staying in the moonlit shadows of the bosque, following nearly the same trail we had followed to Juh's stronghold. Beela-chezzi had the best memory of the trail in Mexico and took the lead as we crossed the border into the land of the *Nakai-yes*.

We were careful to pace the horses and not wear them out

with too fast a gallop or too little water, stopping to rest them when we could two or three times a night near a water source. We continued to ride at night and rest in the heat of the day. When we arose, we waited for the dark and watched for long dust streamers at dusk, a sure sign of the movement of men and an indication of a direction we didn't want to go.

It was strange for us to ride with an *Indah*, and I often caught my brothers watching Rufus. I'm sure they were wondering if an old *Indah* man on a mule, no doubt an honest friend, could keep up with them. But Rufus stayed with us, chewing his tobacco and spitting enough to leave an easy trail to follow across the tops of creosote bushes.

Rufus took a liking to Yibá, and one dawn, he showed him how to load and aim his big buffalo gun. He promised Yibá he could shoot it when we got to a place where the sound wouldn't give us away. I saw Kah and Beela-chezzi watching them, and I knew they wished that they, too, could feel the power of the old thunder boomer in their hands. Yibá told me that Rufus's offer made him want to dance. But he was mature enough to keep his enthusiasm under control and do the job of an apprentice on the war trail. After Rufus made Yibá the shooting offer, Kah and Beela-chezzi became much friendlier toward Rufus.

After two nights of riding west across the rough *llano* south of the border, passing north of Janos, we crossed the Río Janos and soon reached the Río Carretas, which was then not much more than damp sand in a narrow arroyo. Following the Río Carretas, we drew close to Carretas and stayed alert and careful to avoid discovery by a *Nakai-yi* peon or a free-ranging Comanche staying in the *hacienda* of Sangre del Diablo. We found a wagon road toward the springs at Carretas and mixed our tracks in with others to avoid letting the rest of the countryside know new ponies were in the mountains.

The night was more than half-gone as we rode up Higueros

Canyon past the springs where Crook and his scouts stopped for the Chiricahuas to camp nearly two moons earlier. We stopped at the springs and rested the horses before riding on up the canyon and then taking the branch that led to the witch's *hacienda*. I wanted to find a place where we could hide and study the *hacienda* in the daylight in order to pick the best places where we could fire down on hiding Comanches.

Half the moon hid behind the mountains, its shadows growing long, and the stars showed we were not far from dawn. We came to another canyon branch and saw the dark outlines of the *hacienda* and a barn nearby on the top of a low-lying ridge, where I had seen horses and cattle in separate corrals while scouting for General Crook.

The south slope of the canyon was not steep and had thick juniper and piñon cover. We climbed it and stopped at about the same height as the *hacienda,* about three hundred yards away. The air carried the smell of pine, and the spot was warmer than the canyon bottom. Yibá found a place out of sight from the *hacienda,* where there was plenty of grass, to hide and hobble the horses and Rufus's mule. We all rolled out our blankets under low piñon branches in the darkest shadows to sleep a little before the sun came.

CHAPTER 31
ALL ARE GONE

Droplets of light fell through the thick piñon branches over us and filled the shadows with bright puddles of sunlight. I opened one eye, saw Beela-chezzi use his *be'idest'iné* to study the *hacienda*, lower it, and slowly shake his head. The others still slept, wrapped in their blankets, in the heavy shadows.

"What did you see?"

"Nothing. I saw nothing at all. The witch and his Comanches, all are gone."

Bitter bile filled my throat. The witch had escaped once more? I sat up, snapped out the *Shináá Cho*, and scanned the *hacienda*, the corrals, and the barn. The posts with crosspieces where I had seen the big hunting birds were still there, but no birds. The corrals were empty, and around the *hacienda* there were no signs of life, no smoke from fires, no animals of any kind, nothing.

Sleep left the others, too. They stretched and studied the *hacienda*. I looked over at Rufus, who raised his brows and shrugged. I said to him, "I'm going over there. Shoot anyone who comes near me."

He nodded, lifted the long-barreled, heavy Sharps rifle out of his blankets, and pulled the big side-hammer to safety. I pulled the Henry out of my blankets, levered a cartridge into its breech, and let the hammer down to its safety position. Walking and sliding in grass and piñon needles, but staying out of sight from the *hacienda*, I worked my way to the canyon floor.

The wagon road up to the *hacienda* was an easy climb to the top, with three or four switchbacks, but it made it hard for me to stay out of sight. I stayed in the piñons close to the road as I ran from the shadows of one tree to the next. I stayed low in case hidden guards at the top watched the road. In the shadows of a piñon at the top of a ridge, I waited, studying every window and wall around the *hacienda* and the barns and corrals off to one side. Truly, nothing lived there now. I left my hiding place and began to look closely at the *hacienda* and its grounds.

Many tracks, at least four or five suns old, led down from the *hacienda*, but none up. The fine, brown caliche dust showed signs of no more than twenty mounted riders and maybe twice that many ponies. I saw one distinct set of tracks made by *pesh líí'beshkee'é* (iron horseshoes); the rest of the pony tracks were just shallow holes made by hooves covered in rawhide.

At the *hacienda* walls, I felt evil spirits hovering in the light wind blowing through the place. I cocked the Henry and walked through the open gates. Cold charcoal lay gray and black in the big circle of black rocks surrounding the remains of an old fire at the center of the compound. A tall post with a crosspiece, like the one I had been hung on at the witch's *hacienda* near Casas Grandes, stood stinking and streaked with dry, black bloodstains near the old fire.

Something drew my eyes from the post back to the circle of rocks. Prickles grew on the back of my neck as I realized pieces of a burned skull and the outline of partially burned bones forming a skeleton lay in the ashes. I wanted to run out the gates and down the hill far, far away from there, but I forced myself to stay and see it all, hoping I might find some clue to where the witch had vanished.

A breeze pushed through the compound, carrying the smell of gourd flowers and rotting meat, as I walked through empty rooms one by one. I found broken whiskey bottles and clay pots, empty cans with pictures of fruits and vegetables, pieces of broken harness leather and frayed rope, a room with bloodstains on the floor, and a broken knife. Empty rifle cartridges lay scattered throughout the rooms, but nothing else; no chairs or tables or cooking pots, nothing. I had never seen a place so empty of life.

When I had watched this place two moons earlier, the barn and corrals held many horses and longhorn cows. The depth and scatter of their droppings showed that my eyes had not deceived me. A big pile of fresh bones, bits of meat and gristle rotting and making the pile stink like a carcass under big black birds, bleached in the sun behind the big barn. The bone pile said the witch had much dried and jerked meat, evidence he'd planned a long trip. I saw nothing of wagons or buggies, not even any rope or harness chains. I walked back down the ridge following the same path I used coming up, careful not to leave tracks.

When I returned, Yibá brought the water sacks and trail food, and we all sat in a circle to eat. The others asked many questions about what I had seen and what I thought we should we do. I told them of the lifelessness of the place, that it just lay in the bright sunlight, stinking like a dead body, looking like the burned skeleton in the fire's ashes.

When we finished eating, I lighted one of my black *cigarros*, smoked to the four directions, and passed it around the circle.

After finishing the *cigarro*, I said, "Now we must decide what we do."

Kah crossed his arms and stared across the canyon at the empty *hacienda* and said, "The witch is not here? *Ussen* has saved him again? It must mean it's not for us to take our revenge against him. Let's leave this place of evil and return to the land of the *Nakai-yes* no more."

Beela-chezzi frowned and looked at Rufus and then me. I

wanted to frown, too, but kept my face a fixed mask. Rufus cut a chew, rolled his shoulders, and said nothing as he studied Kah through the dust-coated lenses that rode on his nose. Yibá said nothing. As an apprentice, his job was to listen to the warriors and learn, but his eyes showed that he feared we all thought as Kah did.

I said, "This witch has now escaped our vengeance three times. Twice, I nearly killed him. His Power is great, but *Ussen* didn't give me the Power to send him blind to the Happy Land and then save him when we fought. *Ussen* gave you, Kah, Power to save me in my time of great need after the witch nearly killed me. *Ussen* gave me Power, and I vowed to use it.

"Every time we fail or lose, the test is not to quit, but to keep on until we win. This witch must die. I will kill him. If you don't believe this, then return to the reservation. I won't hold it against you. What's your word, Beela-chezzi? Speak."

Beela-chezzi nodded and said, "Yellow Boy speaks true. We may not find the witch before we return to the reservation, but we must try and try again until either we kill him or he kills us. Our will not to quit is *Ussen*'s measure of our strength."

I looked at Rufus, who spat his brown juice to his right side, and said, "I ain't got much say in what ya'll oughter do. I'm kinda like ol' Yibá there, just along for the ride and to help ya if I can. But let me tell ya this, boys. I been around since yore daddies was Yibá's age. If that damned Mex-Comanch mongrel had killed and scalped any of their people, they woulda rid after him till he was a havin' his bald brain roasted over a hot fire and steam's a blowin' out his ears before they sent him to the Happy Land blind and chokin' on his private parts."

Beela-chezzi's eyes filled with the same fire that filled mine. I wanted to jump up and yell for us to find Sangre del Diablo and do to him as Rufus said our fathers would have. But I held back and waited for Kah to speak.

Kah nodded, fire also filling his eyes.

"I haven't spoken as a true warrior. My woman carries our first child. It will never be in danger from this witch. I'm willing to ride any desert, climb any mountain, to help you send him blind to the Happy Land."

The word came from our mouths in a shout. *"Enjuh!"*

Kah said, "How will we find the witch, Yellow Boy?"

I looked out across the canyon to the empty *hacienda* and the words flowed without me even having to think about them. "The witch hunts Apaches for scalp money. Many Apaches go back to San Carlos and Fort Apache with General Crook. Not many left for him to kill and scalp. A few still stay hidden in camps in the mountains around us, and sometimes he even raids the *Nakai-yi* villages to take their hair and claim it is Apache. Juh did not return to San Carlos, and Geronimo still raids for horses and cattle here in the land of the *Nakai-yes* before he goes back to the reservation. Juh's son, Kitsizil Lichoo', planned to make a camp with a few warriors from Elias's camp in the mountains north of here, and the camp of Elias is to the south of where we sit now. There are several other camps we haven't seen.

"I think the witch plans to wipe out the Apache camps, as he did our people, and he knows the place where Elias camps because the two Comanches, who escaped with the witch and that we later killed, knew where it was. I think he rides for the camp of Elias to take scalps. Elias feared the witch would do this and believed lying to us would help the witch and protect his people. He thought wrong, made a bad bargain. I say we go to the camp of Elias as fast as our ponies can get us there. Maybe we will be in time to warn him and ambush the witch. Maybe not, but we move closer to him."

Beela-chezzi, Kah, Rufus, and Yibá nodded their heads.

"Enjuh. We ride."

CHAPTER 32
RÍO PIEDRAS VERDES

We followed the same trail south back into the mountains Crook used to lead the Chiricahuas north to Carretas. John Rope had shown me where the trail to Juh's stronghold crossed the path of the Chiricahuas. I believed that if we rode back to Juh's stronghold trail and then rode for the stronghold, we would find the trail Kitsizil Lichoo' had followed to the camp of Elias. We rode in the daylight, anxious to make fast time and hoping to find the *pesh líí'beshkee'é* (iron horseshoe) mark in the old tracks on the trail, but we didn't see it until we found the trail Kitsizil Lichoo' followed to Elias. Sangre del Diablo must have ridden north and then south around the Sierra del Carcay Mountains to find the trail he knew to Elias's camp, and rode at night to stay out of sight until he was past Juh's stronghold. All this meant he was riding slower and farther than my band, and we might have a chance to get to Elias before he did.

It was a hard ride across the ridges of Crook's Chiricahua trail, but late in the afternoon of our first day out of Carretas, we found the trail to Juh's stronghold. We rode for the stronghold, looking for the trail Kitsizil Lichoo' had followed until, as the sun was hiding behind the western Sierras and setting the sky on fire with reds, oranges, and purples, we found a deep canyon with good water and camped.

After we ate and talked awhile, I sat smoking and cleaning my rifle near the fire when Yibá asked to join me, and I told him I was glad for his company. There were many frogs and insects near the water, and their night sounds made a comforting chorus. Up on the ridge above us Coyote called for his brothers, and Bat darted after insects drawn to the fire.

Yibá stared in the fire and said, "The war trail is a hard one."

I nodded as I finished oiling my rifle. "Yes, a hard one. It's why Apaches train their young from an early age to endure suffering, to be strong, and to outlast their enemies. You see this now?"

"Yes, clearly. I can see I'm with strong warriors on this trail. I am strong but miss my mother and sister. Is this a sign I am weak?"

"You are not weak, Yibá. I miss my wife and child. This trip is the way we protect them. This is a good trip for you to learn all the things a warrior needs to know on the warpath."

"I have learned much. Even your *Indah* friend, Roofoos Peak, teaches me much. Do you think we'll get to the Elias camp before the witch?"

"No. The witch was gone four or five days before we came to his *hacienda*. We can only gain two, maybe three days on him. But, I don't think he'll catch Elias in his camp. Elias knows he'll probably come, so I think Elias has moved to another camping place the witch doesn't know and is watching for him. He has more warriors than the witch, but he won't fight him. He's afraid the witch has the power of demons and will curse his people if they fight. Elias will just stay out of the witch's way."

"Then why do we go to Elias? The witch will have come and gone. There's nothing we can do."

I shook my head. "There's much we can learn. There are only two trails into the canyon camp of Elias. We've gained two or three days on the witch. If he stays a day at the old Elias camp, we'll gain another. We'll have a fresh *pesh líí'beshkee'é* trail to follow when he leaves Elias's camp. If he comes back down the trail, we'll follow and can ambush him. If he takes the other trail out of Elias's camp, we'll find Elias and learn where the witch is heading. Elias watches him come and go. Elias knows."

Yibá nodded and stared into the fire while we listened to the frogs' and insects' songs and the water burbling in the stream. After a while, he said, "A personal question for Yellow Boy?"

"Speak. I'll answer."

Yibá looked at me as a child might when asking his father or mother for something from the sweet jar at Blazer's store. "If I do well on this raid, you and the others have said I will be welcomed as a warrior. In a year or two, I'll have enough ponies for a wife. Soon Moon on the Water will have her *Haheh* and be ready to take a man. Do you think Maria would let Moon accept ponies from me? If Maria accepted my ponies, and if Moon accepted me, we would be brothers."

I had to look at the stars and pretend thought to keep from smiling. "There are many paths in your words. I haven't seen Maria face-to-face since Juanita became my wife. But I know Juanita tells me that Maria thinks good things about all the boys and men now in our camp. How will you get your ponies for Moon? You will need four, maybe five. Moon is a hard worker, pleasant on the eyes, and built for having babies. She'll bring a high price for her mother."

"I'll hunt and trap and maybe work at the sow meal (saw mill) for Blazer, trade up for better ponies, and maybe even gamble a little."

"Be careful of the gambling. You can win big or lose much in the blink of an eye. Who will you ask to stand for you with Maria? I can't look at her."

"I've asked Beela-chezzi. He says he will when the time comes, if I still want him."

"*Enjuh.* Beela-chezzi is a great warrior. He'll do well for you. After Moon has her *Haheh*, dance with her in the round dances, and you'll know soon enough if she's right for you. Give her a

246

good present after you dance, and she'll know you're a strong warrior, worthy of her consideration. Who knows? Perhaps we'll be brothers. It will be a good thing if we are."

The teeth in Yibá's smile were brighter than the moon. "And if we are, will you teach me to shoot?"

I laughed. "I'll teach you even if we are not brothers."

The next day, at the time of shortest shadows, our trail crossed the trail Kitsizil Lichoo' used to lead us to Elias's camp. In the time it takes the sun to travel the width of four fingers across the sky, we found the ridge where we had camped on our rides to Elias's camp. We were less than a day's ride to the camp of Elias, and tracks and other signs showed that twelve to fifteen warriors had camped under the tall trees two or three nights or days earlier. Kah, looking through camp, waved me to come to a thin spot of grass where a little sunlight fell between the tall pine trees. He pointed at a track with his bow and said, "A *pesh lii'beshkee'é* track. Is it the same as you saw at the *hacienda* at Carretas?"

I didn't have to study it. It was exactly the right size and had a minor defect on the inner rim of the *pesh* just like the other track.

I nodded. "Hmmph. The tracks come from the same shoe."

We rode on, but sent Kah in front of us to ride back with warning if the witch and his band were coming back our way. The urge to ride faster on the narrow ledge trails was strong, but not strong enough to overcome being careful. We stopped for the night at dusk on top of a high ridge and made a cold, dry camp back in the trees off the trail in case the witch and his band came our way. After rubbing down and hobbling our ponies to graze the few grassy spots under the tall pine trees, we all sat together for warmth and ate the dried food warriors carry on raids.

Nearly all the day glow was gone when Kah made it to the top of our ridge and paused, trying to see what the trail did going down the other side. Beela-chezzi whistled like a *googé* and Kah turned and rode into the trees where we sat.

He dismounted and, holding his pony's reins, squatted down beside us. Yibá reached for the reins and led the pony to where the others grazed, rubbed him down, and hobbled him for the night.

Kah said, "The boy is a good apprentice. He'll be trustworthy on raids."

He waited until Yibá returned, took a swallow of water, and, smiling, stuck his hand and arm down his long sack of trail food. "The witch passed through Elias's camp, killed no one, but the camp's wickiups had been torn apart, big carry baskets chopped to pieces, tall water jugs broken, and meat drying racks were torn down. My guess is he was looking for food. Elias must have known the witch was coming and left with his people. The witch and his warriors ride on down the trail."

Beela-chezzi grimaced. "Now it becomes a cat-and-mouse game. The witch is in front of us. Unless we can get around him, he can set an ambush and take all our hair when he learns we follow. We must be very careful that he doesn't see, hear, or catch us."

Rufus nodded and spat. "Yes, sir, truer words ain't never been spoke."

The next day, before shadows were shortest, we sat on our ponies on the high ridge above the canyon where Elias's camp had been. I handed my reins to Yibá and asked Rufus to cover me since the range into the village was far too long for all but the best of marksmen with a repeating rifle. I practically ran down the trail into the rancheria and began looking for some sign I might find that would tell me where the witch and his band rode.

As I tried to read the truth of the tracks, an old woman, most of her teeth missing, her old face a *llano* covered with wrinkles, stuck her head out of her hiding place in scrub oak lining the stream banks. When she saw we were Apaches, she came scrambling out of hiding to get close enough to give us a good look over.

"You search for Sangre del Diablo? He's not here. He rode away yesterday. Soon Elias will lead the people back."

"What happened here, Grandmother?"

"You don't ride with Sangre del Diablo and his Comanches?"

"No. I kill witches. Sangre del Diablo must die."

"Yes, yes, he is a witch and must die. Three suns ago, a rider came galloping into our camp and told us an evil demon leading Comanches and *Nakai-yes* was coming. Elias knew this was trouble and told us all to go to the cave downstream and wait until he led us back.

"I'm an old woman. It's too hard for me to walk to the cave. I can disappear as good as any other Apache. I waited here to see this Sangre del Diablo. When he and his warriors came to our camp, he became very angry. He wanted Elias, but Elias had disappeared. Elias is smart like Coyote. It takes a warrior smarter and more skilled than Sangre del Diablo to catch Elias and his people."

I smiled. "Where did this witch go, Grandmother? Did you hear or see anything that might help us find him?"

She giggled, sounding girlish, but showing no more than three or four nearly black teeth in her bare gums. "Oh, yes, I heard him. He stood over there," she said and pointed her shaking, gnarled old fingers at a big boulder near Elias's council place. "He made a big ceremony, standing on that rock to decide what to do. He says his Power tells him to go to another *Indeh* rancheria hidden south of here on the Río Piedras Verdes near a *Nakai-yi* village. He says they can take many scalps and new slaves in both villages. The slaves they can take to Casas Grandes for much *pesh-klitso* (literally, yellow iron—gold). I know this place. We've traded meat for corn and beans there. They're not Apaches, but it is well hidden, and they have good fighters. He'll never find it."

"How far is the rancheria, Grandmother?"

"A day down the trail if a warrior knows the way and rides hard."

CHAPTER 33
SLAVES AND SCALPS

We rode as fast as we dared, but it took us nearly a sun and half the next one to follow the witch's trail to the *Indeh* village on the Río Piedras Verdes. At the time of shortest shadows on the second day, we saw a black, smudgy plume of smoke rising high above the edges of a deep distant canyon until it disappeared in the wind. I knew what we would find under that smoke, for I had seen the work of Sangre del Diablo and his band on my own people, and its memory made my guts clinch like I had eaten bad meat and needed to vomit. I stopped my pony and pulled open the *Shináá Cho*. I could see a second plume, stronger and blacker than the one from the canyon, and maybe eight fingers' ride across the canyon from the first plume. The second plume, I believed, must be from the *Nakai-yi* village.

I scanned the ridges above the twisting canyon and saw no one. The witch's band had to be driving their captives along the river. We could get ahead of him by the next sun if we stuck to the ridges above the river.

By the time we rode down into the river canyon and into the smoking rancheria, the sun had fallen three hand widths from the top of its trail toward the western horizon. The rancheria had been Opata, not Apache. It made no difference to the witch, or to the *Nakai-yes* who paid him, as long as the scalps looked like they had been torn from Apaches. Bodies of men in their prime and the old lay scattered in drying pools of blood turning the sand black amid the debris of lodges reduced to piles of smoking ashes. The men, all shot more than once, lay facedown in the sand or on their backs staring with lifeless eyes at the darkening, turquoise sky, the few surviving their wounds, tortured and gutted, their privates slashed off and stuffed in their mouths. The old ones had their throats cut. All the bodies lay twisted and scalped, but I saw no women or children. Flies gathered in great hoards on the bloody, hairless heads. Great black birds had already begun to feed on some and others, like a gathering thundercloud, wheeled high, darkening the sky, looking for choice meals as the bodies lying in the hot sun out of the shadows of the canyon walls had already started to swell and stink.

I heard Rufus mutter, "Great God! We got to kill those demon bastards, ever damn one of 'em."

Kah and Beela-chezzi sat their horses and stared at the carnage. Killing didn't bother either one of them, but a torturous massacre of grandfathers and grandmothers and the slaughter of their fighting men, all killed for their hair, made the massacre an evil far beyond normal warfare: a witch's evil, something to be despised. Yibá sat his pony, looking sick, as if he had eaten bad meat.

I knew my Mescalero friends would never touch a body, unless it was a relative's. I said to Rufus, "Will you help me gather and burn the bodies? My friends cannot. They fear Ghost Sickness."

He nodded, reaching in his vest pocket for a twist of tobacco. He cut a plug, popped it in his mouth, and started to chew. "Shore, I'll help ya. I seen a pile of wood and some coal oil by a hut over yonder that ought to get a hot fire started. Ghost Sickness ain't never bothered me none. Send yore friends downriver a little way to wash the stink of the day off, and we'll get to work."

As the sun fell behind the jagged horizon, we finished gathering the bodies and turned them into ashes with hot, roaring fires started with the burning oil and wood. The burning bodies smelled worse than those rotting in the sun, and the hot grease from them collected in glistening pools, becoming solid on the thirsty sand as it cooled. At least the ashes of those we burned returned to the land, and the black birds would have to look elsewhere to fill their hunger. *Perhaps,* I thought, *tomorrow if I'm lucky I'll take their revenge on this evil and give the black birds their supper.*

Rufus and I washed in the river and purified ourselves in the smoke of sage we'd found in a basket near a rancheria sweat lodge. Beela-chezzi, Kah, and Yibá waited downstream for us to eat and to talk about attacking the witch's band.

The night chorus of insects and frogs began close to the river in the deep shadows of the canyon. We ate in silence, each lost in his thoughts about the evil he had seen. Beela-chezzi finished his meal and took a long swallow of water from an army canteen Rufus had given him. He rubbed the back of his hand across his wet lips and said, "I studied the tracks out of here while you worked. There are maybe ten Comanches and five *banditos* herding about ten women and maybe fifteen little ones. The oldest cannot be more than ten harvests. It also looks like maybe ten pack animals are loaded with loot and supplies. It's a big crowd to herd down this river. They'll move slow."

Back up the river, we could hear wolves howling and fighting in the rancheria over anything they found to eat. The smell of fresh blood in the sand, charred bones, and melted fat must have been driving them crazy. Beela-chezzi listened to them for a moment, shook his head, and continued.

"With all the women and children, I think the witch will herd them downstream to the *llano* for a trail straight for Casas

Grandes. Just like the old woman at Elias's camp said. Even with the moon, it's too dark to move in that canyon without risking the captives getting hurt, and that would cost them money at the slave market. They'll stop when it's dark and make fires. The canyon walls are so steep the slaves can't get away with two or three guards on either end of the camp. The witch will make his Comanches and *banditos* leave the women alone in order to keep their value in the houses of women or the slave market. They'll have no *fiesta* or whiskey until after they get to Casas Grandes where they can spend their scalp and slave money on supplies, whiskey, and women. The Comanches and *banditos* are three times our number. We must be careful killing these demons, get them in a trap where they can't escape, and kill them, every one."

I nodded and pulled out a *cigarro*. We smoked to the four directions, and then I said, "Beela-chezzi speaks wise words. What does Kah think?"

Kah lay back on his elbows and, looking at the stars, made a face and shook his head. "It is as Beela-chezzi says, we must be careful when we try to kill these demons, or they'll kill us. I want to live to see the child Deer Woman gives me."

Rufus spat, worked his jaws some more, and said, "Beela-chezzi has it about right. The fastest way for that damned witch to git them captives outta here safe is to stay on the river, and they're gonna have to stop at night. We need to ride on the tops of the ridges and keep outta sight while we look for a good, narrow ambush spot down in that there canyon. I 'spect we're gonna have to split up. Two of us got to git down in the canyon behind 'em, and two has to git in front of 'em, and we got to pick a spot where there ain't gonna be much cover for 'em. We oughta figure out where our ambush is gonna be and ride for it. We got to git up on the ridge above the canyon tonight and ride downstream as far as we can in front of 'em so we can ride back toward 'em when they's enough light to find a place for ambushin' 'em."

Beela-chezzi, Kah, and I were all nodding our heads when Rufus finished.

Yibá had our horses and mule watered, fed, and ready to ride. We left the smoldering, stinking rancheria made desolate by Sangre del Diablo, its remains to stay forever in our memories, and the need for vengeance burned in our spirits. Up on the high ridge above us, we followed the canyon rim as far as we could before the dawn came.

We saw and passed around the captives and the witch's fires down in the canyon before the moon was near the top of its trail across the stars. It was very hard to see into the canyon with moonlight shadows covering most of the river. Off to the west clouds had gathered and occasional arrows of lightning flew between them. We rode until the moon was about four hands above the edge of the mountains (about 2 a.m.) and then stopped to rest on a little grassy rise back from the edge of the canyon. The lightning arrows had grown stronger but were so far away we couldn't hear the Wind spirits or Thunder People. We hobbled our horses and mules so they could graze. Kah told us he would keep watch until dawn. We wrapped in our blankets near a thicket of junipers, the pine smell from their sap filling the warm air.

I was tired from the long ride and work of burning the rancheria bodies, but thoughts of the coming day and the destruction and desolation Sangre del Diablo had left in the rancheria kept me awake. I watched the lightning arrows awhile and saw the legs of rain out of clouds walking between them. My mind drifted like a leaf carried by the wind.

And then I lay on the mountaintop, the mountain of my vision, the mountain high above Rufus's lodge. The sky was filled with lightning arrows snapping and crackling and Wind spirits moaning. I heard a voice but not with my ears.

Show the Power I gave you is stronger than that of any witch. Face him first with empty hands. My Power will stand beside you and help you. Let him bring you his hands filled with weapons to kill you. I will make you and your warrior brothers safe. Send him blind to the Happy Land. Do not fear this evil. Wipe it out.

And I saw, as in a dream, a vision in a vision, the witch on a black horse running on white sand by fast-running water as he charged me. There were many faces, many guns behind him, watching, and I stood alone, unafraid, my hands empty, my rifle standing by me. My rifle and I were as one, and the witch was falling and attacking and was no more.

I heard my name called from far away. Light filled my eyes and Kah looked in my face; his hand shook my shoulder.

He said, "Yellow Boy holds his rifle ready to shoot. He has visions? Speak to us."

I said, "*Ussen* is with us. I have seen the day. Let us find the place where the witch will die."

When I returned from my vision, enough light filled the canyon to see features of the river. We began following the ridge trail back toward the witch and his captives as we looked for a place to make an ambush. Off to the southwest, we could see the plumes from the witch's fires rising straight into the cold, bright air until they bent as one over the hills and ridges and drifted toward the rising sun. Beela-chezzi guessed, and we all agreed, that the witch and his captives would be where we could easily see them by the time of shortest shadows. We stayed on top of the ridge above the river looking for the place in my vision. He would ride; I would stand, and he would die.

Not far from where we rested, I saw the place. The walls of the canyon were steep, nearly vertical, on either side of the river, and there was a long, straight stretch of white sand with no trees for cover except for small scrub oaks and an occasional piñon right next to the rising walls of the canyon. I stopped and told my friends the spot I wanted lay below us.

Rufus looked at me, his brows raised in question. He spat a stream of brown juice and said, "They ain't much to hide behind on the stretch of sand, but them trees is gonna make good cover once them demons run. You sure you want this place?"

"This is the place I saw in a vision when we slept before dawn. Beela-chezzi and Kah will stop escapes back upstream. Yibá will stay here with the ponies and shoot when the attack starts. Rufus and I will shoot from downstream. See the little waterfall in the middle of the line of sight along the stretch of sand, and then another that begins about where the river bends north."

I looked at each one before I told them the rest of my vision.

"In my vision, I faced the witch alone with empty hands."

Yibá frowned and shook his head. "Without surprise and facing him alone, the witch will kill you."

Beela-chezzi said, "The boy is right. Our only chance against so many is surprise."

Rufus cut a chew from the tobacco in his vest pocket while he looked at the ground and shook his head. "Yore call to make. I'm ready to die."

Kah sighed. "I'll never see the child Deer Woman brings me."

I waited while they bent their minds to my vision, and then I said, "Wait to shoot until I kill the witch. *Ussen* will bring him to me. The Comanches and *banditos* will see only the struggle between us. They won't realize how exposed they are. Kill as many Comanches and *banditos* as you can as fast as you can when the witch is no more."

Kah and Beela-chezzi nodded, and I knew they believed my

vision came from *Ussen*.

"Try not to kill any captives, but do what you must to wipe out all the Comanches and *banditos*. Don't let one ride away. Today the ghosts of our people find rest at last. When I face the witch, only one of us will walk away.

"Yibá, from this ridge, you'll be able to see them coming a long time before they get down there. Flash me with your mirror down on the river bend there where Rufus and I will wait. One flash means you can see them. Two flashes means use caution. Three flashes means wait to shoot."

Beela-chezzi, Kah, and Yibá looked at me with fire in their eyes. It was a good day to die.

Rufus looked sad and shook his head. "Don't go lettin' that devil do you in, *amigo*. We're all with you."

CHAPTER 34
THE WITCH COMES

The top of the river canyon ridge stood more than two hundred yards above the river. The fastest way down followed a steep wash filled with piñons and scrub oaks and big black boulders made in mountain fire before the time of the grandfathers. Rufus, Beela-chezzi, Kah, and I ran switchbacks from boulder to boulder, tree to tree to as we descended. The light whisper of the river at the ridge top became a steady burbling rumble, and the air grew cool and comfortable as we approached its splashing waterfalls and swirls around boulders scattered along white, sandy banks. It took us four fingers of the sun's trail to reach the river and stand, dirty and beat up, in the cold water drifting past our ankles.

We waded along the river's edge, stepping on big rocks to hide our tracks along a bank of bright, white sand until the river made a sharp turn toward the west with a long stretch of sandy banks practically free of trees and brush where we wanted the ambush. At the turn, and no higher than twenty yards back up the ridge, a jumble of black and brown boulders formed a perfect place for Beela-chezzi and Kah to shoot from behind to stop any escape back up the river. Beela-chezzi and Kah took a quick soak in the river, jumped, shivering, out of the icy water, and climbed up to hide behind their rock wall.

Rufus and I continued to hide our tracks as we waded downstream, working our way around boulders in the waterfalls, each pool where a waterfall ended before the next one began looking like a stair step made for giants. At the end of the stretch of beaches the river made another sharp turn, this time back to the northeast. At that bend Rufus waved good luck, stepped across the river on rocks sticking above swirling water, and climbed into another little jumble of boulders up the far side, about ten yards above the beach. On the near side of the stream, I had found two boulders clumped together that looked like the Rabbit Ears Peaks in the Organ Mountains north of Rufus's *rancho*. Their high points were about my shoulder height. A few other small boulders had nested around them, making perfect cover for looking through the narrow crack between them and shooting upriver.

I sat down on the sand, the boulders at my back, and saw Rufus sitting behind his boulders in the cool shade with his old hat over his eyes. I leaned back, checked my rifle's load, levered a bullet into the chamber, set the safety, and waited, listening to the low rumble of the river across its boulders. Birds whistled and called as they flew and jumped from limb to limb in the brush and trees on the far side. Crows passing high above squawked and cawed at us for disturbing their retreat.

The events on the long trail that brought me to this place on a river high in the Blue Mountains of Chihuahua drifted through my memory like puffs of white clouds across the sky. I remembered the night I was given my Power by *Ussen,* the rage and sorrow I felt when I found my people massacred and scalped, the pleasure and satisfaction Juanita had given me with our life together, and now with our little daughter, Kicking Wren. I thought of my father and He Watches and all they had taught me. I smiled when I realized that one of my teachers was sitting just across the river, ready to help wipe out my enemies.

I picked up a handful of pebbles and flicked them with my thumb to splash one at a time in the swift river current as I thought of Sangre del Diablo, who had tortured and killed my adopted grandfather, He Watches, and had hung me on a cross to die with drying, green rawhide cutting through my joints. I remembered thinking him dead by my hand after he had shot me, as he floated facedown in the great river, leaving a dark, red streamer of blood before he stood and staggered out of the water, somehow finding the strength and will to live, while darkness and dreams filled my eyes.

Now, with the help of *Ussen,* I had another chance to kill this evil witch and make the world smooth again. It had been a long trail, and I was . . .

A bright flash of light fell where I sat. I looked to the top of the ridge where I saw the glint off Yibá's mirror. I waited. There was no second flash. I crawled out of the boulder's shade to find the sun and flashed a golden reflection off my rifle's receiver toward the spot where Kah and Beela-chezzi waited. Beela-chezzi flashed he understood and then flashed twice—caution. I knew they must be able to see or hear the witch's band and their captives approaching. Rufus nodded when I flashed him and raised my eyebrows to ask if he was ready. I flashed once at the top of the ridge to acknowledge Yibá and tell him I understood, and then I crawled behind the boulders to watch the bend in the river upstream and wait for the witch and his captives.

In the span of the sun moving four fingers against the horizon, four Comanches, two on each side of the river, mounted on shining, buckskin ponies, suddenly appeared at the far bend of the river and paused, their long black hair falling from under brown straw hats they had taken from the Opata. They wore white shirts with long sleeves that covered their big, muscular arms and torsos. Canvas pants stuffed in boots protected their legs, and they had bandannas tied loosely around their necks. Even from a short distance, with the exception of the long, black hair, they looked like *vaqueros*. With squinting eyes, they scanned the stretch of sand below them. The two on the left side of the river crossed to join the others because there was no room for a trail on their side, and together, they slowly moved along the white sandy beach toward Rufus and me. Brown, nearly naked children appeared, followed by women in torn blouses and skirts, most barefooted and some with babies in their arms, following the four leaders. Four horsemen were on either side of the group. Each man had a long, slender stick he used to beat any who wandered out of the group or who couldn't keep up. None of the captives appeared tied or roped together. They had learned obedience quickly, for when several pointed toward the river and asked in words I knew must mean they wanted a drink, the leading Comanche shook his head, raised his switch, and no one else asked for water. The group moved on down the bank, stopping by the pool of the first waterfall. Their masters let them sit down to wait and rest.

The witch, with a *bandito* on either side, came around the bend. I had lost memory of how big he was, and I drew back a little when I first saw him. He towered over the men on either side of him and rode with a bandanna tied around his hairless head. Black paint covered his eye sockets. He wore no shirt, but his canvas pants were stuffed in boots like the others, and a shiny repeating rifle, glinting in the sun, lay across the pommel of his saddle that cast myriad glints from silver *conchos*.

He frowned and yelled above the rumble of the fast water, "*Que paso?* What's happening? Why do you stop?"

A horseman in the lead, his face fierce, scowling, eyes painted with black circles like the witch's, perhaps the witch's new *Segundo* (number two), yelled back, "These dogs beg for water."

Sangre del Diablo nodded and said, "We have far to go. I don't want to lose one. Let them drink and rest here."

The riders between the captives and the river turned their

ponies to face the captives, opening a space between them like gates, and motioned them past their horses toward the water with a swing of their long switches. Even with all the horror and abuse they must have seen and endured in the last two days, the little ones yelled with delight as they ran to drink and jump in the water, the women, even ones carrying babies, not far behind.

The witch rode downriver slowly, regally, studying each captive, woman and child, as he passed. Arriving at the four leaders who had dismounted and were loosening cinches to rest their ponies, Sangre del Diablo let his horse, a big black gelding, drink while he twisted in the saddle to look over the canyon and the next bend. He looked directly at the boulders where I waited unmoving, barely breathing, my heart pounding with excitement. His gaze moved from my boulders to the rocks where Rufus, I knew, had his big buffalo rifle sighted on the middle of the witch's chest. Seeing nothing, the witch turned to look back up the river where all his Comanches and *pistoleros* had dismounted to rest and water their horses and the captives rested. The *banditos* who had ridden beside the witch each led five pack animals, and moved to let their ponies and the pack animals drink.

Looking through the crack between the rabbit ears boulder, I studied Sangre del Diablo and saw the bullet scar on his chest where I shot him as he crossed the great river. If my shot had been even half a finger length lower, he would never have staggered out of the great river and walked away. Now *Ussen* had delivered him to me again. Time for deliverance was at hand. I was ready. My thumping heartbeat slowed, and my spirit grew peaceful. This day Sangre del Diablo, so calm, so evil, so deserving to die a long, hard death, would ride into forever darkness in the Happy Land of the grandfathers. I knew it would be so. I had seen it in a dream.

I waited until the image in my dreams became real before I

stepped to the side of the boulders to become visible to the evil I had longed to confront the last three years of my life. I left my rifle, cocked and ready, hidden from view behind the boulder. I faced the witch alone with only the Power *Ussen* had given me, my hands empty, obedient to the voice in my dream. I wanted to face the murderer of our People, my father and grandfather. I wanted to put out the fire of hate and revenge that burned in my guts. The witch turned the gelding toward the bend in the river where I waited, and I could tell I filled his eyes like some unexpected vision.

He stared at me a few seconds as if trying to decide if I were real or a vision. I crossed my arms and stared at his eyes in the middle of the black shadows of his painted skull sockets. He shook his head as if coming out of a dream, and from deep in his belly howled like the wolf I had heard when I chased him across the *llano* to the great river. Comanche warriors, *banditos*, and captives looked at him in terror, and then they saw me. Children stopped their play and stared. Women covered their mouths with their hands, certain they were about to see another man murdered. Comanches and *banditos* dropped the reins of their horses and cocked their rifles and pistols. The canyon became deathly still except for the steady swish and rumble of the river flowing across the waterfalls.

Sangre del Diablo laughed, a great booming sound of delight, and yelled, "Apache! The spirits have blown you into my hands. I'll drink your blood and eat your heart to honor your courage. Warriors! This Apache is mine." The Comanches and *pistoleros* started grinning, looked at each other, and relaxed as they lowered their weapons.

Sangre del Diablo tossed his rifle aside, and pulled from behind his saddle cantle a war club made from a smooth river stone the size of two of his great fists stacked together and fixed with sinew and rawhide to the big jawbone of a mule. He swing the club over his head and jerked back on the reins, making the big black rear up before he charged down the sandy beach toward me. Howling like a wolf, the witch swung the club effortlessly in big looping arcs made by the stretch of his immense arm. He must have thought I was there for no other reason than to give him the honor of him killing me. *Fool,* I thought, *don't you understand* Ussen *has sent me to claim you. Today you go to the Happy Land.*

The distance closed between us in blurred fury as the black's pounding hooves threw puffs of sand high in the air. I didn't move. The Comanches began to shake their rifles and scream, "*Hoya!* Kill him now, Chief of Witches!" The *Nakai-yi banditos* stared unbelieving at me.

Twenty yards, fifteen yards, the swooping deadly arc of the war club began. He came on, the big black running flat out. Howling and slashing the air with his war club, Sangre del Diablo raised up in his stirrups and leaned toward me as he cocked his war club arm for a nice smooth swing that would burst my head like an egg cracked against a cooking pot. Five yards and the war club began to fall fast, with all the power in his great arm behind it. I dodged behind the boulders, the Henry rifle filling my hands as if it had never left. I heard the swish of air from the war club's arc even in the heaving wind and pounding hooves of the big black.

Time seemed to slow like a leaf drifting on wind as the witch thundered past. The Henry came up in flame and thunder, sending a bullet into the black's brain. Its front knees buckled and it began to roll forward. The witch tried but failed to pull his feet from the stirrups to jump free. The black rolled over the top of him and collapsed on its right side, pinning the witch's leg to the ground.

I ran forward to finish him, but with his great strength he braced his free foot against the saddle, pushed free, and rolled to his knees. I brought the Henry up to fire. His war club, faster than a striking rattlesnake as he swung wildly, caught the end of the Henry's barrel with such power that it jerked the rifle out of my hands and sent it spinning, still cocked, to land to one side of and behind the witch. Snarling in fury he pulled the great knife he carried, the kind the *Indah* call *Bowie,* and staggered to his feet as he swung the club and knife back and forth like snakes trying to lull birds into a death trance.

I backed away and pulled my own knife, the one He Watches had given me many harvests before. The witch thrust his knife and swung the club in a backstroke. I dodged his knife and leaned back from the club. My knife slashed his forearm holding the club as it swooshed past my face. The cut made his hand relax and the war club flew out of his grasp as his knife stabbed the air again past my belly.

I stepped back to avoid another thrust at my belly, and my heel slid on a smooth, moss-covered rock. Off balance, I staggered backwards. The witch, very fast for a big man, flew on top of me before I could raise my knife. We hit the sand hard, his blade nipping the side of my ear as he stabbed down. He grabbed for my throat with his free hand as he pushed himself up to stab at me again.

Ussen filled me with a strength I have never known before. I knocked his reaching hand away and jabbed my free thumb in his left eye as his big blade came up. Its downward swing for the middle of my head slowed. He bellowed in agony. I twisted to one side as his blade stabbed again with all his power into the sand by my ear. I jammed his jaw up with the palm of my hand and drove He Watches's blade deep into the muscles of his neck. A bright red shower of blood spewed over us. He rolled to his back, his left hand over his empty eye socket, blood covering his chest and throat, as he reached for He Watches's knife.

The Comanches who had been screaming for my death watched in silence as I rolled to my knees and crawled to pick up the Henry. It filled my hand, and I turned and raised to my knees in time to see Sangre del Diablo, an eye gone, blood streaming and squirting in a fountain from his neck, standing with He Watches's blade in his right hand. He roared like a great bear and staggered toward me.

The Henry thundered, and the witch's head jerked back, his right eye disappearing in a spray of blood and brains out the back of his head. Before he fell, the Henry sent a bullet into the bloody eye socket already empty. Sangre del Diablo flopped on his back, empty eye sockets staring at the deep blue above us, his devil's blood turning the sand around him black.

I thought, *witch, today Ussen has taken your eyes and your life, but you escape my revenge too easy.*

Screaming in fury, the leader of the front four, the *Segundo*, threw his rifle to his shoulder and fired. A stripe of burning fire whipped across my back. In the same instant Rufus's buffalo gun boomed. The *Segundo's* head snapped back as if it had been hit with the witch's club, and he staggered and fell facedown in the river with half the back of his skull gone.

The canyon filled with fury; captives screamed and hid behind boulders in the water. I ran for the boulders I had first hidden behind. The Comanche and *bandito* horses thundered back upstream, tearing their reins from the hands of their dismounted riders, who fired wildly into the brush and canyon sides. Rufus's buffalo gun boomed over the sharp cracks of the Comanche repeating rifles. One of his bullets slammed into a packhorse leader between his shoulder blades as he turned to run back upriver. Rufus was nearly as fast loading his Sharps as I was with the Henry, and he killed the second packhorse leader before he had run five yards beyond the first.

The Comanches, trying to find cover and shoot at the same

time, were easy targets, and I killed the rest of the front four. The side riders ran for cover behind boulders in the river or in scattered bits of brush on the sides of the canyon. They made the mistake of facing Rufus and me, and were killed by Kah and Beela-chezzi. Not a Comanche or a *bandito* escaped.

CHAPTER 35
THE WORLD IS SMOOTH AGAIN

Kah and Beela-chezzi climbed down to the river. As they walked down the bank, checking each body, ready to cut a throat if the Comanche or *bandito* was still alive, they brought the horses that had tried to run upstream, led them to brush growing against the canyon wall, and tied them there. The captives, saying nothing, the children still wide-eyed and trembling, the women solemn, uncertain who we were and what we would do with them, waded out of the river and sat down on the sand in the middle of the bank to look at the bodies of their captors and to watch us. It wasn't long before the younger children began to play in the sand.

Rufus climbed out from behind his boulders and worked his way across the river. The quiet—no birds singing, no babies crying, no guns firing, no men groaning in the grip of death as they entered the Happy Land of the grandfathers—told its own story of what had happened here on the Río Piedras Verdes. The sun burned straight down in the time of shortest shadows and filled the canyon with bright light.

From the ridge top Yibá had watched me face Sangre del Diablo and had seen how I had killed him. As soon as the witch died, Yibá had begun the ride to bring us our ponies by riding along the ridge's edge south and then down a steep canyon trail off the ridge leading to the river.

I checked the bodies of the Comanches I'd killed and then walked back to stand next to the remains of Sangre del Diablo, truly a witch of power. Staring at the gore on the bloodstained sand, I thought, *It is not enough.* My rage flared again, as I used my knife to cut off the witch's clothes. My thought was to cut off his genitals and stuff them into his mouth as he had done to my father, but then I remembered what I'd told Kah years ago when he would have mutilated the Indah scouts that had captured him during our first test of manhood: "My father is a great warrior, and he says he never cut a dead body. It is not good. There are better ways to make the living suffer and humiliate the dead."

I left Sangre del Diablo naked for the vultures and wolves to claim, but suddenly, one of the captive women screamed in rage. She came out of the water, a crying baby tied to her back, her face covered with deep, ugly bruises and one eye swollen shut, wading up the bank, holding high a big, round stone the size of her head. She ran to the body of Sangre del Diablo and swung the stone down with all her might into what was left of his head. As it flew apart, crushed like a ripe melon, she screamed, "For my People, witch!"

I considered the evil he had done, all the Apaches and those from other tribes he had scalped, all the men he had hung on crosses, all the poisons he had made to make men die in agony, all who had had their eyes torn out and killed by his trained *búh* (owl). At last, his end had come by He Watches's blade and my rifle, and a woman had mutilated him. Truly *Ussen* must have a scale in the stars that weighs our fortunes to make them balance.

I heard Rufus's boots crunching the sand. He stood beside me, spat a brown stream on the bloody mess of brain and bone that was once the witch's head, and said, "Just wish that one had died 'fore all the grief he caused ever'body that got within ten mile of him. Son, you amazed me th' way ya killed him. I almost killed him, but decided it had to be yore vict'ry. I'm real proud of ya. You're mighty lucky that's just a scratch across yore back."

I nodded. "*Ussen* made the world smooth again today."

Kah and Beela-chezzi joined us. Beela-chezzi said, "I thought the witch and then, for a heartbeat, the *Segundo* had killed you, but I see it's nothing worse than stripes we took in learning to be warriors. I have grease and herbs that will stop it from becoming red and hot. Truly, Yellow Boy is a Killer of Witches, and this day he has killed a very bad one. Your courage is great, grandson. Live long. What shall we do with the captives? It's still a long walk to Casas Grandes."

"I'll speak with them, and then we'll smoke and decide what to do. Take all the weapons and bullets from the Comanches you can find. We can use them all. Leave the bodies. The black birds, wolves, and coyotes will have their fill. The first flood that comes will wash away what's left of them. All will be gone. Then the land will be free of them and will no more taste their bitterness."

I approached the women and children, who were sitting in the middle of the bank squinting at us in the bright, fiery light. They watched me with sad, but unafraid, eyes. I looked over each one for a moment, and then spoke so they all heard me above the splash and swirl of the river.

"Does anyone here speak the words of the *Nakai-yes* or the Apache?"

A young woman, beginning to grow big with a child, stood and said, "I can speak the words of the *Nakai-yes*."

I motioned to her and we walked to boulders near the canyon wall, a place where we could speak without the others hearing us.

Before I could open my mouth, she asked, "Are you Apaches?"

"Yes, Mescaleros."

"Are you going to kill us? Or keep us as slaves?"

"We won't kill you or keep you as slaves. No slaves live on our reservation. The witch slaughtered and scalped your men for money. He planned to claim their scalps as Apaches, and the *Nakai-yes,* closing their eyes to any difference, would have gladly paid him every penny he demanded because they hate and fear Apaches. The witch planned to take you to Casas Grandes and sell you as slaves to *hacendados* or to houses of women."

She stared at the sand and nodded. "I heard them say this. The one with no hair warned them not to rape or torture us because it would lower our price and cost him money. Why did you kill him?"

"My brothers and I took three years to find this witch and today finally kill him. He killed all our people as he did your men. Now he wanders in darkness, blind in the Happy Place. The world is smooth again. The Mescaleros give you back your life."

She stared at me with big, sad eyes and said, "We're grateful to have our lives back, but the Season of Ghost Face comes soon. We'll starve without our harvests and our men to help and protect us. What can we do? Will you help us?"

"We burned the bodies of your men to save them from the black birds, coyotes, and wolves. We took nothing from your rancheria. The witch took you and ten packhorses of loot from your rancheria and then burned everything, even your crops. There is nothing left for you there. My friends and I return north to our land the *Indah* took from us. Where do you want to go? We will help you if we can, but we must go quickly. The time we can stay away from the reservation grows short."

She looked at the white, glaring sand and the rushing, rumbling river, and held her belly. "My child needs the help of a man to grow strong. He needs him to put food in my belly. I need food to make milk in my breasts, or the child will starve, and I will, too." She looked at me with pleading eyes. "Mescalero, kill us or sell us, but don't leave us to starve."

An idea flew out of my mouth unbidden. "Will you live with Chiricahuas, become part of a band?"

"We are Opata. The Chiricahuas have raided our rancheria many times. How will they treat us? We will work and help their women, but I won't be among them as a slave. They are hard men, raiders and warriors, not farmers, and they make me afraid. I can't speak for the others, but I'd rather die than become a Chiricahua slave. If you choose to sell us to them, I'll run away or kill myself rather than let a Chiricahua use me for his pleasure or work my child like an animal. I know the rest of the women and children think this, too."

I took council with my brothers. We decided to take them to Juh's stronghold and ask that they be adopted into the band as second or third wives. We would not leave them as slaves.

By a few riding double, the Opata women and children all had rides on the ponies of the Comanches. We rode the trail we had followed from Elias's camp. From there, we knew the trail to Juh's stronghold.

The sun was nearing the edge of the western mountains, and the shadows fell deep in the canyon of Elias when I waved at a warrior up the canyon wall who was watching the trail into the camp. He waved back, but I saw him studying us with his *be'idest'iné* as we walked our ponies toward the first wickiups in the rancheria. A crowd of women and children formed as if by magic, and warriors, rifles ready, stood among them. As we approached, they formed two lines for us to ride between and watched us as we passed.

Elias met us at the end of the lines, arms crossed, his face a mask of indifference. Because I had killed the witch, Beela-chezzi said I should ride first, and the others agreed. Stopping in front of Elias, I slid off my pony and walked up to him waving my palm parallel to the ground to show that all was well.

Elias said, "So, Mescalero, you return to the camp of Elias with all your brothers and have many Opata captives on fine ponies. I see you did not find the witch you told grandmother you hunted, but slaves and ponies instead."

I was tempted to remind Elias of how his band had run from the witch, but it is a bad custom, and sometimes makes bad blood, to make fun of your host.

"I've killed the witch and sent him blind forever to the Happy Land, and my brothers and I have wiped out his band to the last warrior and *bandito*. The Opata here were his captives. Now we take them to Juh's stronghold and ask they live free."

A gentle murmur swept through the crowd around us. I saw warriors, their eyebrows raised in surprise, look at each other, and Elias frowned. He cocked his head to one side, crossed his arms, and looked at me in disbelief. "You, Mescalero, killed the great, hairless, demon witch, Sangre del Diablo? You sent him blind to the Happy Land of the grandfathers? How? Everyone I know, in or out of the Blue Mountains, feared and stayed away from him as my People and I did. If he didn't witch you and make you sick and wishing to die, he killed you and took your hair so you had none in the Happy Land."

"Yes, Sangre del Diablo tried to kill me with his war club in a charge on his big black pony. He came snapping his teeth and howling like a wolf. *Ussen* gave me Power to send witches blind to the happy place, Power to shoot out their eyes with my Yellow Boy rifle. I did this to Sangre del Diablo, and a captive woman smashed in his skull after we killed his Comanches and *pistoleros*. We've freed you and your people from fear of the day when Sangre del Diablo comes."

Elias's face cracked into a big smile. "*Enjuh!* You've done a great thing for all Apaches. Be our guests this night. We'll feast you and celebrate your victory while we give Kitsizil Lichoo' a new wife."

Elias let us use all his empty wickiups on the far side of his camp, and he gave a place close by us to the Opata to make their beds and fires. Kitsizil Lichoo', washed and dressed, ready to take a new woman, came to visit us and learn what had happened to the witch.

He sat by our fire, his face shining and happy, and nodded appreciatively as we told the story of the witch's death. When I finished, I said, "And what of you, my friend? Will you stay here with this woman in Elias's band or return to the stronghold of Juh?"

He shook his head. "My new woman is my second wife. She has parents no more, no true relatives in this or any other band. She goes with me to my camp in the Blue Mountains to the north."

Kitsizil Lichoo' laughed when he saw me raise my brows. "Juh moved his camp south when he broke out of San Carlos with Geronimo, Chihuahua, and Loco. Two moons after you left the stronghold to return to Mescalero, I gathered up a few warriors and made a new camp in a Blue Mountain canyon to the north. Sweet, cold water runs by it, and we have made brush corrals for our ponies and mules and lodges with stone walls that will keep us warm in winter and cool in summer. We've found a way from our camp through canyons out to the *llano* so the *Nakai-yes* won't catch us when we raid the great herds of the *hacendados*. I'll never raid my people north of the border. Men from other tribes have joined us. We're still only twelve warriors, and there are only three women and a girl child with us. We must find women to help us grow strong and have children, so we don't have to take them in raids. We grow slow, but well. Our camp is on your path to Mescalero. Come and see."

Light filled my brain like a sunrise. "Do your warriors insist their women be Apaches?"

He looked puzzled and shook his head. "No. In fact, one of our women is a *Nakai-yi*. Why?"

I nodded toward the Opata women and children. "The witch's captives. They need a band, and to survive, the women need men. I was taking them to Juh's stronghold to ask that he take them, not as slaves, but as adopted Chiricahuas. You say Juh camps in another place, and you need women and children for your warriors. Why don't you take them?"

He looked through the trees at the camp of the Opata women and children. "I can see future warriors and strong women there. Ha! I came to the camp of Elias to take another woman back to my wickiup. Now I can return with my woman and enough women and children for all my warriors. In the span of a day, I have gone from a little camp to a big one. Will they come? Will you help me take them there?"

"I want to see this camp of yours. We'll help you. Come, let us ask the women what they choose."

As dusk came, a great fire was lighted and the freshly made tiswin brought out. Drummers began a slow, rumbling beat on a big, stiff hide, filling the camp with its boom-dah-dah-boom rhythm. Kitsizil Lichoo' and I walked to the camp of the Opata women and children. They all sat down with us around a fire, and I told them who he was/ and why he was in the camp of Elias. They frowned in disbelief and slowly shook their heads when I told them he was a son of Juh. No Apache had red hair. He told them how when he was four or five harvests, Juh took him in a raid where his mother was killed. He had survived because the women in Juh's band thought his red hair was good luck. He told them many of the same things he had told me about his new camp to the north. He said his warriors needed wives, and that I had told him they needed men. When he asked if they wanted to become part of his camp and become his warriors' women and adopted children rather than be taken to some *Nakai-yi* village, they all nodded yes.

He said, "My warriors will want you all. Our camp is three suns' ride from here. My new woman and me will not drink too much tiswin after our feast begins. We'll leave at first light before Elias makes trouble. Don't tell his people of our business. Be ready."

"Enjuh," they said as one, and, for the first time since I had found them, I saw a few women smiling.

The drum picked up in tempo, and singing and the wheel dance began around the great fire.

CHAPTER 36
LONG RIDE TO MESCALERO

Kitsizil Lichoo' and his new woman, an easy-on-the-eyes, hardworking widow, Calico Dove, led the long line of Opata women and children, their packhorses, and my brothers and me out of Elias's canyon mists as the sun shot long, golden shafts through the tall trees toward the top of the ridge above the camp. The night before, the camp, with much dancing and singing and tiswin drinking, had celebrated their union and our destruction of Sangre del Diablo and his Comanches. By the time Elias and his warriors awoke with their heads throbbing from too much drinking, our ponies had carried us far away, too far for them to catch us in order to take the Opata from us for camp slaves and wives. All the Apaches in the long string of ponies winding around the narrow cliff's edge trails knew Elias and didn't trust him in any of his words. The Opata seemed to sense the same, although they didn't know him or have any other association with him. We were all glad to be gone from the camp of Elias.

Kitsizil Lichoo' took a trail west out of the Blue Mountains down to the Río Bavispe where the trail near it made riding north much faster than across the mountains. We passed around and stayed out of sight of the villages of Bacerac, Bavispe, and San Miguel, and then took the Carretas Pass to the east side of the Blue Mountains. After a long day's ride, we stopped at the springs near Carretas as the sun sank into the far mountains, changing the white, far horizon clouds into blazing oranges, reds, and purples. The women chopped wood for two or three fires, made little wickiups to sleep under, pulled grass to sleep on, and made us all a meal that filled us up with enough left over to eat for the morning before we rode on. While the women made shelters and cooked, Yibá, Beela-chezzi, Kah, Rufus, and I rubbed down the ponies and mules and hobbled them to graze during the night.

After the warriors ate, we sat around a fire, smoked to the four directions, and spoke with Kitsizil Lichoo' of his camp two days' ride to the north. I said, "Why did you start your own camp so far away from the safety of Juh's stronghold? You're a chief's son. In his rancheria, you would live well."

Kitsizil Lichoo' smiled and nodded. "I left because I'm a chief's son." He saw us frown and laughed aloud. "A chief's son does what his father tells him. Juh has killed a lot of White Eyes. I'll never make war on or raid people of my blood. I didn't want to refuse him when he wanted to take me on a raid north across the border. The best thing for me to do was have my own camp far away from the camps of other Blue Mountain Apaches and Chiricahuas."

He paused for a moment, and we could hear Calico Dove sitting with the Opata women telling them stories of her days in Elias's camp. There was much laughing about her stories, mostly about men trying to court her. Out in the darkness the children played their games of tag and hide.

Kitsizil Lichoo' continued, "One day, three harvests ago, I hunted and rode the mountain trails to the north. I left a trail following a deer and climbed to the top of a long, flat-topped ridge following the tall tree line on the edge of a great meadow. It was there I saw a tall stack of boulders in the middle of the meadow. It stood up straight and tall, like a finger poking out of the ground, and smaller boulders, shaped like eggs, surrounded it. I climbed to the top of the finger and could just see, through the gray haze far to the north, the top of a mountain. I learned later the *Indah* called it Big Hatchet, and that it lay just across the border in the land of the Blue Coats. I liked the top of the boulder stack. It was a place where a guard could watch for enemies coming from a long way off or hide from those who approached from nearby.

"An arrow from a strong bow shot from the boulder toward the east side of the ridge, would reach the edge of a line of trees and brush that covered the sides of the canyon all the way to the bottom. I climbed down from the boulder and led my pony into those trees. I heard flowing water down in the canyon, and I found a game trail down through the trees to the bottom.

"Down on the canyon floor, I found a wide, slow-moving stream flowing around a big bench that stood about two rifle lengths above the water. Brush covered the bench and grew all the way over to the far canyon wall. I crossed the stream, never more than the length of a forearm deep, to the bench and found on the far end a place to ride my pony up on to the bench. The brush and trees thinned out as they approached the canyon wall. Birds called from the trees and great white herons swooped down the long, straight stretch of the water by the bench. It was far from villages or soldier forts of the *Indah* or *Nakai-yes*, hidden in the northern Blue Mountains, very hard to find, and far from the camps of Apaches to the south who raided across the border. I knew *Ussen* had shown me the place for my rancheria.

"I rode back to Juh's stronghold and told him what I had found and that I wanted to start my own rancheria. He argued with me for a while, saying that I should stay with the People in the stronghold, but when he saw I was determined to leave, he told me to go ahead. I told him I wanted to ask warriors in the stronghold to join me in a new camp, and he said that was all right. He didn't think I had much of a chance to get any warriors to join me. Four warriors, two with women whose kin had already died and two without women, surprised us and said they would go with me.

"On the way to the new place, we rested overnight in the camp of Elias. I found many warriors in Elias's camp who wanted to leave because Elias had gotten too many of them killed or wounded in his raids. But few wanted to take the risk of starting a new camp. I talked and smoked a long time with them before eight decided to come with me. That was nearly one in four of Elias's warriors. They were all warriors, but young, and had not yet taken a woman.

"Until now, there are still only three women in our camp, and one of them is my first wife. She says there is too much work to do alone and to find her a sister. My warriors have even talked about slipping off to San Carlos to steal women. These Opata bring us much that I once thought would take a long time to find. Now the warriors won't need to cross the border to steal women. We'll be different from Apaches to the south."

It grew quiet around the fires. The women and children slept. We smoked, alone with our thoughts. Somewhere up the canyon trail, a *googé* (whip-poor-will) called, and a night bird squawked.

I said, "How will your camp be any different from the camps to the south except that you'll only raid *Nakai-yes*?"

Kitsizil Lichoo' poked at the fire's coals with a cane stick and said, "We'll stay in one camp harvest to harvest until we're found by the *Nakai-yes*. Then we'll leave. I've already found another place nearby that's even harder to find than the one we have now. The canyon protects us from wind in Ghost Face time and from most of the sun during the hottest times, from the Season of Many Leaves until the time of Large Fruit. We'll have lodges better than ones with skins or cloth over wickiups or tipis. We'll have lodges with walls made of stone that will be as good and long lasting as any *Nakai-yi* lodge."

He laughed again when I frowned in disbelief. "How will you

do this? Can you make stones obey you?"

"I can't, but we have a warrior who can. He is one with black skin who escaped from the White Eyes when he was a slave on a trader's wagon Juh attacked. He looked so different from the White Eyes that Juh kept him for his own slave. The black slave had worked on stone fences made by the White Eyes to the east. He had learned how to make stones stay where he put them. In the stronghold, he showed us what he knew by building a short fence out of stones. He tried to show some of Juh's warriors how to make the stones obey, but they didn't want to learn. They wouldn't do something slaves did. I remembered that stone fence and asked him if he could make lodge walls. He agreed to come to my camp and show us how. Now every warrior in my camp builds a lodge with walls of stone, cool in the time of Large Fruit, and warm in the Ghost Face Season. He knows how to make a stone lodge by himself.

"We've also made corrals from brush and *Indah pesh-diwozhi* (barbed wire) thorn ropes that will help keep our ponies and mules and the cattle we take from the *hacendados* in one place when we need them. We'll have room for our women to work without fear of attack from Blue Coats or *Nakai-yes*. We'll have many children, and our band will grow strong. Our warriors won't die faster than our women can have children to replace them. Come stay with us. You've killed the witch who destroyed your People. You don't have to live on a reservation."

I nodded. "I'll think on this. Show us your camp."

We left Carretas Springs, as the dawn brought gray light, and moved along the eastern side of the Blue Mountains, passing west, above and hidden from a big *hacienda* built against the steep wall of a high ridge rising alone up out of the *llano*. There were many cattle in small groups scattered across the *llano*, and, from the high trail we followed, I used the *Shináá Cho* to see *vaqueros* in several small camps herding and protecting them from Apaches and *banditos.*

We reached El Paso Pulpito and took a side canyon north. By the time the sun was falling into the western horizon, we came to the end of the canyon and stopped to camp at the beginning of a trail west across the ridges.

With the coming of the sun, we were climbing switchbacks up the first ridge. We crossed four high ridges that day, and when the sun was four fingers above the horizon, we rode down a narrow trail into a deep canyon. From the top of the trail, I heard water flowing in the bottom of the canyon. At the bottom, a wide, shallow stream flowed across wide, flat stones covered with green moss. The sun was nearly gone, and shadows were long and black, but Kitsizil Lichoo' easily followed a trail along the eastern bank until he came to a wide brush-covered bench and turned into the trees where light flickered from fires near the canyon wall.

Warriors surrounded us as if they were ghosts appearing out of the air. Kitsizil Lichoo' raised his rifle in greeting and said, "Ho! Brothers, I come with a new sister for my wife and bring you wives and children saved from the witch, Sangre del Diablo, killed by the Mescalero, Yellow Boy, and his brothers and an *Indah* friend who ride here with us. Welcome them. They are great friends and brothers to us."

I saw the Opata, both women and children, bravely look in the eyes of the warriors who surrounded us and knew their hearts raced with uncertainty. Would they be accepted or driven away? A warrior, tall and strong, who I remembered from Juh's stronghold, stepped toward us, his rifle in the crook of his arm. He nodded and said, as he motioned toward the fires, "*Hondah* (Come in; you are welcome)." Other warriors, saying the same thing, walked, smiling, to the children and women's ponies and helped them dismount. The children were shy and looked at the ground, but I knew they were fast warming to these strange warriors who accepted them. The Opata women smiled at the warriors and seemed relaxed in their company.

Calico Dove slid off her pony and was met by the smiling first wife of Kitsizil Lichoo', Steps in Water, who took her hand and led her toward a large lodge with stone walls and a blanket-covered doorway near one of the fires. The Opata women and children followed them to the fires.

The warriors took the reins of the Opata ponies and led them to a brush corral where they kept their own ponies. They helped my brothers and me unpack the ponies, carrying the loot we had taken back from Sangre del Diablo. The warriors carried the loot back to the fires, and we brushed down all the ponies while the women worked to make a feast.

We left the camp of Kitsizil Lichoo' after five suns. The Apache warriors and three women were happy the Opata had come to them, and they worked well together. I think their mutual need made them a good match.

In the early morning light with mists rising from the stream, they all gathered to watch us ride up the trail to the top of the ridge on the far side. The night before, Kitsizil Lichoo' had said, "My brothers, if you ever need a camp or warriors to help you, come here first." We promised to remember the camp of Kitsizil Lichoo'.

Kitsizil Lichoo' told us of a trail that was shorter than the one we thought to take that took us past Janos and then north toward the great river and around the big village of *Indah* and *Nakai-yes* on the border at the great pass of the north, El Paso del Norte. The trail Kitsizil Lichoo' showed us led from the finger of boulders on top of the far ridge down into a series of canyons along a stream Kitsizil Lichoo' said the *Nakai-yes* called the Río Bonito.

We crossed the border at what the White Eyes called the *playas,* in the Animas Valley, a great, white place where water stood like a great lake a few inches deep in the time of rain, but was soon gone by the Season of Earth is Reddish Brown (late fall). We made our first camp in a canyon in the Little Hatchet Mountains, near a well pumped by a windmill.

We sat and smoked to the four directions, and Rufus, who had said little, except for long talks with Yibá, since the Río Piedras Verdes where we had wiped out the witch, surprised us and said, "Boys, I know yore anxious to git on home, but now we're in the land of the *Indah,* and it just got a lot more dangerous than down there in Mexico. Folks up here see four Apaches with an old *Indah* geezer? They're likely to shoot first and find out later if maybe they made a mistake. I'm thinkin' we ought to be ridin' at night and holin' up during the day. What'd ya think?"

I looked around the fire, and all the Mescaleros were nodding. I'd been thinking the same thing. Beela-chezzi said, "Roofoos Peak speaks wise words. I, too, think we must now ride at night." We all agreed and would have ridden on, but the ponies needed rest.

The next night we rode nearly all the way to the great river and rested at a natural tank that was nearly dry. The following night was an easy ride from the tank to Rufus's rancho in the Organ Mountains. We took care of Rufus's mule and our ponies while he cooked us bread, beans, and chiles.

Before the light showed behind the eastern mountains, we had all found sleep. The Mescaleros slept out by the cattle pool where we had camped before, although Rufus said we were free to sleep on his porch or under the shed at the corral. At the coming of night the next day, we thanked our friend Rufus, promised we would come to his *hacienda* again as he had asked, and rode for our canyon on the reservation.

It was early morning when we saw smoke rising from our ti-pis. I counted the notches on my day stick. We had been gone twenty-eight suns. Sangre del Diablo was no more, and the moon was as bright as it had been when we left to send him blind to the Happy Land.

CHAPTER 37
JICARILLA COME TO MESCALERO

Yibá took the reins to our ponies. "Your families must know you return safe. Go. Make their spirits glad; fill them with happiness that you return. Your ponies, I'll care for."

Beela-chezzi, Kah, and I faced him. Beela-chezzi said, "Yibá, you did well in your apprenticeship. This day, you're a warrior. This day you're a man. We're proud when you ride with us. You honor us with this last favor. Don't make your mother wait a long time for you to return to her tipi."

Yibá held up his chin and looked each of us in the eye. "You're truly my brothers. *Áshood* (thank you) for your approval. Now go."

I crept through the trees until I was just outside the blanket covering the opening into Juanita's tipi and stood there listening to her speak to Kicking Wren like someone grown rather than a two-harvest child barely off the *tsach*. I heard Juanita moving pots and baskets around the fire, slicing and chopping food with her knife against her smooth, flat piece of wood, a gift from the sawmill. I heard her giggle, and my spirit filled with joy and relief. I grew impatient waiting for her to open the blanket and thought, *Maybe she'll stay inside all day.*

I reached to pull the blanket aside when the whole camp heard Beela-chezzi's young son, Shiyé, yell, "Beela-chezzi!"

The door blanket snapped back before I could touch it, and there she stood, squinting against the sun's glow in the early morning mists. Her fingers flew to her lips as if her spirit tried to leave her when she saw me. Kicking Wren held to her skirt, peeped out from behind her, and, seeing me, laughed, covering her mouth like her mother. Faster than Coyote after Rabbit, Juanita grabbed my vest and pulled me inside before wrapping her strong, trembling arms around me.

"My man has returned to us. I'm glad to see him again."

Out of sight of the rest of the camp, she gave me hugs and tears of joy, just on the other side of the door blanket, in our private place, which was the right thing to do. Juanita always did the right thing. She laid her ear against my chest where my heart beat like *dahtiyé* (humming bird) wings. "You found the witch? Did he wound you or the others? Have you killed him? Are we free of his power?"

I whispered, "One question at a time, *Ish-tia-neh* (Woman). The witch is no more. I killed him. I have a long scratch across my back where his *Segundo* nearly killed me before Rufus sent him to the Happy Land with his big thunder rifle. Beela-chezzi has kept grease and herbs on it. Soon it will be only a scar. We're free of this evil. You and Kicking Wren, you're good?"

"Now we're good. You're in the tipi. I would see your wound."

"I'll show you later. Now, I have hunger."

I reached down, grabbed giggling Kicking Wren under her arms, and swung her high. Truly a warrior's heart stays with his family.

Much happiness filled our little camp. My mother, Sons-ee-ah-ray, and her adopted daughter, Lucky Star, Juanita's sister, Moon on the Water, and even Maria, Juanita's mother, who broke the son-in-law avoidance way, visited us to see that I was in fact alive after facing the witch and to thank me for killing him and to wish good things for us. All the women visited all the warriors that morning, welcoming us as if we had come back from the Happy Land of the grandfathers.

Later that morning, my friend, Chawn-clizzay, who looked after my family and relatives while we were gone, stopped at Juanita's tipi. He stood before the tipi entrance blanket, holding his pony's reins, and said, "Juanita, Chawn-clizzay stands before your tipi. Can I provide anything for you or the others before I go to the agency?"

I put the edge of my fingers before my lips for her to be quiet, moved to the blanket, flipped it back, and stepped out to meet him. "You've done enough, my friend. *Áshood* (thank you). We all owe you a great debt."

His jaw dropped, and his face filled with a smile as he grabbed my shoulders and looked in my eyes, not yet certain I wasn't some kind of spirit. "And you, my friend, you and your friends killed the witch? You've done this great thing. I can see it in your eyes. All Mescalero will dance to your return. I must ride today and tell Branigan and Tata Crooked Nose. They ask often if you return."

I motioned for him to join me on a blanket spread in the shade of tall pine nearby. "Come let us smoke to the four directions, and I'll answer all you ask."

Captain Branigan sat at his agency table smoking his pipe when I came to his door. He glanced up through the cloud of smoke floating around his head, saw me, smiled, and, curling his fingers, motioned me toward the chair in front of his desk.

"Mr. Yellow Boy. You return to us. I'm happy to see you, and the eyes of Major Llewellyn will be glad. You resolved your business in Mexico? You come ready to continue your work as a tribal policeman?"

I nodded. "Yes. We finished what *Ussen* gave us to do in the far Blue Mountains. Now I must help my family. It's a big one, and I'm the only warrior in it. The stories between the camps say something big happens soon, but none know the truth. If you need more policemen, the two warriors I traveled with and the apprentice, who became a true warrior at the end of the trip, will help you."

He nodded and groaned, putting his boots up to rest on the edge of his desk, while he stared at the high ceiling, thinking and stroking his pipe. At last he said, "You ever had any dealin's with the Jicarilla?"

I told him, all the while wondering why he asked me such a thing, "The Little Basket people who live in the mountains to the north? Yes, I know them some. When my father lived with Cha's band in the Guadalupe Mountains, a Jicarilla buffalo hunting party rested with Cha's band for a few suns before they moved on. Usually they hunted on the *llano* east of their camps in the mountains, but that year, the buffalo had disappeared from their usual path, and a Jicarilla band had drifted far to the south looking for them. They had little meat to show for their hunt. Cha told them to go for their families, come back to his camp, and help him raid the *Indah* and *Nakai-yes*. Their leader thanked him but said their great warrior spirit from the long ago time, Monster Slayer, demanded they live in their northern mountains or they would be no more. I remember a young man with them. It was his first hunt. *Ussen* had touched his cheek with the shape of a red pony running. He rode his pony better than any of the others, and he showed me a few riding tricks I still use."

Branigan made a half smile on the right side of his face, blew a puff of smoke toward the ceiling, and, looking me in the eye, said, "I suppose you're wonderin' why I asked if you'd dealt with the Jicarilla. The government has decided to combine the Mescalero and Jicarilla agencies, and after some haggling back and forth, the Jicarilla are movin' down here rather than the Mescaleros movin' north. Major Llewellyn will be their agent, too. I'm not gonna mix Jicarilla in with my Mescalero tribal policemen, so you boys is gonna hafta handle enforcing the reservation law for both tribes. There're gonna be twice the Jicarilla as Mescalero, but the Jicarilla will be spread out across the reservation in three camps: one on the Río Tularosa, one on Carrizo Creek, and one at Three Rivers over the mountains. They're startin' on their way here just about today, over seven hundred of 'em. They should be here in a couple of moons. Think you can handle the law for both tribes? I know it won't be easy, and I'm gonna need some more policemen. Tell your friends to come in and talk to me. I might use 'em. What do you say?"

I didn't like what he had just told me. The reservation land belonged to the Mescalero. There would be many confrontations between the tribes over where and how often to hunt, fights and killings over gambling wagers, and competition for women.

"I treat Mescalero and Jicarilla same. Why Jicarilla come here? Mescaleros no want. Jicarilla no want. Why big chief in east do this?"

He made wrinkles on his face and shrugged his shoulders. "I don't know his thinking. I just do what I'm told and ask you boys to help me."

"Hmmph. I went far with Crook in land of the *Nakai-yes,* and my brothers and I finished reason for ride we take there. I ready now to be tribal policeman again. I send my brothers to talk to you."

"Good. Chawn-clizzay looks for old women making new tiswin. We watch for smoke in the deep canyons where they hide and work. You come tomorrow. Ride to help find 'em. When the Jicarilla come, we'll all help to get them settled. I'm glad you're back from Mexico."

"Next sun, I go with Chawn-clizzay."

"Good."

I left Branigan at the agency building and walked to the trading post to see my friend Blazer. I thought maybe he could tell me why Jicarilla were coming, but he couldn't. He thought the big chief in the east had lost his mind.

Tata Crooked Nose moved seven hundred twenty-one Jicarilla over a distance Branigan said was five hundred miles to our reservation. It was in the Season of Large Fruit, and the heat on the *llano* made the walk hard on the old ones and little children. I learned later from a Jicarilla that, on the way, six died from the fever and skin sores the *Indah* call small pox. Tata Crooked Nose never told the Mescalero this. He feared we might fight to keep the sick Jicarilla off our land. The big chief in the east never asked either tribe what it wanted to do, and neither was happy the Jicarilla had come to Mescalero.

Kah, Beela-chezzi, and Yibá talked to Branigan. Branigan liked Yibá and thought him a good warrior, but he didn't think him old enough to handle older warriors without a lot of trouble. He hired Kah and Beela-chezzi and asked me to show them the way tribal policemen did their job.

A moon after Beela-chezzi and Kah began working for the tribal police, we sat smoking by a fire and tried to think what life would be like sharing our reservation with Jicarillas. Kah said, "Mescaleros have much anger over the Jicarilla coming to stay on the reservation."

I looked at Beela-chezzi. He shrugged, indifferent, but said, "Kah is right, but if the big chief in the east says they come, there's nothing we can do. There's nothing the Jicarilla can do."

"Kah, why do you say this? I only remember seeing Jicarilla the time they stopped at Cha's camp when we were boys. I saw nothing then to make me dislike them. I remember my father didn't like them, but I never understood why. Do you know?"

Kah nodded. "Based on that one time they camped with Cha, I, too, would say nothing against them. But, remember, I rode with Victorio and listened to stories the Mimbreño told of the Jicarilla. They said the Jicarilla believe their god, Monster Slayer, told them long ago in the time of the grandfathers that they must live in the northern mountains or be lost. There they live and hunt. They never think, like the Mescalero, about driving the game away or wiping them out by taking too many. They never learned the lesson of the *Indah* fur trappers in the high north mountains who wiped out Beaver's tribe, or how the *Indah* made the buffalo vanish.

"I also remember my father telling me that, in the days before Bosque Redondo, the Jicarilla rode with the Navajo and Utes on raids against the *Indah* and other Apaches. When the Blue Coats made us go to the Bosque after Cadete surrendered to Keet-Kah-sohn (Kit Carson), the Navajo came often to raid our animals and shed much blood. It didn't help when Keet-Kah-sohn sent all those Navajos to the *llano* around Bosque Redondo to make life worse for us day by day. My father remembered the Jicarilla raiding with the Navajo and did not like them at all. I think your father thought the same way."

Beela-chezzi said, "I'm older than you two, and I remember the Navajo raids on Bosque Redondo the first year or two there. We killed many. I wish we'd killed more. A tribe that rode with the Navajo at any time should not be on our land. I don't like them. They don't like us. They should go. But I give my word to Captain Branigan to do as he says. I'll do it."

Within a moon after the Jicarilla came to the reservation, we rode with a group of tribal police, Tata Crooked Nose, and Branigan to the camps of sullen Jicarilla, healing from long, hard days on the trail. At the camps, Captain Branigan explained to the Jicarilla what the tribal police did and the power we had if they made trouble.

At the Río Tularosa camp, a tall, proud Jicarilla warrior stood, a red mark under his right eye there from his birth and looking like a running pony. He threw his blanket off in the cold evening air, crossed his arms, and said with some heat, "Why put Mescalero over us? Tribal police for the Jicarilla must come from Jicarilla warriors." Many heads nodded in agreement, but Branigan shook his head no. "The Jicarilla have great warriors, but the Mescalero tribal police know my rules and ways of doing things and have worked together a long time. For now, only Mescalero are tribal police."

Silence fell like the quiet before a big storm as the Jicarilla looked at each other and frowned and then looked back to Branigan. We sat together behind him and stared back at the crowd as hard as they stared at us. Before hot words flew, Tata Crooked Nose motioned for Branigan to sit down, and, stepping to the speaking place, began telling the Jicarilla how they would be given supplies and how often. He also said they would get cattle to start their own herd. When the tribal police heard that news, we looked at each other and frowned. The Mescaleros had no cattle to start a herd. Were the Jicarilla being favored over the Mescaleros? If so, that would surely start trouble.

I could tell trouble of a different kind was already starting to brew. There were rumors all over the reservation that a witch, one with shape-shifting powers, had come and walked unnoticed among both Jicarilla and Mescalero. This was the kind of belief that might hurt a lot of innocent people. Branigan was smart enough about Apache nature that he told us to keep a close eye out for any indication that might point to someone about to be charged as a shape-shifter by *di-yens* back in the camps scattered over the reservation.

After the Jicarilla talks, not many days passed before Tata Crooked Nose and the Mescalero chiefs had a long council.

After they finished their talks, they smoked to the four directions, and Tata Crooked Nose announced he would buy five hundred head of cattle, half to go to the Jicarilla, half to the Mescalero. He even registered the tribes as part of the Lincoln County Cattle Growers Association. We Apaches thought of ponies as something valuable to care for, but we saw cows as food. *Those herds will grow small quickly,* I thought.

CHAPTER 38
RED PONY

On a cold gray day before the snows of the Ghost Face Season, I stood by the stove in Dr. Blazer's store. The warrior who challenged Captain Branigan for not using Jicarilla for tribal policemen came in with a woman carrying a baby still on its *tsach*. Less than three moons had passed since the tribe made their camps in the places Tata Crooked Nose showed them. I knew this warrior camped on the Río Tularosa. The pile of skins and furs he brought to trade showed him busy hunting and trapping, much more so than a Mescalero for that time of year.

The pile of skins and furs reminded me of the talk I'd had with Beela-chezzi and Kah about the Jicarilla coming to the reservation and how they would pay no attention to overhunting game. I said to the Jicarilla warrior, "I'm called Yellow Boy. When I was young, my father rode with Cha, who camped in the mountains the *Nakai-yes* call Guadalupe. I remember a band of Jicarilla returning from a hunt off the *llano* that rested with us on their way back to their northern mountains. A young warrior with them had the same kind of mark under his eye that you have. Are you that same warrior?"

He stared at me, looking me straight in the eye, nearly insulting me, before he looked away and said, "Yes, I stayed at the camp of Cha with that hunting party. I remember you. You didn't have the name Yellow Boy then. I showed you some horse tricks we used to hunt the buffalo."

"My name was Ish-kay-neh then. How are you called?"

Again, he stared in my eyes and then put a finger to the mark under his eye. "I'm called Red Pony. I remember when you came to our camp with Branigan. Your coat says you're a tribal policeman. I tell you this in a good way. The Jicarilla won't obey Mescalero tribal policemen. If Branigan sends you or your brothers to arrest one of us, you will fail, and blood may flow. We didn't ask to come to mountains we don't own. One day, we'll go back to the mountains Monster Slayer gave us and leave you to the land the *Indah* gave you. Leave us in peace."

I wanted to challenge Red Pony then, but I decided it wouldn't be worth the trouble it might cause. Instead, I stared at his eyes and said, "I hear you, Red Pony. Now hear me. If Branigan sends a tribal policeman to arrest a Jicarilla, the Jicarilla will be taken, blood or no blood. The Mescalero don't want you here, but we do as the big chief in the east says we must. Live in peace, and there'll be no trouble. Break our laws, and there'll be blood if you resist us. That is all I have to say."

He opened his mouth to speak, changed his mind, and turned away.

The Ghost Face Season that year had much snow. Trees popped, cracked, and split from the cold. We stayed by our fires, hunted when we could, and went to the trading post only when we had to. Kicking Wren grew fast before my eyes, learning to speak words and to joke and play with me as the winds blew and the deep snows surrounded us.

Juanita was ready to carry our next child, and we lay together under the blankets by the orange and golden flames of our tipi fires many times during that Ghost Face Season, but no child appeared to make her belly swell with life.

In the Season of Little Eagles, the rivers ran higher than usual, making them hard to cross. This kept the men from hunting. Instead, they spent much time playing Monte, and other card games, around the camps. It was only a matter of time before Jicarilla played cards with the skilled Mescalero and lost much with their bets. This led to disputes ending in fights and even death.

Captain Branigan motioned me into his office one morning. He sighed and slid a reservation pass across his shiny, brown desk.

"A game of Monte went bad last night. A Jicarilla named Red Pony claimed the one who ran the game, a Mescalero, old He Who Catches Horses, refused to give him the pony he had won in a big bet. He Who Catches Horses claimed Red Pony never made the bet. Red Pony didn't say much, disappeared for a while, and then came back with two other Jicarilla who kept their rifles on the other players. Red Pony beat and then cut the old man up pretty good. He took the pony he claimed he had won and claimed an extra one for his trouble.

"The Mescaleros in nearby camps gambling with the Jicarilla want to wipe out Red Pony's camp and any others that get in the way. I told 'em I'd take care of it properly, and they'd damn well better leave the Jicarilla alone. I checked this morning. Red Pony ain't in his camp on the Tularosa, but his woman and children still have their tipi there. Naturally, nobody, including his woman, knows where he went or if he's plannin' to leave the reservation.

"Old Charlie, who works the mules unloading logs over at Blazer's sawmill, said he saw a warrior on a big buckskin leading another pony headed across the mountains on the Three Rivers trail. I'm guessing he'll cross the Tularosa Valley at Three Rivers, ride around the southern end of the Valley of Fires, take the pass across the San Andres to the *Río Grande* bosque, and follow it north. He's likely plannin' to hide out in the mountains he knows and dare us to come after him. I can't let what he did stand. We have to get him back here in the calaboose, or there's gonna be more fightin' and blood than we can handle. If that happens, the big chief back east will send in the army. That's not what I want. Is that what you want?"

I shook my head. "No! No more Blue Coats back on reservation. Bad time. Very bad time."

"Yes, sir. I think you're right about that, and I don't want some fool sheriff and his posse chasin' him, gettin' their tails shot off and gettin' us in more trouble. You're the best shot I got. Catch Red Pony and bring him back here. If you have to kill him, do it. I'd prefer to have him back alive. I want the Jicarilla to learn they ain't gettin' away with breakin' rules and nearly killin' folks—even if they deserve it."

I took Branigan's paper with the tracks he drew on it and folded it to fit in my pocket.

"I go. By and by, I come back with Red Pony."

Branigan smiled, saluted like the Blue Coats do, and waved me out of his office.

I found Beela-chezzi, told him what Branigan said, and asked that he tell Juanita I'd be gone a few days. He said he'd tell her, but that he wanted to come with me. I thanked him but said Branigan's pass was just for me and not to worry, that I'd be careful chasing Red Pony. I took an extra pony from our corral, got some extra cartridges and supplies, and headed for the trail over the mountains to Three Rivers.

CHAPTER 39
CATCHING RED PONY

The trail to Three Rivers from the agency at Mescalero, well used since the Jicarilla began their camps, branched off from the main wagon road to Tularosa. It ran due north up a ridge and through a canyon to another ridge that went all the way to the ridgeline above the Rinconada. From there, a long canyon led into the Rinconada. The trail crossed canyons and ridges and then followed a steep, winding trail up a canyon to the top of the mountains where the Tularosa Valley, the San Andres Mountains on its far side, and, in between, the black, burned rock of the Valley of Fires suddenly spread out west before me. In the middle of the sun's fall from the time of shortest shadows, the canyons below me had already started to show shadows on their northern walls.

I paused to rest my ponies and pulled out the *Shináá Cho* to study the land. Up high where I sat, the air felt cool, smelled of pines, and I could see green pines and piñons descending into the canyons, stretching far below and vanishing into the tan-colored desert. Due west, the San Andres Mountains, a day's ride away, rose tall and rough in the gray haze.

The pass I thought Red Pony rode toward lay just beyond the Valley of Fires. Easy to see even from the ridge where I stood, the pass to the eastern side of the Jornada del Muerto stood out clear and inviting, a clean getaway from the order of the big chief in the east and revenge for the attack on He Who Catches Horses. Stretched out just before the San Andres, the Valley of

Fires lay like a great, black lake except it was not water but a mighty ash heap. Its black rock, black as crows and covered with knife-sharp edges, ashes of fiery liquid the old ones said came burning like wood from a hole in the ground long ago, lay waiting to cut the unsuspecting hand or foot touching it. Only the desperate dared to run across it, much less ride a horse. I knew Red Pony must have spoken to his brothers in the Three Rivers camp who, no doubt, had quietly explored the range below me and told him not to cross it, but to go around it, if he ever used the pass to the great river.

The *Shináá Cho* showed no sign of a dust streamer anywhere on the *llano* stretching across the Tularosa Valley to the Valley of Fires. I figured Red Pony had already stopped in Three Rivers and passed to the other side of the Valley of Fires. He had not yet begun his ride across the *llano*, or, somewhere out on the *llano*, he waited in ambush. I put the *Shináá Cho* away, lighted a *cigarro*, and smoked while I thought about what to do. I decided Red Pony waited on the *llano* for the tribal policemen, who were sure to follow him. He would not stop in Three Rivers if he believed a policeman followed, and he had to know, after his attack on He Catches Horses, at least one must surely come. The distance to the pass, too far for him to have made it already, meant there had to be a dust streamer if he were riding. I decided what I had to do, finished my *cigarro*, and rode down off the mountaintop along the edges of the world.

The trail down from the mountain was narrow and winding. It used long and short switchbacks, the drop-offs from the trail edges as bad as anything I saw with General Crook's scouts in the Blue Mountains. Down off the mountains, I rode south across the foothills in the deepening darkness of the late afternoon mountain shadows before I stopped at a spring with enough flow to make a small waterfall as it rushed to the thirsty desert ready to gobble it up. At the spring, my ponies and I rested and waited for moonrise.

The moon, glowing bright white, popped over the mountains behind me, casting inky black shadows from the pines and piñons. Swapping ponies to give the one I had ridden all day more rest, I rode a little south and then down a deep twisting arroyo that emptied runoff water from the mountains and foothills into the Three Rivers arroyo that drained out on to the *llano*. Down in the valley, I followed the western fork of the Three Rivers arroyo, which drained into the *llano* south of the southern end of the Valley of Fires. From there, I rode straight for the mountains and passed south of the southern end of the Valley of Fires by a distance of about a pony ride in two fingers of time (about half an hour) long (three or four miles).

There are two pass entrances through the mountains at the southern end of the Valley of Fires, but they come out at the same place on the Jornada del Muerto. The moon was setting in the Blue Mountains with dawn soon to come, when I rode down the white, sandy trail of the northernmost pass entrance.

Deep in the pass, a long straight stretch ends in a sharp turn north and then turns west and south again just before the pass ends at the Jornada del Muerto. At that turn is a small water seep surrounded by brush and a good place to hide and rest ponies. I decided to wait there for Red Pony, who would tire of waiting to ambush me at the southern end of the Lake of Fires and ride on, using the pass to head for the great river.

I made a lookout place behind some small piñons on a ledge on the opposite wall of the canyon. From there I could see Red Pony coming from more than a thousand yards away, and from behind me I could see over five hundred yards out of the canyon toward the Jornada. The water seep lay less than a hundred-fifty yards away, and it was easy to see my ponies as they stood resting in the shade, their tails driving away flies after their blood. I crawled into the shade at my lookout and made a nest to wait, watch, and think with a full canteen of water, extra cartridges, my blanket, and some trail food.

I ate my trail food and thought a long time about Red Pony, a strong warrior in his prime years, forced to live with a people he didn't choose or want. It wouldn't take much to make his anger boil over beyond his control. But a strong man, a warrior, didn't lose control of himself, or he didn't live long to dance his victories.

Branigan didn't mix Mescalero and Jicarilla in his tribal police because he knew he had to have harmony among his policemen, or he would fast lose control of the reservation, and the Blue Coats would come back. Nobody wanted the Blue Coats back. Still, Red Pony wanted Jicarilla warriors in the tribal police who had as much authority over Mescalero as Mescalero over Jicarilla. Fair enough, but without the Jicarilla obeying Mescalero tribal police, I knew there would be many events like the one I faced now, and the Jicarilla would never get their own tribal police. None of the events like this one would end well, and all of them would be remembered and used to stoke the fires already burning in the bellies of the Jicarilla.

I didn't want to kill Red Pony. I had seen his woman and children. They needed him to keep from starving in the next Ghost Face Season. But if I let him get away, many others might try it, too. I realized then that both tribes were waiting to see what happened with Red Pony.

I cocked my rifle, set it to safety, and waited, dozing in the hot shade, but alert for my pony's hearing something in the canyon I might not yet see or hear. At the time of shortest shadows, a coyote came trotting down the trail, his tongue hanging out, panting, heading for water at the little seep tank. He had almost rounded the bend to the seep when he stopped, and sniffing the air, got low to the ground. Staying close to the canyon wall, he crawled around the bend and cautiously raised his head to look at the seep. He saw my ponies and saddle but no sign of the source of the man smell. He sniffed again and waited. When the man smell source never appeared, he crept up to the little tank and slaked his thirst, noisily lapping the water with his big red tongue. The ponies' ears went up when he approached, and they eyed his every move. When they saw he only wanted water, they were still. I smiled. Even Coyote and ponies could get along for common need. His thirst gone, Coyote trotted on, heading for the Jornada. Later a family of quail came out of the low brush around the seep, and they, too, drank before running back into the brush.

The sun had fallen close to the western mountains, and shadows began to appear on the southern canyon wall and on the bend wall in front of me. I heard from far back up the canyon the dim echoes of rocks clicking together like those scattered by a moving pony. The *Shináá Cho* did not show anything yet. Maybe the changing heat made a few rocks roll down the sides of the canyon. I waited. As if by magic, he suddenly appeared, his pony trotting on the edge of the trail, Red Pony floating smooth and easy on its back. My ponies stared at the bend in the trail, their ears up.

I waited. The distance closed at a good pace. I knew the shadows on the bend in the canyon wall where I waited made me all but invisible to him. Five hundred yards, four hundred yards, three hundred yards, I waited until I knew I wouldn't miss if he tried to run.

Two hundred yards, I yelled, "Hold! Stop, or I'll kill you!" My yell echoed down the canyon walls, making it impossible for Red Pony to find my location. He jerked back on the reins and the pony stopped. Even in the falling light, I saw his head scanning the canyon walls for me, the temptation to charge ahead great.

Wise man, he waited, and yelled back, "What do you want?"

"Get off your pony. Lay your rifle, pistol, and knife in the middle of the trail and step back."

He hesitated for a moment before sliding off his pony. He laid the weapons before him and took a step back, apparently still trying to decide whether to risk running.

"Now what?"

"Reach down and pick up the pistol."

He scowled and reached for the pistol he had just laid down. When his hand was a less than an elbow length away I shot the pistol. It jumped in the air, its handle destroyed. The booming thunder from the rifle echoed across the canyon. He jerked back, his eyes filled with surprise, his arm and upper body stung by the flying sand. In the blink of an eye, I shattered the stock of his rifle and, with another shot, made it flop in the sand like something just killed. I shot again and his knife, its blade shiny even in the shadows, went tumbling somewhere off to the side, and the thunder from the shots made the canyon roar like some huge, wounded animal.

He scowled in the direction where he saw the flames from my rifle and yelled as the echoes died out, "Tell me what you want!"

"I want you to understand I do not miss. If you run, I will kill you. Do you believe what I say?"

He nodded slowly. "I believe it. Tell me what you want. It must be something, or you would have killed me already."

"I want you. I'm Yellow Boy, Mescalero tribal policeman sent to bring you back for nearly killing old man He Catches Horses. Tata Crooked Nose will judge you fairly. If He Catches Horses cheated you, you will not stay many days in the calaboose. Lie facedown on the trail. If you move, I'll shoot you. You won't die, but I'll cripple you worse than I did your pistol and rifle. Do you understand?"

He nodded, disgust filling his face. "I understand," and then lay down on the trail. I came down the side of the canyon carefully, never taking my eyes off him. Reaching him, I kneeled on his back, tied his hands behind him with a piece of rawhide, and then tied his feet. I gathered what was left of his weapons and my gear, gave his ponies water, swapped saddles on his ponies, and saddled mine.

It was nearly dark in the canyon when we rode east for Three Rivers and Mescalero.

Tata Crooked Nose heard the charges against Red Pony. A Jicarilla witness contradicted every Mescalero witness. He Catches Horses, who had suffered several bad cuts and whose face was many colors from the beating, refused to speak of their fight, and so did Red Pony. He Catches Horses said he and Red Pony would settle their own differences. Tata Crooked Nose gave He Catches Horses back the ponies Red Pony took, and warned Red Pony that if anything like this happened again he would spend many days in the calaboose if he didn't get killed trying to escape. Red Pony, his face an unmoving mask, said nothing. He nodded he understood and walked away.

I don't believe Red Pony and He Catches Horses ever settled anything. Two moons after I brought Red Pony back, his wife didn't show up at the agency for rations. Branigan sent Kah to check on them at the Río Tularosa camp, and he learned that the entire family had disappeared six suns before. Branigan decided that with his family with him, Red Pony would be slow to make trouble and ordered no one after him.

Two harvests later, after two hundred Jicarilla disappeared from the reservation and camped outside of Santa Fe demanding the governor see them and give them their own reservation, I learned that one of their leaders was Red Pony.

CHAPTER 40
TIME OF THE GHOST FACE

After I took Red Pony back to Tata Crooked Nose, I had no more chases or hard cases that year. The tribal police took care of the people who needed help with their rations, collected drunks, broke up gambling fights and arguments, and hunted the reservation for *Indah* who made whiskey to trade and took in exchange everything a Mescalero or Jicarilla might own. Stories began to bubble out of the reservation camps about a witch that could change shapes, and *di-yens* often started trouble by claiming they knew a particular man in another camp who was a shape-shifter. After a young warrior named Kadinshin was accused and nearly killed because an old *di-yen* believed he was a shape-shifter, Tata Crooked Nose called all the *di-yens* to the agency and warned them to keep their beliefs to themselves. He said if they didn't shut up, they'd be spending long times in the calaboose. After that, rumors and stories about a shape-shifter became whispers but never fully went away.

Tata Crooked Nose believed the People better off if they knew what the *Indah* knew. He encouraged the fathers to send their children to the boarding school near the agency. Although many fathers refused to send their children to the boarding school, between the Mescaleros and Jicarilla, enough children went to the school near the agency that Tata Crooked Nose started another one at the Three Rivers Jicarilla camp.

I didn't blame the fathers for keeping their children out of the *Indah* school. If a child went there, he had to live there and wear the same costume every day, do work for the *Indah,* and learn all their ways, besides learning to read and count, counting we already knew how to do, and making tracks to read on paper. I didn't want Kicking Wren away from her family. We needed her there to help her mother and to learn what was proper for a Mescalero woman. I didn't want her to forget the customs of her people that we'd taught her. I wanted her to be Apache, not *Indah.* She needed the kind of *Indah* schooling I'd had with Rufus Pike, not to be a little slave for the *Indah* teachers. I decided I wouldn't send her to the agency school.

That harvest, late in the Season of Earth is Reddish Brown, Tata Crooked Nose called all the chiefs and tribal police together and told us he would not be an agent anymore. He said Captain Branigan would stay to oversee things until a new agent came and that we should help him all we could. I thought then and still believe Tata Crooked Nose was one of the best agents we had in all the years I lived on the reservation. All the policemen promised to do the best we could to help Captain Branigan.

The Ghost Face Season came with much snowfall and hard, bitter cold, so cold that when the horses made water, it froze in balls before it hit the ground and stuck to their legs. We stayed in our canyon close to our tipi fires to stay warm, and protected the horses in the shallow cave we used for camp councils. Juanita worked nearly every day with her sister, Moon on the Water, to make baskets they could trade at Blazer's store for supplies, cloth, beads, and sweets that did not come with issued rations.

Moon on the Water, whom all the people called Moon, started her growth into womanhood. Her breasts grew and her hips began to take on the shape of a grown woman's. Juanita and Maria thought they might have to do her *Haheh* in the snow, but the sign of her womanhood did not come.

Yibá came to our tipi often. I showed him how to make the

best arrows, the right size for him, straight and true, with sharp, deadly iron points we filed from iron barrel bands. He learned quickly, but played dumb, as he sat by the fire working with me, but exchanging glances with Moon. I knew after her *Haheh*, Yibá planned to make Maria an early offer for Moon. Many young men in the other camps knew Moon. She beat them often in foot races when the camps came together, and her fine looks made young men's heads turn in all the reservation camps.

Juanita wanted to have another child and stayed close to me under the blankets as the fires burned low, sharing her secrets and her needs. Her need for me to have a son grew by the day. I wanted another child, too, but I didn't feel the pull she did to have one then. Still, it pleasured me much to keep trying. I didn't complain.

Kicking Wren, a sweet child even at her very young age, followed her mother's instructions around the cooking fire, learning the ways of women. I carved the child a doll, which she held to her breast when she decided it needed feeding as she had seen grown women feed their babies. I even found a few scraps of wood and leather and made her doll a *tsach*. She laughed and giggled, playing with them in the cold times of the Ghost Face Season.

One day Juanita, Kicking Wren, and I sat eating by the fire. As we ate, Juanita told Kicking Wren how important it was to learn how to find food in the wilderness even when the cold wind blew and the snow was deep. Kicking Wren sat nodding she understood, but her eyes wandered from Juanita to me.

She said in her soft little voice, "Father, can I ask you a question?"

"Hmmph. Ask and I'll answer."

"Will I go to the agency school like my friend Little Flower in Chief Roman's camp?"

I was surprised. Where had this question come from? I looked at Juanita. She glanced at me and frowned. She didn't know either.

"Why do you ask?"

"Little Flower told me it's not any fun. The school chief does not let the girls race or chase the boys in Touch-Me-If-You-Can. They can't throw rocks or shoot their reed arrows. She said they have to work all the time. That is what the *Indah* do, work all the time. They don't play like we do here. I don't want to go to the agency school. Will you make me go, Father?"

I sighed and looked at the ground before I looked at her. "No, child, you don't have to go to the agency school, but you must learn the lessons well your mother and grandmothers and I teach you."

Her face filled with relief, and she giggled as she said, "Yes, Father, I'll learn them."

A harvest after Tata Crooked Nose left, the new agent to replace him came to Mescalero. Captain Branigan left, but not before telling the tribal police he was proud of the way we helped him and told us he would never forget us and for us to continue to do ourselves proud for the new agent.

I didn't like the new agent. Where Tata Crooked Nose saw soil for growing crops, the new agent, Cowart, saw only dirt and weeds. He tried to make men work in the fields when they didn't want to by cutting off their rations. Fathers who didn't want their children in the *Indah* schools hid them or sent them to the mountains, but Cowart sent the tribal police after them to make them go. I had to do this once. It was a job I didn't want or like, and I promised myself I wouldn't be a policeman if I had to do it again. I knew that when Cowart insisted all children of the tribal police had to go to school, I wouldn't be a tribal policeman anymore.

One day in the Season of Earth is Reddish Brown, in the year the *Indah* named 1886, two hundred Jicarilla disappeared from their camps on the reservation. Cowart, the agent when they left, tried to order the tribal police into going after them, but we refused to go. We said there were too many Jicarilla and not enough of us. Much blood might spill for no good reason if we tried to force them back. Cowart finally understood why we let the Jicarilla go after he spoke into the box (a telephone) that talked to the Blue Coats at Fort Stanton and demanded action. The Blue Coat chief said as long as the Jicarilla didn't attack White Eyes, the Blue Coats would leave them alone, and the tribal police should, too. He said he didn't have enough soldiers to chase Jicarilla, guard the country, and force Geronimo and his warriors to surrender and go far away to a camp at a place called Florida.

The Jicarilla followed Red Pony's path across the Tularosa Valley and pass through the San Andres Mountains to the great river. On the ride up the great river, many were starving and barely survived on the food they found in the bosque. I think the Blue Coats decided to let them starve after they camped by the great river outside Santa Fe, refused to leave, and demanded the *Indah* chief give them land in their mountains for their reservation. Santa Fe *Indah* and *Nakai-yes*, afraid the Jicarilla might go on the warpath, insisted they be given food and said in one voice and many words that the *Indah* chief had to find a way to make them move. In four moons, during the Season of Little Eagles, the next harvest, the *Indah* chief gave the Jicarilla their own reservation in the mountains at a place called Tierra Amarilla.

When word came to Mescalero of what had happened to the Jicarilla waiting outside Santa Fe, the rest of the Jicarilla packed up, left the reservation, and were soon all gone to Tierra Amarilla. Cowart didn't try to follow them or bring them back. We

Mescalero smiled and danced to see them go, and the Jicarilla laughed and sang all the way home.

I could find no deer or elk to hunt in the Ghost Face Season after the Jicarilla went north. They had taken nearly all of the big game in the two harvests they had stayed on the reservation. After four hunts where I returned with nothing but rabbits, I worked on my arrows and played with Kicking Wren while Juanita and Moon sat by the flickering orange and blue fire making baskets. Kicking Wren asked me to make many of the things girl children ask of their fathers. I carved her more dolls so she had a family—a warrior, his women, and their children. I cut a piece of feedbag cloth so she could wrap it around little lodge poles she cut from arrow wood to make a tipi for her doll family.

While Juanita and Moon worked on their baskets and I my arrows and other weapons, Kicking Wren played between Juanita and me with the toys I made her. I asked her, "Kicking Wren, what will you give your man for his evening meal tonight?" She would grin shyly and whisper, "Don't tell him, Father. It's a surprise. I have mesquite bread, roast deer, beans, and potatoes. Then we will have a big circle dance." I soon learned her menu was usually the same as Juanita's.

One day, I noticed she didn't have the father doll I had made for her, and her baby was wrapped warmly in a moss bed she had made. As I smoothed and straightened an arrow shaft, I said, "Wren, is your man gone off hunting today? Do you need meat?" She looked at the tipi floor and slowly shook her head. "My man goes to bring a *di-yen*. Our baby is sick. It's too hot."

I was surprised that Kicking Wren knew about sickness or *di-yens* curing anything. Juanita looked at her and raised a questioning eyebrow, too. I said, "How do you know your baby needs a *di-yen*? She looks good to me."

She picked the doll up out of its moss and held it to her chest as though to feed it and said, "I dreamed she was sick. I dreamed she went to the Happy Land before my man came with a *di-yen*."

I thought, *This child should not be having dreams like that.* I said, "Do you want me to sing a *di-yen* song for your baby and make it well?"

She smiled, "Yes, please, Father. My man may not get back in time."

I put aside my arrow work and went through the motions of a *di-yen* sing for someone with fever. I chanted and sang, but used unintelligible words as I made up the ceremony. Juanita and Moon sat back and continued their basket making, but they weren't happy. Making up a *di-yen* ceremony, especially if you were not a *di-yen*, could lead to trouble. Sometimes a *di-yen* might attack you. I knew it, but I didn't think there would be any trouble because it all took place inside our tipi. No one else would know.

When I finished chanting over the doll, I gave it back to Kicking Wren and said, "Daughter, your baby is sick no more." Her laughter of delight lit up the tipi. Even Juanita and Moon smiled, and I thought, *I wish all di-yens were this successful.*

The next day was warmer than it had been in a couple of moons and the children were out of the tipis playing in the snow and bright sunlight. It was a fine time to hunt, even if we found only rabbits. I took my brother, Little Rabbit, who had passed seven harvests, out of the children's games and took him to hunt up on the ridge that led to the Rinconada. With my bow, we took four rabbits and divided them equally between us. I showed Little Rabbit how Sons-ee-ah-ray liked them dressed for her fire. When we returned to her tipi, she was very complimentary of her youngest son and said one day he would be a great hunter, for I taught him well.

When I entered my tipi, I didn't hear the happy talk I usually heard between Juanita and Kicking Wren. They sat together wrapped in a blanket staring into the fire, saying nothing. I had never seen my woman and daughter act this way before. I frowned and pointed my nose at them. "What has happened? Are you hurt or insulted?"

Kicking Wren pulled a piece of the blanket over to hide all but her eyes from me. Juanita shook her head and pointed at a parfleche sitting on the ground across the fire from them. "Look and see."

I laid my blanket aside, took off my coat, and put my bow away before I squatted by the parfleche and opened the lid and saw a carved wooden figure. It was a roosting bird of some kind, its height about the width of my hand. I picked it up and looked at it in the firelight and wavering shadows. My hand trembled when I realized it was an owl. My People believed live owls carried the ghosts of evil men. I threw the carving in the fire and watched it flare up and quickly burn with a bright yellow and orange flame. I waited until it burned no more and broke its cinder apart until there was nothing at all left of it.

It had turned dark outside, and I could hear sounds from other tipis of the People having an evening meal. I said to both of them, "Where did you find this?"

Juanita looked at Kicking Wren, who had dropped the blanket covering her face and looked surprised that I had burnt the carving. Kicking Wren said in her soft little voice, "I showed it to Mother, and she took it away from me."

"But, where did you find it?"

"I was playing with the others in the pine straw under the tall trees, and we found a warrior watching us play. He sat leaning against one of the trees that stood away from the others."

"Who was it?"

314

"I don't know. I'd never seen him before."

"What did he want? What did he say?"

"He said, 'Who is the child of Killer of Witches?'"

"I said, 'I am! He's a great warrior.'"

"He smiled and said, 'I have a gift for you.' He reached in his medicine bag, pulled out that carving, and gave it to me. He said it was for my dolls to have because you carved them for me, and he had carved this for me to go with them. Father, why did you burn the new carving for my dolls?"

I made a hard face at Kicking Wren, not intending to, but because she had much to learn that Juanita and I had not yet taught her. She bowed her head and looked away, afraid I was angry with her. I stroked her face gently and explained, "Owls are where the ghosts of dead bad men go. The owl brings news of death. Avoid it whenever you can. Don't listen to its words. The carving is a symbol of death. He is saying he plans to witch us by giving you this symbol of his evil. Tell me what the warrior looked like who gave this to you."

Kicking Wren stared at the fire for a few moments. Juanita stood up and left the blanket around Kicking Wren while she began to make our evening meal with the rabbits I had brought.

Kicking Wren said, "He was wrapped in a black blanket. He had the skin of a cougar across his shoulders, and his bow case and arrow quiver were made from cougar hide, too. There were three long scars side-by-side on top of his left hand that ended on his fingers. His hair was long and gray like Beela-chezzi's, and he wore it in braids. That is all I remember of him, Father."

"Hmmph. I'm sorry I had to burn your carving, little one, but it's a symbol of evil and would have brought bad things to our tipi. Tomorrow, show me this tree where you saw him, and I'll try to find him. Remember to always be careful around strangers, even ones who offer you gifts. They may be witches who want to do you evil."

She nodded with wide eyes. "Yes, Father. I'll always do this."

The next day Kicking Wren showed me the tree where the children found the unknown warrior. I found his tracks leading up the ridge and followed them. He wore moccasins of a style I had never seen before, very wide at the ball of the foot and quickly narrowing toward the heel. I lost the tracks in the rocks near the top of a high ridge. I circled wide, expecting to pick them up again, but found only cougar tracks following a deer over the ridge toward the reservation.

Although the Ghost Face Season that harvest did not ache with the cold of the one before, the game driven away by Jicarilla hunting brought a big hungry cougar down from the high mountains to take our ponies and cattle. Several of the camps near the agency had lost one or two animals over a moon's time. Although not many animals had been killed yet, it was enough to make some people poor without their horses and hungry without their beef.

Agent Cowart asked Chief Nautzile to send out his best hunter to take the cougar. Nautzile asked several. No one went because Nautzile's *di-yen* had told the People that the cougar formed from a shape-shifter who could only die by the hands of a Killer of Witches. I had helped Nautzile several times as a tribal policeman. He knew the story of my Power and that I had killed Sangre del Diablo. The day after I lost the tracks of the warrior who had given Kicking Wren the owl carving, Nautzile and his *di-yen,* an ancient old medicine man with three teeth and one eye, came to Juanita's tipi and asked to smoke with me.

We welcomed them and asked that they warm by the fire and then take a meal with me. They had honored my family and me with their long ride in the Ghost Face wind. I put their horses up out of the wind and fed them with hay the women had cut with long knives Dr. Blazer let us use in the Season of Large Leaves.

When I returned from taking care of the horses, we sat down together and Juanita and Kicking Wren handed them steaming gourds of roasted meat, wild potatoes, slices of mescal, acorn bread, and nuts and dried juniper berries. Very grateful for the hot food and the coffee flavored with ground piñon nuts, Nautzile and the *di-yen* let Juanita fill their gourds twice.

While we ate, we discussed how families camping close to the agency had made it through the season. Cracking a bone for its marrow, Nautzile shook his head and said several older people had gone to the Happy Land, taken by a sickness that wouldn't let them breathe. He knew this was true. He had seen them before they were taken. The *di-yen* said in a thin, whispery voice a witch had taken them, but claimed, and I believed him, Cowart refused to let him say so aloud. Nautzile coughed hard and spat in the fire. He nodded, yes, true, but said nothing else about it.

When we finished eating, Nautzile had a long coughing spell. I worried he might not have the strength to return to his rancheria or might even die in Juanita's tipi. When he finally stopped coughing, I pulled out a *cigarro,* lighted it with splinter from a fire log, and we smoked to the four directions. Nautzile coughed and wheezed as he blew smoke while the wind moaned and rattled the trees over our tipi. After the *cigarro* came back to me, he said that when he left his tipi, he felt the Ghost Face might take him on this trip, and it nearly had, but that now he felt much better.

I frowned and asked, "Why did you come and not send someone stronger and younger?"

He smiled and said, "A chief does the work of his people. I believed I had to come now and convince you to hunt the shape-shifting witch as soon as I could. I want it taken before its cougar eats more cattle and leaves my People hungry while it creeps off with a full belly. I know of your Power and skill with your rifle, Yellow Boy. I know that if a witch can change its shape into a cougar, then you still have the Power to kill it. I ask you to do this thing for our People."

I didn't hesitate to answer. "*Ussen* gave me a Power to help the People. I'll go with you tomorrow to kill the witch that can become a cougar."

Behind us, Juanita and Kicking Wren listened, and I heard sighs from both of them. I knew Juanita was considering the same thing as I in my thoughts. Was this the same witch who gave Kicking Wren the owl carving?

CHAPTER 41
SHAPE-SHIFTER HUNT

The world spread out before me in black and white. Black from shadows, black from tall trees and twisted branches, black from the sky, white from the full moon's light, white from the snow covering the canyon in smooth waves over brush and rocks, and white from stars. Wrapped in a good, thick Navajo blanket and, around it, an ancient buffalo robe, I waited for Cougar in a little wickiup covered by snow, moving only my eyes, slowly breathing in the cold, brittle air, and exhaling warm, misty steam into the scarf wrapped around my neck and lower face for warmth.

I watched the canyon and the nearby corral surrounding the few cattle of No Foot, a warrior whose name was given because he left no sign when he traveled and was the best of trackers. No Foot had a good name. He didn't even leave a trail in the snow when he left after he helped me build the wickiup under the tall pines above the corral.

As the sun fell into the mountains and the shadows grew long, I saw the dark outline of a figure in a stand of pine two hundred yards from the cattle. He looked Apache, and he appeared to wear a dark blanket with some kind of animal skin on his shoulders. I tried using the *Shináá Cho* to see him better, but he stood in deep shadows, and I could not tell any more about him. He stayed there until darkness came, and then disappeared in the long shadows made by the rising moon.

The moon, big and bright, floated above the eastern mountains to the north, sailed across the black, star-covered sky filled with cold, brittle air, and began falling into the mountains to the southwest. I watched, waited, and thought a long time about the Apache I had seen. From where I sat, I could not see his tracks. Nautzile's *di-yen* said the Cougar came from a shape-shifting witch. Only a Killer of Witches had the Power to kill it or drive it away without being haunted. Was the Apache I had seen a witch, the same one who gave Kicking Wren the owl carving, merely a curious hunter, or even just No Foot? I couldn't tell. I didn't know, but whether a true cougar or a shape-shifting witch came to take No Foot's cattle, I would kill it. I hoped it was the same one with the owl carving. My father, Caballo Negro, grandfather, He Watches, and Rufus had taught me over the early years of my life to believe only what I saw with my eyes, not what a *di-yen* or other man of importance believed. Even the witch I had killed, I knew only to be an evil man who claimed he was Chief of Witches to control those Comanches and *banditos* who rode with him and to keep Apaches away who might come after him. Still, I knew there were many things I did not understand or know. I listened and learned.

The cattle hovering close together near the center of the corral became restless and started moving around, occasionally bellowing when their crowding together shoved some against the corral fence. The bull with great spike horns, the chief of the little herd, bellowed a challenge and turned to face the deep black shadows stretching from the trees on the far side of the canyon where I had seen the Apache earlier. The other cattle, three cows and two yearlings, stopped their milling about and bunched together behind the bull. He stood with his head up, intently watching the growing shadows, snorted once or twice, shaking his head, pawed the ground, and bellowed his challenge again.

I felt my heart beat faster and my body tingle with excitement, ready to face the challenge given me because of my Power. I concentrated my attention where the bull watched and forced myself to steady. My breathing slowed, and I watched the scene, intent and easy like a warrior making a straight arrow. I cocked my rifle and put it against my shoulder, easing it out the open place in the snow wickiup to make sight pictures in the moonlight and shadow edges near the middle of the canyon, but the light made it hard to see the black sights on the rifle, and I saw nothing I could even practice sighting on.

I stared at the same spot the bull watched, the end of tall pine shadows stretching toward the corral. The bull bellowed his challenge again, stomping and pawing the ground. There was something strange about the tree shadows stretching out from the stand of pines on the far side of the canyon toward the corral. One spot in the shadows seemed to be lying on a wave of snow, but it looked darker than the surrounding shadow. I thought it might be a rock pushing out of the top of the snow. Then the rock moved.

Slowly my eyes began to see the shape of the big cougar in the shadows surrounding it. It was the biggest cat I had ever seen. The idea of the shape-shifter drifted through my mind. I thought, *Maybe Sangre del Diablo has somehow come back to haunt me, even with my Power.* I drove the idea from my mind. Sangre del Diablo was no more. I had killed him, sent him blind to wander forever in the land of the grandfathers. The wounds I had from our battles no longer ached, even in the cold. If he had been a witch, he would never be one again. If this cougar were a witch, a shape-shifter, it was one I had never faced before. I shivered with excitement, and my teeth chattered. I clenched my jaws to stop and told myself to relax and do what *Ussen* had given me the Power to do.

I knew I could hit the cougar from where I sat if I had a good sight picture, but the light was tricky and the air cold with shifting breezes. Uncertain I could hit anything, I waited for a better shot, hoping the bull or the cat didn't force my hand before I was ready. A puff of wind passed through the tops of trees moving their shadows as they bent and returned. For a moment, the moving shadow exposed the cat where it crouched, its muscles gathered, making its skin ripple, its ears back, its tail swishing back and forth over the hard crust of the snow, its yellow eyes a peculiar white in the low light. Ready to charge and make meat, it took the measure of the bull's great horns and hesitated. The puff of wind passed and the shadows returned.

The cat bounded straight for the corral in great, long, graceful jumps, puffs of snow flying every time its paws hit the ice-covered snow. The bull backed up and bellowed, shaking his head, his shiny horns like big drawn knives ready to take an enemy. With Cougar in the moonlight, the sight picture improved but still was not good enough to kill a witch. In another slow count of five, Cougar would be over the corral fence and in a death match with the bull. I waited to fire hoping that in one more jump or two by Cougar I would have the light and the range I needed to kill it if it were a witch and to be certain I'd kill it if it were just Cougar.

I waited to fire until Cougar made his long leap into the corral. Time slowed, as it always seemed to when the shot had to be quick and perfect. I aimed for his chest, knowing the light was just too poor to aim for his eyes. The bull charged forward, its head down and twisted left and up to spike Cougar on his great horns. The rifle kicked against my shoulder, its crack of angry thunder making snow slide off my wickiup and fall out of the tree over it. I threw off the blanket and buffalo robe and jumped out of the wickiup to run for the corral, where Cougar, a long bloody streak running from just below the front of his shoulder across his back and disappearing near his hindquarters, snarled and crouched, ready to take the bull as it held its head down and twisted to one side. Cougar saw me coming and jumped over the corral fence, headed for the same pine grove where he started.

I glanced toward the bull, still snorting and shaking its head, and then looked directly at the place where Cougar had been. It had disappeared. I couldn't believe it ran that fast and rubbed my eyes, but nothing changed, except to see little glittering places where it had broken through the ice crust as it ran. The bull relaxed and returned to his family. The tip of his right horn somehow didn't look normal. I climbed on the fence and looked him over. He didn't seem hurt, but a scar about a hand-length long lay freshly plowed on the horn he tried to use. I understood why my shot had not killed Cougar. The bullet had clipped the horn of the charging bull and deflected just enough to tear a furrow through Cougar's hide.

Wrapped in my blanket and buffalo robe the rest of the night, I guarded the cattle in case Cougar returned. Studying the path between the far trees and the corral, I tried to understand, with no success, how Cougar got to the spot where I first saw him without my seeing him sooner.

A golden glow appeared behind the eastern mountains; then a seam of gold outlined the mountains, and the sun slowly rose above the jagged horizon. I shook the snow off my buffalo robe and walked, stiff and slow, out of the trees on my side of the canyon to the trail where the big cat had run. The air was cold and numbing. Even wrapped in a fine wool blanket and buffalo robe, I had to flex my fingers often to pull a fast trigger if I had to.

The hard crust of the snow broke and cracked into small pieces at the spots where Cougar's paws landed as he ran away, making the shape of the tracks impossible to identify. Blood spots were sprinkled along the way and said the damage to

Cougar was more than just a scratch. I followed it into the trees, sinking in the snow in some places up to my knees. A big tree, its ancient spreading branches starting near the ground, stood close to the canyon wall and showed the cat's claw marks as it had climbed toward the treetop before jumping to ledges up the side of the canyon wall that carried him like the steps on Blazer's store to the top of the canyon where he'd disappeared.

I returned to No Foot's tipi. My story of first seeing some Apache, definitely not No Foot, and a while thereafter a big cougar that seemed to disappear when it needed, convinced No Foot the cougar came from a shape-shifting witch. I knew only it made cougar tracks, that it bled like an animal, and that I had seen a man in the trees a long time before I saw it. Big and smart and not afraid to raid around men, the cougar might well be a shape-shifter, but I didn't know.

No Foot's woman gave me hot, tasty venison, mescal, potatoes, and coffee with mesquite flour bread she had just made. I ate like a starving wolf. The meal brought me back to life while No Foot and his woman sat by the fire and watched me eat. As I drank another cup of coffee, I thought of ways to take Cougar. The only satisfactory one meant tracking and killing it rather than waiting for its return.

I asked No Foot to let me borrow his snowshoes. He rummaged in his gear behind him to find a pair and handing them to me said, "I go with you. Two trackers are better than one. I track better than you anyway. I can track anything anywhere."

I grinned and nodded, "*Enjuh*. I'm glad you come, brother. This is a dangerous animal. He's hurt and won't hesitate to fight. If he's a witch and I find him, he'll go to the Happy Place blind."

★　★　★　★　★

We found Cougar's trail on top of the ridge above No Foot's corral and followed it all day toward the great White Mountain across two windswept ridges leading up a deep canyon thick with tall pines and high, steep sides that had many places a cougar might make a den. Near the mouth of the canyon, we found a big tree with a high snow wall built up by snow falling off its branches all the way around it and up into its branches, the thing we looked for to catch deer after a big snow. We dug a tunnel through the wall to the bare inside place, cut a few low branches, made a small fire, and camped for the night, out of the wind, eating trail food No Foot's woman had given us, and sharing stories of the old days. No Foot and I became good friends sharing this hunt and with the memories we had of being surrounded by the thick snow wall under a tall pine tree.

Light was coming, but had not yet appeared, when we built up our little fire, ate again, uncovered, and crawled out our hole through the snow wall. I stood up outside looking for a place to make water, but what my eyes saw, I did not at believe at first. I wondered if I dreamed. Cougar tracks were there. They went all the way up to the hole in the snow wall, and one step inside, backed out, and circled the snow wall before heading down the canyon following the path we had made the day before.

No Foot took one look at the tracks and said, "It's the witch. It goes back and leaves us here. We must hurry."

We ran all day in snowshoes. It was harder than running every day, day after day, when I had scouted for General Crook in the Blue Mountains, but we were able, and fear for No Foot's woman and animals drove us. No Foot knew a shorter path back than the one we followed the day before, and we returned to his tipi when the sun was four fingers above the horizon. The fresh tracks of No Foot's woman showed her running for the corral. We followed her down the canyon. In the distance, we heard the bull bellow, Cougar scream, and No Foot's woman answer with a screaming yell, "Hi! Hi! Cougar! You go! You go!"

No Foot's woman, strong and brave, stood with her back to the corral fence, her ax handle in both hands above her head defending her man's property against the cougar, which was crouching, tail switching back and forth, one good jump from the fence and food. He hesitated, as if deciding whether to take the woman first or the beef. I thought, *If he's a witch, he'll take the woman first.*

I didn't wait. The light was good. But I was tired and breathing hard in the cold air. The rifle's hammer came all the way back, and my eye found the shaky sights. I paused, took a deep breath, and steadied on the cat's left eye. The rifle sent sharp, cracking thunder echoing across the canyon. Cougar, starting to rise into his jump for No Foot's woman, dropped like a full feed sack, and I had hit the other eye before it lay stretched in the blood-splattered snow.

No Foot and his woman stared at me in disbelief. No Foot, his heaving breath coming in puffs of steam, said, "Yellow Boy, you've saved my woman and my cattle. Never have I seen such shooting. Truly you're Killer of Witches. We owe you much."

I said, "*Ussen* gave me this gift for the People. I used it as he wanted."

I kneeled by Cougar's front legs. Side-by-side beginning in the middle of its left leg, three scars without any fur ran clear and straight down its leg and across its paw. Shaking my head, I thought, *Now you no longer threaten my daughter, witch.*

CHAPTER 42
PASSAGES

No Foot and I carried Cougar to Nautzile's camp. It was nearly dark when we got to his tipi, and all in the camp came crowding around to look at the cougar while we spoke with Nautzile and his *di-yen* to tell them all that had happened. We could hear every gurgling breath Nautzile took, and when he coughed, it lasted a long time as he struggled to breathe, his face red, nearly the color of blood and his hair, damp with sweat in the cold night air, but he smiled when he heard our story, glad we had sent Cougar blind to the Happy Land.

The *di-yen*, wrapped in an ancient, ragged blanket, stood by Nautzile and listened carefully, asking us many questions during the story. When we finished, the old man nodded and said, "I don't doubt that you've killed a shape-shifter with your Power. It will wander blind in the Happy Land for all time. You've done a powerful thing. Our people are very grateful. We must burn this Cougar to rid ourselves of any evil it left behind."

We burned Cougar in a big fire that night after the *di-yen* told the people what had happened and that they must stay away from it or risk getting Ghost Sickness. Everyone in the camp gave me a little present in thanks for saving them from the shape-shifter. I took them all, but I gave them to my new friend No Foot and his woman. The next morning, I left No Foot's tipi, glad that I had a chance to use the Power *Ussen* gave me to help the People, but still not certain I had killed a shape-shifter.

I stopped at Dr. Blazer's store on my way back home to tell him what happened. When I walked in the door, the clerk was warming by the big, black *pesh* (iron) fire barrel the *Indah* called stove. He looked surprised and said, "Howdy, Yellow Boy. That was mighty quick. How'd you get here so fast?"

"What you mean? I leave No Foot when sun comes. No ride fast. Three hand spans against horizon (about three hours) on trail."

"You mean you weren't in Nautzile's camp this morning?"

"No. I was in No Foot's camp, a hand span's ride away from Nautzile camp. Why?"

The frown on the clerk's face worried me. He said, "First light this morning, a man from your camp, I think his name is Beela-chezzi, woke up Dr. Blazer about dawn a poundin' on his door. He told Doc he needed him to come to the camp and he had to find you. Doc told him he thought you'd gone to Nautzile's camp to do some cougar huntin'. Doc asked him why he was needin' him and to find you. Beela-chezzi said your little daughter was mighty sick and her mother asked that he come quick. Doc, he got his bag of medicines, told Beela-chezzi he'd send old man Parsons over to Nautzile's camp to fetch you, and said for Beela-chezzi to get him back to your camp as fast as he could. They lit outta here a couple of hours ago."

I turned to run out the door, but the clerk caught my coat sleeve and yelled, "Wait! Wait! I know you're hot to ride, but drink some of this here coffee and eat some of these biscuits before you take off, or you're liable to get sick. I'll saddle you a fresh horse while you're eatin'. Doc will be there takin' care of the child a long time before you can get there."

He let my sleeve go. I nodded I understood his wisdom and waited while he poured the coffee and handed me the bread he called biscuit before he put on his coat and ran out the door into the bright, freezing air to put up my pony and saddle a fresh one out of Doc's barn.

I rode the pony hard and took no rest following the trail of Beela-chezzi and Dr. Blazer to my tipi. All the way, I tried to think what might have happened to Kicking Wren during the five suns I had been gone. The only thing I knew that took other Mescalero children in the dead of winter came from the poisoned air, the breathing sickness, of the *Indah*. But she had not been around any *Indah* except those at the agency, and they all seemed well. As my pony picked its way down the icy trail, I sang and asked *Ussen* to leave her with Juanita and me and the family who wanted her.

The trail up our canyon showed smoke, gray against the brilliant whiteness of the snow, pushing through the top of the lodge poles of every tipi. Many feet at the door of my tipi had tamped down much snow. I saw Blazer's horse eating fresh hay in the corral with Beela-chezzi's pony. Silence covered the camp. No birds called. No one laughed or spoke loud. Everyone stayed inside their tipis. The animals in the corral, with their ears pricked up, watching me ride into our camp, didn't snort.

Shiyé looked out of Beela-chezzi's tipi, saw me coming, and ran to take my horse. As I dismounted he said, "I have great fear for Kicking Wren. She has not felt good since the day after you left when we played outside. She came running to tell me she saw a warrior in the trees above us with a cougar skin headdress and a big rifle. I ran to look but saw nothing. I told Beela-chezzi. He looked and saw tracks, but decided it was just someone hunting. We look again the next day but the tracks were gone in the wind and blowing snow. Now he wishes he had followed them."

"Thank you for telling me this, Shiyé. You are a good friend to Kicking Wren." I thought as I clenched my teeth in anger and ran for Juanita's tipi, *Was it you, Shape-shifter, who made my little daughter sick? You won't do anything like it again. I've killed you.*

I pulled back the door cover and stepped inside. I would have rather entered the cave of a bear with cubs than enter my lodge and see my only child so sick that Juanita had called the most powerful *di-yen*, Dr. Blazer, she knew to help her. My feet moved like they had great stones tied to them.

Kicking Wren, her face covered with sweat, lay wrapped in a blanket with her feet to the fire, her pillow, Moon's knees. Juanita knelt beside Kicking Wren bathing her face with a wet cloth as the child fought to pull air into her gurgling lungs. Dr. Blazer knelt by Kicking Wren's other side, his left-hand fingers stroking his jaw as he stared at her with a frown of worry wrinkles across his brow and around his eyes. The smooth black ropes he held to his ears to listen to her heart and lungs were around his neck.

They all glanced at me when I came through the tipi's blanket door, then turned their attention back to Kicking Wren. I knelt by Juanita and touched Kicking Wren's face with the back of my fingers. Even with Juanita's wet cloth wiping away the sweat to cool her off, Kicking Wren's face felt hot, on fire. I trembled inside. I knew anyone burning up with fever this hot rarely lived.

I heard Juanita whisper, "Yellow Boy comes. His woman is glad. Their child tries to stay away from the Happy Land, but the spirits call her. She may leave soon. The great *di-yen* and your friend works hard to help us to call her back."

Blazer looked at me and nodded. Juanita spoke true. Moon kept her head bowed as she sang a prayer to *Ussen*. Behind Blazer, Maria kept her face hidden in the shadows of a blanket over her head so I could not see her, as the custom required, even in a bad time such as this, although none of us believed in it. Sons-ee-ah-ray kneeled beside Maria with Lucky Star, my adopted sister, and my young brother, Little Rabbit, as they, too, prayed to *Ussen*.

Dr. Blazer had us give Kicking Wren many swallows of water and helped her to sit up to keep from choking when a hard, ragged cough started. He mixed medicine from the bottle in his leather satchel and gave it to us for her to drink. It was bitter water, but she slept in my arms after she drank it. The day stretched toward the night, her fever stayed high, and she often whispered to me, "Father, I think there's an arrow in my side. Please pull it out," or, "Father, I feel so hot, and I can't breathe. Are we in a bad place, Father?" But Dr. Blazer said that was the way the disease made people feel.

Holding Kicking Wren that day, my mind wrestled with trying to answer what I had done to make an evil spirit attack my little child. She didn't do anything to them. Why not attack me? I was ready for any attack by evil. Could this have been the shape-shifter or even the ghost of Sangre del Diablo come to take their revenge? I didn't think so. I'd sent Sangre del Diablo blind to the Happy Land, and there he must stay. Maybe the shape-shifter had come earlier and had attacked us. I didn't know. I just wanted something solid about them that I could get my hands around and squeeze until they stopped. Throughout that day, I asked, *Why Kicking Wren and not me?* All that long day, Juanita was by my side, whispers coming from her great heart to her daughter's ears and to mine as the gurgle and growl of Kicking Wren's cough grew worse. I saw water in Moon's eyes, and she chewed on her lower lip as she moved to sit back in the shadows with Lucky Star. Prayers never stopped from Sons-ee-ah-ray, Maria, Moon, Little Rabbit, and Lucky Star.

As the shadows grew long from the falling sun, I had to go out, and Dr. Blazer came with me. We went to the corral spot under the cave ledge where we were out of the swirl of cold air, and sat down wrapped in our blankets. I lighted a *cigarro,* and we smoked to the four directions.

I said, "Why are the evil spirits attacking my little daughter child? Why don't they attack me? I'll give them a good fight. I know they want it. Why little Kicking Wren?"

Dr. Blazer shook his head and said, "Kicking Wren has what the *Indah* call a sickness. Witches aren't after her. I'm only a dentist, a *di-yen* of teeth, but I help when I can, and I've seen this sickness many times on the reservation." He looked me in the eye and said, "Your little Kicking Wren probably will go to the Happy Land before the next sun. I've seen it happen this way too many times with Mescalero children. They fight hard for their lives, but the sickness is too powerful and takes them. This happens to Kicking Wren now. I, too, have prayed to *Ussen* for the Power to save her, but He hasn't given it to me. A new *di-yen,* more powerful than me, soon comes to the reservation. But even his power won't save children with this sickness. I'll stay with her until she grows stronger or goes to the Happy Land and leaves us with our sorrow."

My chest felt like I had been stabbed in the heart, but I thanked *Ussen* that the best *di-yen* on the reservation was here to do all he could for Kicking Wren and I said, "Dr. Blazer is a good friend to the Mescaleros."

I held Kicking Wren in my arms as she fought the breathing sickness all night until her last gasping breath left her and escaped in the wind. I looked up through our tipi smoke hole and saw the gray light of dawn coming as the dark night of our spirits settled on us. Dr. Blazer crawled to me and held his listening ropes against her chest. He breathed a deep sigh and, with sad eyes, looked at me and shook his head.

Juanita held out her arms, and I gave her what was left of our child. She held her and rocked back and forth while her grandmothers, aunt, and cousins wailed and chanted. Juanita, in a croaking voice from a throat I knew was filled with cactus thorns and ached like mine, whispered in my ear, "Go. Help the *di-yen*. He tried all his medicine, but the sickness was too strong. Let Little Rabbit go to Beela-cheezi. My mothers, sisters, and I will make her ready. Go. There's much for us to do."

Dr. Blazer thrust his big, strong arms into a heavy coat in the cold dawn light outside our tipi entrance, his breath making a steam cloud around his head high above mine. All was stillness in the camp except for the soft popping and cracking of the trees in the cold air. He followed me down the path to the corral. The warm smell of the horses huddled together under the rock shelf overhang filled my nose, and I breathed it in deeply. The smells of life told me I still walked in the land of the living, even if a piece of me was gone to the Happy Land.

As I helped Dr. Blazer feed and saddle his big pony, Yibá appeared at the fence and nodded to me, indicating he knew the heavy heart I carried. He said, "My mother asks the great *di-yen* to come to her fire and eat before he begins the long ride to the agency. The good friend of the Mescaleros must not leave the camp hungry. She also asks the Killer of Witches, Yellow Boy, to come and eat and be warm in this time of great grief."

I nodded when Blazer glanced at me, and he said, "I'm honored to eat at your mother's fire. We'll come with you."

I buried our daughter in a secret place high on the great White Mountain. All in the camp came with us in the freezing, brilliant sunlight and made many prayers and songs to *Ussen* for our daughter. Juanita never wailed or wept. She had the spiritual strength of a man, but I saw in her eyes that her spirit stumbled in grief and bitterness, confused, not understanding why the Happy Land took our daughter from us.

When we returned, cold and aching in our spirits, we built a roaring fire in front of the shallow cave where the camp often gathered. Everything of our daughter's we burned, her *tsach*, her blankets, her clothes, her gourd for eating, spoon and knife, the toys I had carved for her, her little bow and arrows, her sling, the cloth Juanita and the grandmothers had used to bathe her. Everything we burned. If we had not, her ghost might have come back, wanting something left behind, some piece of itself, and the ghost's nearness could make everyone in the camp sick; all, that is, except me.

That night, after everyone in the camp went to their tipis, Juanita and I sat together wrapped in a blanket by the remains of the great fire and watched the orange and golden coals slowly turn to gray ash just as the life of our little daughter had done. I knew how much my woman ached for the life and suffering of our daughter, but I could find no words to comfort her as eye water came and she shook against me in her grief.

CHAPTER 43
LUCKY STAR'S *Haheh*

In the Season of Little Eagles, after our daughter left for the Happy Land, the reservation agent, Cowart, ordered the tribal police to find school age children hidden by their fathers and make their fathers bring them to the agency school. I had promised my daughter she would not have to go, and the thought of Cowart's order forcing a father to do with their children as the agent pleased made my stomach roll. This was not right, and my brothers in the tribal police knew it, but they did it anyway. I quit rather than hunt children, but the chief told me I could come back any time I wanted. I said, "Maybe when the new agent comes." The new agent only made things worse. I stayed away from the tribal police for a long time.

Most of the girls across the reservation, who came to their maturity during a harvest's turn of the seasons, became marriageable women after their *Haheh* (puberty ceremony) at a big tribal celebration, usually late in the Season of Large Leaves (July). When our women rode over the ridges to trade for supplies at Blazer's store for the first time after the Ghost Face Season, Sons-ee-ah-ray saw how the young men stared at Lucky Star. She acted properly and ignored them, which made the young men watch her even more closely. Sons-ee-ah-ray knew they understood, just by looking at her swelling breasts and rounded hips that she had passed her maturity, and they had only to wait for her *Haheh* ceremony before they could chase and perhaps catch her after the ceremony or, later, formally ask her mother for her.

After the women returned from Blazer's store, they all met around a big fire late in the evening. They decided that when one of their girls came to maturity, then the camp would immediately give them their *Haheh* and not wait for the tribe. This would give our girls a chance to avoid being chased and caught by some man she didn't want at the big tribal ceremony, and it could make them early choices of the best of warriors who didn't want to wait until the tribe's big celebration. Since Nautzile's *di-yen* knew our camp, the women decided to ask him to lead the ceremony.

Lucky Star had thirteen harvests before she reached her maturity. Moon on the Water had nearly sixteen harvests. With her long black hair, heart-shaped lips, sloe eyes, and her body built to work hard, run all day, and have many children, she still waited for her maturity. Juanita and I heard her whines and complaints from inside Maria's tipi, as they worked cooking good things for Lucky Star's *Haheh* feast.

Moon said in angry frustration, "I should already have a man by now. If things had happened in the right order, I might even have a child by now. But no, my body, like some hanging fruit, refuses to ripen. It looks ready but cannot be eaten. Will I ever have a man? Who would want me but some old, worn-out warrior who might not even be able to consummate our marriage, much less give me a child? Why do the Mountain Spirits treat me this way?"

Maria listened to this complaining as long as she could stand it, then slapped Moon and told her to shut up her whining. Suffering made her stronger. She must at least act strong even if she had no heart for strength.

Maria said, "Your time will come. A good warrior will take you even if you never have a *Haheh*." After that talk, even my warrior's eyes, dim to the ways of women, saw Moon change from a complaining crow to a dove, soothing an anxious Lucky Star and telling her to stand strong against life's hard times.

I rode over to Nautzile's camp and asked the *di-yen* to come perform and direct the ceremony, and he did. The men built the big, specially shaped tipi, the *kotulh*, where the *di-yen* holds the *Haheh*. The poles have to be pine, about a tall man's height, longer than normal, and the tops left with a tuft of green branches to cover the smoke hole and prevent evil spirits from getting in during the ceremony. The *kotulh* has a trench that goes from five paces beyond the opening, facing the rising sun, all the way around the western back, and returns to the east five paces beyond the opening on the other side. We stuck branches of green oak and willow in the trench bottom to form a screen to keep away the evil spirits of the earth. In this way, the screen and the rising sun, pouring light into the eastern opening of the *kotulh*, maintained its purification. Ten steps east from the green screen, we built a big fire and kept it burning all night to bring light to the *kotulh* when the sun left us. Evil spirits do not come to bright light and do not pass through green leaves.

My mother made Lucky Star a beautiful, ornamented doeskin shift, leggings, and moccasins for her *Haheh*. Four days before the ceremony, Sleepy, Yibá's mother, instructed her at my mother's request in the requirements of being a woman and the importance of chastity.

During the ceremony, the old *di-yen* made many prayers and songs for Lucky Star, and used much golden pollen to bless her. The prayers and ceremonies went on over four nights. During the day, we feasted and celebrated the coming of a new woman. As dawn came at the end of the songs and prayers of the fourth night, the "devil's pit," a square outline scratched in the dust in front of the *kotulh*, made it possible for any evil spirit still lingering nearby to hide from the rising sun. My mother spread rawhide over the square, and then Sleepy covered the rawhide with buckskin. The *di-yen* used golden pollen to outline four footsteps on the buckskin that led to a pollen symbol of the sun.

Juanita gave Lucky Star a finely made basket. The basket held many things of tradition given her during the *Haheh* that would make up her medicine when the ceremony finished. One of these things was an eagle feather. The *di-yen* took the feather by the quill and had Lucky Star take the barbs. He led her across the four footsteps he had outlined with his pollen to the symbol of the sun where her spirit as a newly made woman went for the day to be with *Ussen*.

Our small camp had only one young man eligible to chase Lucky Star, but Yibá still had eyes for Moon and left Lucky Star alone. For the rest of the day, we feasted, danced, and enjoyed our friends while Lucky Star did anything she pleased while her spirit met with *Ussen*.

Juanita ended her time of grief for our daughter at Lucky Star's *Haheh,* and she came to me many times hoping a child might once more grow in her belly. I knew the women whispered among themselves, and the men privately thought that perhaps Juanita could have no more children because an enemy in the tribe had bewitched her with infertility. Some even thought the shape-shifter had done this before I killed it. Moon's long time to maturity showed she had a worse problem than Juanita. Most women her age already had one child, maybe two.

The Ghost Face Season following Lucky Star's *Haheh* passed without the bitter cold of the previous season when our daughter left for the Happy Land. In the Season of Little Eagles, Moon finally reached her maturity. We held a *Haheh* for her, and the old *di-yen* who had performed Lucky Star's *Haheh* came back again. *Now,* I thought, *Yibá will chase and catch Moon.* Juanita told me if Yibá chased Moon that she would not run very fast, but, at the end of Moon's *Haheh* ceremony, Yibá did not chase her. I felt bad for Moon. I knew she wanted Yibá and that she was ready to become a good wife with many skills. Her face showed her disappointment. No one wanted her for his wife. Maria told her to be strong, that life has many surprises.

Life brought me a surprise a few moons later one evening in the Season of Large Fruit. I sat on a blanket smoking and talking with Kah and Beela-chezzi. Our mouths dropped open in surprise as we watched Beela-chezzi's son, Shiyé, now thirteen harvests, lead a fine black pony to the door of my mother's tipi and tie it there. The pony belonged to Yibá and was an offer of interest to take Lucky Star as his woman. If Lucky Star brought the pony back to Yibá, she signaled her willingness to become his woman if her mother accepted his offer of a gift of suitable value for her.

Watching the black pony nibble at grass where Shiyé tied him, I remembered Yibá telling me on our hunt for Sangre del Diablo that he when he became a warrior, he would ask for Moon on the Water. That winter when we had made arrows two or three harvests earlier, he couldn't keep his eyes off her, nor she him. He'd never given me any indication of interest in Lucky Star. I didn't understand why he'd changed his mind, and I knew Moon would be sick in spirit that he didn't choose her, but I didn't doubt Juanita and Moon already knew this would happen. I asked Kah and Beela-chezzi if they knew why Yibá chose Lucky Star, but they shook their heads.

Yibá had become a man of substance, a man ready to take care of a woman and have children. He had won horses in bets on hoop and pole games. He didn't eat, or lose in Monte card games, the cattle Tata Crooked Nose gave him, and their number had more than doubled since he received them. He kept them in a box canyon where there was good grass and water and, with Shiyé, protected them from hungry wolves, cats, bears, coyotes, and men.

That night, as Juanita rested her head on my shoulder and we watched the red and orange coals of the fire send little spirals of smoke toward the stars through the tipi smoke hole and listened to Coyote and his brothers howling on the far ridges, she said, "I know you saw Shiyé tie Yibá's pony in front of Sons-ee-ah-ray's tipi in hopes Lucky Star would bring it back."

"I saw it. Yibá has done well with his animals, and they increase in number. He's ready for a wife. Why did he not ask Moon on the Water? He told me he wanted her when he became a man. Do you know why he chose Lucky Star instead?"

She made a face and said, "He chose Lucky Star because of me." She saw me frowning in the flickering shadows. "It's been over seven harvests since I've had a child, but you know we've tried." She looked at me and made a face. "Stop laughing. This is serious. Some women think I probably won't have more children. Perhaps they speak the future, perhaps not."

I pulled the blanket up to our chins, the night air becoming cold, our breath looking like steam as the fire ashes grew gray and its heat slowly left us. Birds in the trees squawked, and far down the canyon a wolf called his brothers. "But what does this have to do with Moon on the Water and Yibá?"

She blew steam from her puffing sigh up toward the smoke hole. "Moon on the Water had her *Haheh* much later than most girls, who, by her age, would have a man and his child. Moon is my sister. We're from the same mother and father, as close in blood as we can be. After her *Haheh*, people waited to see if my belly grew with another child so they could expect Moon to start having babies, too. I still wait for our child. Now, no man wants her. They fear she could never have children."

"Hmmph. This makes no sense. How can anyone blame you for Moon's slow maturity? She is built to have many children, just as you."

"You speak true, husband. I'm certain, even from my dreams, that she'll have all the children she and her husband want. But the men who might give Maria a good bride price also think she'll be barren. Until she marries and has a child, there's no way to know, and they won't marry her until then."

My head hurt from thinking about such mindless riddles and settled for pulling the blanket over our heads to look for another child.

After Yibá had the pony led to the front of Maria's tipi, Lucky Star, like Juanita, waited a night and a day to return it. That way, she didn't appear too eager and, by waiting, might even cause Yibá to raise her bride price. His mother, Sleepy, his representative to Sons-ee-ah-ray, negotiated the bride price to be four fast ponies and a tipi cover.

Yibá and Lucky Star accepted each other as husband and wife in the bright, morning light eight suns later and left the camp for a hidden place Yibá fixed for them after a day of feasting and celebrating. I thought them a good match, but wondered if Moon would ever find a husband.

CHAPTER 44
SECOND WIFE

Ten suns after they joined as husband and wife, Yibá and Lucky Star returned to the canyon camp and entered the tipi we set up near Sons-ee-ah-ray. Their happy time brought good times and fun to everyone in the camp, including Moon, who had accepted her life and the good fortune Lucky Star had in finding a good husband, young and strong, like Yibá.

The seasons marched toward Ghost Face. In the evenings, I often sat outside the tipi on my blanket and listened to the night animals and insects while I cleaned my rifle or sharpened my knife. Moon came often to sit by the tipi fire and weave baskets with Juanita. I could hear the jingle-jangle of their talk, too low to understand, and then the occasional deep-in-the-belly laugh of Juanita or the lilting giggle of Moon. Hearing them, I never failed to wonder why Juanita couldn't make another baby and why Moon had no husband.

One day early in the Season of Earth is Reddish Brown, a female rain fell all day in the cool canyon air. All the camp stayed in their tipis and did chores put off until a day of rain or the long, dark days of Ghost Face.

I spent the day making new arrows and repairing old ones. Game was coming back to the mountains. To save bullets, I hunted with my bow and enjoyed the challenge of getting close to an animal to make a shot that I could have made at three times the distance with my rifle. As I used the bow more and more often, the deadly accuracy I had developed as a boy returned.

Juanita started the slow roast of a haunch of venison. Its fine, powerful smells of roasting meat and fat dripping in the fire filled the tipi. She used mesquite flour to prepare bread dough for baking when we were ready. Finished, she made bowls of wild potatoes, mescal, and nuts and dried fruit. My mouth watered as I smelled the roasting meat and watched her making the bread and other good things.

She finished her food work and brought out an unfinished basket, a large one with black and red geometric designs that would bring much in trade at Blazer's store after Ghost Face passed. We worked across the fire from each other, enjoying the moment and glancing up to show eyes filling with desire. But before we moved to anything more interesting, we heard by the door blanket, "I stand at your door." Juanita smiled and shook her head at my obvious look of disappointment. She said, "We hear you. Come." The blanket over the door pulled back and Moon put her glistening wet head inside the door and asked to join us while she worked on her unfinished basket. She said Maria wanted to nap, but the creak and swish sounds of Moon's basket weaving kept her awake. Juanita smiled and, motioning her to come inside, patted a place for Moon to sit down beside her.

We worked, laughed, and spoke our memories throughout the day. Despite having no marriage prospects, Moon laughed at our stories of early marriage and told us her stories, which Juanita knew well, about Maria's peculiarities. Since married men do not often associate with eligible young women, Moon pleased and surprised me with her smiles, quick thinking, and lively talk that left us laughing and giggling past the sun's fall into the far mountains.

After taking a gourd of venison and potatoes to Maria, Moon returned to eat with us. The smell and taste of baked mesquite bean flour bread, sweet mescal, juniper berries, and roasted potatoes and venison raised our spirits. In the early night, the gentle rain became a ground cloud. Long after Moon left us for her blankets in Maria's tipi, Juanita and I lay together enjoying each other and the mist-padded stillness of the night by our glimmering tipi fire.

My eyes were finding sleep when Juanita, nestled in my arms, said in the warm darkness, "Yellow Boy, man of Juanita, your woman needs something from you."

My closing eyes snapped open, as this was unusual. "Speak, woman, and I'll give you whatever I can."

A long pause and then she said, "I have never asked anything from you. Now I beg your help."

"Speak. Say what's in your mind. I'll answer."

She sighed and said, "I want you to have a child, a son or a daughter. You don't care if another girl child comes to us, do you?"

"No, I don't care if it's a girl child or a boy. But what do you ask of me? You know we've tried to make a child many times since our daughter left us. No child yet grows in your belly. I can no longer raid and take a child from the *Indah* or go to Chihuahua or Sonora to steal one there. After losing a child of our own, I couldn't stand to steal one anyway. We must be patient. When the spirits are ready, a child will come from you. There's no other way."

Again she paused. My brain knew her answer sure to come, but I feared to hear it.

"There's another way. You must take a second wife."

"What are you saying?"

"She can have our children while the spirits make up their minds about me. As your first wife, I can claim them as much as the woman who carries them in her belly. Please, husband, take another wife and give us a child, give us children. The years fly on hawk's wings. Soon, I'm too old to make a child. You're a strong man. You can still make sons and daughters for a long time. Take a young woman, and let her live with us. I don't care. I won't cry on the blankets while you lie with her to make a child or leave me to go to her tipi." She whispered again in desperation, "Please help me."

I knew my woman well. She always thought things through and planned carefully before she spoke. She already had some woman waiting for me to ask her, ready to become my second wife, ready to bear our children.

I puffed steam into the cold air. "Who do you want me to take as a wife? I know you've already picked her."

She snuggled closer. "Moon on the Water wants to be your second wife."

"What? The people say Moon has less chance of having children than you do. How can she make a child when you can't?"

"She's younger. Her moon times say she will have many children. She suffers like she's been witched because no one takes her. We must help her before she does something foolish so no man ever takes her. She'll have children. Dreams and visions tell me so. Take Moon, and our children will come. The whispers about her will stop."

"What whispers?"

"The whispers that say witches don't bear children. The whispers that say she must be avoided. Be strong, Killer of Witches. Take another woman. Take her."

A little wind came up and shook the trees over us, making pine needles fall on our tipi, and, on the next ridge, a wolf howled my name.

★ ★ ★ ★ ★

The nights grew colder. On a day before the first snow in Ghost Face, while the women gathered acorns and walnuts down the canyon, I washed my best pony, groomed his mane and tail, brushed him until his heavy coat glistened in the light, fed him plenty of grain, and let him drink often. I asked Shiyé to tie him in front of Maria's tipi in the afternoon but before the women returned. Men in the camp doing chores readying for Ghost Face walked by it, recognized it belonged to me, and looked with raised eyebrows toward me sitting at the fire outside my tipi. I nodded, and, smiling, they nodded back and went on with their business.

The women returned in the falling dusk leading a couple of mules loaded with sacks of nuts. I sat back in the shadows unseen and watched Maria's tipi. She and her two daughters saw the pony from far down the path. All three raced for the tipi, but Moon easily won. She stared at the black and white pinto for a moment before recognizing it belonged to me. A hand flew to her lips. Her stare moved from the pony to Juanita's tipi, to all the others in camp, but she never saw me watching in the shadows. Maria and Juanita, running hard, fast approached. Moon pulled back the blanket and disappeared inside, soon followed by Maria and Juanita, who stopped for a moment to look at the pony. I heard loud sounds from inside the tipi, but could not tell if they laughed in joy or yelled in anger.

When Juanita joined me in the tipi, she laughed and said, "Husband you have done a good thing. Moon is happier than I have seen her in many harvests. We'll be good wives and hard workers for you. You'll be proud of us. Who will you ask to speak with Maria?"

"I choose Beela-chezzi. How many ponies will Maria want

for her? I need to decide on what I can offer before he goes."

"Truth be known, Maria feels so bad for her, she would probably give you ponies. Moon will return your pony late tomorrow night. Will you ask Beela-chezzi to visit Maria the next day?"

"Hmmph. I'll ask Beela-chezzi to go and offer four ponies. He will go. He makes a good friend."

When he returned from speaking with Maria, Beela-chezzi said, "She accepts the four ponies with a condition. You must speak with her face to face. This isn't good. You shouldn't break avoidance. Anyone who sees his mother-in-law, his marriage dies. He loses much. He—"

"*Ussen* gave me Power to kill witches. I'm not afraid to look on the face of my first wife's mother. I'll go."

Beela-chezzi nodded. "Your choice to make. She said to tell you she waits in her tipi. Go."

I walked the few paces between our tipis and waited at the blanket door. A woman's voice from inside said, "Who stands at my tipi?"

"Mother of my first wife, I have come to speak with you, as you ask."

"Come inside where it is warm, if you're not afraid to see me."

I pulled back the blanket and stepped through the door. Maria sat on the far side of a small fire that barely lit her face. She motioned me forward to sit by the fire opposite her. She pointed to an old, blue, speckled *Indah* coffee pot. "I've coffee from Blazer's store. Will you have a cup?"

"I'll drink your coffee, Mother of my first wife. Tell me why I'm here."

She smiled and, setting out two cups the same color as the coffee pot, poured us each coffee. My cup was scalding hot but had the best flavored coffee I'd tasted in a long time. I slurped the hot brew, smacked my lips, and slurped again. Maria took a swallow and blew air to cool her gullet. "Good," she croaked.

I waited for her to begin, but she drank the entire cup, folded her hands in her lap, looked at me out of the shadows, and said, "Juanita has been happy with you. She has wanted Moon on the Water to have the same happiness for a long time and speaks of you often. Moon on the Water wants you, even if she will be second wife. You're a good man. Remember when I asked you not to take Juanita even if she offered herself to you when she went on the raid to the *vaquero* camp with you. You said you would not take her virtue. You kept your word. Your marriage has been a good one. I think this marriage will be a good thing. I know Moon on the Water thinks her marriage to you will be good."

Doves fluttered and called outside in the tree limbs above us.

"I don't understand why you choose a second wife who, like your first wife, probably cannot give you sons and daughters. Why do you do this? I'll not have my child any man's slave, if that's what you plan. Watch my face when you answer. I would see the truth in your eyes. Speak."

I stared at Maria's face as I answered. "I chose Moon on the Water as second wife because of dreams."

Maria frowned. "Dreams?"

"Juanita's dreams. She says she wants children for our family. No man wants her sister because they think Moon on the Water will be as barren as she. Juanita's dreams show Moon will give us children and that, in time, they both will be mothers together, regardless of who bears the child. She asked me to take Moon as second wife. I honor her wishes."

Maria stared at me a long time in the silence of the cold, late sun and then smiled. "Yellow Boy speaks as true as he did when we came here from the destruction of our homes and families in the Guadalupes. Take Moon on the Water as your second wife. Treat her well. Give me many grandchildren as Juanita dreams."

Then she looked down for a moment at her hands folded in her lap and said, "Now I must tell you something that may change your mind. Not even Juanita knows this. Moon on the Water has bad dreams. Maybe once every five to ten suns one comes. She awakes moaning and crying, fearful of what she has seen in the land of visions and dreams."

"What dreams does she have?"

"It's only one dream about the time the Blue Coats put our people in that stone wall corral filled more than a hand span's depth of dirt from horses. She's had this dream since we returned from Juh's stronghold. It never came when we stayed in Chihuahua. I spoke with Nautzile's *di-yen* about this at her *Haheh* ceremony. He said ghosts from that time haunt her in this land and that, if it happens long enough, she might become a witch, and others might try to burn her. I think the *di-yen* speaks nonsense. I have told no others. If you withdraw your gift for her, I'll understand and never blame you."

I crossed my arms and stared at her. "I tell you your child may dream dreams, but she'll never be a witch. She'll be second wife to Yellow Boy, Killer of Witches, killer of Sangre del Diablo. I want Moon on the Water. Give her to me that I might yet have children."

Maria held up her hands palms out. "Moon on the Water is your second wife. Let's smoke to *Ussen* on this good day that I give her to you."

"Hmmph. It is a good day, Grandmother."

CHAPTER 45
CAMP OF KITSIZIL LICHOO'

For the next three days, the women in the camp sat with Moon on the Water and taught her their knowledge of good husbandry. I realized, in remembering the talks Juanita had had with Moon while I sat outside the tipi on my blanket, able only to hear mumbles, laughs, and giggles between them, that Juanita had told her sister what she needed to know to make me a good wife.

Juanita rearranged the tipi to make room for Moon and her things. We talked about how she planned to share the work with Moon and that, in matters of intimacy, she would sleep in Maria's tipi when Moon and I wanted privacy, and that Moon would do the same for us. She laughed and said, "Husband, you're a strong man. Now you double the chances of having a child if you don't neglect either of us. We don't expect that you will."

I thought, *Pretty soon now, I'll need to go on a long hunt.*

On the fourth day after Maria accepted my bridal gift, the camp had a feast and dance around a big fire in front of the shallow cave we used for councils and meetings. Our hunters had taken a blacktail deer and an elk cow, and Yibá, who saw me as friend and teacher, traded one of his cows for *Indah* canned goods and sweets that the women prepared. No one even thought of using the food stores the women had set aside for Ghost Face for a celebration so close to the cold, hard times.

I sat between Moon and Juanita surrounded by our friends.

We ate and told stories about the old times, and Bear and Coyote tales. Kah and Deer Woman, happy with their first child, now just off the *tsach,* were anxious to have another. Lucky Star, wife of Yibá, carried their first child. Shiyé, Beela-chezzi and Carmen Rosario's son, soon would come to us for manhood training, and so would my little brother, two harvests younger than Shiyé.

We had good fortune for our celebration. No snow had yet fallen, and the day grew surprisingly warm with little wind. As the sun fell into the distant mountains, the sky filled with blood reds, deep purples, gold, and orange colors painted on clouds coming filled with snow and ice and hard, cold times.

Moon, Juanita, and I left the celebration among well wishes for happy times, many children, and long life. We walked together to the tipi. At the blanket door, Juanita hugged Moon and whispered, "A good night comes, my sister. Make our man proud and give us the children we all want. Come for me when you're ready."

Moon hugged Juanita and said, "You've given me a great gift, my sister. I'll make my new husband happy."

Juanita hugged me. "The spirit of my husband is great. It makes me glad for this day. I wait for you in Maria's tipi. Call, and I will come."

I held her by the shoulders and looked in her eyes. "You're always with me Woman of Great Heart."

She smiled and turned away to Maria's tipi. I pulled back the blanket and motioned for Moon to enter. "I'll wait here. Don't hurry. Take your time. Call me when you're ready." She nodded and stepped inside the tipi. It was growing cold fast, and there was a smell of snow in the air. I squatted by the tipi door and pulled the good, thicket blanket around my shoulders over the top of my head while I smoked a *cigarro.*

I had not finished the *cigarro* when I heard her call, "Come, husband." I went inside. Moon on the Water lay under her blankets, only her face, calm and peaceful, and her shining hair, loose and spread over the ground blanket and her pillow like black fire, lay uncovered. I could see her high shaft moccasins and soft, beaded buckskins neatly folded and set on her side of the tipi. She whispered, "I'm ready. Come to me, my husband."

I knelt beside her and stroked the sides of her face. "I can wait if you fear this and need to get used to me." She shook her head. "I've waited for this since my *Haheh* ceremony. I've waited too long. Come and be my man. You stir me with desire."

I spread my blanket over her to give us more warmth against the growing cold. My skin prickled in the cold air as my best clothes came off. Her eyes, big, dark pools, never left me as I slid under the blankets beside her and her arms closed around me. Her scent filled my head and her soft caresses stirred me. She made me feel like a young man again and gladly received me many times that night before we slept, her head upon my shoulder and her arms around my middle in the newness of discovering ourselves in each other.

Deep in the Ghost Face, the usual rhythms of life returned. I hunted often, but game was still scarce. Juanita and Moon divided the tipi labor so life was easier for them, and they made more baskets and finer tanned buckskin than they had done before. Eventually, they overcame their modesty and stayed in the tipi even when the other was under the blankets with me.

We had only one problem with our living arrangement. Moon's dreams shocked us awake about every ten suns. We knew when she had them by the low moans of terror that woke Juanita and me. When I shook Moon awake, they grew louder, and she would jerk upright, her eyes wide but unseeing, as she came back to this world. When I asked her what she had dreamed, it was nearly always the same. Blue Coats were watching and laughing at her as she sank in a big stone-lined hole overflowing with horse dirt that had no bottom. She always woke up moaning for help when she was about to disappear in it. Juanita would hug her, and I would rub her back until she returned to the land of dreams unafraid.

A harvest passed, and Moon still had the same dream. Neither of my wives' bellies yet swelled with the life of a child. I found a *di-yen* on the reservation who claimed to know how to drive away bad dreams. He came to the camp late one sun during the Season of Large Leaves. That night by a small fire in front of the cave we used when the whole camp gathered, he spread his special medicine blanket covered with strange signs, and asked Moon to sit on it facing the east while he made symbols with golden pollen on the blanket and on her and sang his ceremony. His ceremony was long and difficult to follow, and it went on most of the night. He finished by placing his right hand on top of her head and singing a special, short song to draw out the bad dreams; he then gave her a blue stone to wear when she slept that he said would capture the bad dreams and never let them go.

I gave the *di-yen* a pony for his services. Moon told me she didn't feel any different and didn't know if the dream had left. In twelve suns, it returned. The camp worried witchcraft made the dream come, especially since a strong, young woman taken by a respected warrior gave no signs of producing a child and the *di-yen* had not made the dream leave.

A dark time came to our tipi. Moon asked if I wanted her to return to her mother. I said, "That won't happen." The other women in camp began to avoid her and stayed far from her. Now she frowned much more than she laughed. All the camp listened for Moon's dream that brought her terror deep in the night and talked about it, staring at her from a distance on the days after it happened.

I sat outside the tipi often, now by myself, for my friends feared to come near anyone who might be under the spell of a strong witch. One evening as the golden glow of the moon filled the night sky, Moon on the Water helped Maria in her tipi, leaving Juanita and me alone together. Juanita came outside and sat down beside me.

"I would speak with my husband in a good way."

"My first wife always speaks in a good way. I listen."

"My sister, your second wife, needs to leave the camp for a while. Our good People fear her. They shun and whisper about her when no one thinks she sees, but she sees and feels great sorrow. She speaks of you divorcing her so she can go away and live by herself. I know Maria told you about her dreams and how they didn't come when we stayed in Juh's camp. I've never seen her more happy than there. I've thought about this a long time. I give you a thought."

Golden light filled the mountains as the moon drifted up over the ridges east of the great White Mountain. Trees and ridges stood in sharp, black shadows.

"Tell me your thought. I will listen."

"Take Moon on the Water to live in an Apache camp in the Blue Mountains. Her dream won't come there, and the camp where she stays won't shun her. Stay a moon or two with her, then come back and stay a moon or two with me. The times we're apart will be no worse than the days when Apaches raided often and the warriors were gone for a moon or longer. Being with one woman during a month should make your blood stronger and both your wives more likely to make a child. I know five or six days of riding every month will be hard on you, but it will save your wife, my sister, from becoming an outcast from her People. What do you think, husband?"

I heard a wolf call my name in the bright moonlight and thought if Juanita had been born in a man's body, we would have driven the *Indah* from our lands. Two camps over a five or six days' ride apart, a wife anxious to give their husband a child in each one, I had never heard of such a thing. Yet, for our problem, the thought made much sense.

"It's a good thought. I'll think on it. Have you talked with Moon about this?"

"If you decide to do this, then we'll all talk together before anything is done."

I nodded. *"Enjuh."*

I thought on Juanita's plan until Moon's next dream and decided I needed to take her to the Blue Mountains. I knew Kitsizil Lichoo' had a camp in the mountains a day's ride south from the American border. *Perhaps,* I thought, *he'll take us into his camp.* A couple of days after Moon's last dream, I had my wives sit with me, and I told them what I planned.

Juanita nodded and looked at Moon. "It won't be a good time when my husband is gone, but I think this will be a good thing for you, my sister."

Moon bowed her head and mumbled, "Whatever my husband and his first wife decide, I'll do."

I shook my head. "We must do what will best serve you and make this witch's dream that's haunting you go away. If you have another thought, speak. We'll find the best way."

Moon looked at both of us and shook her head. "I have no better way than for you to divorce me and send me away to live by myself."

"Then we'll pack our ponies and leave when the sun leaves tomorrow."

Moon and I left the next night. We rode all night, and we hid and slept during the day. I decided to go to the camp of Kitsizil Lichoo' by way of what the *Indah* called the Animas Valley and

Hatchet Mountains. Once in the Blue Mountains, I found the Río Bonito and followed the trail I remembered using when my brothers and I left the Opata women and children in Kitsizil Lichoo's camp. The trail led us to the rock formation I remembered looking like a finger pointing to the sky.

From the rock formation, we worked our way down into the canyon where the camp lay hidden on a bench above a wide, full-flowing creek. We rode up the stream a short way and then up on to the bench, through tall brush, until suddenly the camp spread out before us with its people staring in surprise at the unannounced arrivals. There were more lodges in the camp than I remembered, but this did not surprise me. Kitsizil Lichoo' had told me at that time that he expected the camp to grow larger with refugees from San Carlos and Elias's camp, and it had.

It was still early in the day, and Kitsizil Lichoo' sat talking with several warriors around a fire in front of his stonewall lodge. When he saw us, I could see his teeth in a grin from all the way across the camp. He came directly to us and held up his arms in welcome, his red hair hanging long over his shoulders. He said, "My great friend, Yellow Boy, Killer of Witches, destroyer of Sangre del Diablo, welcome to our camp. I remember well the woman with you. Welcome, Moon on the Water, sister of Juanita. Climb down from your ponies and sit by our fire. Our young men will take care of them and bring your supplies to my lodge. Come."

I recognized two of the young men who came forward to take our ponies. They were Opata we had saved from Sangre del Diablo. I recognized Calico Dove, Kitsizil Lichoo's second wife from the camp of Elias, and several of the Opata women we had saved who had taken warriors for husbands in the camp. It felt almost like returning to our home camp.

Kitsizil Lichoo' and I sat by the fire and talked most of the day. I told him all that had happened at the reservation since we returned, and why I had taken Moon on the Water as my second wife. I told him about her dream and why she needed to leave our little Mescalero camp. I asked him if we could join his camp with her to stay and me to be gone every other moon. He assured me that everyone in his camp knew me and would be glad if we stayed.

That night we feasted and the next night, in council, all the warriors agreed they wanted us to come and stay with them as long as we wanted and would support Moon when I returned to Mescalero. The following day I, with the help of the black warrior who knew the secrets of the stones and had shown the other warriors how to build their lodges, started building a stonewall lodge for Moon and me.

CHAPTER 46
Indah BOY COMES

I rode in the night following the same trail I had used to the Blue Mountains and returned to Mescalero after I had built a lodge for Moon on the Water. On the way, I stopped and stayed a day with my friend Rufus Pike, who told me to stay for a meal and tell him the news of the Mescaleros and our friend Kitsizil Lichoo' in the Blue Mountains.

Two days later, I came to Juanita's lodge in the morning sunlight and found her waiting with the door blanket thrown back to let light in her tipi and to warm her face. She looked at me with shining eyes, "My husband returns. I've waited by the door every day since you left. Come. Your meal is ready, and so am I."

She pulled the blanket door closed and sat with me as I ate and told her of the trip to the Blue Mountains, of the camp of Kitsizil Lichoo', the stonewall lodge I built for Moon on the Water, and that Moon had yet to have a bad dream before I left. When I finished eating, I lay down to rest, and Juanita came to me, and in our embrace, the passion and joy of the first night of our marriage came again.

Whether I was going to the Blue Mountains or returning, I stopped to visit Rufus Pike. It was a good place for a little rest before two more days of steady riding to Juanita.

Early in the Season of Earth is Reddish Brown, four moons passing since I had taken Moon on the Water to the camp of Kitsizil Lichoo', I made ready to return to the Blue Mountains.

Juanita came to me with a smile, put my hand on her belly, and said, "A child grows here. My dreams say it's a son."

I thought my heart would burst with the good news. I hugged her without thinking or caring what the rest of the camp might think about it. "I'll stay a little longer with Moon, but I'll return for the winter before snow blocks the passes, and then I'll stay until our son comes."

"My husband is wise. *Enjuh.*"

In the Blue Mountain camp of Kitsizil Lichoo, Moon on the Water heard Juanita's news with great happiness. "Juanita has waited a long time to give you a son. She shows that I, too, soon will carry a child. I'll make a fine basket, a present for you to carry back to her."

"I'll stay in one place or the other when snow fills the passes and canyons. Since Juanita carries our child, due early in the Season of Little Eagles, I'll stay with her through the Ghost Face until the child comes before I return to you."

"That's wise. I have plenty to do and Kitsizil Lichoo' and the camps other warriors look after me, but I'll long to see my husband. Come to me often while you're here, that I, too, might carry your child."

I smiled. "Woman, while I'm here, you won't be alone under the blankets."

She laughed and scrambled to her sleeping pallet. "*Enjuh.* I'm under them now!"

I stayed all the extra time I could before returning to Juanita a few days before the first heavy snows came in the Blue Mountains. Our first son, a big, strapping baby boy with the grip of a wolf's jaws on the throat of a whitetail came early in the Season of Little Eagles. Maria said we should give name him He Comes because he had finally appeared after a long time, and that's what we called him. Four days after his *tsach* ceremony, I rode west to give Moon our good news and help her make her own child.

On the way to the Blue Mountains, I stopped to visit Rufus and tell him my news. The way he whooped and danced, you might have thought the child his. He gave me a big *cigarro* and poured a little glass of whiskey for each of us. He had never given me whiskey before, but I had tasted it while I was a tribal police-man. We lighted the *cigarros* and drank the whiskey. No matter the glass, if I held it, soon it went empty, and I wanted more. When I asked for more whiskey, Rufus shook his head. "One glass is enough. Too much will make you sick. Your people don't handle whiskey well. I know you know that, bein' a tribal police-man an' all."

I nodded and turned the little glass upside down on his table. "Rufus Pike is a good friend to the Mescaleros."

"Just don't wanna see you in no trouble is all. Let's eat."

He filled me up on steak, beans, chiles, thick toasted tortillas, and coffee. I ate so much my swollen belly made me sleepy. I told Rufus I wanted to sleep out by his cattle pool where my People camped when we ran from the Blue Coats' Chiricahua scouts, and Juanita nearly killed a scout, Soldado Fiero, with a stone from her sling to keep him from starting a massacre. I smiled at the irony. Soldado Fiero was the same scout I had killed in Chihuahua to save Tzoe's life.

Rufus said, "It's still cold at night. You'll freeze sleepin' by that standin' water. If you won't stay in my shack, at least take one of these here heavy army blankets to put over yours to stay warm."

I was glad he offered it and went off down the path to the pool. The velvety, black night sky, filled with the points of light from an uncountable number of stars, wrapped me in its cold air as I lay down in warm blankets with my feet to the east. Turning my head a little, I saw the black outline of the mountain against the milky river of stars where I heard *Ussen* speak and then give me Power to kill witches.

The blankets kept me warm and comfortable, and soon the mists of sleep filled my mind. I became an eagle soaring on great wings high over the mountains above me. I flew in the Season of the Ghost Face. Patches of snow lay scattered across the Tularosa basin far below me, and breaking clouds, heavy and dark with snow, sailed above me. The brown *Indah* wagon road came out of the mountains of the Mescalero and, like a scar on the face of the land, made a line past the great waves of white sand straight for the pass the *Indah* call San Agustin. I swooped down close to the road and, rising high again, saw a wagon driven by an *Indah* and beside him a young boy wrapped in a heavy blanket. Leading the wagon toward the pass, three *vaqueros* rode far ahead. I circled the wagon and *vaqueros*, two, three times, and then a strong wind caught and lifted me higher and higher into the sky, making the wagon and riders disappear, and a voice came, saying, *The Indah boy comes. You have Power. Be ready.*

My eyes fluttered open. I was no longer an eagle soaring above the mountains and basin floor. I was a weary man staring at the stars. I wondered at the meaning of the dream, but told no one, and for a long time thought of it often to learn its meaning.

Three harvests passed and I continued my trips to my second wife in the Blue Mountains and back to my first wife and son. My son grew strong and was a happy child. I taught him much even in his early years and brought him and his mother little presents often when I came back from the Blue Mountains. But I did not neglect my second wife and carried gifts and supplies to Moon on the Water, who never wavered in her belief that she, too, would give me a child as her sister, Juanita, had.

I had learned to follow the canyons the camp of Kitsizil Lichoo' used to take cattle from the *hacendado* ranchos. This trail let me reach the camp in the Ghost Face Season when the high passes across the Blue Mountains were blocked. I only used the *hacendado* trail in the Ghost Face Season because it took me an extra day to reach Moon on the Water this way, and sometimes even the canyons along the cattle trail might fill with snow.

In the Ghost Face Season of the fifth harvest since Moon and I settled in the camp of Kitsizil Lichoo', she came to meet me at the corral when I returned from the reservation. She took my arm, something Apache women didn't do with their husbands often, as we walked to our stonewall lodge. I could feel the trembling energy in her fingers and wondered at her news.

Inside the lodge, she wrapped her arms around my waist, looked at me, and laughed. "*Ussen* has smiled on us," she said. "I carry your child."

I embraced her and smoothed her thick black hair blown by the wind and felt happiness fill me. "My happiness covers all the trails I ride. I'm a man blessed. I'm a man with a good and fruitful a wife."

"I don't know if it's a boy or a girl child, but I think it comes in the Season of Large Leaves, and the women here say they'll help me. Will you be here when my time comes?"

"I'll be here. You and our child mean much to me."

"*Enjuh,* husband. *Enjuh.*"

I stayed a little longer than planned that trip because a storm blew over the mountains from the west. It didn't drop much snow in the canyons, but it still made travel hard so I waited it out.

The ride back to Rufus's rancho was cold and hard, but the wind was at my back, and since possible enemies like the *Nakai-yes* had sense and stayed inside, I rode during the day. Rufus said I had to stay inside with him, and I didn't argue. I told Rufus of the child Moon on the Water carried. He whooped again and did his dance like he had for Juanita when she carried He Comes. We smoked a *cigarro,* and he poured me a glass of whiskey. The firewater felt good in my belly after the long, cold day on the trail from the Blue Mountains.

The next morning when I left Rufus, the wind blew hard, and the light came cold and gray under heavy clouds racing toward the east. I knew it would be a slow day for me. I stopped a little distance down from over the top of Baylor Pass, let my pony rest, and scanned the basin floor with the *Shináá Cho,* looking for *vaqueros* moving cattle or travelers I might meet. In this way, I could avoid them and not provoke concerns that a wild Apache was loose from the reservation and hunted them.

I stopped to scan the basin about the time of shortest shadows, although I couldn't be sure about the time because the sun hid its face behind the clouds. Luck was against me. *Vaqueros* were moving a small herd south across the trail I wanted to follow to the Jarilla Mountains, and another crew gathered scattered groups of cattle into a large herd moving south and west. Two wagons traveled east on the brown, sand-covered road that ran past the waves of white sand. I saw three men and their ponies at the place Rufus called Aguirre Springs where we had waited nearly sixteen harvests ago to ambush the Chiricahua scouts chasing after us for leaving the reservation. I studied the men. They passed a bottle of whiskey between them and the sight of it made me thirsty for some. One of the men had a great ugly red bush of hair on his face and had an eye covered with a black patch.

I waited and watched to learn when I might pass in the clear. I got my blanket from my pony, found a comfortable place to sit between two big creosote bushes with my back resting against a boulder, and studied the valley. After a while, the men at the spring mounted their ponies and rode off toward the road. They stopped at the west end of a long dip in the road and hid their horses behind them in an arroyo off to one side. I knew little of *Indah* ways, but any fool could tell an ambush was in the making. I looked down the road and saw three men far in front of a wagon like they led it, and on the wagon sat a man with a rifle across his knees and a small boy by his side. I had seen this before.

ADDITIONAL READING

Ball, Eve, Lynda A. Sánchez, and Norah Henn, *Indeh: An Apache Odyssey*, University of Oklahoma Press, Norman, OK, 1988.

Ball, Eve, *In the Days of Victorio: Recollections of a Warm Springs Apache*, University of Arizona Press, Tucson, AZ, 1970.

Blazer, Almer N., *Santana: War Chief of the Mescalero Apache*, Dog Soldier Press, Taos, NM, 2000.

Bourke, John G., *An Apache Campaign in the Sierra Madre*, University of Nebraska Press, Lincoln, NE, 1987. Reprinted from the 1886 edition published by Charles Scribner and Sons.

Bray, Dorothy, editor, *Western Apache–English Dictionary: A Community-Generated Bilingual Dictionary*, Bilingual Press/ Editorial Bilingue, Tempe, AZ, 1998.

Goodwin, Grenville, Edited by Keith H. Basso, *Western Apache Raiding and Warfare*, University of Arizona Press, Tucson, AZ, 1971.

Goodwin, Grenville, and Neil Goodwin, *The Apache Diaries, A Father-Son Journey*, University of Nebraska Press, Lincoln, NE, 2000.

Haley, James L., *Apaches: A History and Culture Portrait*, University of Oklahoma Press, Norman, OK, 1981.

Mails, Thomas E., *The People Called Apache*, BDD Illustrated Books, New York, NY, 1993.

Opler, Morris, E., *Apache Odyssey: A Journey Between Two Worlds*, University of Nebraska Press, Lincoln, NE, 2002.

Opler, Morris Edward, *An Apache Life-Way: The Economic, Social, & Religious Institutions of the Chiricahua Indians,* University of Nebraska Press, Lincoln, NE, 1996.

Robinson, Sherry, *Apache Voices: Their Stories of Survival as Told to Eve Ball,* University of New Mexico Press, Albuquerque, NM, 2003.

Sánchez, Lynda A., *Apache Legends and Lore of Southern New Mexico: From the Sacred Mountain,* The History Press, Charleston, SC, 2014.

Sonnichsen, C.L., *The Mescalero Apaches,* University of Oklahoma Press, Norman, OK, 1958.

Thrapp, Dan L., *The Conquest of Apacheria,* University of Oklahoma Press, Norman, OK, 1967.

Thrapp, Dan L., *Al Sieber: Chief of Scouts,* University of Oklahoma Press, Norman, OK, 1964.

Worchester, Donald E., *The Apaches: Eagles of the Southwest,* University of Oklahoma Press, Norman, OK, 1992.

ABOUT THE AUTHOR

W. Michael Farmer, a member of the Western Writers of America, learned about the rich mosaic of historic figures depicted in his books while living in Las Cruces, New Mexico, for fifteen years. He has a Ph.D. in Physics and has conducted atmospheric research with laser-based instruments he developed. He has published short stories in anthologies, won awards for essays, and published essays in magazines. His first novel, *Hombrecito's War,* won a Western Writers of America Spur Award Finalist for Best First Novel in 2006 and was a New Mexico Book Award Finalist for Historical Fiction in 2007. His other novels include: *Hombrecito's Search; Tiger, Tiger, Burning Bright: The Betrayals of Pancho Villa; Conspiracy: The Trial of Oliver Lee and James Gililland;* and *Killer of Witches, The Life and Times of Yellow Boy, Mescalero Apache, Book 1,* winner of a 2016 Will Rogers Medallion Award and a Finalist for the 2016 New Mexico-Arizona Book Awards in Historical Fiction and in Adventure-Drama, and *Mariana's Knight, The Revenge of Henry Fountain, Legends of the Desert, Book 1.*

The employees of Five Star Publishing hope you have enjoyed this book.

Our Five Star novels explore little-known chapters from America's history, stories told from unique perspectives that will entertain a broad range of readers.

Other Five Star books are available at your local library, bookstore, all major book distributors, and directly from Five Star/Gale.

Connect with Five Star Publishing

Visit us on Facebook:
https://www.facebook.com/FiveStarCengage

Email:
FiveStar@cengage.com

For information about titles and placing orders:
(800) 223-1244
gale.orders@cengage.com

To share your comments, write to us:
Five Star Publishing
Attn: Publisher
10 Water St., Suite 310
Waterville, ME 04901